O U T R U S H

OUTRUSH

The Mer Chronicles, Book 3

Errin Stevens

OUTRUSH

An Errin Stevens

E-book edition / February 2019

Paperback edition / February 2019

Copyright (c) 2019 by Errin Stevens

Library of Congress Catalog Card Number: On File

Series illustrations and design: Randy Tatum, pilot-adv.com

ISBN 978-0-9982961-8-0

Published simultaneously in the US and Canada

PRINTED IN THE UNITED STATES OF AMERICA

For Mike and Jack. You guys are my heart.

Praise for Updrift:

"I loved this book. Stevens took the Hans Christian Andersen story of 'The Little Mermaid' and de-Disneyfied it, replacing it with a tale that will haunt you. This is one of, if not *the* best Mermaid/Siren tale I have ever read. Run, do not walk to read this."
– Andrea Stoeckel, Book Reviewer

"This story was beautiful! Errin's writing style is GORGEOUS, and the last page made me cry."
– Ellen Cummins, Author of "Nineteen Days" & "Butterfly Ruins"

"Some stories work wonderfully in audiobook format, this is definitely one of those books."
– Tasha and Megan Mahoney, Audiobook Reviewers

"Updrift is a beautifully crafted romance novel that involves fantasy and a wider scope of events. One of my favorite things about this romance was that it wasn't just merely a romance; instead, it was a fantasy adventure as well as a mystery, and that added tantalizing substance to the story."
– A. Aarones, Reviewer

"If you're into mermaids, cute romances with a side of paranormal, or you just need a chill read, look no more because Updrift is what you're looking for."
– Vampress Bathory, Instagram/#bookstagram Reviewer

"This book was hands down one of the best that I've read this year. I love books about fantasy creatures and Updrift doesn't disappoint."
– *bibliophagist_omnilegent, Instagram/ Bookstagram Reviewer*

"I loved the world that the author created with this tale of Mer people! Immensely interesting and intricate, there were also some great family values presented."
– *Sweatpea, Goodreads Reviewer*

"This book came as a complete surprise. It is unlike any Mer story I've read. Not only is the book really well written but the dialogue is fantastic."
– *Tangled 'n Books Reviews*

Praise for Breakwater:

"The storyline is complex and amazing. Ms. Stevens is an author who packs a lot into a story and adds in small side stories along the way."
– *Judi Easley for Blue Cat Review*

"I loved this. I dreamed about it."
– *Cloud S. Riser, Author of "Jack & Hyde"*

"Rarely, if ever, is a second book in a series as good as the first; in this case, I felt Breakwater to be, in fact, better than Updrift!"

Acknowledgements

Mom, Greg, close and distant family, Jillian Jenkins
– you continued to be fearsome players on my
personal O line for this one, and my thanks here in
no way represents the depth of my gratitude to you
for all your support. Beth and Martha C., I owe you
wine, dinner and a mermaid-free conversation,
maybe over that Outlander marathon? T. Petrie was
invaluable in helping me characterize the antics of a
real-life financial deviant and it probably says
something really bad about me how fascinating I
found our phone conversation… Martha Moran,
you are a fabulous editor and a goddess among
women. I'm erecting a shrine to you as we speak.
MJ's proofing was beyond competent and saved me
from death by embarrassment; please will your
brain to me when you die.

To Ruth and my colleagues on the Lifelong
Learning Committee at St. Catherine University,
your accommodations and inclusions these past two
years have meant more to me than you'll ever know.

I also continued to collect new and far-flung online
fans during this journey, folks I've never met in
person but who have taken it upon themselves to
showcase my stories on their Instagram, Twitter and
Facebook feeds. Y'all are crazy and I love you.

"Out of the rolling ocean, the crowd, came a drop gently to me,
Whispering, I love you, before long I die,
I have travel'd a long way, merely to look on you, to touch
you…"
—Walt Whitman

Prologue

Maya took a break from her laptop to stretch in her chair, using the activity as an excuse to check if the men following her were still across the street.

Yep. The Undertaker was behind the wheel of his car, reading a newspaper as usual; and Jethro was in the window of the café opposite hers, texting on his phone.

These weren't their real names – she didn't know the men assigned to watch her every move. But she'd needed to call them something, and one was a gaunt, cadaverous-looking guy she just knew was draining the blood of the dead in some dungeon-like, basement mortuary during his off hours. Every time she saw him, she pictured herself laid out before him on a cold, stone slab, a macabre smile on his face as he stood over her with a bouquet of axillary drain tubes. She shuddered and looked toward his companion.

Jethro was the Undertaker's opposite, seemed even less the detective, but at least she could convince herself he was harmless. He was just too fresh-faced and beefy and wholesome; and too cheerful compared to the stern-faced urbanites surrounding him. Her made-up story for him was he'd been waylaid en route to an ad audition – a toothpaste ad, she decided. "Pssst, buddy," rasped a Mafioso lurking in the shadows and waving a wad of cash. "Wanna spy on a rich girl?"

Maya was a little proud she'd won out over dental hygiene.

She sighed and rubbed her tired eyes. *Week twelve,* she thought, and almost three months since she'd noticed she was being followed or watched or whatever. Most people would have run, she supposed, and at first she'd wanted to, not that she'd done anything wrong. But being the subject of someone's surveillance mission was creepy, made her want to slink off even if she was innocent. The scientist in her had prevailed, however, meaning instead of acting to avoid scrutiny, she'd done the opposite. She'd maintained an even stricter schedule, leaving and returning to her apartment at the same times each day, running errands to the same places, even stopping for coffee at the Bean Machine each afternoon as she was doing now. If she found her regular table taken, she took her second regular table instead, and then moved if her first choice opened up.

This constancy, which she knew made her easier to track, also allowed her to verify she was being followed and by whom. Now, she easily recognized the cast of characters sent to attend her, no matter how careful the men were, which they weren't. Physical appearances aside, their quirks showed and showed big. The Undertaker, for example, tended to drum his fingers; and Jethro had a fondness for bubble gum, making him the only adult she'd ever seen who periodically sprouted small, pink balloons from his mouth.

But she'd trained them well during their tenure; like good little ducks following her mother duck lead, they'd fallen into the pattern she'd dictated, meaning they took up the same posts in the same places each time she took up hers, and wasn't that just a sad testament to their spying competence. There were four of them on rotation, assigned in pairs, Monday through Sunday. Porky and Popeye had the day off today, which she could predict at this point since it was Tuesday, and Tuesdays were Jethro and Undertaker days.

One thing for sure, these guys weren't the low-level paparazzi who occasionally dogged her socialite in-laws. They didn't have the look – no cameras, no lurking around in what appeared to be permanently slept-in clothing. Even their expressions were wrong, devoid of that mixture of desperation and defiance Maya considered a kind of trade calling card.

No, these men were paid babysitters looking for something other than media currency, which was the variable in this situation she couldn't, no matter how hard she racked her brain, figure out. What could they want? What had she done to warrant all this attention? She stared at her notebook screen again and pretended to take interest in her search…

…and then she felt an overwhelming sense of peace she sometimes, heaven knew not often enough, experienced like a gift, always when she was teetering on the edge of a nervous breakdown. Her last reprieve had been months ago. But here it was again out of nowhere, comforting her like an embrace from her mother, and oh, how lovely to feel so cared for and protected. Like everything was going to be okay. She understood just how tightly wound she must be if a fantasy encouragement could so undo her. She thought she'd been coping just fine with her disaster of a life and smashed-up emotions. Apparently not.

But for the moment, her feeling of well-being was complete, and better yet, intensifying.

Someone approached, and she opened her eyes, realizing only then that she'd had them closed. A man walked toward her table, no one she knew… but she instinctively identified him as the source of her comfort. When he reached her, she smiled at him as if they were old friends.

He stopped to rest a hand on her shoulder, a hand she clasped and held against her cheek.

Everything will get better. I'm going to help.

She heard the words as if he'd spoken them, and she was so grateful, she wanted to cry. She turned her face to press her forehead against his arm.

Thankyouthankyouthankyou pleasestaybyme, she thought. The man looked out the window and frowned, and then gently disengaged his hand. After a stroke to her hair, he walked away.

Maya noticed the alarmed expressions of her watchers across the street but couldn't be induced to care at first. She was reveling in her break from anxiety, felt too light and free to give in to her usual moodiness and fear, even if it looked like a little fear might be warranted. Jethro spoke grimly into his headset while staring at her in a way that looked sinister and specific. He no longer pretended anonymity, no longer appeared cheerful. Maya toasted him with her coffee cup. The Undertaker made a reckless exit from his car, attracting curses and the blares of car horns from several angry drivers. Maya shook her head and smirked. *So much for stealth*, she thought as he stumbled after the man she considered her angel of mercy. All in all, she thought her guards looked like comic book villains instead of real people posing an actual threat.

She knew she had her just-departed visitor to thank for her lack of concern, but as he retreated, so did his influence, and worry once again seeped into her consciousness. Especially when Jethro began marching in her direction. She watched his mouth form commands as he talked into his wireless, and she heard his words as if they were whispered in her ear, words that came with an explicit warning by their translator to take heed.

You need to know what's going on, Maya.

"Contact's been made," Jethro reported. "Looked like a lover but it had to be a front. Been here all month and never seen the guy before. May have passed a message. We're following."

Anger at the men she saw as responsible for her exile welled inside her like roiling lava, bursting her bubble of complacency and destroying her reprieve from all the pressure. Her inner competitor – the one that had made her an all-star on the volleyball court during college – hardened her resolve to face this challenge head-on.

All right, boys. I'm here to play offense.

Maya abandoned her coffee, stood up from her seat and deliberately held Jethro's gaze through the glass, her stare a refusal to be intimidated any longer. It felt good to be obvious, and she realized just how tired she was of all this, of pretending to be unaware, of all the stupidity and furtiveness, and especially how her current situation – her life in suspension – had no expiration date she could foresee. Whatever the fallout, she was done: done with waiting, done with trying to figure out why she was hiding and from whom.

Jethro paused and raised an eyebrow, discreetly moving a panel of his jacket aside so she could see his holstered gun. Then he smiled, the big creep.

Run! The panicked command echoed in Maya's mind... and adrenaline coursed through her body like a shot of jet fuel to a primed engine. She didn't pause to think, just bolted away from the window. She ran through the kitchen and into the back alley.

*Dreadful sounds betokened the breaking up of the ship,
and the roaring waters poured in on all sides.*

From "The Swiss Family Robinson" by Johann David Wyss

PART ONE

Chapter One

Seven years was a long time to be in a wrecked marriage. Maya likened her existence these days to a kind of permanent post-trauma, where she was consigned to forever tip-toe around in her own personal life, picking through her relationship with her husband for signs of compassion like she might search the debris of a catastrophe for something – anything at all – salvageable.

When she thought about their digression from where she was now, she determined her last and perhaps only feelings of optimism had occurred at the altar, when she'd believed fervently in their ceremony and all it represented. How she'd cried during their promises to cherish and protect, and how brightly her conviction in their future had burned. When Stu delivered his vows, he'd stood so tall and strong… she would never have believed such sincerity could fade. However, she fast learned it would last only as long as it took them to walk out the cathedral doors after the reverend pronounced them mister and missus.

"The guys are going to steal me for a quick pub tour before the reception, okay?" Stu whispered in her ear. "Mother!" he called over his shoulder. "Take Maya home to rest before dinner, all right?" He placed a swift kiss on Maya's temple and was gone, leaving her struggling to cover her anger with an over-bright smile.

Really? He was so hard up for a scotch he would abandon her on the church steps to toss one back with his buddies? She turned to her new mother-in-law to decline her offer of company and avoid the very real possibility of a bridal tantrum in front of her. Maya's best friend, Kate Blake – along with Maya's sisters, bless them – intervened.

"We've got you," Kate murmured so only Maya could hear, and then more loudly, "We'll see everyone at the dance!" She flashed the milling guests a grin, and along with the other bridesmaids, pulled Maya toward the church parking lot and into one of the cars.

Her girls had taken good care of her, too, plying her with humor and champagne until she set aside the bitter resentment that had her fuming and willing to skip the reception altogether. She even believed Stuart's disregard for her at the church was an aberration, although truthfully, she knew better. No one else was surprised either, Maya noted. Which depressed her.

But she'd pretended everything was fine, both at her wedding reception and all the public gatherings thereafter through the years. Stuart's willingness to leave her side for any and all excuses continued to embarrass her, even if she could plausibly attribute his departures to their busy schedules and need to stay in touch with a large circle of friends and associates. And she was determined to prove everyone wrong, to earn through forbearance if she must the casual, bedrock-like intimacy that drew her to the idea of marriage in the first place and convinced her she needed to keep trying.

She was thankful the palpable doubt she'd felt from her friends and family – and if she was being honest, herself – no longer distressed her to the extent it had in the beginning, when she was forever steeling herself against anger and tears; when she felt destroyed for days after one of Stuart's blithe escapes. His constancy in this area had inured her, eventually blunting the sharp stab she used to feel when faced with his lack of devotion.

Her medical training helped in a morbid kind of way, too, partly because medical school and residency took everything she had to give. She didn't have the intellectual or emotional resources to brood when she faced, every day, twenty hours of class and studying; or when she worked back-to-back twelve-hour shifts on rotation for her residency. In light of these demands on her time, she'd come to view her relationship with Stuart like she would a patient who came into her emergency room: it was anemic and listless but alive, while others were rushing through the doors with fragile aortas and potentially fatal knife wounds. She focused on the truly dying, telling herself she'd get to that other guy as soon as she could.

Still, over the years, she'd come to suspect there was nothing more she could do, that she would either have to leave – an unthinkable prospect – or accept her marriage as it was, which was barely a friendship. She never believed she would be the kind of woman to settle for an apathetic husband, partly because she'd assumed at first Stuart's love for her would draw them closer once they'd married. It hadn't. And that he didn't love her – at least not in the idealized way she thought he should – revealed more of her own ugliness than Stuart's. She knew her pride hurt more than her heart; and she understood her determination to stick it out was a testament to her desire not to fail, not because she loved Stuart as she should.

Early on, their home life had provided a sufficiently fascinating diversion from her dissatisfaction, enough for Maya to wonder later how big a factor public pressure had been on their efforts to carry on. Maya's in-laws were members of an elite social milieu in New York she knew nothing about growing up, aside from what most people knew of old families with big money. To Maya, the Evans patriarchs, like the Rockefellers or Vanderbilts, occupied the same place in American lore as other historical detritus she'd been forced to consider in grade school, like the rise and fall of riverboat commerce, or the washed-out and distant images of dead presidents on daguerreotypes. But the effect of the Evans wealth on her day-to-day life now was significant, and not something she could have understood until she was part of it, when their extravagances separated her from what she'd always assumed was reality. She and Stu had a housekeeper for crying out loud, a fact she vowed never to reveal to her parents. They wouldn't understand, and she could well predict their disapproval should they find out. If she was being honest, she shared it.

Maya had adjusted to a more intrusive public life, too, most of which revolved around her father-in-law, Thad. He was frequently pictured in the society pages, of course, but he was also chief executive for the country's largest insurance company; was in fact responsible for catapulting his organization into its premier market position via a massive public-private deal he was credited with creating. Stu had told her about it when they were engaged, reporting with pride on the intricacy of his father's campaign and how the effort had required more than a decade of legislative lobbying and aggressive political contributions. It brought billions to the company's bottom line and solidified Thad's candidacy for top dog.

Unfortunately, this meant Thad became the face of an unpopular kind of corporate policy, and subsequently a lighting rod for protesters and similar unpleasantness. Maya and Stuart weren't directly targeted, but close enough in Maya's experience. This meant they all had drivers and a security contingent whenever they went out.

Maya had stayed out of the limelight to sidestep the more disturbing attention Thad and those closest to him suffered, but she'd still had to change her habits out of caution. She never, for instance, took a spontaneous walk in the park or made an unaccompanied trip to the grocery store, not that she shopped for groceries any longer. For the first time in her life, she was fluent in the strange privacy characterizing interactions between the wealthy and their attendants, people who witnessed the personal lives of those they served without being included in them. She'd been so uncomfortable with these relationships in the beginning, was still plagued with guilt over the underlying premise: how another human being was hired to make her bed, fold her clothes, or put his or her life on the line for a job. She minimized interactions with these people as much as she could, sneaking her own laundry to the drycleaners to be washed or ironed, and keeping her personal clutter to a minimum so no one had to pick up after her.

She no longer fought the need for a security escort, however. On more than one occasion, Maya had witnessed thwarted physical attacks on Thad by crazed strangers, the kind who often appeared at public events Thad attended. Usually the attacks were verbal, comprised of a few protesters carrying signs in the hopes of capitalizing on media attention, and their real aim was to garner visibility, not inflict bodily harm. Then again, she'd been hurt once when she was between Thad and a man running to tackle him. Maya was knocked to the ground hard enough to sprain one of her wrists. Thereafter, she took better care when she was in public with her father-in-law close by, a situation she made every effort to avoid.

She was adopted by one guard in particular who, no matter how hard she tried to drive him away, faithfully showed up to both protect and torment her over the years, although she didn't believe he intended to trouble her as he did. But she wouldn't have been so loyal given how deliberately, relentlessly rude she was to him.

It was a defense. Mitch Donovan was hired by her father-in-law about a year after Maya and Stu's wedding, and since she'd had no complaints about the guard he replaced, she didn't understand why she needed someone new. The head of the Evans security team introduced her to him on a day Stu traveled for work. Mr. Donovan would be available whenever she or the younger Mr. Evans wanted to step out, and here were his pager and cell numbers. Mitch had been reluctant to shake her hand, which she'd found offensive until it happened, at which point she was overwhelmed by a sense of grief so acute her knees buckled. Mitch grasped her elbow to steady her, support she quickly shrugged off in her embarrassment.

"It's just... you remind me of someone," she blurted after a lengthy, uncomfortable pause. And he did. Something about his eyes, and a sheen of vitality she associated with a family she used to socialize with back in North Carolina, the Blakes. The likeness was superficial, but it made her horribly homesick, and if possible, even sadder over her empty, soul-sucking marriage.

Maya realized everyone was waiting for her to explain her strange greeting, or maybe they simply hoped she'd resolve the awkwardness she'd created. Sweat bloomed on her forehead and she became aware of the shallow, insufficient breaths she took, which she worried were too loud. She felt unanchored and bizarre and very much hoped she didn't look it. She checked Mitch's expression. It did not encourage her.

Her lack of composure was obvious. Worse, she felt like Mitch had shone a spotlight on her most private fears, ones she preferred to pretend she didn't have and most definitely wanted to keep hidden.

Her marriage was disappointing and unlikely to improve. Her absorbing career was no more than a convenient place to hide. And if she couldn't achieve happiness with an M.D. under her belt and marriage to a beautiful, wealthy man, something was very, very wrong with her.

And there it was, dang it, the path to the ultimate no-no of all her memories: Aiden. It was Mitch's fault for bringing him to mind, she decided, since he looked at her in the same penetrating way and exhibited the same physical markers. Aiden symbolized all her missteps up to now, his name synonymous with the more unpleasant consequences of her running away – from him and North Carolina and all the possibly destructive super-secrets he wore like a cloying aftershave. With just a glance in Mitch's direction, Maya saw starkly the unhappiness of her future as Mrs. Evans, understood too well what she didn't and never would have with Stu.

She despised Aiden – or at least, she wanted to – for stealing her peace of mind so thoroughly after her wedding, she'd never regained it. That awful dance at the reception, where every second felt like an accusation. His recriminations, issued without actual speech, were like an internal battering ram ripping through her insides from the center of her liver. *This marriage is a lie you cannot turn into truth. I'm the one you wanted. You've made a terrible mistake.* When Mitch Donovan shook her hand, his touch was a direct transmission line to the whole, miserable litany.

And no. Just... *no.* She would *not* feel that draw again, the attraction to Aiden that had solidified her decision to marry Stu when she was finishing college. Back then, she was struggling for purchase on adult life with very little hope she'd achieve it, thinking maybe she had it in her to go to medical school, and how, if she was lucky, she might be able to build a life with Stuart Evans. Stuart had been a guy who, unlike Aiden, didn't seem like he'd die without her. Stuart was maybe predictable by comparison, bland even... but he never freaked her out with intense, hungry stares that gave her the impression she was about to fall off a thousand-foot ledge. Mostly he never made her feel crazy, like she could suddenly smell the ocean, or feel a sea breeze on her skin; or think she wanted nothing more than to dive into the biggest, deepest body of salt water she could find. She hated swimming in the ocean. All she could think about when she waded in was a statistic on shark attacks, how most of them happened in three feet of water.

"There are about a gazillion things waiting to kill you out there," Maya explained once when her friend, Kate, questioned her on her saltwater reticence. "People don't belong in oceans. That's why God invented swimming pools." Kate snickered.

"Laugh all you want, Blake," Maya retorted. "I'll be your ER doc when you come in with shark's teeth lodged in your sternum. Or a Man-O-War wrapped around your neck. Don't think I'll forget this conversation, either."

Interactions with Aiden back then felt like a free-fall into chaos when she was already too at odds with herself to cope. And even though she'd refused what Aiden represented – by running to what she thought was safety with Stuart – the memory of Aiden continued to niggle away at her tenuous stability, no outside reminders necessary.

She couldn't afford to feel gutted every time she ran into Mitch the Security Guard. In fact, she wouldn't. Her unprompted self-negotiations concerning love and marriage were taxing enough, and she decided she'd do anything to preclude repeat panic attacks triggered by something she could control.

"I would prefer, Mr. Donovan, that you stay out of my personal space as much as possible. I don't want to be aware of you, so no casual comments, no taking my arm. In fact, if you must address me, don't make eye contact. Are we clear?"

Mitch's boss appeared stricken, but Mitch smiled at her indulgently, as if she'd made a weak joke and he wanted to make her feel better about it.

"Of course, Maya." He stared, without apology, directly in her eyes.

So much for her attempt at a firewall, which meant she'd just have to try harder. "That's Mrs. Evans to you," she snapped, pivoting on her heel and hurrying off.

Thereafter she went to heroic lengths to avoid him and repeatedly stated her request for a different escort when one was needed. Everyone except her – and Mitch she supposed, since he always showed up looking all confident and like he had her number – suffered from inexplicable amnesia in these situations; no matter who she spoke with beforehand, no matter how many times she complained about Mitch's unsuitability, no one listened to her. No one seemed to even remember her complaints, and Mitch was the one who came, without fail, to take her out.

"Did everyone in security get bashed in the head?" she finally asked him. "I don't want you around. Why can't you guys understand this?"

"Oh, I understand, Maya."

Eventually she gave up her public campaign against him and settled for being as hateful as she could to him personally. She texted her need to leave in thirty minutes, then either left immediately to make him scramble, or kept him waiting another two hours. She was dismissive and haughty, impatient and willing to criticize him for all manner of imaginary missteps. Mitch responded by ignoring her. Or he gave her probing looks that dared her to continue her tantrum, until she couldn't sustain her conviction, and her tirades died without the bloodletting she intended. Then she undid all her hard work with an apology.

"I'm sorry to be so spiteful," she'd mumble.

Mitch always forgave her, which made her feel even more exposed. "It's okay, Maya. I get it," he said, and then he stroked her hair, or squeezed her hand. She had to run – literally turn from him and run – to get away from what he made her feel.

In what Maya considered the most perverse irony of all, she came to find periodic comfort in Mitch's constant reminders of love, loss, and that guy back home who got away. Thad's extra-curricular romantic habits, which became much less discreet following his wife's death due to cancer, had grown to include Maya's husband, where Stu would play wing man with any number of suspiciously sexy young women, ones who didn't hesitate to drape themselves all over a married man – at their house or in public, it didn't matter. Maya seethed at what she saw as Stu's complicity, and because she thought he made her look weak in front of their friends.

"It's not like your dad's personal life is any of my business," she complained one evening as they prepared for bed, "but I don't understand why you're part of it. All those women... it's like you're double dating, and you're not exactly discouraging any of them." Maya suspected this was precisely the case but hoped she was wrong. This was the first time she'd brought it up, and she badly wanted her husband to take her in his arms and deny he was choosing casual affection with strangers over real intimacy with her.

Instead, Stuart bristled, and she knew she was in for a scolding. "Give the guy a break, Maya," he said shortly, his condescending tone one she knew too well. She could almost hear the words "you idiot" tacked on the end of his comment, and she slumped to sit on the edge of the bed. *Another dead-end conversation where I get to feel guilty over his indiscretions*, she mused. Should she point out she was concerned about his behavior, not Thad's?

"He's under a lot of pressure at work," Stu continued. "And Mom's illness was a terrific drag, something I'd expect you to understand. He deserves to kick up his heels. I'm just along for the ride. It's like… I don't know. A father-son bonding thing."

Riiiight.

Her hopes for marital enlightenment sank for the nine hundredth time. She realized how, once again, she'd believed Stuart would act differently if only he understood he was hurting her. He had demonstrated – once again – her feelings were not a consideration for him. Even worse, Stuart's dalliances became more blatant after this conversation. This was when she came to welcome those pesky introspections Mitch Donovan prompted.

Maya was never aware of asking for relief, but whenever Stuart and Buffy-Number-Whatever went too far in her presence, she felt as though Mitch channeled Aiden, and her fantasy-man, himself, appeared to comfort her. Sometimes when she was truly desperate, she even saw him. In these situations, she no longer cared if Aiden was a made-up psychological defense; he eased the ache of betrayal and shame, and he saved her from making a scene that would have broken her carefully built image of a strong and stable wife, one confident enough in her marriage to overlook a little friendly flirting.

But inside she would be anxious and miserable… and then a moment later, she felt removed, in the same way she used to when she experienced what she thought of as one of Aiden's mind-wipes, and oh, what she wouldn't give to have *that* prescription on re-order. She could witness something offensive and then find herself unable to recall it, or the event seemed so absurd it no longer mattered. Best of all, she felt cherished after these illusions, truly loved. This sense of herself as attractive and worthy lasted for hours, and nothing – not Stuart's continued disregard for her, not his most puerile escapades with other women – nothing upset her.

Maya's favorite of these experiences followed a public demonstration she could not clearly remember. Perhaps it was a kiss Stuart shared with some female guest in their kitchen during a party they hosted, the woman in his lap, their hands inching beneath each other's shirts, while friends milled around as if the couple's behavior was nothing unusual. Stuart was no doubt drunk and would use that as his excuse, but Maya would have been appalled and angry and on the verge of tears...

The actual image of them had disappeared from her mind, however, or maybe it was so overshadowed by the contentment that followed, she no longer cared. Aiden was before her and said... she didn't know what he said, but it launched a reverie that erased her heartbreak and removed all her devastation. By the time Maya was aware again, she felt better than she ever had after one of these compromises. In fact, she felt not only strong, but free, and as if Stuart's penchant for public fondling might never affect her again. Not her happiness, not her plans for her future, not her confidence in her own ability to love and care for another.

And she finally knew how it felt to be in Aiden's arms. Amid an intimate crowd and seconds from a volcanic emotional breakdown, Maya had the impression she'd been wrapped in a bubble, a protective cocoon insulating her not just from her own hurt and anger, but also the perceptions of everyone else there. None of the other guests appeared to even see her any longer, meaning no one scrutinized her response to Stu's make-out session, or worse, looked at her with pity. It was as if her mind manifested her most private wish, and the partygoers all disappeared so she could fully enjoy it.

This time, Aiden came to her like an avenging angel, one sent to protect her and dispense with her agony using violence if necessary. She breathed deeply as her trouble dissipated, lifting away like it was helium-injected; and she felt stable for the first time that evening. Maybe for the first time in months. She found she could also stand tall and open her eyes without dreading what she'd see.

She saw Aiden's shirtfront clenched in her fists, and Aiden's face when she looked up. Enfolded in his embrace, Aiden's voice calmed her, the concern he expressed healing the ragged cuts to the heart she'd received with each and every one of Stuart's tactless romantic displays.

She felt steady and strong, but also, despite Aiden's pull on her senses, aware of herself. Which was unusual when Aiden was around. She welcomed the clarity this time.

She faced her dilemma without a preconceived idea of how things should work out between her and Stu; and without censure, she evaluated her own contributions to her marital problems. She saw she was not responsible for Stuart's myriad discourtesies, but she was guilty of running scared from truths she should have faced years ago.

She was sorry for her dishonesty. She recalled her many misjudgments, starting with those she'd made in Griffins Bay as a senior in college. She regretted her unfair treatment of Aiden, how her efforts to drive away her own fear had compromised not just her, but him, as well. Her confession to him now, conflicting beliefs and all, was immediate.

She thought the words as she focused on his shirtfront. *I am so sorry. But I can't be here with you like this, won't do this to Stu. Even if he doesn't care, we're married and I won't betray him.* Then she raised her gaze to offer Aiden the first clean sentiments she ever had, with no attempt at evasion. *But you were right. I shouldn't have run from you. I'm sorry I wasn't brave enough.* She forced a few inches of distance between them and crossed her arms to keep herself from clinging, not just physically, but also to the hope of escape he represented.

Aiden cradled Maya's face in his hands and swept her tears away with his thumbs. "It's okay, love. I think you're going to get the chance to be brave again soon. I just want you to know there's more out there for you, that this doesn't have to be enough." When he released her, his devotion remained behind, a glowing warmth within her fortifying her against what she knew was coming.

Which was the end of her belief that she could and should save her relationship with her husband.

This time, she knew how her frustrations with Stu would play out, and it wasn't with them together. Stu wasn't leaving her any choice.

Chapter Two

Thad hunched over his desk and rubbed his eyes. He'd been on edge these past weeks, but he probably shouldn't be as agitated as he was. Considering the crushing demands of his professional life over the previous two decades – and Gloria's horrifying and ultimately fatal fight with cancer a few years back – nothing should rattle him to this extent.

He distracted himself with thoughts of all the things *not* bothering him at the moment: people suing, vicious public relations attacks, picketing over some moral wrong his company inflicted on humanity… these had been part of his daily life for so many years they were normal, had been since he joined upper management at Health & Wellness Prescriptives, or "The Hell Well," as he called it privately.

No, his work, which had been his wife and lover, his church and God since age twenty-seven, did not factor at the moment. His problems had to do with his daughter-in-law. Or he hoped they did.

She didn't seem cutthroat enough to outright damage him, but he couldn't afford to risk that possibility. He wouldn't have hesitated to act against her if their roles were reversed, but then he'd been more ruthless at her age, had needed to be to break out from under the pall of expectation placed over him by his father. Maya's expectations were self-inflicted, her motivations born from a softer, more introspective place than his own. Thad believed she lacked the killer instinct that came with an external, environment-sponsored drive to achieve... although he couldn't be altogether sure.

His winner-take-all upbringing was not typically something he pondered, but he was obsessed with the idea Maya might be talking and couldn't shut off his need to evaluate her inclinations, an analysis based on his extensive experience with human behavior. If he planned to remove the threat she posed, he needed to know he had definitive cause. If he did? Well, he didn't like to think of himself as the kind of man who would make the decisions that would follow.

He felt pushed, though, and he was too aware of the stifling effects of being pushed. His family had beaten him over the head with the mandate to become a legend whether or not he wanted to, or if he even could. There had been many, many mornings before grade school when he'd hid in his room, sick with nerves, wishing the spelling or math test he had to take meant the same thing to his father as it seemed to mean to the other kids' dads. He hoped he'd spared his own son that particular torture; that Stuart knew his performance in school was about his own growth and progression, not about upholding the Evans name in the world.

Thad's one big act of rebellion – going into general business instead of securities banking – didn't appear so daring in retrospect, but it had led to Thad, Sr.'s profound disappointment in him and created a rift between them that had never mended. Conformity, if the elder Evans were asked, meant more than almost anything. It had been the source of the Evans wealth and the foundation of their high stature in the community; and it was the key to continuing the epic social and economic legacies established by Thad's father, grandfather, and great-grandfather. By choosing not to follow in his dad's footsteps, the younger Thad felt like he might as well have told his parents, "I'm off to become a professional pornographer!"

That he'd made good – as *the* top executive at the country's largest insurance provider – gave him little comfort by the time it happened. The elder Thad had not been alive to see it, and by then his perceived insubordinations had propelled him beyond the point of redemption. Sadly, his infractions, which had felt like victories in his twenties and thirties, no longer offered any satisfaction. Turned out being ultra successful in a different business sector, refusing to sit in your grandfather's chair, and naming your son something other than Thaddeus were not the visionary departures he'd meant them to be. Turned out these petty stands didn't take him away from his father's hopes for him after all, which meant he'd wasted a *lot* of time congratulating himself for breaking a mold he didn't really break. Thad pictured what must be his dad's smug assessment from the afterlife, a fat smile on the man's face as he peered at him from his stoop behind some eternal desk.

It was funny how all his engineering to forge a separate path, the rigid categories he'd created to make a life that would turn him into his own man, had done nothing of the sort. When he looked at photographs of his father at his age, he saw himself as nearly identical. He sat on the same kinds of boards, supported the same causes, and was solicited for donations from the same breed of pandering hangers-on who had followed his mom and dad around when he was little. Most damning was the definition of himself he saw reflected in his interactions with others, a definition he couldn't influence no matter who was in front of him, be it a life-long friend or someone newly introduced. He was an Evans, he was a Hell Well executive, and these positions established him as a de facto authority on any and all subject matters whether he knew a single thing about them or not. If a dispute arose in conversation, the group looked to him to resolve it. He was the man on whose shoulders the needs of others could be placed; the bequeathor of power, money, and opportunity; and he was the person ultimately responsible for fulfilling the individual dreams – or soothing the disappointments – of his underlings.

He was allowed no variation in this role, so that he sometimes felt like a caricature drawn by a stranger, someone who hadn't quite gotten the lines right. It didn't matter; others expected the image he provided – refused, in fact, to recognize any deviation from it he exhibited. He believed he saw this situation for what it was: he was a yardstick for others to measure their own accomplishments against, and he was a convenient scapegoat for their failures to live up to all they hoped for themselves. His own dreams didn't factor because, after all, what more could one want out of life?

Yet for all the lack of nirvana at the top of the socioeconomic food chain, Thad was unwilling to give any of it up. He wasn't unhappy, was better off in this regard than most, he believed. No one had it any easier as far as he could see, and the conniving antics of all the folks vying for a secure place in the world... well, people were as lacking in integrity at the bottom of the ladder as they were at the top. Many times, Thad thought the lower-end supplicants were worse, and at least he was free of the uglier competitions that festered among the mid-level management types at HWP, people who believed since they wanted more, they deserved more. And who would undermine anyone and everyone around them for the smallest shot at advancement.

Maya had never struggled with these issues because her life was hers to direct, and because, in Thad's opinion, she hadn't experienced enough of other human beings to know their motivations were never black and white, no matter what kind of background they had. She could afford to be philosophical about social status and class, was even unaware of how shortsighted and self-specific her own worldview was. She'd never had her job threatened or future traded as collateral for someone else's ridiculous utopian scheme.

Over dinner a few months after Maya and Stuart's wedding, Thad had solicited her opinions, curious as to what she thought of her new, lavish lifestyle. There were eight of them seated in the dining room in Thad's penthouse, where the view of the city lights out the window was only slightly more impressive than the apartment itself. The rest of the family engaged in separate conversations, and Maya kept her voice low to avoid drawing attention to their talk.

"I believe concentration of wealth like this," she gestured around them, "is bad for society. It's too destabilizing. There's no reason for this much disparity."

"Probably not," Thad allowed. "But your argument doesn't have as much merit as you think, Maya. For all we do – and we do a lot – our social problems never go away."

Maya's response was polite but stiff. "I believe we can do better."

Maya had really tried to understand his perspective, Thad knew, and he was aware she now relied on many of the perks that came with wealth, so she'd come a long way since that first exchange. But he also knew she remained uncomfortable with her elevated status. As with non-family, his surname and title at work were barriers to further confidence, meaning he could only guess at how strongly she felt about the obesity of his trust fund and multi-million-dollar salary. These matters were enough to incite others from her class to public attacks, and he suspected Maya was partially sympathetic to those, too.

Which meant when he found her in his home office that evening staring at a cryptic but damning handwritten note, he'd had reason for concern. He caught her by accident and knew she lied when he asked, "What are you doing here?" He couldn't figure out how she'd gotten in, since he kept his office locked when he wasn't there.

"I... I was just taking a break from the party and figured no one would think to look for me here," she stammered. Her gaze kept flickering behind him toward the door, demonstrating her reluctance to talk with him and suggestive, he thought, of deceit.

Her reaction alarmed him more than the situation. Did she know what she was looking at? If she hadn't seemed upset, he would have assumed he'd left the door unlocked and she'd wandered in for his stapler. But she was visibly shaken, and with no one else around and nothing to attribute her agitation to, he had to assume she reacted to something she saw. He stared too hard at the folder in front of her, the one containing his cousin's note. It was unsigned but scribbled on personal stationery with a stylized "E" at the top, and clipped to a copy of a client's account record. Thad had tucked these items into a folder marked "Planned Giving – Evans Charitable Trust," which he was sure he'd placed under the pile it now topped. He'd chosen a title he thought suitably dull; in the unlikely event anyone did see it, he couldn't imagine they would have any interest in the contents.

Had she read it? If she had, did she know what it meant?

He glanced at the scanner on the credenza behind her to see if it was on. It was, as usual, which didn't mean anything. She wasn't carrying a purse or something that could hold a photocopy, and her dress didn't have any pockets... but of course a thumb drive could be easily hidden. She could have one tucked into her hair, for all he knew. She could have taken a photo with her phone and already sent it off somewhere.

In all likelihood, Maya's presence had nothing to do with Nate's missive. And if only he could be certain of that.

Thad had received the envelope late in the day according to a protocol he'd established at the outset: electronic missives could be traced, whereas paper messages were read and burned. Explicit communications, if necessary, were conducted in person, were brief, and were made intentionally vague. According to Nate's scribblings, Thad needed to take care of a particular transaction when the market was open, which was why he'd retained the packet instead of tossing it in the fireplace. Nate had followed the rules, and Thad should have nothing to worry about... yet here he was, staring at an obviously distressed daughter-in-law who very much seemed like she'd been doing something she shouldn't.

"Why are you behind my desk, and what are you looking for?" he asked bluntly.

His sharpness appeared to surprise her, because her eyes widened. "You think I'm snooping," she stated. Then her gaze dropped – guiltily? – as she denied it. "I'm... I'm not. Not really. I just had to come here to think. I just had to see if…" Her mouth trembled as she tried to control either anger or tears. Thad couldn't tell. Whatever else she thought to say, she swallowed back. She straightened and leveled a challenging look at him. "I'm not doing anything wrong, and I don't owe you an explanation. In fact, I'm tired. And I'm leaving."

Thad turned aside reluctantly to let her pass. She was shaking, and there was definitely something she hadn't told him. Was it what he feared?

He conducted a more thorough inspection of things. The surface of his desk was warm, he noted, and he found a trace of perspiration on the lip above his center drawer. He pictured Maya leaning there on folded arms as she pored over the account report. He sat in his chair.

He had no idea how long he remained there, speculating and stewing. Eventually, however, he decided Maya's actual guilt didn't matter; he needed to take precautions. He summoned his security manager, Harlowe, to his office. He reviewed Nate's file and account notes, and he mulled over his interaction with Maya again and again while he waited.

Harlowe rapped on the door. "Mr. Evans?" Thad called for him to enter.

Thad was in no mood to be civil and he delayed saying anything in the hopes he could compose himself, or at least refrain from barking at someone whose discretion he required. He felt as if he stood at the opening of a long, narrow tunnel, one in danger of collapse that he nevertheless had to walk through. And there was Harlowe at the other end, a soldier whose loyalty he would test with his next words. Thad had to hope his man would be true, that he would not cause a crash that could annihilate them all.

God, he wished he didn't have to do this. He hesitated even longer before speaking, before taking this first step to defend a deception he hoped very soon to erase from his life. He thought through his circumstances again, following the course he considered to its rational end. At best, intimidation tactics would scare his son's wife into keeping her mouth shut, he'd deal with his troublesome client and have nothing further to worry about. At worst, however…

Well. He needn't think beyond his current dilemma. This action, after all, would save them all from exposure, right? Yes. He was in the process of fixing everything, anyway. This situation was temporary, and Harlowe's oversight would keep it that way.

"Sir?" Harlow prompted.

Thad released a breath and spoke. "I need you to tail my daughter-in-law, Maya. Be discreet, and no matter what you see, do not confront her."

Harlowe waited expectantly. When Thad offered nothing more, he inquired, "If you don't mind my asking, sir, it will be easier to keep you informed if we know what we're looking for."

Thad studied him longer than he should have. Because the risks of talking about his side business were too many to count. Moreover, voicing his concerns aloud, saying he wanted Maya watched because he felt threatened… well again, it gave solidity to the idea he was in trouble, and he badly wanted to believe otherwise. He needed to offer something for the security team to go on, however… so, he'd need Harlowe's assurance this conversation would stay between them.

"She may have taken information she could use to blackmail me. If this is her intent, I have to stop her." He scribbled Nate's phone number on a scrap of paper and handed it over. "I want you to leave a message at this number if you see…" Here, Thad stumbled. If he saw what, exactly? Maya talking to a federal agent? Anyone bureaucratic-looking, nosing around Maya's home or workplace? "…if you see something that looks like a meeting to pass along information," he concluded. God, he sounded ridiculous. But it was the best he could do.

"You should know," Thad continued, "if you are discovered and questioned – by anyone at all – you are to call this number, and this number alone." He pointed to the note he'd just given him. "I personally want to hear nothing further from you. Do not reveal any association between this effort and me or my family, and certainly refrain from sharing we had this conversation. If anyone comes to me asking about your assignment, I will deny I know anything about it. And, Harlowe, if you compromise me, I will personally destroy you."

Harlowe inspected him closely, and Thad saw he'd shocked him, which was understandable since he'd never engaged in hyperbole with his employees. But Thad also believed Harlowe had become dependent on him over the years, particularly around Christmastime when the Evans family awarded generous bonuses to its longtime help.

So, Thad expected Harlowe's attempt at reassurance, although he was still glad to receive it.

"I've worked for you for fifteen years, Mr. Evans," Harlowe said stiffly. "Our company has dozens of clients. We wouldn't necessarily be linked to you. And I would never do anything to put you at risk. Please know you can count on me and my team."

Thad relaxed a little and forced a smile. "Very good. Please show yourself out."

After the door closed, Thad pulled out his phone and called his son. "Stuart, I need you to come to the penthouse. Right now."

"Really, Dad? It can't wait?" Thad heard low, feminine laughter in the background, not Maya's.

"I'm sorry, Stu. It's urgent. Get here."

Chapter Three

Maya wasn't supposed to be at Thad's party and she hadn't called ahead, so Stu didn't expect to encounter her at his father's place. He certainly didn't appear to be thinking of her now, as he and Annette stumbled down the hallway together, so lost in their groping and clothes-shedding they almost bumped into her as they passed. Maya had just arrived and was on her way to the kitchen when they burst into the corridor. She'd scurried into an empty room to hide. And spy.

Maybe I would have been better off at home, nursing that quart of butter pecan, she reflected glumly as she watched them through a crack in the door.

She'd traded shifts with another resident late in the day and gained a rare reprieve: an unexpected night off. A week earlier she would have sworn that, given a choice, she'd spend the evening in stretch clothes in front of the idiot box; or curled up in bed with a novel in anticipation of an early date with her pillow. But she'd been restless that morning, was irritated by the constant stress attending a job comprised of incessant medical emergencies on too little sleep. She was also fed up with her own insular thinking, which had her so inwardly focused all the time, she wondered if she twitched or spoke to herself aloud in front of others.

Mostly she wondered if she would ever be fulfilled and happy again. Probably not, since all she ever did was work, and she got nothing but heartache from her husband. She foresaw no relief on the horizon, either... and this put her in a rebellious mood.

She didn't want to be alone on the couch, disconnected from friends and family and stuck in her own head, so, hang it, she wouldn't be. She wanted empty companionship and irresponsibility for a change. She decided to show up at Thad's, surprise Stu, and have a drink or three like a normal, overworked twenty-something about to go out of her mind.

As Maya watched Stuart's hands roam all over Annette, she guessed her husband would, indeed, be surprised to see her right about now.

She considered confronting them but didn't, something she briefly regretted later, because doing so would have meant a clean break then and there; no follow-up explanations required, no need to regurgitate any drama related to what she saw as the final insult to their marriage. She would have felt better, too, if she had for once slipped out of the role of tolerant, supportive wife. Or if she could have given her upper-crust man a dose of the same disapproval he shared so easily with her, all on matters that didn't count.

This counted. Not, she realized, because it was any new affront, but because this time Stu and Annette thought they were alone. They were not in someone's kitchen during a party or out at a bar putting on a show, which made their current flirtation seem more personal... and way more deviant. With no one else around to buffer her – or remind her why she wanted to keep up a façade – Maya saw her circumstances in severe and unflattering detail. Like she really was on the outside of her marriage looking in, which she supposed she was. This was actual adultery, not superficial flirting. She could not pretend otherwise.

It all put too fine a point on her predicament, Maya thought, because it concentrated the loneliness that had come to characterize her home life, loneliness she alone seemed to feel in their marriage. Not because she begrudged Stu his need for fun – she really didn't – but she felt begrudged, maybe because she didn't have it in her to cheat. And she'd refused to give up and leave. Was this what Stu hoped, that she'd cat around like he did and be the one to end them? Maybe. Maybe he wanted her permission to be faithless and feel blameless.

She couldn't give it, but neither could she go back on her word, the one she'd given on her wedding day before God and family… and cue the standard mental review of what had gotten her here and what she was going to do about it. She always arrived at the same place during these reflections, where her choices were to stay put and endure or leave and start over, neither prospect tenable to her. Her mental habits on the subject were now rote, her responses had become mere reflex.

They were also tiresome and frustrating.

Earlier in the week, she'd been sick enough of thinking through the same dead-end cycle of what-ifs, she'd reached out to talk to someone, a first for her. She'd called Kate, who was not shocked by what Maya revealed of Stu's extramarital doings. Maya acknowledged to herself that no one who knew him would be. Kate had a lot to say on the matter, too, although she did not interrupt as Maya related the whole of her conundrum.

Maya told her everything, starting with her misgivings from before her move to New York, followed by what she'd believed of Stuart at their wedding and then immediately after. She described her steady, careful reactions over the years when Stu had left her hurt and floundering in front of friends. Mostly, Maya unburdened herself, sharing her worries over how she had contributed to her own dissatisfaction, her ongoing self-doubts, and her unrelenting and escalating unhappiness no matter what she said or did about Stu. Kate listened without comment, but afterwards, she was furious, and Maya thought she might be angrier with her than Stuart.

"You've been living with this for seven years?" Kate inquired acidly. "And you haven't talked with anyone?"

"More or less."

"Your sisters? Your mother?"

"No."

Kate all but yelled at her then. "*Why*, Maya? We love you. We could have helped."

Maya massaged her forehead. "I don't see how. It's not like any of you could have said anything to my husband."

"No, but we could have said something to *you*, honey. Stu's a jerk, but that's his problem, not yours."

Maya's laugh was humorless. "That actually makes me feel better, that you think it's all on him. It isn't."

Kate answered her after a long pause, during which Maya sensed her friend's struggle to curb her anger, to come off as reasonable. "You should leave him, Maya. Life's too short – or maybe it's too long – to live with someone who doesn't care."

Maya hesitated enough to let Kate know her advice was considered. "I can't do it, Kate. I just can't."

Kate sighed. "Yes, you can. You're strong and brave. And gorgeous. And you're too young to spend the rest of your days doing... I don't know, let's call it romantic solitary confinement." She huffed and muttered, "I know someone who could spring you."

Kate's comment prodded a deep and dormant hope in Maya, one she couldn't afford to have awakened. She didn't think she could survive the disappointment if Kate's inklings – and her own, as well – proved false. A lump formed in her throat, precluding her attempt at a reply.

Kate responded as if she'd commented anyway. "I shouldn't have said that. Gabe would kill me for even thinking it." Then before Maya could speak, she rushed to add, "Maybe we could light a candle at church. Or chant prayers or make a burnt offering. Ooo! I have a copy of *Anna Karenina* we could set on fire! How perfect would that be?"

Now, watching Stu and Annette fall all over each other, Maya wished she'd taken Kate up on her suggestion and relied on something other than her own powers of reason to get her out of this misery. In fact, she wondered if her friend wasn't right, if she should have aired her problems sooner to friends and family. Maybe she would have gained a clearer understanding of her options, could have spared everyone, Stuart included, some of the heaviness and angst they'd lived with since their wedding day. Whether due to stubbornness or pride though, she'd elected to keep her own counsel; the years had passed, nothing changed, and she'd stayed stuck.

She sensed she might be getting unstuck at the moment, though. By the time Stu and Annette had reached the end of the hallway, Maya was contemplating one of her previously unthinkable options without her usual resistance, maybe even a little hope. Stu fumbled with his key, opened the door to his father's office, and disappeared inside with his lover. The latch didn't quite catch, meaning the door shifted open slightly, allowing a sliver of a view into the room. Maya crept forward.

Her first inclination – to confront them – quickly fled, because out of sight she felt protected, and she preferred to observe their actions dispassionately so she could choose her response rather than react in haste. She also figured a scene would shake her up more than them, a situation she really didn't want. So, she studied the pair, Stuart especially, as she would a patient.

The exercise was instructive. Within seconds she could interpret what she observed, concluding Stu's fevered expression was identical to what she saw on the faces of drug users who wound up on her table. She also guessed he wasn't truly enjoying his interplay with Annette, any more than the addicts she treated enjoyed begging or stealing to get their fix. She turned her scrutiny to Stu's partner, and her findings further supported her analysis: Stu was self-absorbed, his actions frenzied and blunt... and he had something else lurking behind his eyes, maybe despair? He refused to look at Annette directly, while Annette's responses to him were outwardly focused, adoring even. Stuart appeared withdrawn, Annette open and reaching.

Maya felt an impending sense of release, one tied to her much-sought understanding of all she'd been doing wrong; or maybe over what she might do to repair things between her and her wayward man. An epiphany loomed, one she badly wanted, and it changed the scene before her so it brimmed with promise instead of calamity. Her skin prickled with anticipation.

There really is a way out of this.

Her spirits lifted. She felt as if she'd been sitting in an overheated sauna for too long and someone had propped open a window to let in cool, outside air. The oppressiveness cooking her steamed away bit by bit. It was replaced by something tolerable, something like peace.

What she saw before her truly was, at long last, the death knell to all that had tortured her where Stuart was concerned, an uncaging of the wretched conviction she would be forever obligated to dig in and try to make their relationship work, no matter what. She would never have the power to fix them. She really couldn't change Stu, or make him happy, or do more than she already had to bring the two of them closer together.

As these truths sank in, Maya knew she hadn't understood until now how fiercely she'd resisted this knowledge, hadn't noticed how insidious and adamant a voice inside her had become, the one insisting she could and should get them around their shortcomings. Stuart's proclivities concerning intimacy were in place long before she'd met him, and she acknowledged they'd never changed, not even when their romance was fresh and he was devoted.

Maybe, just maybe, she'd been free all along and hadn't known it, like Dorothy in Oz. Maybe she'd played jailor to herself instead of prisoner to the larger world of marital fidelity, fidelity she alone had respected. *Ah. What a lovely possibility.* Her body relaxed. Her mood rose on an endorphin-induced high.

But after several seconds of unqualified bliss, her self-criticism returned to pick at her. Euphoria, after all, was probably not the correct response when one was deciding to leave one's husband, right? She could have missed something, and maybe she shouldn't trust her newly drawn conclusions, which could be nothing more than her battered psyche trying to give her an out. She didn't think so… but she decided a little more reconnaissance might relieve her. She snuck into an empty room and waited for them to finish.

When Stu and Annette left Thad's office several minutes later – Stu looking agitated and like he couldn't get back to the party fast enough, Annette dawdling and clingy, suggesting they sneak out for a bite – Maya waited for them to exit the hall, then went into their vacated space looking for justification. In his haste to get out of there, Stu had left the office door unlocked, which Maya took as a sign from the universe she was doing just what she should.

She walked behind the sleek, substantial desk – which probably cost more than her father made in a year – and she turned in place. Yes. This helped, being here so soon after, because everything she saw confirmed her perceptions. She wasn't nuts, her responses were not just a coping mechanism concocted by her subconscious. The very air was still thick with humidity from the sex they'd had, the surface of the desk still warm. Maya leaned down and fogged the area over the center drawer with her breath, noting the outline of what she presumed was Annette's derriere. She saw exactly how it had happened, Annette seated on the desk, Stuart standing in front of her, order hastily restored to Thad's papers before they left.

Maya rolled her shoulders and breathed out tension she hadn't known she held. It was over. Even if she wanted to – and she didn't – she could no longer think of her relationship with Stu as she previously had. Because there was no mistaking the stench of the dead, stinking body in the room now, the unavoidable evidence their marriage was not just sick, but an actual corpse.

Relief hit her on a cellular level. What had gone on here had nothing to do with her. Nothing. Not the kind of person or wife she was; not her inadequacies or failures of intimacy; not even her unenlightened reasons for marrying Stu in the first place. This was the last bit of information she needed to know her role in Stuart's infidelities was miniscule. She finally understood her ability to influence him was and would always be peripheral at best.

As relieved as she was, she no longer felt wonderful, however. She felt stunned. The decision she'd fought so long and so hard was all but made, and she was sitting in her father-in-law's house possibly for the last time. She slumped into Thad's chair to give herself a moment…

…and this was how Thad found her, engrossed in her fresh revelations and too distracted to respond to his alarm as she should have. He apparently had a big problem with her being there, but she couldn't think why. Neither could she recall him ever being this discomposed in front of her, or guess as to what had him all in a lather.

But she couldn't be expected to do more tonight than she already had. She decided to cut herself some slack and deny Thad the inquisition he seemed driven to deliver. In the aftermath of her little spy-fest on Stu and Annette – and the rush it had given her – she was now in the post-adrenaline crash phase, and fatigue hit her like a wrecking ball to the forehead. She had to pull herself up from the chair and hope her legs would hold her long enough to get her out of there. Thad was still… well, he was in a bad way and dying to talk to her about it, but really, no, thank you. She'd had enough for one evening.

She needed to go somewhere safe to recuperate, which first of all meant sleep. She didn't need to stay and explain herself to Thad or figure out what was eating him. Thad's expression when she slid past him still worried her – it was some mixture of hostility and fear. Maybe intimidation? This was not for her to clear up, though. Not today. She made her way unsteadily down the corridor, one foot in front of the other, her vision fixed on the door and her exit out of there.

Chapter Four

Hard as it had sucked to pretend, Aiden had kept his cover with Maya.

On his side of the behavioral ledger, any announcement concerning his identity – or if he'd revealed just how far he was willing to go to be by the object of his affection – would have meant breaking his word to the folks back home, a violation sure to bring all kinds of personal trouble. If caught, he could be ostracized, which was tantamount to a death sentence for most sirens. At best, he risked getting carted into the sea by his cousins and forcibly kept off the mainland until his girl died of old age. That option wasn't even a little bit better since he wouldn't survive being cut off from her, not that any of the sirens he'd complained to believed him. Well, his brother, Simon, did. But no one higher up got how he could be in a one-sided, bonded relationship with a woman he hadn't actually bonded with. No other siren had ever had such an experience.

And even Simon didn't encourage him.

"Kill the melodrama," he'd snapped after yet another of Aiden's brooding self-reviews. "She's not available. So what? Just chill, already. Or hang out at Shaddox and find someone there."

"That's rich, coming from you," Aiden rejoined. "When you were told 'no,' you hazed Sylvia and took her to Antarctica. *The literal ends of the earth.*"

Simon stopped scolding him after that, although Aiden knew his attachment disorder still rankled fraternal relations. Which was too bad. He'd been unable to change how he felt.

But since two of Maya's sisters had already married in – one of them to Simon, in fact – the community felt they'd pushed past the allowable quota of siren exposure to one group of humans, meaning Aiden was as banned as a guy could be from all things Maya Wilkes. Or Maya Evans, now. Consequently, he'd had to be sneaky.

He'd made a cursory attempt at compliance in the beginning, had heeded Xanthe's directive to walk away and steer clear, although he couldn't "find someone else to obsess over" as she'd directed. Why everyone thought this was an obvious and easy answer to his problems was beyond him. But he'd physically separated from Maya, first by returning to his government's seat at Shaddox Island, where he'd been resigned if not hopeful he could make a fresh start. He'd even attended one of Carmen's ludicrous matchmaking sessions in Griffins Bay to see if he could fall for one of his own kind, which turned out to be the ultimate exercise in futility. Still, he'd twice put himself in Carmen's hands… with demoralizing consequences, which meant he'd returned afterwards to Shaddox even more depressed and lonesome, something he hadn't thought possible.

It seemed even the community's most celebrated marriage broker couldn't undo the faulty biological wiring that made his insides so certain of the wrong girl.

So he gave up his quest for an alternate mate and sequestered himself offshore, hoping to bury himself in work instead. This approach worked a little better for him. But not much.

In one respect, his misery opened the door for his return to land. During those first weeks back at the palace as his introspection deepened, his ability to explain why – and honestly, to appear socially competent – diminished. No one was fooled by his attempts to seem normal, anyway, so soon enough the whole proposition became too tiresome and awful to uphold. He began to hide, to choose solitude over engagement.

The sirens who saw him meander off on his own were fascinated, since as a rule his kind chased interconnectedness all the time but really chased it when troubled. To his frustration, he became even more worthy of oversight, although he was not the first to hole up like this; in fact, he followed the same behavioral protocols established by their former crown prince, Peter Loughlin. A few other notables – Simon, among them – had also preferred to contemplate private dilemmas in private.

So, Aiden couldn't figure out what had everyone flustered.

But the disengagement trend, while tiny, had thrown siren leadership into a snit; the individualism of human society was rubbing off, they surmised, and if more of their kind continued to veer from cultural norms, their mutual dependency – fundamental to their stability – was at risk. Where would it end? Those governing feared that it wouldn't.

Aiden's response to such crisis mongering was to retreat further, to brood even more but hide what he was doing so as not to get picked apart every hour of every day. In short, he developed a low-level ability to cloak, just enough to mask his dissatisfaction. To his surprise, the bloodhounds trailing him bought it.

It took him a few days to figure out what had happened, but when he realized what he'd done, he was thrilled since it meant distance – if not freedom – at long last from his pseudo-jailors. His internal organs could be disintegrating in a stew of corrosive, unrelenting angst; but Xanthe's spies – her obvious, overbearing spies – were sold on the image he fronted, the one where he looked like he was coping. Beauty. Aiden actually felt Xanthe's remote sigh of relief as she accepted the report, "Aiden is re-assimilating."

Ha. More like 'Aiden is getting really good at lying,' he thought. Regardless, he was given more leeway, so he didn't care.

The community was not so lenient after his next trick, the one where he completely disappeared.

If only he could have managed to vanish in private, but no. He had to cloak – really cloak – in a crowd for the first time, which made sense after the fact since his new outlook on life was defined by distrust and the desire to escape when pressed. Which is exactly how he felt among the siren social police. Meaning, maybe his downfall was inevitable. But by the time Xanthe's oppressively friendly guard surrounded him, he no longer had the ability to smile and engage and roll with it.

They'd been sent to bring him in for a final lecture on the importance of societal integration and his role in maintaining it, and they wanted him to come along nicely. He wanted out of there, and the longer he endured their incessant emotional inquiries – *How are you today, Aiden? Still contemplating insurrection, heh-heh? Acceptance and inclusion feel so much better, don't you think?* – the more desperate he was to run. And voilà, his big reveal as to how unimproved he really was.

Since Peter had already established a precedent for such demonstrations, Aiden's companions knew right away what he was up to. His first blatant cloak – the kind to truly hide him from others' perceptions, not just veil his troubles – showed his sadness had not been brought to heel after all. The smiles and nods of approval transformed to looks of alarm, maybe even fear.

He also became in the space of a few seconds a lost cause in the eyes of those in charge.

"He's too far gone, could become dangerous," Xanthe was told. "And you don't send seals to bring a Great White in line. We can no longer help."

Which meant he was now a candidate for the new, rag-tag brigade of protectors-in-training comprised of other counter-cultural sirens flirting with permanent dissatisfaction. All that turning inward, hiding your feelings…well, it just made everyone confused and uncomfortable. Aiden was dispatched to train with the other misfits.

Simon was there too, had in fact paved the way for the team's creation by rebelling against convention himself back in the day, enough to attract notice from *the* master cloaker, Peter Loughlin. Peter held the unofficial title of 'Deposed Siren Prince Gone Rogue' and was by far the scariest example of subversion their world had ever seen. Perhaps because he was so personally powerful, no one could best him in combat, not that sirens engaged in combat. Or perhaps because he refused to live by the standards he at one time personified. Regardless, Peter was the man who had in a big, big way started the whole dissension trend worrying the traditionals. Evidenced by the fact that no one in mainstream society wanted anything to do with guy.

During Maya's wedding reception, Peter had found Simon and consulted with him on the topic of what to do with wayward sirens henceforth, since Peter knew Simon labored under his own behavioral black marks and was consequently also on the outs. Aiden had been peripheral to their discussion at the time... and their plans had seemed too theoretical. They'd also been inconsequential, considering he had his own pet neurosis to feed. But according to Simon's later accounting, that exchange launched the creation of a group he would soon join. Peter went on to analyze the happiness levels of other siren attendees at the reception, concluded more were on the verge of disunity, and declared, "The trend toward individualism will not be contained," to Xanthe.

"We have more potential cloakers among us than you know," he'd gone on to say. "And they're going to cause you the same headaches Simon did. Why not put their skills to good use?"

Peter had suggested the formation of a first-ever siren security force, one he would train to interface with humans and employ to protect the siren community from too much integration, a very real risk given the growing level of curiosity among sirens increasingly eager for those delicious emotional encounters with their land-bound brethren. Peter warned that the unraveling was underway, and the focus should be on human containment since the pull for sirens couldn't be quelled, not really. "We'd be better off forming a buffer," he'd argued, "comprised of those among us able to control ourselves."

The other benefit to Peter's suggestion was the removal of those misbehaving, the taking away of potential unhappiness-spreaders who would instead have their proclivities channeled toward a constructive end. Kind of like when a crew of them had been sent off to Antarctica for a year... and Aiden could proudly claim membership in that club, too.

To Xanthe, Peter had continued, "Simon is stable now, but he's never going to integrate as you'd like. I can turn his anti-social leanings – and those of others like him – to our advantage." Xanthe approved his request on the spot.

Peter – and Aiden too – knew she found the idea of a siren militia preposterous, mostly because she desperately needed to believe their community was above such base needs. But the idea of a formal training program for sirens who could cloak intrigued her, and she was especially hungry to get all the siren malcontents popping up these days off her docket of state problems. Also, if society's wild cards could all be cordoned off somewhere, they would no longer bother – or worse, infect – the larger population.

"Hopefully, we'll never need such a force. But yes, build your team," she'd directed.

Simon had reported favorably to Aiden on the whole endeavor. Compared to the rest of the trainees, Simon was, for the first time ever, a paragon of stability. Aiden knew much of his brother's newfound happiness relied on his more fulfilling home life, since the guy now had a wife and family to go home to every day. Meaning Aiden couldn't count on enjoying the same contentment, seeing as how his mate was both married to another and forbidden. He doubted his errant romantic compass could be repaired no matter where they put him. Nonetheless, Simon had been given a tempting level of personal freedom in Peter's little army, so Aiden entered military exile willingly, hopeful he'd find some comfort.

And he didn't wither away; in fact, he felt as balanced as he believed he could given his circumstances. At least he no longer writhed under Xanthe's suffocating watch, and he experienced a semblance of the interconnectedness he'd enjoyed with other sirens pre-Maya, enough to contain the worst of his anti-social tendencies. The other trainees were also disenfranchised and irritable, although for different reasons, which was why true harmony remained out of reach for all of them. But their common dissatisfaction birthed a solidarity that helped them muddle along better than they had before. They'd each undergone the same attempted manipulations, weathered the same condemnations from the community, and longed for a more autonomous existence than Xanthe et. al. found permissible. And they'd all cloaked too, meaning here was the only place they *could* fit in. Aiden felt as settled as he'd been in Antarctica.

Not that he confused this experience with true happiness, because he still pined. But he could see this life as maybe an adequate distraction from his discontent, or at least close enough, especially when his cloaking talent became sufficiently prodigious – and Peter's sponsorship sufficiently influential – to earn him a shot at what he really wanted.

Which was the freedom to pursue Maya.

After his first year of training, wherein Aiden had acquitted himself admirably by all accounts, he floated a proposal for a land-based assignment past his higher-ups. He could make it happen cloaking as Mitch Donovan, would volunteer to learn human security protocols they might want to mimic. He then perfected his artifice well enough to snow his brothers-in-arms, which garnered him the respect of everyone he trained with but Peter most importantly. Aiden was sent ashore without drawing suspicion to his true motives. Well, Simon knew, of course; and Aiden suspected Peter had figured him out, as well, since the guy was freaking omniscient. But he'd let him go.

Aiden had made straight for Maya, studied her living situation, and then found out who ran security for the Evans family. He got himself hired onto her team within a week.

He'd been by her ever since and vowed he wouldn't leave her again no matter the personal consequences. If the siren governing body would see him banished and broken over his compulsion, he no longer much cared. His need to be with her outweighed his need for self-preservation, not that he wanted to have to choose.

Of course, he'd been summoned home for a prolonged debriefing at the very moment Maya had finally accepted the real state of her marriage. And he'd have to go soon or Xanthe's minions would come for him and find out what he'd been up to, after which all his choices would be taken away for good. He wasn't quite sure how he was going to carry his lies forward this time. Hopefully by keeping the reporting structure small, staying by Peter, et. al.; and by avoiding a broader inquiry in front of Xanthe and her ilk.

At least this current threat of separation had also clarified his tolerances, since he no longer had to wonder if he'd be better off peripherally bound to his mate or toeing the siren line and remaining in the fold. He was so sick of wallowing in that bitter soup, the one comprised of small either/ors and narrow what-ifs to characterize not just his present, but also his future. He finally knew which choice he would make. And he'd take a pseudo-life lurking around the woman he loved, with or without the possibility of permanence.

He looked at the time and realized Maya should be off-shift by now. He started back to her townhouse... and then on a whim veered toward Manhattan. He should check in at Thad's instead, maybe see if he could get close to the guy and figure out what was behind his increasingly reckless quest for... whatever Thad was after. For whatever rotten personal egg the man sat on like an evil mother hen these days. Aiden's intuition warned him he'd need to figure that situation out and soon.

He was headed to the Evans penthouse when he was caught by a particular call from the ocean... and he changed direction abruptly, this time toward the old sea wall. He evaluated the negligible crowd, and when he deemed it thin enough, cloaked to slip unnoticed into the water. Ah, how he missed the ability to transform as he liked. He should just leave now to make his report... but he could steal a few more hours, couldn't he? He decided it didn't matter, he'd remain as long as he could. He stayed close to the embankment as he swam, weaving lazily out and back just under the surface as he thought and wondered and hoped.

Peter surveyed the water to the north of where he stood, which was on the balcony of the private home he'd built to anchor his siren military compound seven years ago. He searched the waves – with his intuition as well as visually – for Aiden Blake.

He'd expected him days ago, although he understood better than he cared to the dynamics behind Aiden's reluctance to return. Still, Peter would have preferred promptness, since the longer the delay, the more anxious everyone at Shaddox became. And the more scrutiny Aiden was likely to receive when he did finally show up. Peter wasn't particularly sympathetic to Aiden's plight with Maya Wilkes, but he wasn't heartless, either.

He walked a romantic tightrope of sorts himself these days.

His affections were more complicated, not to mention unspoken; as yet, he'd acknowledged his interest grudgingly to himself and no one else. He'd mostly avoided thinking about her, and certainly no one else knew of his considerations, including the woman he considered. She might be unpleasantly surprised if he were to declare himself, could well reject directly a relationship with him, especially given his history. And while he didn't intend to pursue her, neither did he relish the prospect of her negative response should he decide to.

So, he ruminated over whether or not he would approach her, and after accepting that he might, how. He'd prefer to wait everything out a bit longer, daydreamed he might get over his fascination, as if it were the flu. He'd been hoping this for months now.

The more he thought about her, the closer he wanted to be, however; and he suspected her own isolation – a function of her profession, just as his had been for him – called to him most profoundly. Aside from himself, she was the loneliest person he knew. And he was the only one who seemed to notice; she, herself, hadn't identified her own sadness, had consistently ignored it by busying herself with others' problems.

Peter knew exactly what she needed. Moreover, he wanted to bring her to his side, show her what she didn't know she lacked. He anticipated feeling complete should he succeed, although for once, this was not what drove him. He suspected her well-being preoccupied him more than his own, which was an odd situation to find himself in. He knew first-hand the grief she'd feel when he revealed her blind spot... and the prospect of hurting her stopped him.

He also didn't believe she'd think fondly of him if he did facilitate her awakening. Meaning he had two options: he could either leave her alone and never get close to her, or obliterate her belief in who she was, then hope she'd be drawn to him. He feared he'd lose either way.

But if he didn't help her, no one would, although he tried to convince himself of the wisdom of leaving things as they were. The consequences of doing nothing were slight, because she could just continue on and so could he. He was used to un-fulfillment, and she was used to attributing her own angst to the wrong source.

Peter rested his forearms on the balcony railing and rubbed his eyes. Given the growing number of hours each day he puzzled over this semi-obsession, he understood he would soon seek her out even if doing so was a bad idea. And when they connected, he knew he wouldn't be able to stop himself from trying to correct her misperceptions. He moved his head around to stretch his neck, then searched the water once more.

Aiden had better come distract him soon or Xanthe's emotional solo act was finished.

Peter pushed himself back from the railing and headed downstairs to the sea. He would swim north and pay a visit to Gabe and Kate's house, maybe wait for Aiden there. And give himself something to do other than brood over a woman he didn't want to want.

Chapter Five

Stu grinned to himself as he buttoned his shirt, ignoring the petulant pleas of his lover to stay in bed. He'd been summoned.

The prospect of a late-night meeting with his dad – and it sounded like he was wanted for an actual reason for once, not just a photo op – excited him, which admittedly didn't take much these days. His pretty, pretty life, which made him the envy of most people on the planet, was deadly boring much of the time, not that anyone cried over it, including him. But the chance to make an appearance on the larger, high-energy stage where his dad played... well, it sounded like a thrill ride and he wanted on. Especially since his current thrill, Annette, wasn't delivering of late.

This wasn't her fault, just as it hadn't been the fault of any of the women who'd kept him company before her. None of them understood – and he expected Annette would soon fall into the same category – how the failure of his romantic attentions to them was nothing personal; that these sorts of relationships were a sideshow for him, a diversion he relied on to blow off steam and feel... *right* inside. At any rate, the women would never be more to him than this, no matter how beautiful or interesting they were, and no matter how compelling their reasons might be for extending their affair when he inevitably broke things off.

"But you were so intense about us," or, "You were so into me, Stu," were common responses when he informed them he was moving on. Well, yes. That was no doubt true in the beginning, but since by now he'd juiced everything he could from their association and could no longer say he felt the same way, these objections didn't matter. Not that he said as much.

He didn't dislike any of his girlfriends, and he certainly didn't judge them, a worry he saw again and again in their eyes when he was saying goodbye. *Am I not good enough? Was I too easy?* His only concession to what might be called regret was the scant attention he paid to a niggling voice in his head, the one warning him his liaisons carried an insidious emotional threat – not to others, but to himself. If he was wise, the inner voice cautioned, he would deny his compulsions and find a constructive replacement for the high he got from illicit sex. Or rather, the chasing of it.

He always scorned the idea of restraint, though; his entertainments were a requirement if he wanted to continue to look and act like the Stuart Evans people knew. When he'd tried abstinence in the past, his mental health quickly unraveled. He became distractible and unable to focus at work, and things that shouldn't bother him, like the buzz of his phone or a loud laugh at a restaurant, sent him into a rage. He also spent his days in a constant state of paranoia, as if everyone he met knew how strange and disconnected he was just by looking at him. He worried he failed to pass some test of normalcy, one he imagined was administered by everyone he met, passersby on the street and colleagues at the office included.

At least he was familiar with the tangled subway of his own psyche, knew it well enough to take evasive measures when his composure began to slide. He recognized the paranoia for what it was, too, knew it meant it was time for a fix. He hated that feeling, where he teetered on the edge of self-control and was about to misbehave, maybe get himself arrested for a Drunk & Disorderly. Then it was either a quickie with a lover and all would be well, or he'd have to sign up for shark whispering lessons or some such nonsense, and better to stick with a little action on the side, especially since no one was being damaged by what he did, not really. He told himself he was a considerate lover, and hurt feelings were the burden of every human being, not an indication of true harm. He'd learned that lesson when he was no more than five.

Anyway. His companions were always there by choice, and if he was looking for something he shouldn't, well, so were they. People cheated all the time, so these relationships couldn't be *that* wrong, especially not when he considered the stabilizing effect they had on him. He wouldn't allow himself to be troubled by something so restorative, although he actively avoided thinking about the serial, predictable nature of his affairs. Or the expressions of distaste he sometimes read on the faces of friends when he flirted in public.

Which was where his wife got inserted into his mental health formula. In fact, Maya's reactions to his diversions had come to play an ever more meaningful role in the unknotting of his insides. He was acutely aware of the anxiety he caused her during his overtures to other women, knew he courted her distress when he rested a hand on another woman's back or pulled her into his lap. He also knew he should have curtailed these displays – not for Maya's sake, but to pre-empt a potential problem with his paramours. Maya was a loyal, dig-in-and-make-things-work kind of gal, whereas a vengeful lover… unfortunately, he could see how someday one might make public accusations against his character. A couple of the guys at work had ended up in that gutter, meaning Stuart had witnessed firsthand how a well-timed slander campaign – or lawsuit – could take a good man down.

But in a way he refused to consider too closely, Maya's anguish now added to the pay-off for him, to the point he could no longer stop himself from seeking it. When he flaunted his indiscretions in front of his wife and saw how they devastated her… well, it was really something. It was something to see how hurt she was, to test her promise to love him and stick around no matter what. And her ongoing efforts to reach him were miraculous, how she continued to try and build something intimate and real between them. In addition to the sexual rise he got from all his Annettes, including Maya as a spectator made him feel strangely worthy, if only for a little while.

It was his one source of guilt in all this, but again, he needed the release too badly to stop. He needed the reassurance, as well, that he was more than a two-dimensional human being, more than some rich socialite who was shiny on the outside and corroded on the inside. Just because he didn't sleep in a paper mâché box in the suburbs or wear off-the-rack suits didn't mean he struggled less than anyone else. Besides, the affairs were simply something he did, like drink scotch with his buddies, or work out at the club. His extramarital activities kept him in check, his dissatisfaction hidden. He thought they might also have a steadying effect on his marriage, since they chilled him out around a wife who was frazzled from medical school on top of the social challenges that came with being an Evans. He told himself what he did was for her benefit as well as his.

And he lived for the adrenaline rush. He'd never liked feeling as if his life was all decided, or foreseeing the plodding progression of his days until their end. He could picture himself exactly as he would be in another thirty years, an easy enough proposition if he perused the portraits of the Evans forefathers hanging in his parents' home. He would be practicing law and attending charity functions, posing for the camera with the same artificial smile, taking the same vacations, probably eating off the same china and drinking the same brand of liquor, too. Was this all there was? He might as well be dead already.

Fundamentally he felt cheated, as if his painless upbringing, provided via all sorts of handholding and sponsorship from birth onward, had deprived him somehow, and his incompleteness now showed like a limp. How different he felt from those he saw around him, even those who'd grown up in the same milieu. He wondered if it would have made any difference if he'd chosen a more divergent path; if he would have felt a stronger sense of purpose if life hadn't simply been handed to him, or if the expectations he'd had to meet weren't all but met at the outset. Now, he had the impression others were privy to some universal truth about humanity he wasn't in on. Whatever he'd missed, he felt marginalized because of it and, at least when it came to interactions with people outside his class, like the brunt of a joke.

Maya had given him real hope, had convinced him he could be, if not fulfilled, then no longer so concerned over his inadequacies.

He remembered the first time he saw her, the electric charge that had surged through him when she walked onto the volleyball court at Penn State. His attention fastened itself on her the entire game, which he attended with a work colleague who had a sister on Maya's team. Stu didn't remember a thing about the sister, nor any of the other players, for that matter.

Maya had looked like... like liquid energy, her movements so fluid and sure, her performance addictive. Her strength, her grace – she glowed with it, radiating the most seductive aura of health he'd ever encountered. He actually rocked backward after each spike, as if her hit had connected with him instead of the poor blocker she demolished at center court. He found himself hanging around after the game, feeling very out of place among a crowd of teenage girls waiting to meet the university's star middle hitter.

"She can hit outside, too," one of them remarked to her friend. "And her left kills are as good as her right."

The friend bounced with excitement. "I know! And did you see all those short hits? She was amazing!"

Stuart had no idea what they were talking about but made a mental note to brush up on his volleyball terminology. Maya was someone he wanted to appear competent in front of.

She emerged with two of her teammates from the building, all of them jostling giant athletic totes with the ease of people who'd done it a thousand times. They stopped when they saw the small crowd awaiting them, their heads turning in unison toward their entourage of fans. "Maya! Maya! Over here!" they called.

"Don't keep her too long, ladies," one of Maya's companions instructed the throng. "We need her at practice tomorrow." Then all three women looked Stu's way.

He knew he was hard to miss, since he was the only man there and towered over the adolescents around him. He thought Maya and her cohorts scanned him suspiciously, like they were checking for guns or knives. This made sense; they didn't know him, and they maybe had to worry about stalkers? He rushed to make himself look harmless, folding his hands in front of him and offering his warmest smile.

They frowned. "Do you want a security escort?" the friend on the left asked.

"I'm Stuart Evans," he interjected quickly. "I work with Stan Barrett, Missy Barrett's brother, and we just watched the game. Stan took Missy to dinner… but I had to join your admirers here." He gestured around him, then addressed Maya. "You're fantastic. It was a pleasure to watch you play."

Maya had been assessing him during his introduction and must have decided he was worth talking to because she dismissed her sidekicks.

"I'm good here," she assured them. "You guys can take off." The teammate to Maya's right took out a phone and snapped a picture, the flash temporarily blinding him. He blinked to refocus his eyes.

"In case we have to file a police report on you," she explained brightly. "See you, Maya!" She and her companion walked away.

Maya interacted easily with her fan club, Stuart saw, handling the barrage of compliments and questions like a pro. She was patient as they all asked the same thing ten different ways, and she was thoughtful with her answers so every girl received individual attention, which was what each of them most wanted from her. She was responsible, too, encouraging them all to enjoy the game for its own sake, not for fame or the possibility of a scholarship. She ended with a spiel that sounded coached but no less sincere on the role sports involvement should play in a young woman's life.

"I love volleyball, but school comes first," she asserted. "Your education is what will carry you in life, not how high your vertical is at age twenty. If it ever came to a choice between my game and my schooling, I'd quit the game, don't you doubt it."

After signing a couple dozen T-shirts and volleyballs, she wished the crowd good night and headed Stuart's way.

"Thanks for coming to watch," she offered. "I know Missy was excited her brother was coming, and we don't get many guys who aren't relatives."

"It was a blast," he told her earnestly. "More people should know about this. You could be bigger than the Yankees." Maya laughed. Stuart then decided to show off his newly gained knowledge of her sport by commenting on her skills as if he knew what "middle," "outside," and "short" were. She saw through him, though, and he ended up confessing he knew absolutely nothing about volleyball other than that there was a net between two teams and a certain number of players on either side. Maya nudged him with her shoulder and smiled slyly.

"There are six on a team," she informed him. But she wasn't offended, and she patiently explained the terms he'd fumbled over.

Stu fell into step with her as she walked toward student housing. By the time they reached the Commons, he'd talked her into going out with him to meet Stan and Missy, although she'd hesitated initially.

"I don't have an official practice tomorrow, but I have class in the morning and the team will go over clips with the coach tomorrow afternoon. I'll look bad if I fall asleep during the review." He promised to have her back by midnight, and she agreed to go.

When the evening was over, he delivered her to the front of her dorm as promised. He thanked her for coming out with him and told her, sincerely, he'd had a great time. "Look," he said while she fished for her keys. "I'd... I'd really like to see you again." To his surprise, he was nervous. He truly didn't know if Maya would say yes, which was a novel situation for him. Once a woman knew who he was, he didn't typically need to sell himself to get her to meet him when and where he chose. Maya had seemed interested – they'd flirted lightly all night – but he didn't have the impression she was on fire to start anything. He resolved to change her mind about that.

Years later, he would think of Maya's demonstrations of self-reliance as the dynamic that solidified his attraction to her. Maybe it was a result of her athletic training, but she was fearless and funny, and he found himself struggling not to appear over-eager. He was convinced after several encounters that he was spending time with a truly whole woman, one who knew herself and didn't dwell on the petty shortcomings that threw his other girlfriends into destructive bouts of insecurity. She ate actual meals, for instance, and enjoyed them without drawing attention to how much or how little she consumed. He couldn't remember the last time he was so at ease at dinner with a date. She was witty but kind, and her overall vitality – again, to Stu, she glowed with it – fascinated him. Stu found her irresistible, and the more of her confidence he witnessed, the closer he wanted to be.

Most of all, he loved how little Maya asked of him, starting the night they met and continuing through the rest of her college career. He never understood how society – strangers, mostly – believed he had a responsibility to take care of their little gripes and problems. Like because of his last name, he was required to give a rip about everyone else's well-being before his own.

Maya was such a relief in this respect. When he was with her, he never felt solicited for a kind of attention he could not deliver, interactions that so often left him drained, irritable, and lonesome even among friends. He wondered whether his father ever felt the same way.

Somewhere in Maya's senior year, Stuart decided to make a permanent bid for her companionship. She was so self-sufficient, he figured she could be happy with any number of guys, so why not him? For his part, he truly needed her; she continued to make him feel free to be himself when he had, he thought, precious little opportunity otherwise.

She'd never failed to take care of herself without him, except briefly during the spring before her graduation, when she spent several weeks wrestling with uncertainty over a career path. She righted herself, however, chose to pursue a hot-shot degree in medicine, and then navigated all the corollary decisions related to that choice without leaning on him. Which he appreciated. Once again, he felt bolstered by their association, and he could well envision how introducing her around as his doctor wife would come off. Just by showing up with her on his arm, he would more appear solid. Others, he predicted, would see the depth he tried unsuccessfully to portray on his own, and what an asset that would be. The prospect tantalized.

To his way of thinking, their wedding day was like a victory tour, and he'd meant every one of the vows he'd spoken at the altar. Gone in that moment was the cloying mantle of inadequacy mixed with ennui; satisfaction, he was sure, had finally been delivered to him whole, placed at his feet, and he would trouble himself no further for the wanting of it.

His contentment failed within a month, as did his attempts to regulate his disappointment in reaction. The frustration from that particular crash had simply been too much, and he'd gone on a weeklong tear so depraved, he still couldn't bear to think of it. Afterwards, he'd opted for the relatively tame approach of taking lovers like a normal guy. It was only in the last couple of years Maya's participation had come into play, as the high he chased became more elusive. Now, Maya's responses to his flirtations filled a nagging void. Because the more agitated she was, the more satisfying his pursuit became. The paradox of their marriage, from his point of view, was that the harder Maya tried to save them – the more she cared – the more driven he was to make her suffer. He needed her to watch.

He knew Maya could have no way of understanding all the intricacies of these internal machinations, or that his sexcapades with other women had nothing to do with her own romantic suitability. But as long as she questioned herself and what she could do better or differently, Stu didn't have to justify his actions, which meant he did not work to enlighten her. As it was, she continued to pay him the attention a wife should in these situations, and in doing so bore more and more the burden of his efforts to feel stable and happy. God help him if she ever figured out how little her own appeal factored in what he did.

Now, as he sat in his father's home office, Stu considered the information the elder Evans revealed in light of his wife's purported presence there earlier. Something about a high-risk mutual fund his dad and his dad's cousin, Nate, had launched a while back. Stu was stunned to learn of the venture, or rather, was stunned to hear his dad would embark on it. *Why would you bother?* he wanted to ask. There was no reason he could imagine, no ensuing attainment all of them didn't already have. Money? Social status? Professional prestige? Stu couldn't foresee any outcome that made the effort worth undertaking. He studied his dad for signs of health problems.

He was brought out of his musings by the sound of his wife's name, and he forced himself to listen more closely to the details Thad relayed thereafter, about how his fund was solid but didn't need any bad press at the moment; how he'd found Maya snooping in his office that evening, and unlikely as it seemed, maybe she wanted to make an example of him, to make some public stand against the inequities of capitalism...

"I'm sorry, Dad. When did you say Maya was in here?"

"Stu. Pay attention," his dad scolded. "She was here during the party."

Stu's stomach did a slow, sickening roll. As fulfilling as it was to have his wife suffer through foreplay in public, she'd never watched him take off from a gathering in another woman's company. He'd always thought such a move would be too disrespectful – and the one insult that might actually drive Maya to leave him. So he'd kept his obvious flirtations and actual seductions separate.

He considered his earlier progression through the corridor with Annette from an onlooker's – Maya's, in this case – perspective. She must have hid in one of the guest rooms and… well. There would have been no question as to what he and Annette were up to. Maya's timing alone, how she must have gone into Thad's office immediately after he and Annette had vacated it, filled Stu with dread. He checked his phone. If she'd been at work – which she apparently had not been – she would have texted when she got off-shift. She should have been done hours ago.

She hadn't messaged him.

Meaning she hadn't been at work, had decided to drop by his dad's, and her reasons for her visit to Thad's office had most likely been his fault, an insight he didn't much care to share with his father but would. He made a last-ditch, desperate effort to convince himself he was mistaken.

"Maya was here tonight," Stu reiterated, hoping Thad would deny it by saying, "Did I say tonight? Stuart, I meant *last* night!" But, no.

"I haven't left this room since I found her in it."

Stu stared at the spot on his dad's desk where he and Annette had satisfied each other earlier. Thad was off again on his diatribe, explaining how he'd dispatched a security team after Maya… and Stu again forced himself to listen to this next report, the one informing him his wife would soon be followed by armed men. Which he thought was going too far. He had to come clean.

"Dad," he began. "I don't think Maya was spying. I was down here earlier. With Annette, and we – "

Thad snorted. "Stu. I saw you two leave the party, hanging all over each other. I knew what you were doing. Everyone did." Stu drew a breath to contradict him, but Thad kept talking. "Maya's seen you at a hundred parties with some woman or another. It's never landed her in my office, looking through my papers." Thad picked up a folder for emphasis. "Even if she came in here to check up on you, she saw this." He flung the file onto his desk.

Stu hesitated. Was his father right? Had Maya seen something, even unintentionally, to warrant Thad's reaction? He checked his phone again, which still showed no attempt at contact. "I'll try to call her," he offered. After several rings, he reached Maya's voicemail. He hung up without leaving a message.

Thad glared at him accusingly. "She's gone, isn't she."

"I don't know," Stu admitted. "She's not at home, and I haven't heard from her."

"Dammit, Stuart. Find her."

Chapter Six

Three months later…

Maya let herself into her apartment, thumbing through her mail as she ambled into the kitchen, knowing she'd throw most of today's take in the trash. She'd find no personal correspondence because no one knew she was here, except for those men following her for reasons unknown. And since they hadn't ventured past security in the lobby, she suspected they only knew her building, not her unit. She hoped.

Plus if those guys wanted to talk with her, she doubted they'd send a letter.

So all she ever got was junk mail addressed to "Current Resident," or bills addressed to the person who had agreed to sublet to her, a guy she'd never met. She paid the bills along with her rent in cash, which she put in an envelope and deposited in a box next to the first-floor administrative offices on the first of each month according to the arrangement she and Mitch had made to secure her hideaway. She included no note, nothing with her name or signature, nothing to even specify what the money was for. In fact, she'd avoided attaching her name to anything related to where she lived, something she was pleased to verify each day when she scanned the ads and fliers she pulled from her mailbox. She threw the entire pile in the garbage bin and took her first easy breath of the day.

At first her dissociation from the rest of the world gratified her more than she would have predicted, the sense of peace that accompanied being unreachable and unaccountable a surprise pleasure given the hard-charging, plugged-in life she'd lived up until now. And while she hated hiding from her job – she truly worried she was throwing away seven years of schooling – she preferred to think of herself as on hiatus, not as a permanent dropout. Somehow, some way, she would resume her residency and complete her training, launch herself as a bona fide doctor.

Still, her current circumstances were kind of freeing. She no longer used her cell phone, although she turned it on once each evening to check for messages. Which meant she wasn't tied to endless texts, nor was she obliged to keep constant track of her calls, or hurry to get back to people. And while she fretted over the worry her disappearance had surely caused friends and family, she did not reach out to anyone, wouldn't until she felt she could without risk to them. Which meant living off the grid for the time being; so no car, no credit cards, no accessing her personal financial accounts. The only account she kept now was at a local pawn shop, where the owner was delighted to front periodic transactions in exchange for the luxury items she sold him for pennies on the dollar. Gone were her Tiffany's wedding ring, her Cartier watch, as well as several other pieces of high-end jewelry she no longer had reason to wear. Some of the bigger items she'd agreed to sell on consignment, so she wouldn't see full payment until they were purchased from the store, but the broker had bought enough to keep Maya in cash for the next several months. She very much hoped to be back in circulation before her current funds ran out and never mind how much she could scare up if she kept on selling. She could probably exist like this indefinitely, a depressing prospect no matter how much she enjoyed her invisibility.

She'd begged to be able to keep in touch a little, though, and she'd refused to let her parents wonder if she was dead under a bridge somewhere. For this reason, Mitch had set her up with what he called a "ghost" computer, one that shifted servers and networks, disabled all cookies, and generally ensured her searches and location would remain untraceable. He'd promised to reassure her parents, too, although she never understood how. But between her one email – sent from an anonymous account, saying she was okay but would be unreachable for a while – and Mitch's undisclosed efforts, Maya's parents had been mollified. Or at least they hadn't launched a missing persons campaign, which would have made hiding out more difficult. She hadn't heard a peep from anyone else.

Now, three months into her exile, the pleasure of her break from responsibility was, she acknowledged, fading. The solitude in particular wore on her, as did the whole wait-and-see approach she'd adopted since her last encounter with Mitch, which she'd had shortly after her epiphany in Thad's office.

She believed Mitch had advised her honestly when he'd convinced her to disappear, to take seriously the perceived threats from Thad, ones she suspected were indeed dangerous. But she'd had the impression he was only a little better informed than she was on the specifics, details he'd promised to research and defuse, although he hadn't yet, since here she still was and there were her intrepid followers. In the end, though, she'd been convinced the risks warranted her drastic duck and run.

Mitch had told her Thad was in some kind of trouble, but he hadn't been able to get close enough to him to ascertain the particulars. Financial trouble, Mitch thought, as incongruous as that sounded, and Stu might even be involved. Mitch hoped so. "I want... well, just let me at him," he'd reported darkly.

But between his efforts to monitor his Evans security colleagues and challenges from "problematic parties back home," Mitch said he hadn't gotten his arms around the whole of what had turned into in his words a complicated game with too many players. He lamented being the only one "of his kind" to be charged with figuring everything out, complained how frustrating it was for him to not have a better grasp on everyone's motivations. And intentions.

"Your kind?" Maya inquired. "You mean other security guards of Irish descent?"

Mitch pretended she hadn't spoken. "All I know is Thad's beefed up his security detail, and the new team members are armed and scary." As if this development wasn't troubling enough, Mitch suspected a new contingent had also entered the fray, *another* group of actors operating under stealth. Thad et. al. were unaware of these new participants, from what Mitch could deduce; and Mitch himself had no idea what they were looking for, who employed them, or how far they were willing to go to get whatever it was they wanted.

Maya agreed to skedaddle after that declaration, had actively participated in plans to make herself scarce. The effort had felt like she was lopping off her own limbs, as if she might actually be destroying everything she'd achieved even as she thought of every possible detail she could to facilitate her own demise.

In quiet hours, the totality of all she'd surrendered undid her. She'd had to abandon her job at the hospital to make it look like she'd skipped town, a decision she'd found as gut-wrenching as the one to leave her husband and that was saying something. Why should her hard-won degree, which she was on the cusp of completing after years of discipline and sleeplessness – the whole of her adulthood, when she thought about it – be sacrificed? Why did her professional goals *and* personal life have to be incinerated, and why was she obliged to light the fire that turned it all to ash? From her vantage point after the fact – and considering the lack of resolution she still lived with – she wondered if perhaps she'd placed too much confidence in Mitch.

He'd been pretty convincing after the Stu and Annette incident, however, when she'd realized her marriage was over.

Mitch showed up that night like he was conjured, she recalled. How he'd known where to find her, and to come when he did…

well, she'd never figure that one out. Whatever his method though, she owed her life to his intervention that evening.

She'd felt so strange leaving Thad's office, more disturbed than she'd ever been at work, which didn't make sense when the medical emergencies she dealt with, one after the other, should have unsettled her way more than snooping after Stu to verify the obvious. She'd never broken down as a physician, though, never felt this shaken as she staunched a gunshot wound or stitched someone's intestines back in place. On any given Friday night, she and the other ER docs even joked about what they called 'The Midnight Show,' since they could almost time the influx of gang violence victims they'd be treating.

She was not as cavalier about her own internal injuries, apparently. Her revelation in Thad's office had left her in shock, and way more wrung out than any blood-based trauma she'd dealt with as a resident.

After brushing past her very agitated father-in-law, she'd made it halfway down the hall before she had to stop. She'd intended to walk out the door and check into the nearest hotel for some anonymity and sleep, but all those rapid-fire emotions, along with the heavy import of the decisions she'd just made, left her woozy. She braced a hand against the wall to steady herself. The corridor, when she looked up, had taken on the characteristics of a carnival fun house, like she was walking in one of those tunnels where the floor rolled under her in waves, and the place looked to have been built at odd angles. She closed her eyes and breathed, trying to contain the loopy feeling in her stomach. Maybe if she checked again, the world would straighten out and she would feel normal… but a peek had her quickly squeezing her eyelids shut again. Nope.

Someone had altered the earth's gravity, she decided, so she'd best stay put for a minute. She focused on the turmoil inside her instead, on bringing order to the ideas and sensations careening around inside her like bumper cars. This approach seemed to work, since the next time she braved a look at her surroundings, she understood them. Moreover, she knew where she needed to be, and it wasn't at a hotel.

She didn't fight the compulsion this time – she just went. Couples and late-night runners roamed the walkway behind her as she rested her forearms on the sea wall. She stared out at the water, letting the wind and the sound of the waves deliver the magic she'd come for. A call and an answer meant just for her, like a promise from a lover.

Yes. This. Just this, she thought on a sigh.

She let her musings settle where they would, eventually bringing her to Aiden. She rarely gave herself this permission to think about him, but tonight she felt she could. And maybe ought to.

She considered how she'd behaved toward him when she was still in Griffins Bay and unattached. Away from Stu and his family and all their damage, she allowed herself to remember her early interactions with Aiden – and her selfish, fearful responses to him – without self-criticism, and without her usual stranglehold on the difficult emotions that attended these recollections. Which she'd resisted hard because they highlighted too sharply her isolation, as well as her uncertainties over her future.

But she was in the process of changing her future, was no longer going to be stuck with bad decisions she'd made eight years ago. She nursed a burgeoning, fragile sense of compassion for herself over her failures and all she'd done to bring them about. For trying however poorly to create a good and meaningful life.

I was just young and figuring things out, she realized.

She wished she could tell this to Aiden, wished she could apologize to him truly and in person this time for the hurt she'd caused both of them. *I thought of love all wrong. I'd do better if I could go back.*

The sound of the water calmed her. Her heart unclenched, as if the ocean leeched away her misdeeds and told her she was, indeed, forgiven. She began to imagine how it would feel to be submerged, floating in that sweet darkness; how the buoyancy of the water would lift her out of all the heaviness she carried. She would be loved and know everything would be all right. The vision so enticed her, she dropped her arm over the sea wall and reached toward the waves.

The next thing she knew, she sat on the sand, huddled and dripping salt water as Mitch knelt over her, also drenched. His chest heaved, either with emotion or from exertion, she couldn't tell.

"How did I...?" she sputtered.

Mitch dragged a soaked forearm across his eyes. "You're lucky I was around," he grated. She couldn't tell if he was angry with her or just really, really worried.

"I fell in?" she guessed.

"You *jumped* in, Maya. You nearly gave me a heart attack."

"That's ridiculous," she countered. "I would never... I mean, I don't even like the ocean. And it's so cold..." Then, realizing they were at risk for hypothermia, she straightened. "We have to get inside. Right now."

Before she could push herself up however, Mitch captured her hand and held it against his chest. Maya became still, astonished at the sensations she felt from him. As she watched, a sleepy expression crept over his face.

"I've got us covered, Maya. Feel. You're not cold. I'm not either."

And she wasn't. In fact, Mitch seemed to radiate a kind of self-generating, personalized heat. Feverish, maybe?

"No," he said, leaning closer. Maya didn't realize she'd voiced her concern. But she must have. "You won't... I came to you... we were only in the water a minute," he murmured. "And I made sure... I mean, you won't freeze."

For no reason she could ascertain, she *was* warm. Even though she could see her breath in the air. Huh.

Their next progression was so dreamlike and disjointed, she couldn't have described it afterwards if asked. It began with Mitch interlacing his fingers with her own, then circling her wrist with his other hand, his thumb pressed to the sensitive underside of her wrist. The gesture – the fact that he held her hand at all – was too loving, too intimate, and Maya tensed, caught between a sudden need to run from… whatever this was; and a colossal hunger to get closer, to allow the intimacy blossoming between them to expand. Mitch's pull on her soon darkened, however, until all the prettiness, all that was gentle in his demeanor, fled. In a matter of seconds, he'd exposed a raw secret looming within her, one he knew as well as she did. She experienced a familiar flutter of panic in her stomach, made all the more distressing because she understood neither of them could escape the affinity Mitch had just revealed… and he didn't want to. His stare became a brutal mandate to be present for this, to stay with him.

The ghost of Aiden visited her now, his voice an echo in her head. *You said if you could go back, if you could try again, you wouldn't run*, he reminded her.

Of course she'd been brave when this situation had been hypothetical. How foolish of her, because out of context, she could forget why she'd resisted Aiden as diligently as she had. Now she faced another guy with the same fantastical attributes, ones that looked like a departure from any reality she was still willing to accept. It was too much. Especially now, when she was not yet free of her commitments to Stuart… and the man before her was not the man in her head. She looked away in an effort to guard her self-possession.

"We shouldn't be doing this," she said desperately, her feelings a festering swamp of hope, want, and shame.

"Maya. Look at me." She did, and under his regard, her worries and convictions steadily waned.

She remembered this, having her ability to hold onto herself taken during an onslaught of small, tender tugs from some outside source she could neither defend against nor deflect. She dimly considered protesting… but soon she no longer cared to. She leaned forward, losing the struggle not just internally, but also physically. Even as she continued to believe she shouldn't give in.

Mitch said nothing, but the hunger pouring off him was like a deluge of warm water melting the fortress of ice encasing her. When had she last felt so wanted? Still, she fought to protect her last, tiny bit of restraint... until she lost it in a languid, lovely outpouring. She couldn't fight this and didn't want to, not really. Here was someone so lost in love with her, he would welcome her wholly, her ugly and graceless past included; a man who might, given a chance, erase every doubt she'd had since becoming Maya Evans. She exhaled a breath she hadn't known she held, and she searched Mitch's expression. *Did* what she feel come from him?

It did. She somehow knew. Mitch drew her close, without explanation or apology, and buried his nose in her hair.

His seduction – or maybe her own longing – leveled the last of her fight. She felt a peculiar, orchestrated release within her, a loosening of the internal discipline she relied on to protect her vulnerabilities. Mitch had obliterated her barriers and was now a vortex of solicitation for her deepest, most private contemplations. He asked for everything – her thoughts, her fears, her hopes and desires – and they flowed from her unchecked, leaving an emptiness, a kind of serenity, in their wake.

Life outside them ceased to exist for her, as if the universe beyond the two of them had fallen away and they floated in a disembodied void. She reveled in their closeness even as a small part of her acknowledged this was not right. Because she was still too entangled in her old life, and Mitch was not the man she would choose even if she were free. A silken thread of despair penetrated her euphoria... and she begged Mitch to let her go, not because she wanted him to, but because she couldn't stand the thought of making another wrong choice. She demanded a reprieve even as she arched into him, into his hands on her body and his lips at her throat.

You are not Aiden, and I am not free.

Mitch froze and time stopped with him, leaving them adrift in a dim, fathomless dimension as still as death, a death Maya craved. Then after several additional, surreal seconds, her senses revived, and the world she knew started again around them, like a warped music box hitching faultily up to speed. She became aware of the sounds of the wind and surf, felt once again the grit of sand beneath her knees and the rush of cool air into her lungs.

Her return to reality was bittersweet since she knew it meant Mitch had resisted just as she'd asked, that he'd succeeded in withdrawing from her. She was grateful for his effort. She hadn't had the wherewithal to divide them, would have given herself to him no matter how much regret she might suffer later. Even so, she pressed her cheek into his shoulder so he would not see her disappointment. She should help, she knew, should force herself away from him. But his touch was a solace she could not refuse.

She wished fervently she wasn't so messed up. If her circumstances were different, she could have met this man on open, uncluttered terms instead of as she was. Which was ignorant and drowning in madness.

A minute later – or so it seemed – Maya opened her eyes. Her surroundings disoriented her, since she wasn't at her townhouse, nor did she appear to be in a hotel.

Uh-oh.

She leapt out of the bed, relieved to note the stale, grungy state of her clothes. She'd slept in them – and they were still on her, which was encouraging.

Mitch startled her from the doorway. "We're at my place. I slept on the couch," he confirmed. He appeared equally rumpled, still wearing what he had last night, too. She relaxed, could even smile at him. She should have worried given her last recollection of them together… but as she took him in, she couldn't. She knew – *knew* – she could trust him.

Although, truthfully, she should leave. Starved though she might be for love and affection, now was not a good time to explore new romantic horizons. Plus, she'd accustomed herself to her deprivations and knew how to cope on her own. She had no confidence she could navigate the next stretch of her existence while protecting someone else from all her craziness.

My life has all the stability of gravy on a stick, she thought bitterly. And until she got out of her marriage, completed her medical training, found a place to live and started making her own breakfast again, she had no business pretending she had anything to offer a lover.

She also couldn't predict how difficult the Evans family was going to be when she filed for divorce. She didn't plan to ask for anything, but her soon-to-be jilted husband and questionably upstanding father-in-law might still decide to make the next several months an ugly lesson in humiliation. Unlikely, given their distaste for media attention, but Thad's behavior in his office had been so erratic – and Stuart's so sick – she didn't dare guess what they might or might not do.

She also dreaded the prospect of either dodging or facing the bottom-feeding, publicity-hounds who would love to hear about all this, the ones who lived to expose the interpersonal dramas of the rich and famous. If she was seen with anyone in public, her decisions – and those of the man with her – would be thrown out on the street for public mastication like a side of beef to a pack of vicious, mannerless dogs. No, thank you.

To her surprise, Mitch did not need excuses or explanations from her. He didn't protest at all when she started to explain why she would not be continuing whatever they'd started on the beach last night. "I'm not in a good place to..." she began. "I mean, I can't even think about, well, not before..." She tried a different tack, the one concerning her faithless husband. "See, I have to do some things on my own, because I can't stand to feel like a doormat anymore."

Mitch snorted. "You're not a doormat, Maya. Stuart's an idiot. Soon he'll be showing the world just how much, I'm sure. Also I've got to leave town in two days, and I won't be back for... a few weeks? I think. So you're off the hook where you and I are concerned." His expression became ominous. "For now."

Disappointment flooded her in spite of her belief they should stay uninvolved. She looked away to hide her hurt feelings, reminding herself she really did have to let Mitch be and get out of there, had to start taking care of her problems. Mitch sighed. He spoke again, this time more gently. "Don't be sad. It makes this too hard for me." He pushed himself off the door jamb. "I've worked out a plan I'd like you to think about."

Unable to talk past the obstruction in her throat, Maya nodded. He was doing what she'd asked him to do, after all, and in a way that saved either of them from saying words like, "I reject this. I reject you." But she kept silent so as not to reveal how close she was to throwing herself at him and pleading with him to stick around...

Although part of her wished he wanted her so badly he'd come to her regardless of their impediments. Mitch issued a short, bark-like laugh. "I'm going to remind you of that wish when I get back."

She grasped at the first distraction that came to her. "Tell me about your plan," she blurted, a little wildly. Because if she stayed in this emotional state another second – where she tried to contain the unreasonable want constricting her chest – she would suffocate. She needed a different effort to put her shoulder into. Maybe an actual direction to take herself, preparations she could make to stabilize her existence tomorrow, or the next day, or the day or week after that. *Anything* to interrupt the compulsion to explore what hovered between the two of them here and now.

And she did feel better after they talked, although she initially balked at Mitch's proposal for a total retreat. His patient explanations convinced her, though; Thad was up to something nefarious, and he was inclined to blame her – possibly punish her – for things not going his way. Together, she and Mitch worked out her entire escape plan, step by step, at his kitchen table. Then they put their plan into action.

Both Stu and Thad were taken in by Maya's ploy to convince them she'd left the city, which she created by buying a bus ticket to Santa Fe. She used her credit card so the purchase could be traced – and as part of the Evans security team, Mitch made sure it was.

Then she'd given her ticket away to a woman further back in line. The woman distrusted her at first, but the offer of a free fare eventually had her clinging to Maya like she was her long-lost baby girl. She grabbed the ticket to her chest, hugged Maya again, and then released her with the promise to keep her cover. "Run along, sister," she whispered, squeezing Maya's hand. "Disappear like you needs to." As Maya exited the station, she heard the woman introduce herself as Maya Evans to her fellow travelers.

Before executing this ploy, Mitch had encouraged her to gather whatever cash she could and warned her away from any procurement methods that could be tracked after the bus ticket caper. Meaning just before heading to the depot, she'd made a twenty-thousand-dollar withdraw from checking, money she was supposed to use for shoes and a gown to the annual Evans charity gala.

She went back to Mitch's place and waited until he showed up with a van full of personal items from the townhouse she'd shared with Stu, which he'd extracted without attracting attention from Stu or his father. Maya thought that was a neat trick, one he didn't explain and she didn't ask about. What was one more inconsistency in this bizarre situation? Mitch then dropped her off at her new "safe house," an apartment he'd secured from "a friend." He left her with a set of keys, twenty-one unopened boxes from her former life, and a host of uncertainties, among them the reason for his departure and his plans to return. He would only say he'd be gone a while, and she shouldn't worry if he failed to check in. He'd get back as soon as he could.

He'd made his frustration at having to go evident, although that hadn't translated to the disclosure of any rationale related to his trip. "Believe me, I'd do anything to get out of it. It's mandatory, it's personal, and if I don't show up, they'll come get me." He assured her she looked like she was on the other side of the country to the Evans family. She was safe here, he promised. He'd try to call her next week sometime. She waited until she saw his cab drive away and returned to the privacy of her condo before indulging in tears.

That had been twelve weeks ago – shortly before her goon babysitters had begun tailing her – and she hadn't heard from Mitch once. He could be dead for all she knew. God, she hoped he wasn't dead, or in trouble because of her.

But for whatever reason, he hadn't returned and hadn't tried to contact her... and she had to consider the possibility he never would. Which caused her to start thinking of her situation differently.

Mitch had been the one to ferret out her new digs, where her unknown sublettor would presumably return one day. She had no way to determine when that might be or where she might go when that happened. She didn't even know how to get in touch with the guy, assuming he had someone else check the deposit box for him downstairs. Would a note tucked into her rent envelope be too risky? Possibly. Maybe her pursuers had already cut her off from everyone, and the urgency to follow her stopped on the front steps of her building because they could come in and get her at any time. She stood at her window, stared down at the street, and scanned for her surveillance goons. The Undertaker's car was, sadly, in its usual place; and Jethro's broad-shouldered swagger – as well as his gum chewing – helped her pick him out in seconds.

Disgust over her lack of progress – and over the possibility of being stuck here forever, alone and jobless – caused her to pivot away from the view and pace the room. She had to wonder how hidden she'd been all along, and how un-vulnerable she was now. The tone of Stu's daily texts, which had been comprised of desperate, predictable attempts to call her in... well, they'd even changed, a worrisome development that roughly coincided with her realization she was being followed. Today's message had been straight-up alarming:

I know ur around, hon. Grab a taxi home and we'll work it out.

She'd assumed he was bluffing. But maybe he wasn't?

She hadn't responded – she never did. This time though, she fumbled in her haste to turn the device off, flung it to the couch across the room to distance herself from Stu's offer. Because her seven-year lesson on why they could not "work it out" must not be unlearned at this point, right? She mostly needed to deny the surge of longing she felt, a desire to go back and live with things as they'd been. For the first time since she'd gone into hiding, she wanted her old problems instead of her new ones, wished she and Stu did not have to un-marry and abandon every hope they'd had for themselves when they'd begun.

Logically, she knew loneliness drove these musings, and if she were smart, she'd stop rehearsing old questions she already knew the answers to. She should watch TV or read a novel or bake some cookies or go for a walk... anything to avoid the tired, fruitless mental rut this kind of contemplation dumped her into.

But her phone made other distractions impossible. It pulsed like a tiny black hole on the vast expanse of her couch; its silence, its stillness, served as a thundering contradiction to the bustle and noise of life being lived outside her window. *There's your answer, Maya,* she thought. *Relief is just four steps and seven digits away.* She really thought about it. She couldn't help herself.

Her job. Her inviting, beautiful brownstone. All she had to do was put up with Stuart, something she knew how to do well enough, and she could have those things back. In fact, she could reboot her former life with the press of a button and the phrase, "I'm on my way." She stared hard at that phone and dreamt of deliverance.

Something – she couldn't have said what – stopped her from acting, and a few seconds later she regained her perspective, the one that had prompted her to put herself in her current circumstances. She could never go back, wouldn't be able to make herself stay in a stifling, joyless relationship with Stu no matter the upside. As soon as she pictured it – really pictured herself scrapping for emotional crumbs again within her own marriage – she felt ashamed. There could be no reunion, no resurrection. She had not been wrong in her analysis when she left, and she couldn't allow herself to throw away this hard-won chance at freedom after all she'd gone through to have it. The idea to return was just boredom and isolation talking.

But the extent to which she'd reconsidered her decisions jolted her. If she was this tempted to throw in the towel tonight, she knew one of these days she would. And if her options were her profession and Stu, or unending seclusion and misery, how much longer would she last? A week? Maybe not even that. She approached the window to gaze again at the cityscape, thinking how she was almost in the same oppressive situation she'd worked so hard to leave. Her set-up was eerily similar, since she didn't know anything, didn't know when she would, and didn't do anything other than wait around and hope things would change.

She pressed her face to the glass and peered at the people below hurrying along the street. She felt jealous of every single one of them, every person out and about striving to make something of him- or herself. Even if they were overworked or socially awkward or stressed out over their families or jobs, at least they had families and jobs, and at least they were out there trying. Everywhere Maya looked she saw evidence of human energy she wasn't part of.

This is intolerable. Surely, she could come up with a better way to address her problems. She pushed herself back from the visuals feeding her discontent and resumed pacing. She thought about what she could do substantively to extricate herself.

For starters she needed to stop hiding, or at least stop hiding here. And she needed to figure out who was following her and why. Then she would either run again – truly run, where no one, including Mitch and his apartment-leasing friends, would know where she was – or she would figure out where to go for help. It wasn't much of a starting point, but she achieved enough resolution to calm down. She checked the locks, turned out the lights, and retired to her bedroom, determined to start fresh after a night of sleep.

Chapter Seven

The next morning, Maya grabbed her computer and headed outside.

At the Bean Machine, she set up at her regular table and studied her options. She knew certain places in the country would take her, remote areas where they were hard up for medical practitioners and might overlook the fact that she was only ninety-eight percent a doctor. Appalachia? An Indian reservation where she could work under someone? Or she could disappear overseas, maybe in Haiti or Nepal; or some sprawling, densely populated city in South America. The idea of living as a low-level fugitive, even in poverty among people she didn't know, was preferable to wasting away here.

But she decided to focus her search within the contiguous U.S.; she didn't really want to mess with passports and the State Department, not when she could quietly vanish without a fuss in her own back yard. Yes. This idea felt right.

Instantly her mood brightened. A grim form of happiness settled like a warm shadow within her, her first flirtation with honest-to-God hope since forever. Her body tingled in preparation, anticipating action like it used to when she and her teammates were about to take the court before a big game. How glorious to feel competent again, and how strange to not have had this feeling in her emotional repertoire all these weeks. Here she was, taking her life back into her own hands, and all she'd needed to feel self-sufficient again was a cup of coffee and a tour around the internet.

She would escape the scrutiny of her unknown stalkers and get away from the pressure, from loneliness, from everything bugging her and making her crazy.

She could go now if she wanted.

At this thought, authentic optimism took root in her heart. *Why not? Why don't I just pick up my computer and leave?* She envisioned living a simple, unencumbered existence somewhere quiet, helping in a rural clinic, maybe coaching a girls' sports team at the local school... and she had no further desire to play it safe. After all, what was the risk? On someone's order, one of her pet watchdogs might take a shot at her. Or gang up on her curbside, duct tape her and cart her off in the trunk of a car. Honestly, this whole situation was so unpredictable, she couldn't guess what might happen if she stuck around.

The Evans boys apparently knew she was in town.

Mitch hadn't tried to get in touch in months.

And she had no one else she could rely on to help her, at least no one she could trust. Why *was* she still here?

She took a sip from her cup and stretched as an excuse to look around, and yes, there were her guards, just where she expected them to be and doing what they always did. Man, was she ever tired of this drill...

Which was when her mystery man – her angel of mercy – appeared, tossed her an insubstantial lifeline then walked blithely away, causing Jethro and the Undertaker to scramble and come after her for real.

Forty minutes later, Maya slid into the back seat of a cab, intent on showing her father-in-law precisely how un-enthused she was over his assault on her peace of mind. Her savior, the one who'd so recently visited her at the café and made her believe she was no longer alone in this fight had somehow found her again. He followed her into the back seat of the taxi, vomiting a list of instructions. Which she ignored.

She was *done* letting others steer her.

"Ten West 54th Street," she told the driver as he pulled into traffic. She felt her companion's alarm, although she was certain she hadn't stated her intentions aloud. He grasped her shoulders.

"Maya. Please. Don't go to him. Don't risk yourself."

Maya twisted away and spoke calmly to the cabbie. "Make it fast and I'll pay double. Cash."

The driver grinned into the rearview mirror. "Yes, ma'am."

Following Jethro's artless threat, where he'd pulled his jacket aside to reveal a gun – as if that was supposed to make her stay put – she'd run out the back door of the café. He thought she would just sit there? Wait for him to either threaten her some more or walk up and shoot her? What an idiot. "Prick," she'd mouthed before pivoting away from the window.

She was furious. And so fed up with waiting around for salvation, she refused to do it any longer. She would have to stop back at her condo for money, but then she would hire a driver to take her literally anywhere else. She was *finished* playing by the rules, certainly these rules. She headed for her apartment.

Jethro must have anticipated her decision to go home, however, because when Maya checked over her shoulder, he was four blocks behind her and running hard in her direction. She took off in a sprint.

Seconds later, her gentleman stranger from the café stepped in front of her, bracing her when she collided into his chest. His attention was on her pursuer as he attempted to shift her behind him, but she stood her ground and clutched his arms to get him to look at her. "Who are you?!? No, wait – never mind – I'm being chased and he has a gun and there might be others and *we have to get away*!"

The man scanned her face before releasing her. "Go. Get what you need from your apartment and meet me back here." He gestured with his chin at her pursuer. "I'll take care of Magnum over there."

Maya didn't stay to argue. She fled, slowing only after she made the lobby of her building. She composed herself on her walk to the elevator, straightened her clothes and smoothed her hair; and she mentally mapped out her game plan, the bag she would use, the belongings she would grab, just things she absolutely needed.

She'd left the street with every intention of returning to her new friend... but as she crammed bundles of cash and her hairbrush into a shoulder bag, she decided she wouldn't. She didn't know him, had no reason to believe he could help her. And relying blindly on others had consigned her to her current predicament. She wanted no part of it.

She couldn't let her desire for relief convince her to team up with a stranger. Even if the guy truly believed he could save her from the undefined threats closing in on her, he might not know any more than she did.

She briefly toyed with the idea of returning to him out of courtesy, just to inform him in person she was declining his offer of help... but she immediately rejected the thought, because what if he tried to come with her anyway? She'd be smarter to just take off, make a clean escape. She zipped her bag shut and closed her apartment door for the last time. She hoped.

Outside, she walked briskly in the opposite direction of her would-be partner. She jumped three feet when he tapped her on the shoulder.

"You're going the wrong way."

She bristled and looked longingly toward downtown and its plethora of drivers for hire. "No, actually. I'm not."

Was there no activity of hers that others – even strangers, apparently – didn't feel they had the right to oversee? Frustration flared in a white-hot flash behind her eyes... and for a second, she envisioned perpetrating violence. Not that she knew how to fight because she didn't and would probably have her fanny handed to her by any and all, the fit male before her especially. But she had to keep to her original goal, which was autonomy and ultimately freedom.

She decided the quickest means to her end was to not explain herself. She was about to turn on her heel and march off when she eyed a suspicious lump in his jacket pocket, one heavy enough to make his coat list off his shoulders to one side. In an instant, she understood it was the gun he'd retrieved from Jethro... and with dim consciousness, she equated possession of that firearm with independence.

Before she'd considered her actions, she snatched the weapon and tucked it into the folds of her own coat. *Thank you, years of athletic training and quick reflexes,* she thought smugly.

Her escort stood motionless. "Okay. I didn't expect that."

They faced off warily in the middle of the sidewalk, with industrious members of the city streaming around them as if they were rocks in a river. Maya assumed her new friend probably wanted to take the gun back, but she didn't think he'd make a scene. When he reached for her, she avoided him, or more specifically, avoided his touch, which she instinctively knew would compromise her. Because she wanted him to touch her, suspected the comfort she would feel... even without contact, she felt the beginnings of her undoing, an experience she knew too well. She stepped backward.

But she was too late. A familiar lethargy had already blunted her resolve, just as it had around Aiden when she started to act one way and then couldn't follow through. She'd fared no better with Mitch over the years... meaning she didn't doubt her imminent downfall.

Getting away was too important to her this time, however. She couldn't let herself cave, couldn't return to a life of confinement... the idea hurt like the stab of a blade into her side.

Don't. Please, she pleaded. Her adversary smiled.

"Give the gun back, Maya," he insisted, not unkindly. She took another step back and shook her head. This was the first time she'd had any leverage since she'd gone into hiding, and she wouldn't concede it.

"No. Not until I figure out who those men are and who sent them." At his knowing look, she pressed, "Who was Jethro working for?" And then, because she was worried, "Also, what did you do to him?"

"He works for your father-in-law. And I knocked him out, but he's not hurt. Not seriously, anyway."

Maya was alarmed for all of two seconds: this stranger knew a lot about her, including her association with Thad. How long had he been following her? As what he'd just reported sunk in, however – that Thad was the one having her watched – a fury big enough to burn the city down seared through her, obliterating every rational thought. She no longer even saw the man with her, or heard whatever he continued to spew her way.

So. Mitch had been right about Thad's paranoia, not that he was around to offer insight. She was so upset she shook, until the seasoned competitor within her took over, allowing her to crystallize her intention with the single-mindedness she would need to carry it out. She didn't care the least little bit if she got into trouble now.

Thad had upended her entire life using intimidation. He'd done it like a coward, hiding behind the likes of Jethro and Porky. She resolved to show him in the clearest terms possible he'd messed with the wrong girl. She now had a use for that gun.

Which was when she'd stepped to the curb and called, "Taxi!"

Now en route to settle up with the guy responsible for her persecution, she faced forward and let her tagalong friend plead with her, then demand she let him handle things. Rather than respond, she sat with her arms crossed and kept her focus outside the car, marking each street sign they passed. The closer they came to her destination, the hungrier she grew for her showdown. Her companion seemed apprised of her plan, although she hadn't discussed it. But truthfully, she didn't care what he knew, or that he disapproved of her intentions.

When his last attempt to talk her down failed, he slumped in his seat. He rubbed his eyes with his fingertips. "Okay, Maya. Fine. Confront him. But you can't do it without my help."

This, she felt, warranted her attention, so she turned from the window to face him. Which brought to mind her earlier suspicions, ones she'd do well to consider before she allowed him to accompany her further. Who did this guy think he was? And what made him believe she'd risk herself – or him, for that matter – by including him on this quest? She'd met him less than two hours ago, didn't even know his name, which pretty much made her a perfect idiot. He looked like she'd just hurt his feelings. She studied her feet and forced herself to ignore both the urge to acquiesce and the remorse she felt in denying him. *Sell that to someone else, buddy. I don't owe you a thing.* She attempted to give him an uncompromising stare.

But as she looked in his eyes, she felt a tremendous pressure to believe in him, and to accommodate his next request. "I'll get you through security so you won't be disturbed, at least for a while," he said. "You can even go up by yourself. I'll babysit downstairs. Then, afterwards, I want you to come right back down to the lobby. Back to me. All right?"

Maya didn't want to trust him, but she did. *Because I'm desperate*, she thought in disgust. Although she *would* need help getting through security where they were going, and thank goodness one of them had the sense to remember this. She was also sick to death – and apparently incapable – of figuring out on her own all that was going on around her. She would dearly love some help moving the barge that seemed to be parked on her future. She squeezed her eyes shut to cut off her companion's visual appeal, and she spoke for the first time since they'd entered the cab.

"Fine. Yes. Thank you. Now, who are you? And how did you find me?"

His hesitation told her he didn't want to answer, and annoyance flared again within her. Maybe she wouldn't accept him into her confidence. Maybe she couldn't afford to. She shook her head and returned to gazing out the window. He sighed.

"You can count on me, Maya. Just... be careful around him, okay?"

"Whatever."

Once they'd left the taxi, Maya walked to the doorman, airily announced her posh, married name and flipped out her ID as proof. "My father-in-law will want to see me immediately," she informed him. She cringed at how snobbish she sounded, but if the act got her in front of Thad, she didn't care.

Thoughts of all that could trip her up raced like miniature comets through her brain. As she watched the support staff discreetly call upstairs and greet other entrants, she stewed in her growing anxiety, wondering if the attendants were already apprised she was no longer in the Evans fold. She'd filed for a no-fault divorce six weeks ago, and it might have gone through, not that she'd know, since she'd used her and Stu's address for notification. She hadn't shared her new email address on the form for fear of being tracked. Still, a status check might have been smart before embarking on her current crusade.

Even if Thad was unaware of her legal efforts, though, he likely mistrusted her motives – as he should – and might have the police show up. He might have no interest in seeing her here and would leave her to be stonewalled by a security guard, or the club manager. Or maybe her incompetent watchmen were lying in wait to take her out of commission. She again envisioned herself bound with duct tape and locked in the trunk of a car.

Just as she thought she should give up and walk away, the concierge replaced his phone and gestured toward the entrance, where a man in livery held the door for her.

"Mr. Evans is awaiting you upstairs," the concierge reported. She walked past him in what she hoped was a stately, confident manner.

Once inside, though, she realized she'd lost her sidekick. She looked over her shoulder to confirm his absence... and she was, in fact, alone, which was worrisome. Because where the heck had he gone, and thanks a lot Mister 'I'm-Here-To-Help' because now everyone's focus would be all on her. And her gun. If she had to walk through the metal detector now – which was directly in front of her with one of the security agents motioning for to her to proceed through – she'd be spending the afternoon in handcuffs down at the precinct. Dammit. She should have questioned her volunteer bodyguard more closely before they'd arrived...

He spoke from behind her, which should have startled her but didn't because she was too relieved he'd stuck around – which was kind of stupid.

"They can't see or hear me, Maya," he offered. She twisted around to verify this statement. Sure enough, no one was there. But his voice was close, and he seemed willing to explain himself, for once. "I've, ah... how to describe – I've temporarily disabled their alarms. And I've projected a kind of, let's call it a *spell*. On me, and on you too. So you can get upstairs without being stopped. But it won't last, okay? Don't mess around up there, and don't do anything showy, like wave your piece in the air or grandstand. Because I can't keep you that far under cover. Not from here."

A spell. Why not? From an intermittently present guy who could get her and her firearm into a prominent New York social club. Maya decided she was good with that and wouldn't think about how silly such a proposition was. She was just glad for the resurgence of confidence she felt, as well as her new friend's improbable, possibly unreliable assistance. She was determined to give Thad a day in her court... and she'd risk just about anything to make that happen, including herself and her dubiously trustworthy comrade. Whose name she still didn't know. *Because I refuse to let that rat-fink coward Thad think he can muscle me around, and I'm too pissed off to care about the peripherals*, she thought.

Her friend chuckled as he urged her through the archway of the security scanner. "Yeah. He does have it coming."

The guards stared vacantly at the front entrance, didn't even glance Maya's way as she and what's-his-name breezed toward the bank of elevators. Phew. Another obstacle down. Maya sent a silent thanks to the gods of lax oversight or whatever drug dealer had provided the guards with their barbiturates that morning. She pressed the button to call the elevator, then stretched her neck and breathed. Her vengeance was nigh. She couldn't wait.

Before stepping into the open elevator car, she found herself with her back pressed against the pocket doors so her feet straddled the threshold. Her co-perpetrator held her there, settling one hand at her ribs, his thumb pressing lightly into her midriff... and Maya experienced something like vertigo. As well as the certainty she was about to be overwhelmed à la Aiden Blake.

She closed her eyes, which didn't help.

She felt that familiar, hollow yearning, the very one that had plagued her during every encounter with Aiden and several with Mitch Donovan. It filled her with equal parts elation and despair as her internal holds on herself were pried loose, until she felt like a receptacle whose sides had collapsed. She frantically tried to retrieve all the liquid parts of her pouring out, even though she knew she couldn't. This was the stage where she fought for control and failed; the part where she yearned for the man before her to take her in his arms, hold her together, and erase her emptiness, her desolation.

What is wrong with me? she wondered listlessly. Was she so needy she would now yearn for every man who paid her two minutes of attention? It seemed so, since she'd responded in just this way to Mitch and now to... she realized she *still* didn't know this guy's name. How pathetic.

No. You weren't like this with Stuart. Not with your fellow students or colleagues at the hospital or your patients, either. Her companion's words were intoned somewhere inside her mind... and she became grateful for them. Her worries loosened their grip, and a kind of inner sunshine burst within her, driving away all the dark cares that had smothered her during this last, endless stretch of time. She reached for her source of comfort, palming the back of his head to draw him closer.

"Kiss me," she pleaded, her voice like a soft rustle, textured and seductive and rife with want. If she'd practiced the line, she couldn't have sounded so sultry. He shuddered in her arms.

"That's, ah, not a good idea. Unless you want to ditch this plan of yours to visit Thad?" He sounded hopeful.

Maya tensed, returning to herself with ice-cold clarity. Because in an instant she pictured herself back in her apartment, lonely and frustrated and stuck under surveillance, her freedom in a chokehold once again. Could she risk it? Let Thad believe he'd scared her into submission? She didn't even have to consider her answer. She slumped against the pocket door.

"No. I can't," she replied.

He sighed. "Then we're going to have to wait for more of this." He dropped the hand at her ribs to grasp her hip, and then pulled her against him, which had her straining into him for more – more contact, more warmth, more of the delicious promise unfurling between them.

His expression became pained, and the set of his mouth suggested he had something he badly wanted to say. Something she almost understood, anyway.

If he felt like talking, though, she would listen this time. She would have *all* the bad news at this juncture, not just an overview. She could no longer endure – or enforce – living in a state of perpetual ignorance, couldn't tolerate the experience of wandering around as if her lack of awareness wouldn't hurt her.

She still wanted upstairs, though. "Later, then?" she suggested.

He shifted reluctantly away from her, just a few inches. He retained his one-handed hold on her hip... and Maya hated this new separation. With his other hand, he lifted a lock of hair framing her face, then brushed it behind her shoulder and cupped the base of her neck. "We'll talk when you get back. Remember, I'll be waiting for you right here." He pushed himself fully away and walked toward the front of the building.

After a few steps, he paused, turned around, and grinned. "Oh, and Maya? I'll be hanging onto your bag and your cash." He held up her carry-all on two fingers.

"Of course you will," Maya muttered sourly. But she wasn't going to try and wrestle it away from him. She slid into the elevator and punched the button for club level, marveling over how, once again, she'd been paying so little attention to anything outside her own head, she'd conceded something she couldn't afford to lose. This time it was her getaway money.

She supposed the upside of all these lapses was the amount of practice she had recovering from them. Within seconds she had a solution to her dilemma, even though it involved a return to her apartment.

A project I'll tackle after I settle up with Thad, she decided.

She mused instead over her slippery grasp on reality, one she'd spent years justifying and had been sure of not six months ago, although she'd definitely been expelled from her paradigm. What kind of signals did she emit, giving folks everywhere permission to trample all over her? No one at any other time would have dared to treat her this way – not when she was a stubborn, abrasive teenager; definitely not when she was an ace offensive hitter for Penn State. And her position as a would-be physician should have completely insulated her from these kinds of compromises. She felt like she maybe walked under a flashing sign that read, "Gullible! Manipulate me!" Her siren song, apparently, for too high a percentage of the guys she'd encountered since leaving Stu. Now she'd snared a stranger in a café, one who could hold her breathless against an elevator door while he stole all her cash.

She reached her floor and put aside these extraneous considerations to concentrate on the confrontation at hand. Her focus became absolute as she rehearsed all of it – her approach, the expression she'd wear, and what she would say when she faced the man who'd forced her to abandon everyone and everything she loved.

The maître d' stood at the entrance to the dining room, all smiles when he greeted her, although Maya thought his perusal held a furtive edge.

"How lovely to see you again, Mrs. Evans. The senior Mr. Evans is expecting you."

He grasped her elbow, ostensibly to guide her into the dining hall but more likely, Maya believed, under orders from Thad. She could almost read her father-in-law's directive in the furrows on the man's forehead and via his shaky grip on her arm. He'd been told to bring her directly to Thad's table and hurry up about it… and she'd guess Thad had forgotten his instructions were to a restaurant worker, one who didn't have the constitution for the type of physical oversight he'd been asked to provide. Maya shook him off firmly but politely.

"I see him. I'll take myself from here. Thank you." She walked away quickly. Her escort fretted but stayed behind.

Thad's habit was to take lunch here every Thursday and Maya had hoped today would be no different. It wasn't, since here he was, although he had only one dining companion today. This man – older, roughly the same age and social rank as Thad if Maya were to guess – remained seated but watched her advance. Thad stood and faced her, a broad smile on his face, his arms open in welcome.

He expected them to embrace? The man was high. *No more kiss-kiss play nice from this chick, Thad.*

She fixed him with a hard, unblinking stare as she strode his way, hoping to communicate how very un-open she was to being charmed.

When she was within ten paces of Thad's table, she nabbed a linen napkin from the hands of a guest she passed – a guest who, curiously, didn't react – wrapped it around the stock of the gun in her waistband and then withdrew the firearm so it hung, draped by the napkin, at her side. People she passed should have worried she concealed something… and a weapon should have crossed their minds.

No one paid her any undue attention, however. Which was odd, but she focused on why she was here: to face the man who'd tried to destroy her life.

She wondered if Thad had any idea how upset she was.

The answer was yes, yes he did; and how gratifying to at last see concern color his regard. His eyes went to the draped gun at her side. His smile faltered and his arms drooped.

Now you're getting the picture, loser.

Thad's geniality had completely subsided by the time Maya placed the gun on the tabletop, the muzzle sticking out from under its cloth and aimed in his direction. She could almost see his mind working, reactions flickering across his face like scenes in a film, his anxiety growing frame by frame.

"No, Thad," she announced. "I did not come to make up with you or Stu, if that's what you had in mind."

She kept her piece anchored under her hand, her finger over the trigger. Thad's lunch date reached discreetly for his phone, which Maya knocked away with her free hand.

"Don't even." She kept her attention on Thad.

The friend spread his palms before him on the table – to placate her? – and sat very still. He was calm… and Maya thought he might also be sympathetic. He confirmed this impression with his next statement to Thad, "So. You were just assuring me you've got everything under control, and I have nothing to worry about. Have I got that right?" To Maya he said quietly, "There's no reason to take this any further, miss. I'm sure if you leave without a fuss, no one will follow you. No one will get hurt."

Pfft. Maya was certain neither of those things was true. She inched the gun forward as she leaned toward Thad and bit out, "We took this off of one of the four you sicced on me three months ago." She leaned closer. "I'm here because I do *not* appreciate that, Thad."

Thad's gaze darted around anxiously before returning to her. He did not want a spectacle, Maya saw. Good. Though they weren't making one, which was odd. The people around them continued their lunch as if they didn't have a seething, armed woman in their midst. No one noticed Thad's distress, either… and she thought again about her sidekick's witchy promise downstairs. She was again glad for whatever he'd set in motion, for however he'd managed to facilitate this encounter. Maya realized Thad's unwillingness to make a scene was clutch, because it meant she could control their interaction. She delivered what she hoped was an evil smile. Thad swallowed.

"Maya, listen to me," he said softly. "I'm sorry. I never meant to cause trouble for you, I promise. I needed to protect all of us, you included…"

"Sending armed men after me is *not* protection, Thad," she hissed. She straightened then, dragging her weapon backwards until it rested on the table's lip in front of her. She kept the barrel aimed at her father-in-law's chest. Thad's eyes made a nervous back-and-forth between it and her face.

Maya liked what she saw, so very much. He was cowed and perspiring; nervous and sorry. She pulled the gun so it hung once again at her side, draped under the napkin.

"I see we understand each other. Not so fun to have this kind of threat hanging over you, is it? I'll be going now, but I expect you to remember this little visit. And how pissed off I am. The next time you decide to intimidate me? Well." Maya lifted the gun gently in his direction. Thad dropped woodenly into his seat. Maya nodded once, turned away, and retreated at a calm pace.

She attracted a few wary glances as she neared the exit… and she felt the veil of protection she'd worn since she'd arrived thin. No one stopped her or called for security, but she sensed she needed to hurry, and she walked more briskly toward the lobby. The maître d's' face was now devoid of professionalism – he was on the verge of hysterics – but she brushed by him. He didn't appear to notice the gun she held, which she thought fortunate. She deposited it on a side table outside the dining room – draped under its napkin and hopefully free of fingerprints – then sped onto the waiting elevator. She watched the scene in the dining room disappear as the doors slid shut.

Chapter Eight

Aiden became increasingly worried as first ten minutes passed, then twenty. Eventually, he realized Maya wasn't coming back downstairs to meet him, had likely already left the building.

He knew his frequent presence at her side the last several years – even if she hadn't been aware of him – had given her a degree of immunity to his manipulations… and considering her anger at Thad, as well as her desperation to end her confinement, she'd probably mustered the emotional resistance to slink away.

She never could have given him the slip when he first came to her. Then, he would have felt her absence immediately, could have followed her exact path away from him and called her back to him effortlessly. He sure wouldn't be stuck wondering if she was around or not; he'd know.

He'd seen her withdraw into herself before, when she felt vulnerable or unable to trust those around her, a coping mechanism he well understood, seeing as how it was the one he'd adopted himself. She wasn't aware of the effect this response had – the buffer she created that undermined Aiden's ability to sense her – and he mostly admired her for it. Few humans could pull it off, even people like Kate who'd lived closely with sirens a lot longer than Maya had. Anyway, he really should have anticipated this possibility before he'd sent her upstairs, assumed she'd mask her output and try to disappear.

He sighed and mentally reviewed the layout of the building, wondering where she would have exited. And what better inducement he could have offered for her return aside from holding her money hostage, her stash still in the bag at his feet.

He could have told her who he was, for instance.

But a reveal presented its own problems, among them her present marital status. Acting as Mitch, he'd queried her thoughts often enough to know how important her independence from Stuart was... and how necessary a finalized divorce was to her ability to move on. He believed her divorce was likely official – both Thad and Stu were aware she'd filed and enough time had passed for the case to have been processed. He hadn't verified anything, however.

Maya wouldn't embark on a new relationship before she was free to do so, though... and truthfully, he also wanted to see an inked divorce decree. Maybe he'd check in at City Hall before he tracked his girl. Again.

At least he had leave from his siren overseers to come here and act as he wished, since leadership at Shaddox remained unaware of his real intentions. As it happened, he'd procrastinated long enough to cause concern, meaning he'd had to spend extra time back home, showing everyone what a dedicated, reliable guy he was.

But his sojourn had been a success, the in-person debriefing on human security protocols had, in fact, protected what he wanted, especially with Xanthe, although he'd exhausted weeks more than he'd meant to. When he'd thought he couldn't stand to stay another hour, he finally received leadership's blessing to return to New York alone. Apparently, his argument that a larger contingent of sirens would draw attention and get in the way had gone over, too.

He hoped to figure out a permanent way to be with Maya this time.

Simon was and always had been his biggest vulnerability in this regard, because an interrogation of Simon by higher-ups could get him to reveal Aiden's less-than-truthful representations of his efforts. So far, Simon had lied for him, a courtesy Aiden expected but appreciated anyway. Aiden had supported Simon, after all, when he'd needed help running away with Sylvia. Which had been directly contrary to Aiden's own need to court Maya. So, in Aiden's opinion, Simon pretty much owed him an eternity of allegiance.

So far, Simon's evasions combined with Aiden's rock star ability to mask any troubling output meant Aiden's 'professional development' smokescreen had held.

Not that Simon participated graciously – he didn't, badgering him whenever he could when they were alone. "It's stupid and you're going to get caught and there has to be a better way," he griped. He'd also employed scare tactics, using terms like "treason" and "expulsion" to try and bully Aiden out of his heartsickness. "It's like, I don't know, zombie love with you, because it's freaky and makes no sense… and *it just won't die*."

"Riiight, Simon," Aiden crooned. "I'll get over this, because risking all of us is *fun* for me." Simon had shut up but periodically voiced his hope Aiden would reconsider his fixation. As time went on, Aiden knew his brother began to understand him better, perhaps better than anyone else; Aiden really wasn't melodramatizing when he said leaving Maya would kill him. And in every instance, Simon *had* protected Aiden. The fact that he was bonded to Maya's sister, Sylvia, probably helped.

Now, as Aiden mulled over his options on the ground floor of Thad's club, he wished his brother were here, because Simon could have handled cleanup with the guards while Aiden went on reconnaissance. *Can't be helped, though. I'm outta here*, Aiden thought. He left his post – as well as tons of siren tampering evidence – behind.

He reasoned his loyalties weren't on the side of siren law, though, hadn't been for several years, so what was one more indiscretion? Plus, who was around to check up on him? No one, that's who. Aiden threaded his way to a corridor he suspected Maya had used to escape him… and caught a trace of her. Excellent.

Nonetheless, he realized he had a unique opportunity to interview Thad upstairs, was possibly ditching his only chance to query the guy one-on-one... and he *really* needed to know what was motivating him. Maya might be on the run, but she would be quick and careful, he knew. He also knew he couldn't operate effectively without knowing what Thad intended. With his emotions riled and close to the surface – and how could they not be? – Thad would be ripe for mental plundering. Aiden could, despite being out of the water, probably glean anything he wanted from him, including what his business gig was and why he'd sent armed men out to tail his daughter-in-law.

Aiden might also ascertain the status of Maya and Stu's divorce... which should be final, but wouldn't that be excellent information to take back to Maya.

He had to risk it.

He hurried back to the elevator, entered an empty car and ascended. He'd spend a few short minutes with Thad, and he could influence him to cause no further harm. Then he'd chase Maya.

He honed himself, steeling his mind as he and his fellow trainees had been taught during their inaugural sessions of pseudo-military instruction eight years ago. Consequently, he no longer struggled to shut out all peripheral pulls on his attention as he first had, when their professor and drill sergeant, Peter Loughlin, had schooled them relentlessly until they could all achieve absolute concentration. He understood the importance of these preparations, how the ability was fundamental to the deeper cloaks they'd also become fluent in... and the platform under their more lethal skills, ones few other sirens were aware of and none had sought to master.

But Aiden had become adept at all sorts of behaviors antithetical to siren nature during his tutelage under Peter – cloaking was one example, resisting the pull of humans another, although he still struggled occasionally. And he'd practiced killing, which was still monumentally difficult for all of them, but for the first time in his people's history, possible. Along with several of the other trainees, Aiden could retreat almost as well as Peter, could mask his identity so thoroughly, all outside markers announcing his physical presence disappeared. He could even confuse siren perceptions.

Humans were a lot easier to snow, of course. He glided without notice past the maître 'd and into the dining room.

Thaddeus Evans, III, was not doing well. On Aiden's way in, he'd run into Thad's departing lunch companion... and received the man's disgorging anger like a blast from an iron forge. Aiden had stopped him, gripping the man's forearm to scan him for useful intel, which he got.

The friend believed Thad had deserved Maya's firearm-forward challenge. In fact, rather than have her arrested, he wished he could find her, query her on Thad's exact doings and commiserate with her. Which was laughable. *Another Evans-hater to add to the growing roster*, Aiden mused as he released the guy and continued toward the paranoid, trouble-mongering human he'd actually come to interrogate.

He read Thad's misery from twenty feet out, no problem. The man sat hunched at his table, nursing the suspicion he'd finally depleted the last of his morality. He was so buried in his own head, so oblivious to his surroundings already, reading him was going to be a walk on the beach.

Thad had just been treated to an invective-rich dressing down from his departing friend, which in his mind had thrown the wisdom of his actions into question even more profoundly than Maya's confrontation. He stared vacantly and at his half-eaten soup, unaware he had company. Aiden cloaked anyway, pulled out a chair and sat down, briefly examining his quarry before deciding how best to mine him.

Thad was *really* vulnerable, so he leaked a crazy amount of information just by proximity, but Aiden wanted to apprehend all of it fast, and that meant touch. He grasped Thad's forearm... and Thad didn't register a thing. Aiden influenced him to further relax his hold on himself.

When Thad was completely open and suggestible, Aiden began to pull out the details he sought, starting with the status of Maya and Stu's divorce. Was it final? Thad had seen the decree, so the marriage was legally dissolved. Beauty. Aiden then prompted a review of Thad's recent interaction with his former daughter-in-law.

What a goddess, he thought. She'd been magnificent. Unfortunately, though, he and Maya had both underestimated Thad's reaction – or more specifically, how desperate he was to protect himself. Before today, the senior Evans had been reluctant to engage in violence or attach himself to intimidation efforts more obviously than he already had. But Maya's demonstration had scared him past what he'd deemed "precautionary measures."

At least Aiden was finally able to ferret out the particulars of Thad's side business, which Thad believed warranted his extreme response where Maya was concerned. Aiden disagreed, thought Thad's decisions deserved *a lot* stronger scrutiny than he'd given them. Gloria's illness had affected Thad to a greater extent than the man was willing to admit, and this drove many of his faulty decisions. Aiden scoured Thad's psyche to better apprehend his whole story.

His troubles were rooted in a fraudulent investment scheme, which the senior Evans had been running illegally for the past eighteen months. He'd set up a legitimate fund a while back at the urging of his cousin, Nate, a securities broker who wasn't breaking into the same stratosphere as his colleagues when it came to year-end bonuses. As in, Nate's take had hovered around two million while other senior VPs scored ten or more, so he'd been looking for a new road to stardom. Nate had appealed to Thad on and off with a proposal to start a fund of their own; until his wife's diagnosis with cancer, though, Thad hadn't been interested.

Around the time of Gloria's decline, Thad had finally agreed. He'd been susceptible, Aiden saw, mostly due to his wife's failing health, but also because he was under pressure from his board for public relations issues that seemed to intensify no matter what measures Thad took to address them. Thad was beginning to hate his position, and he'd started wondering if his cousin's sketchy plan might provide a dignified way out.

The potential success Nate pitched was not the inducement he imagined. Thad had been lured by the promise of independence and redemption – independence from the charmless yoke of corporate life, and redemption in the form of decisive action he could take, an option he hadn't had during his wife's horrific illness.

Once Thad indicated receptiveness, Nate had registered the fund before Thad could change his mind. He'd promised Thad he could steer as much or as little as he wanted until they grew. Aiden saw Thad had maintained his skepticism throughout his dealings with Nate, was as dubious now as he'd been initially. As Thad recalled the conversation that had started it all, Aiden teased out the full interaction.

"You truly want to start a mutual fund, and you want my help?" Thad had asked.

"A hedge fund. It'll be easier to administer from a regulatory standpoint. And with your name on it, it'll be a success the second it launches. Look at it this way: we'll run it as a side business until it's big enough for you to take over. If you want to leave HWP, I mean."

Leave one of the world's most prominent and coveted positions on his terms? Gloria would have hated the idea. But then, Gloria was dead and unable to argue, here.

"All right," Thad had agreed. "Let's talk."

Nate's obsequious responses had almost killed Thad's shaky interest in the scheme. Almost. *Wouldn't your father and grandfather be proud?* Nate had fawned, and think of the good they would do, the individual attention they'd pay their clients, the economic boost they'd give people outside their class.

Thad had only half-listened to him, remembering instead the waxen, wasted form of his wife hitching through her last breaths on her wheel-in bed from hospice. His silent supplications to her at that time, which had brought forth no response at all, somehow morphed into his father's non-silent preaching, endured ad nauseum, also during the old man's final days. Thad made his decision very quickly then.

Why not? he thought. If nothing else, he was sick – truly sick and tired – of fighting ghosts. Maybe Nate's plan would deliver the exorcism Thad craved. He interrupted his cousin's supplicating. "Nate, enough. I'm in."

And they'd done great in the beginning. As Nate predicted, Thad's name made the launch all but effortless; and he found the hands-on, tactical nature of managing the investment – without the shackles of big corporate bureaucracy – refreshing. It was certainly a departure from the stifling rigidity of the Hell Well.

The fund was initially stable, too, would probably have done just fine if they'd let it be, but Nate thought it best to appear like they were outperforming the market. Not by a large amount, just enough to build confidence among current and prospective shareholders. Thad had left the matter with him. By the time Thad understood they were behind, payouts had outpaced returns... and Thad genuinely worried how they would contain their lie. He started to watch their progression with alarm; and then he decided to do whatever necessary to make the fund self-supporting.

For a while, he'd hoped a miracle surge in the market would wipe out their deficit, but that hadn't happened. A few days before the house party where Maya had made her surprise appearance, a man holding the third largest position in the fund – a guy from Italy – got nervous first, then angry. He may have been bluffing, but he hinted at foul play and threatened public redress if he didn't immediately receive a check for his full initial investment plus a high return. Thad had agreed to personally cover his demands the day after the party, was just waiting to conduct transactions during normal trading hours.

Meaning, Aiden realized, Maya's presence in Thad's office that night had been nothing more than really bad timing. Why hadn't the guy equated his disarranged desk to his hound dog son and companion of the month, though? Why had he concluded Maya had betrayed him?

Talk about paranoid.

Aiden brought Thad back to the immediate past, reviewing his exchange with his lunch associate, who had been a longtime friend and seminal investor in Thad's venture. No longer. They'd been discussing Thad's pursuits and the friend's instincts that something was awry before Maya's visit… so his lunch date had harsh words following Maya's stop at their table. Naturally, he promised immediate liquidation of his shares. He'd also said he wanted nothing further to do with Thad – not professionally, not personally.

"What in God's name have you been doing?" he'd fumed once Maya was away. "I know you have managers for your affairs. I can't imagine even one of them endorsed anything remotely illegal. You'd better talk with them about what's next, Evans. And set yourself up for life in prison. I'd think hard on that outcome if I were you."

Even with everything else running through Thad's mind, those parting words clanged around in the man's head like tacks in a coffee can. Getting cut down by a lifelong peer had made Thad, if possible, more desperate to save himself… which, Aiden saw to his dismay, had led to a truly wicked plan. One Thad had already acted on.

Aiden now wished he wasn't here, even though he'd needed the information Thad had just provided. But Maya was out there at this very minute on her own, and Aiden had arrived in the dining room too late to preclude Thad's evil directive.

Terror electrified him. He retrieved Thad's phone and verified what he'd already gleaned. Thad's most recent text read, *Two cleanings at 58 and 05 from addresses given. Discreet. Half transferred will cover rest on finish.*

It wasn't even code. Aiden hardly had to scan Thad for confirmation the "05" indicated the month of May – a reference to Maya. The doomed lunch friend was apparently born in 1958.

Aiden once more grasped Thad's forearm and concentrated... and Thad didn't want a public execution to draw attention. He'd thought of this possibility weeks ago and set up the approach he'd just green lighted.

He wanted the deaths to appear accidental or random, discretion was a must. He had wired half of the payment for the job and would transfer the other half when the targets were confirmed dead.

Aiden panicked. He couldn't influence anyone via phone, so his siren gifts wouldn't deter the recipient of Thad's text. Neither could he track from an IP address. How ironic that Thad's life should be saved by a smart phone. Because even if Aiden badly wanted to end Thad's ability to inflict further harm – a concentrated squeeze to the heart, a few minutes of constricted blood flow to the brain and, nighty-night, Thad – Aiden couldn't do it. He might need the guy to cancel this or other insidious orders, or confess and put an end to all this lunacy. Plus, Aiden couldn't un-send the order for Maya's murder, couldn't unwire compensation to her murderer... and the effort to end another might well debilitate Aiden, himself. Which would leave Maya alone and even more vulnerable.

He'd never actually killed before... so who knew what fallout he'd experience? He'd heard the repercussions could mean death for the siren perpetrator as well as the victim. He again wished his brother were here, and maybe Aiden could recruit him later to help.

But first things first.

Aiden pivoted toward the door with Thad's phone, leaving Thad in a semi-aware state he wouldn't soon come out of. He then called up Thad's text to the death squad and initiated a call to the recipient. A man answered with a terse "Sir," and Aiden offered what must have been a convincing facsimile of Thad's voice because he wasn't questioned.

"Hold off. I think I can contain the situation," Aiden instructed.

"Too late. Already dispatched. First asset is located, communication's cut until after."

"Which target? Where?" Aiden couldn't quell the raw alarm in his voice. He started for the door.

"Oh-five. Tracking device in her jacket... reads at Café on Front Street. Our guy is twenty minutes out."

Aiden hung up and tossed the phone to the floor. He ran. Twenty minutes before she was taken away somewhere for a quiet kill.

He knew as he ran alongside traffic on the bridge he'd be too late. Fast as he was, he wasn't fast enough – no one was. His path – the sidewalk between the thoroughfare and a free-fall into the river – seemed to roll under him like shifting sand, as if every footfall slid him backwards half a pace.

He stopped midway, breathing heavily. He considered the distance between here and Front Street. He braced his hands on his knees... and thought of another plan.

He quickly studied the barriers to his left, ones authorities had put in place years ago to discourage jumpers; three layers of thick metal mesh overlaying one another. Using the knife from the tether he kept under his clothes, he sawed through it. If his knife could slice up a 450-pound tuna, he reasoned, it could cut through the barricade. It could. He opened a hole and stepped onto the two-foot lip separating the platform from nothing. He estimated the distance to the water to be three hundred feet, which was high up... but this could work.

He faced the opposite bank, concentrated with everything he had in him, and made his call: *"Maya! Come to me!"*

*Way out at sea, the water is as blue as the petals on the loveliest
cornflower,
and as clear as the purest glass, but it's very deep,
deeper than any anchor rope can reach.*

From "The Little Mermaid" by Hans Christian Andersen

PART TWO

Chapter Nine

Maya had always loved falling. Or maybe she craved the sensation of floating, since the joy came before, not during, her descent. It was that soul-freeing catharsis at the apex of an arc, the half-second of suspension at the top of a bounce off a trampoline; or the heady, gravity-less moment after a launch from the seat of a swing she'd pumped too high. As a little girl she'd limped home with skinned knees and a bruised backside so often, she'd been forbidden from that last practice, although she still connived her way to the playground every chance she got to swing and fly.

She blamed her father, Jeremy, who'd fostered this affinity when she was just a toddler. Their play in the front yard was her earliest, most poignant memory, where she was tossed in the air and caught, tossed and caught again, Jeremy's strong hands propelling and releasing her with such force she thought she might travel up forever. The prospect almost – but not quite – terrified her as much as it thrilled. Still, she chased whatever unknown awaited her at the top of her fling, a savage sort of joy building and building until fear threatened, fear she might be swallowed into some skyward abyss and disappear. And then in the instant before terror overtook her, she fell back to earth loose and weightless and happier than ever, her father's embrace like an extra dessert after dinner.

"Do it again, Daddy," she begged.

She thought on this memory now as she ran alongside the clog of honking, irate drivers on the bridge. Aiden awaited her ahead, his summons a promise she knew he meant to keep: soon she would fly and fall through the air, and he would catch her.

It had been years since her last volleyball game at Penn State, but the adrenaline rush she experienced now was precisely the one she'd had before taking the court before a match. Her innate compulsion to perform physically, to play at her very best under pressure, swelled within her like a song her whole body knew the lyrics to. She hadn't played since college but had kept in shape, was still strong and lithe, and what a pleasure to experience her athletic gifts again. She ran as hard as she could without knowing all that awaited her.

The urgency of Aiden's call furthered her anticipation... because he was desperate for her to reach him, and because she would soon see him, be with him. Nothing could dim the euphoria of that prospect. And nothing would interrupt her focus on their reunion – not the complaints voiced by the drivers she passed, not the police cars amassing on the bridge, sirens screeching.

Just minutes ago, when she was still on Front Street, she'd believed herself safe at last. She'd sneaked away from Thad's club without her stalker friend's knowledge; had stealthily entered her apartment building, then convinced the super to let her into her condo, since she didn't have her keys. She'd gathered what she needed in under thirty seconds – she'd timed herself – then completed another trade of jewelry for cash from her favorite pawnbroker. He'd complained he felt like he was stealing these last pieces, to which Maya replied curtly, "Then pay me more for them." But she hadn't been upset, not really, even if she'd received a pittance compared to what the broker would make. He'd given her the means to be independent for the foreseeable future, so she held no grudges.

After her sales stop, she'd avoided her usual haunt, settling herself instead into a dim corner at an obscure diner near the water while she mulled over the specifics of her next disappearing act. It was an internet café with public terminals… a resource she appreciated since her laptop was stowed with the cash currently in Mystery Man's possession.

Aiden's summons broke into her concentration with the force of an explosion. One moment she was calmly searching for remote, off-the-grid communities where she could hide out and start over; and the next, she was out the door, sprinting down the sidewalk. She didn't even remember having left her chair.

Run, Maya! Run! She heard his command shouted inside her head, and her heart filled with hope despite the fear-filled undercurrent behind the entreaty. Aiden was here, she would see him in mere minutes, and they would figure things out together. She ran flat out.

Traffic slowed and then stopped as she approached the bridge's center. Along the way, snippets of conversation from drivers frustrated by the delay rang in her ears. Apparently, someone was outside the barriers and about to jump.

"Aiden! I'm coming!" she yelled.

Emergency vehicles blared as they muscled their way through the jammed lanes. Maya was determined to reach Aiden before they did.

You gotta love New York, she thought, laughter threatening her air supply, something she couldn't afford to waste if she wanted to finish this trek. Which meant she swallowed her hysteria in spite of the comedy playing out around her. *Eye on the prize, Wilkes*, she instructed herself.

"This is New York City, buddy!" someone yelled. "You couldn't have thought this plan up in, say, Boise?" And then from a man in a delivery truck, "Hey, pal – I gotta get to my kid's recital! Dance or get off the floor!" A younger guy in a suit yelled, "Dude, you wanna die? 'Cause about five hundred people here want to kill you…"

Her favorite came from a little old lady who sounded dead-on like the East-Coast grandmother of one of her university friends, her r's truncated and e's like long a's. She leaned from the window of her ancient sedan and groused, "What? You're depressed, so *I* should suffer?"

It all showed an appalling lack of sympathy, although maybe they could sense – as she did – that this was no suicide attempt. She didn't know what it was, but it wasn't despair and tragedy awaiting her.

In the last moments of her run, the voices around her as well as the clamor of sirens and car horns faded. Because she saw only the man outside the walkway, and his presence muffled everything else. Her lungs burned now and a slight, pleasant asphyxia blurred her senses. Finally at the barricade, she perceived – in addition to Aiden's figure before her – her own breath and heartbeat, then his, but no other sight or sound.

She didn't remember climbing through the mesh... but she must have because Aiden had her crushed against him. She heard the loud click of a gun being cocked, and dimly registered the shouted warnings from police to stay back.

Aiden's smile reflected pure, uncomplicated joy, however. He set her down and cradled her face in his hands. "God. It's so good to see you, Maya."

He was happy? Sweet heaven, so was she. An easy lightness blossomed in her chest, expanding like a balloon that threatened to lift her bodily from where she stood. In the ensuing contentment that took her over, she realized again how careworn she'd become, how small her definition of happiness had shrunk since her days in Griffins Bay, especially this past year. She smiled openly in response to him, indifferent to the context of their reunion and their precarious perch on the lip of the bridge.

Aiden stared at her intently, kindly. *This will be okay*, he assured her. And of course they would be okay – they were together. He then tucked her forehead into his neck, wrapped her tightly against him, and leaned toward the water.

Their fall went on for ages, as if they'd started at the very top of the earth's atmosphere instead of a few hundred feet up... and she reveled in that same fulfillment she'd chased as a girl, the suspension from time and gravity. She sensed a transformation in his body, which lengthened and further enfolded her, and she did not think the experience strange. They plunged without resistance into the soft, welcoming river below, and then floated downward as if on a light breeze. They stopped when the sounds of the world above no longer penetrated, Aiden's hands resting at her waist, hers at his.

They won't catch us now, he promised.

Sunlight filtered weakly around them, the dimness a veil protecting their privacy… and in the gloom and silence, Maya felt a delicious unburdening from every worry she'd held onto since coming to New York.

A stunning change, isn't it? She heard Aiden's words within her. She was unclear which transition he meant. From air to water? To her, the bigger conversion was internal.

As she'd planned her most recent solitary escape back at the diner, she'd convinced herself she could delay fulfillment yet again, that she was willing to flee one last time for a chance at the life she wanted. Aiden's call obliterated that notion; not because she didn't yearn for what she always had, but because his offer of immediate relief was too seductive. She knew in an instant she couldn't think about safety as she had up until now, couldn't embark on yet another exile and remove herself again from everyone she cared about.

And she wouldn't wait any longer for love.

His response closely matched her own. *We've already tried avoiding each other. You've already tried running. It's miserable.* She wondered again why she'd resisted Aiden before now and instantly had her answer: because she'd been afraid of what he brought out in her, of the unpredictability he represented.

Or maybe because of what he was.

But she no longer had it in her to deny herself, much less him. As they drifted in this dream world where their former problems didn't touch them, she envisioned a future with him rather than without… which caused a thousand bits of wire to untwist within her, releasing her from a cage she hadn't known imprisoned her. *This truly is a fall into love*, she mused, and Aiden smiled at her. He spoke against her temple. *I fell for you years ago. And yes, it felt just like this.*

Chapter Ten

Thad knew he was paranoid and overreacting, his business decisions ill conceived. Reckless, even. Like he willfully masterminded his own demise. But he did not check his compulsions.

Maybe he could have avoided his current problems if he'd taken the advice of his physician – and more than a few friends – to talk with a therapist after Gloria's death. But he couldn't stomach the prospect of prolonging what had already been an intolerable trial, extending his loss with some multi-session, probing psychological review. In effect, he didn't want to acknowledge his wife's corporeal death wasn't the end of the whole, awful experience.

After it had happened, he'd swung between blissful emptiness, for which he'd been grateful; and wallowing in a brutish stew of relief and shame, two sentiments that mixed like lard and lemonade and gave him heartburn. Although even that had been preferable to the impotence he'd felt watching Gloria's decline. Plus, he was clear on his reactions, so he didn't require any shrink-induced epiphanies: he needed no revelations as to what he'd lost, on how oppressed he'd been, or angry or sad or whatever. His genuine relief Gloria's illness was finally behind them didn't keep him up at night, because of course he preferred an existence free from sickness and an end to all those barbaric medical regimens.

They'd both tired long ago of hoping the worst was over only to experience an ever more appalling progression of decline. They'd both badly wanted to disengage from a life that was not a life, one that consisted of vomiting and fecal incontinence and pharmaceutical oversight for every blessed bodily function.

In a way, they'd needed to be as stupid as they'd been at the outset, when their money had afforded them immediate access to the most advanced treatments on the cancer menu. Had they known how constant her disease would be, how grotesque their definition of normal would become; or the escalating threshold of tolerance they'd need for the more insidious failures of the human body subjected to these protocols... well, Thad believed they would have foregone much of it to welcome sooner the end that was coming anyway. Her cancer had pushed each of them leagues past their ability to ask why, and eons beyond any belief in a benevolent God.

So, yes, he'd been relieved when death had, at long last, put a stop to it all. To the emotional and physical slavery inflicted by Gloria's illness as well as the proverbial carrot that medicine had dangled before them – the lie she might miraculously recover or enjoy 'a better quality of life.' Hell, he'd have settled for the ability to enjoy a meal with her or a stroll outside during her final months.

But. These were his prettier reflections on Gloria's final fight.

"Of course you're glad it's over. Gloria's at peace, her pain's gone," was the pat response he'd received from ever so many. He didn't mention his focus wasn't on Gloria, because that would have necessitated an explanation too monstrous to trot out to the polite world.

When the hospice nurse had confirmed his wife had drawn her final breath, Thad folded his hands on the rail of the bed, braced his forehead on them and wept. The nurse gripped his shoulder in a gesture of comfort, one he didn't deserve.

I'm free, was all he could think at the time. By then, he'd officially spent a year and a half suffocating in depression and failure – truly, there had been *nothing* he could do to either expedite or forestall Gloria's death march. He could barely manage the appearance of solemnity at her bedside, had to steel himself against the desire to stand up, spread his arms to heaven and cheer. All these months of powerlessness, the tortuous waiting for an end that had far, far overextended them both.

He didn't celebrate, of course. Instead, he reveled silently in his new sense of peace. He contemplated Gloria's stillness, the utter absence of life he took as sure evidence that, this time, their ordeal had passed. Her lax expression, her poor, frail body devoid of medical contrivances. He interpreted the tableau before him as justification for the quiet happiness he felt, deciding privately he had also been among the ravaged and she no longer mattered because she was gone. He couldn't help but be glad for it.

He'd wanted everything removed right away – the body, the bed, the monitoring equipment and oxygen machine, the IV bags and reeking, institutional stench – he'd wished he could shove it all out the window. As it was, the funeral home came in under an hour to recover Gloria's remains, the hospice coordinators took minutes to clean up the rest of death's detritus. He'd called Stu as the nurse collected Gloria's various medications.

Stu picked up right away, probably because he was expecting the news, although he still took it hard. He was traveling for work but promised to catch the first flight home. Emotionally disconnected, Thad delivered the correct characterizations of Gloria's last moments in an appropriately somber voice, then assured Stu he would not be alone tonight and no one needed to come over. Stu didn't delve, thankfully. Thad then reported to the nurse that his son was on his way. She could go ahead and leave.

He played a game on his phone for several minutes to ensure he wouldn't run into the departing crew and all they'd just carted out his door. The very second he felt he could, he called for his driver and checked into a discreetly posh neighborhood hotel in lower Manhattan. Once there, he contacted his housekeeper, ostensibly to update her on Gloria's status.

His true aim was exorcism.

He slogged through Mrs. Strand's condolences like a mechanical version of himself. He believed this conversation and ones like it to come were just punctuation, his signature on the bottom of a contract that had been hashed out months ago. He didn't need to revisit all the details therein, just authorize and file everything away. He got to the real reason for his call.

"I need…" His mind reeled ahead to the picture he imagined of his life cleansed of the last year and a half. "I need everything stripped. Add to your crew if you like, but send the furniture and carpets out to be cleaned, the drapes, too. Hire painters and have them paint every wall. White. I want the place scrubbed." He tried to interject a note of apology in his tone. "I can't tolerate the smell of all the medicines, you see." He told her he'd be at Stu's, or with other family. He hoped six weeks would give her adequate time to go through everything.

Afterwards, he'd lounged on the balcony outside his suite and lifted his face to the sun. A new life, a self-directed future. He was at last free to pursue it, unfettered.

Now, well after the fact, Thad understood how naïve he'd been during those first months. Death, it turned out, was more complicated than one human being's physical expiration. In a way, he felt as if he'd caught Gloria's cancer, since the memory of it remained to leach away his appetite for life, diminish his capacity for joy.

He'd had no choice but to rebel. And if he wasn't ever to recover from it all – his pressured upbringing, his wife's desertion, his lucrative but depressing job – he could at least establish a new direction that might lead to autonomy. This was perhaps the biggest impetus behind his acquiescence to Nate. Just a little more effort, too, and he'd have everything straight.

He checked his phone and saw no update on Maya. Sometime in those first weeks following her disappearance after the penthouse party, he'd changed his mind about managing her, had redirected Harlowe to report her whereabouts to him instead of Nate. His cousin hadn't liked the implications of the assignment…

and had refused to be part of any oversight effort that might lead to unpleasant decisions. After Maya's visit to the club, Thad conceded Nate had been wise to dissociate from this part of their campaign to stabilize. Thinking on that gun she'd pointed at him and the anger with which she'd wielded it, Thad needed to be the one to direct the situation.

Although he couldn't figure out why his order hadn't already been carried out, or why none of his operatives were returning his calls. He realized something in this game had shifted dramatically... and he preferred not to think too closely on what that might be.

At least part of his problem had been solved. Later in the week, he'd be attending the funeral of his lunch friend, who'd broken his neck in an unfortunate fall off the deck of his house.

Thad practiced deep, calming breaths until his equilibrium returned.

Chapter Eleven

Maya's eyelids cracked open, prodded by the early morning light filtering through the sheers. She still craved unconsciousness, probably because she'd been so depleted when they'd finally stopped last night. Sensing she had more to confront today than she cared to, she pulled the sheet over her face.

Depleted or not, though, her body would not go under again. She flipped the covers back and surrendered to wakefulness, then took a visual inventory of her surroundings. The cabin was temporarily theirs, thanks to Aiden's mysterious ability to talk strangers out of their keys to it. She'd found the experience almost funny, watching her guy basically hypnotize the couple out for a hike… but they'd happily promised to get a hotel the next town over and leave the two of them alone. There were steaks in the fridge that could be grilled the next day. Enjoy! They'd shuffled off with blank, mildly confused expressions, and she knew just how they felt. Chalk that up to yet another anomaly she didn't care to question too closely at the moment. Not with the bigger issues hanging over her.

She hardly remembered crawling into bed, didn't, in fact, recall the lights going out. She'd never been so tired in her life, which for a former medical student was saying something. She stretched now – carefully – so as not to disturb her sleeping companion.

He'd curved himself in a half-moon around her, and even slumbering and unaware, his devotion enveloped her like a warm bath. Or maybe what she felt was her devotion for him? She could no longer separate their individual emotions, a phenomenon that had overtaken her somewhere in the water during their journey here. Now, the delineation seemed permanently smudged, which was too wonderful since she felt sated and happy for the first time in ages.

Snippets of their descent into the river, broken and surreal, glitched through her mind like a stream of transparent holographs, the recollections flat and insubstantial.

They hardly registered against the prevailing peace of this moment. She craned her neck to better contemplate the source of her newfound fulfillment… and realized she couldn't be awake, not really. Because here was Aiden, and he was too much the fantasy, too rumpled and warm and approachable, down to the velvety stubble on his chin and soft, sleep-matted hair.

Also, the two of them were together, a most unlikely circumstance.

Echoes of their escape, increasingly disturbing recollections, inserted themselves into her thoughts, and they pushed her further off balance. Had they really jumped off a bridge in New York, and then spent a day and a half *swimming* to get here? No way. That had to have been a dream. The mental replay of their dive continued to insist upon her awareness, though – their tip forward from outside the trusses, that endless fall. It had to be the idea, not an actual memory, that was so vivid.

But could it be true? she wondered.

Aiden opened his eyes and treated her to a lazy smile that blazed a hole right through her stupor… and caused her to jolt upright. He sat up as well, raised a hand to brush her hair from her face, then cupped the back of her neck with his palm.

"Morning, love."

She eyed him suspiciously. This trill inside her was too sharp, Aiden's presence too intense to qualify as delusion.

"Did we just... I mean, how did we get here?" Her words were edged with desperation, because she so wanted this to be real even if the narrative playing in her head didn't add up. It was all so unlikely, though, starting with Aiden's telepathic summons – which, truthfully, she could be talked into given her past run-ins with him – to their foolish vault from a worrisome height; followed by the lush, abiding intimacy that had encompassed them during their liquid sojourn. This last memory tugged hardest at a lurking cache of despair, because she felt she might die of sadness if what she saw now were untrue.

She switched her review to the more reasonable, less upsetting particulars of her flashbacks, such as how she'd felt just before her headlong, Aiden-focused sprint. Her fear had been justified, since Thad's subversions where she was concerned were established, his craziness verified. Murderous thugs were on their way to get her? Of course they were; Jethro & Co. had been armed and dogging her for months, and not to take her out for ice cream.

During their swim, Aiden had shared the details of his mental post-mortem on Thad, one he'd performed at the club after she'd left the dining room... because apparently he could accomplish that sort of thing. Anyway, Thad had ordered a hit on her as soon as she'd walked away, meaning her confrontation, gratifying as it had been, had escalated her circumstances instead of freeing her from them. Which galled her. She'd been so sure they'd understood one another...

But another piece of Aiden's examination yielded a welcome surprise: an image of her divorce decree, as detailed as if she herself had opened the envelope containing it. She didn't even question the document's existence – its dry charmlessness, the uneven notary stamp and double stapling, like it was a shipping order for construction materials. So prosaic. It certainly didn't look like the epitaph to years of emotional contortions and teeth-gnashing, and what an artless coda to the fanfare that had started it all. She didn't doubt she was legally divorced, though.

If only what she saw at present was so convincing.

Her replay insinuated itself incessantly now – the falling, the floating, just her and Aiden distancing themselves from the rest of the world. They'd never had such freedom from other parts of their lives, from individual distractions and the compound host of undefined issues that had kept them apart. So she *had* to consider the likelihood she and Aiden weren't really here, that they hadn't reconciled their insurmountable divisions in some glorious, fairytale swim.

But how awful if what she saw and felt now was an illusion.

In an instant, her old internal fetters resurrected themselves to constrict like metal bands around her rib cage, bleeding the strength from her limbs and killing the joy she'd awoken with. Tears overfilled her eyes, because if reality was being hunted and lonely in New York? Then she vowed to be done with reality, would just abandon her former ambitions altogether. Maya thought of a film she'd once seen where the timid heroine faked her death to escape an abusive husband. Maya wasn't timid, just careful, but she would change her name and become a checkout girl at a convenience store rather than go back to what she'd had.

Aiden interrupted her reverie, answering her thoughts, not her actual words. "No need to go that far, love. Okay, maybe there's a need, and working at a gas station might be a plan, but only if I get to be your stock boy and we're both hiding out." He winced. "Which is a possibility, I should warn you. Okay, more than a possibility, but I'll cover that later. After we take care of this internal wrestling match you've got going on. Look at me, Maya."

Aiden's thumb caressed her cheek, and as he held her stare, her improbable half-memories took on solidity.

They really had met on that bridge and flung themselves into the river. They really had gotten away and declared themselves underwater...

...and Aiden had always looked different to her because he *was* different. Both in and out of the East River, but mostly in, and no. No, she *really* didn't want to think too specifically about what she'd seen there.

But he secured her face in both of his hands, so she couldn't look away. "Not this time, love. This is the last wall between us, and I won't have it."

Falling, falling – Maya was airborne again, suspended between a landless platform above and an inscrutable expanse of water below.

Brilliant images of him flickered through her mind, of light playing across his skin in the shallows, the sharpness of his eyes – how they'd changed in shape and intensity during those first seconds of submersion. The way his body had shifted against her, the control he'd exerted over both of them while they swam.

Her understanding of biology – his as well as her own – changed when she was with him.

Yes, Maya. Keep going.

Their journey from sky to river looped repetitively in her head, drumming against her ability to reason. Her thoughts and feelings during that fall – the dreamier reflections it had prompted – commanded her focus more than what she'd actually seen and heard, and as she relived their downward progression again and again, she felt the veil dividing her conscious and subconscious mind rip.

An atemporal mishmash of memories rushed forth: her father throwing her up and catching her as a toddler. White clouds over Griffins Bay during a picnic. A volleyball game on the beach when she'd chased the ball into the ocean and stood in water up to her knees, mesmerized and convinced someone else was there.

She thought of the dozens of interactions she'd had with Aiden over the years, of his addictive, incessant pull... along with all those physical oddities she'd tried so hard not to see.

She knew what he wanted from her.

The transformation preoccupying her thoughts had been inside her, not the gargantuan, external one she was supposed to face. Obvious as the truth was, it remained uncomfortable to contemplate directly, like a too-bright light that would scorch her corneas if she stared at it straight on.

Aiden's voice rustled like dry leaves against pavement, an abrasion against the concrete acknowledgement she'd prefer not to make. "Name what you see, Maya. Let's move on from this," he pressed.

Well. Of course she knew what he was. Anyone would. Still, she hedged. "You're a myth," she ventured. She hesitated, grimaced, then apologized. "I can't say the word, Aiden. It feels too ridiculous."

"Siren," he supplied. "And here. I'll make this easier for you."

He flattened one of her palms against his chest, securing it with his own splayed hand. With the thumb of his other hand, he skimmed the inside of her forearm from elbow to wrist... which prompted yet another reminiscence of their free-fall, this time of their actual plunge.

From the moment they'd become immersed, she'd felt welcomed and wanted. And forgiven. Like a troublesome teenager returned home after an ugly, destructive rebellion, her earlier crimes no longer mattering. Aiden's joy as he'd held her during those first seconds was a force of nature every bit as overwhelming as his external metamorphosis. It was also, in her estimation, a miracle.

He offered her unquestioning acceptance, wasn't even a little concerned about the thousand and one things she'd done out of selfishness and fear. She could offer him the same in return. With such an understanding between them, who cared if he occasionally changed into a fish?

Maya recalled their swim in the river vividly now, not as a memory but as a physical recurrence. She relaxed just as she had beneath the waves, with Aiden keeping her physically and emotionally anchored, holding her from a drift away into chaos. She'd loved him for this, for containing them both, for keeping them together and apart from the world above. How buoyant and free she'd been in that dense, foreign place. And in his arms. Her vision faded.

Gravity reasserted itself until she felt the bed beneath them, the sheets against her skin. Framed by the sunlight streaming through the window, Aiden's face glowed with triumph.

"You've been with me all along, haven't you," she stated.

Because she knew, *knew*, he'd been around. Something about his touch, his familiarity, the continuity she felt in their connection. Combined with the raw, fantastical truth they'd just unraveled, she believed anything was possible, certainly his secret presence at her side in New York.

She understood Aiden must have trailed her to the city, witnessed her personal struggles and helped her all those times she'd sensed him. Of course he had. They were bound to one another, had circled around their mutual attraction since she'd been in college, so where else would he be but by her? She would have done same if he'd been the one to leave. If Aiden had married someone faithless and dismissive – if he'd become a surveillance target by gun-toting PIs – she would have installed herself right next to him, too, would have done anything to shield him, comfort him. Somehow Aiden had accomplished their companionship. She studied him for clues and asked, "Okay, my sneaky siren. How'd you do it?"

She was only mildly phased when Aiden demonstrated, appearing first as Mitch... and then, as an added surprise, her savior from the café. Which was one she hadn't thought of. Still, she watched his serial transformations without alarm.

But why hadn't he appeared to her as Mitch at the café and Thad's club? Why the extra disguise?

"I couldn't let the guys tailing you see me as Mitch, because they knew me," he reminded her. "I'd worked for the same security company for Thad, right?"

To which she said, "Huh."

Given Aiden's impossible revelation a few minutes ago, she didn't have it in her to feel shock over this new 'ta-da.' She stared over his shoulder at an undefined spot on the wall, her thoughts focused inward.

Their couple-hood finally made sense, from their last interactions at SeaCakes when she was in college, to her conviction she could make a go of things with Stu, to the deconstruction of the ideals she'd brought to her ill-fated marriage. She remembered the times she'd sensed Aiden during Stu's smarmy public exhibitions, the familiar presence next to her alleviating her feelings of sadness and failure. She recalled how shaken she'd been during her introduction to Mitch, how like Aiden he'd seemed. Finally, she considered the support she'd had from her mystery man during her confrontation with Thad. The experiences were cohesive… and she knew why she hadn't hesitated to heed Aiden's desperate call to her from the bridge.

She genuinely wasn't freaked out by any of it – not his marine provenance, not his ability to turn into other people, not over the fact he'd kept such close tabs on her. She was grateful they'd remained associated throughout her marriage, for the knowledge she hadn't been alone. She didn't need to explain the complexities of her life to him, which was a lovely relief – no justifications, no apologies – he already knew it all, including what she'd resisted each and every time she'd behaved rudely to him. He'd even put his own shoulder into her challenges to help her.

All the while, he'd refrained from judging her, and what a devastating instruction in kindness that was to her smaller, too-insular self. Her final, meager stand against the truth wilted.

Siren. She tested the word silently in her mouth. At least now she understood his strange intensity, as well as their insuperable attraction to one another. His otherworldly physical traits – and apparently his ability to take on the appearance of another – all of it normalized. She released a tiny, frustrated laugh.

"I've been running from you and longing for you my whole adult life, without knowing why. I finally understand what we are to each other."

Aiden's intensity sharpened. "Yes. And there's more to talk about on that front. But for now…" He trailed off and stared at her mouth, then dipped forward to kiss her. When he drew back, his eyes were silvery bright. "We have other catching up to do," he whispered.

Which brought Maya abruptly up against another monumental emotional roadblock, revealing a problem she hadn't given *any* previous consideration... because she'd never expected to find herself in this situation.

Physical intimacy with Aiden as a distant, unlikely possibility had been a daydream she'd dismissed, but now she and her daydream were cuddling in bed together. And he'd fought for her, protected her from her evil in-laws, and he loved and wanted her. She loved and wanted him, too... but. Her past – specifically her listless, infrequent, and invariably depressing bedroom encounters with her husband – loomed over her like a shakily suspended axe.

Stu hadn't ever, ever been this into her, hadn't cared for her fulfillment beyond a kind of perfunctory petting. He'd never touched her with Aiden's earnestness, or focused on her so absolutely.

She'd never in her life felt this vulnerable... and the experience undid her.

By contrast, every caress, every look from Aiden was for her and her alone; not generically sensual, not part of an interaction some anonymous person could have with another anonymous person. What flourished between them in this place and in this moment was deeply, unavoidably personal, leaving her as uncertain and anxious as a teenager contemplating her first kiss.

She was supposed to be an experienced, sexually confident woman at this stage of her life, and damn it, she wasn't. She should be comfortable with Aiden's desires, know how to function within this realm of intimacy. She didn't. In fact, she'd resigned herself years ago to the idea she wasn't a very sexual person, that she didn't have it in her to get lost in the act the way other people did. The way Kate and her sisters said they did, or like the heroes and heroines in the novels she read.

Which brought her face-on with an acknowledgement she'd have to make right here and right now, and where was the justice in that? Seriously. What past sins consigned her to these back-to-back, excoriating confessions that left her off balance and over exposed?

Put on your big girl panties, Maya, she instructed herself. If she intended to wriggle out of intimacy with Aiden right now, she owed him an explanation.

"Aiden, I don't think I can do this. I don't want to disappoint you, and I don't... I mean, I'm just not..." She trailed off, twisting her face away to glare at the opposite wall. "Why do all my interactions with you feel like you're holding a gun, and I'm handing you bullets to shoot me with every time I open my mouth?"

Aiden didn't appear to take her seriously, since he reached for and casually twirled a lock of her hair around one of his fingers. She turned back to him, and he grinned at her. "So, you're nervous, and that's *my* fault?" he teased.

She was in no mood to banter. "It's just... I'm just not good at this sort of thing..." and to her astonishment, he chuckled.

"No, hon – I'm not laughing at you, I swear. It's just so sweet... but you know how we're kind of able to read each other's thoughts? I mean, when we're together?"

Maya wanted to crawl under the bed and hide. No, she just wanted to find someplace she could breathe. He already knew she was frigid? She preferred the earlier embarrassment she'd felt over her marriage to a sex addict, how she'd believed it would last. She'd never felt so ludicrous in her life, and the feeling cut a bloody, painful path through her gut.

Thankfully, dispassion – her crutch whenever her confidence flagged – came to her like a well-trained dog. She grabbed its leash and let it pull her up from this pit of stupidness. She rose fluidly from the bed, turned, and regarded Aiden calmly.

She'd assumed the brisk, ready-for-anything persona she'd first developed at the net when she was defending against some monstrously talented hitter intent on cramming a volleyball down her throat. Medical school further honed this façade, since the appearance of competence went a long way toward coping with emotionally unstable patients and never mind that she was the unstable one here. After all, what good was a truly excellent, ice-goddess front if you couldn't hide behind it at times? Here went nothing.

She would reason both of them out of Aiden's intention, would divert their conversation toward something other than her inadequacies, maybe launch into a deeper inquiry of Aiden's siren ways and why they should talk about them for a few months before engaging further. She would lead them into a detailed discussion of his world and how they might negotiate their way in it as a couple, which should, she hoped, defuse the urgency between them. She opened her mouth to speak…

…and said nothing, because, no. He wasn't going to play.

With a penetrating gaze and single shake of his head, Aiden dispatched her words before she formed them. She almost heard them evaporate from her mind like droplets of water hitting a hot skillet. Then the idea she could and should execute some sort of dodge disappeared, just floated off into the atmosphere. She couldn't quite recall why the effort to stop him had been so important. What had she wanted? To protect herself? Pfft. Her concern frayed around the edges before unraveling altogether.

Now she badly wished she hadn't moved away from him. The small distance between them started to feel like an ugly chasm, one that yawned wider with every passing second and left in its wake a proportionately broadening despair… and she realized how appallingly lonely she was, all because they weren't touching. Could she afford to show him how much she wanted to be back in his arms? Couldn't he see how forlorn she was? She stood rigidly, vibrating with tension.

Within a few more seconds, a cavernous grief blossomed inside her like an actual wound, one she could mend in an instant if only she would rejoin him. She knew she would never feel whole again unless he held her.

Did he want her as badly? She checked his expression and took comfort in his apparent misery.

"Come here, lover," he said gently, then rose to his knees to catch her as she swayed toward the bed. He snagged her waist, and in one smooth movement aligned her length to his. In another instant she was tucked under him, each of her hands clasped in his by her head, her arms bracketing her face like commas.

God, but his touch was heaven itself, their connectedness better than anything she'd ever felt. Her former worries over her sexual reticence – and she truly could no longer feel any – staged a comical side-insurgency in her mind, like a tiny, drunken bat careening in front of a gigantic and luminous moon. Its by-play was laughably small against the hypnotic glow of Aiden's hunger and devotion, which penetrated through her pores and made her feel as if she also glowed.

"You can't compare me to Stu," Aiden commented hoarsely, his starved gaze dispatching the last of her ability to reason. He ran his lips up the side of her neck to whisper in her ear, "And you're not frigid." She shivered and softened against him, and she felt his smile at her throat. She closed her eyes.

"You can't know that." Her voice shook. She drew another breath to say anything that might contain this unease within her. She scanned his face... and relaxed.

Aiden pressed her wrists into the bed as he leveraged himself over her, dropping the lightest of kisses on her mouth before replying, "Yes. I can." He settled his hips between hers. "And you're way off, Maya. This belief that you don't get excited? It's wrong. That was all Stu. His sickness, his problem. It was never about you, what you did or didn't do." He hovered closely above her. "You think you're not into to this?" His low laugh caressed her skin like heavy, cool satin. The planes of her body shifted and pressed against his...

...and her desire for him released itself like a flood, like a mighty rush of water that had beat too long against the deteriorating wall of a dam, and now the dam broke. Ahhh. This was so much better. Her reservations – as well as any thought to her own inabilities – surged out of her and away.

Dimly, she realized she'd compartmentalized her marriage to Stu, and she shouldn't have. She'd accepted her lack of control over her husband's outward behavior but still assumed their lukewarm physical connection was her issue, not his. In fact, it was exclusive to him, to their marriage, not anyone or anything outside of it.

The neediness building within her now certainly bore no resemblance to any of her prior experiences, not with Stu or any man before him. She felt Aiden's yearning minutely; every caress, every pleasure a balm and an offering. Not an escape. Not an antidote to boredom or insecurity.

He was different, and so their union would be different.

"Yesss," she sighed.

Aiden released her wrists, slid one of his palms to the middle of her back and arched her torso, tucking her hips into his as he did. Maya wept at the perfection of their fit, at how right they were. She hooked her arms under his shoulders and pressed her forehead to his chest. Why hadn't they done this years ago? If he'd held her like this back in Griffins Bay, before there was a Stu, it would have clarified so much.

His response came to her like an apology. *I had to be careful. I wanted you... but I could never be this close. Not if I was going to walk away.*

I wouldn't have let you go, she answered swiftly. And she realized it was true. If they'd shared what they were sharing now, she would have followed him around like a beggar.

He entered her smoothly, holding himself still those first seconds. She felt a surreal and shattering closeness, a heart-stopping intensity she initially squirmed against... and then didn't. Because she didn't want to get away even if she could never control her feelings for him again. She embraced him tenderly.

Their exchange was grounded in his familiar emotional solicitation, which this time drew a more open response from her, as easy as if resistance had never occurred to her. Her world stabilized, her insides breathed... because this was something they'd both craved for too long.

The hidden parts of herself she gave up were given back to her in kind, with Aiden yielding his own intimacies. She absorbed everything he offered – his loyalty; his strength; his fierce, unshakable attachment to her; all of which bound her to him more tightly than an opulent ceremony in a church ever would.

Again she regretted the times she'd run from him back in Griffins Bay, not only because of what they shared now, but also for what she was able to give. For what he wanted from her and the joy they both experienced as they shared themselves. With their emotions and bodies intertwined, the encounter broke and remade them both, destroying her former understanding of love even as it forged a new one.

One that felt like an identifying mark, like a brand they would each wear hereafter.

"In a way, we *are* branded," Aiden told her. "Other sirens will see what's between us, know we belong together."

Maya hid her smile against him. They were established, just like that? Everyone would simply know they were a couple? Providence had finally paid her a visit. Because she wouldn't have to justify or defend her romantic choices to anyone, could assume what was obvious to her was also obvious to others, no public announcement needed. "I wish we could have that in my world," she lamented.

Aiden fisted the back of her hair and tugged gently to tilt her face to him. "We will. Depend on it." His kiss was a vow she thrilled to.

Aiden's desires commanded their progression now. He was everywhere, with his mouth, his hands, his ranging, enveloping hunger. Maya relinquished herself to sensation, and to the longings spurring them toward mutual bliss. This was so simple, so easy. She felt like a dancer trained from birth to partner him, their performance fluid and lovely.

When they were spent, they faced each other on their sides, Aiden caressing her – her face, her neck, her hair. Maya placed a hand against his heart, which he responded to first with a kiss to the underside of her wrist, then by pressing his fingertips to her pulse point.

This time, she felt the action differently, in the form of a dull vibration of her heartbeat, the sound like the boom of a far-off explosion. The resonance suggested something other than the rhythm of her circulatory system, more premonition than physical function.

Her eyes opened fully. "What is that?"

For some reason, Aiden looked uncomfortable. "Our desire for each other will change according to your cycle." He held up her wrist. "This is how I read you. I can feel how close you are to ovulation."

"I'm on birth control," she blurted.

His smile was warm. "I can tell. And it's probably wise."

"I just never felt confident enough, you know, with Stu. And then medical school was…" she shook her head. "There was just no way."

Aiden closed his eyes. "I want things to be different because it's my nature. But a baby would be a bad idea. I know that."

She searched his face. "Would it, really? For you? Why? I mean, I'm not advocating, I just want to know what you think. What you want."

He ran the back of his hand along her cheek and jaw. "I have what I want. But part of bonding for us happens when you're most fertile." He settled his chin on top of her head, and she heard the frown in his next statement. "Not that I'm the norm where you're concerned, since I've been unable to leave you alone, even without the fun part." He huffed, almost a laugh. "I will say it would go easier for us back home if you were pregnant, because there would be *no* further arguments against us."

"Aiden…. I… I just can't see how I'd juggle…"

He pulled back. "No, love. Don't worry. We have a bond, and it will show enough." His brows drew together. "I hope. Or at least enough to the people who count." He searched her face. "Seriously, there's no rush. And I might be able to coerce those who need coercing."

"Meaning...?"

"My aunt – you know her – Carmen Blake? She's the reigning siren queen, meaning what she says goes. She dotes on me. I have good cause to think she's sympathetic..."

Maya gripped his arm. "*Carmen* is a mermaid queen?"

"Mm-hmm. Although Maya, we *really* prefer the term 'siren.'"

"And you think she'll go to bat for us?"

"Yep." But he frowned again. "Maybe."

"Does that mean we get to go to siren-land or wherever and plead our case?"

Aiden shuddered. "God, no. Not for a while. The longer we're gone, the more time we spend bonded, the less likely they are to try and undo us. I mean, if we show up now, they'd haze you so you don't remember me and haul me off and... I don't know. Chain me up or something. To keep me away from you."

"That's... that's appalling. And for the record, we will *not* be living among other sirens if that's how they treat people." She sat up and hugged her knees. "Seriously. Why would they intervene? What business is it of theirs?"

Aiden shifted uncomfortably. "You'd be the third Wilkes daughter to marry in, which our people think is too risky. From an exposure standpoint."

Maya stilled. "Simon and Luke. Oh my God, Aiden..." He placed a hand over her mouth. "Let me finish, love. I know it's a shock and you have things to say about it all." Maya quieted and Aiden dropped his hand to re-clasp one of hers. "Our problem is bigger than you know. Because things tend to go badly when people are aware of us.

"The primary issue is internal, though. To you – to humans on land – individuality is its own end. You act based on singular wants and needs, for self-expression or fulfillment or other internal drives. Sirens are individuals too, but we're a lot more dependent on each other, especially when it comes to our emotions. We need each other to process what we feel, every day, so we function in a hierarchy of 'community first, individual second.' Or third or fourth if you've got other collective interests ahead of you – your job, maybe, or your family. But anyway, independence for each of us requires stability of the whole, and those who are unhappy or rebel or are different... well, they have a big impact. They create unrest that disturbs everyone, even sirens you don't know or interact with." He studied their joined hands.

"That's why I was sent to train with the siren militia, as was Simon. All of us in the program didn't fit in right, couldn't integrate, not that we didn't try. And our inability had a community-wide effect."

Maya peered at him doubtfully. "Really? You didn't want to play in their Little League so they kicked you off the field?"

Aiden smiled and tucked her hair behind her ear. "Not quite. In a population our size, my antics – and Simon's and the rest of us in the corps – have broad consequences." His expression turned wry. "This is actually the big leagues, and a significant problem for our leaders. None of us have known what to do about sirens like me, including sirens like me." His whole demeanor soured. "But we've had to do something. Ostracism would literally kill us, so we can't be 'kicked off the field,' as you call it. The next best option was to isolate us, send us off to, I don't know, a kind of group home, one where we have each other but don't trouble our happier brethren."

Maya fumed. "Excuse the term, but how inhumane."

Aiden rubbed his eyes. "We're not the same as humans, Maya. We're anxious and unhappy when others are, and our contributions, emotional and otherwise, are vital to our well-being. To our physical and mental health as individuals and as a group. You can ask Simon about this sometime, but not wanting what everyone else around you wants is a huge drag. So much, we all learned to hide. As in 'super hide' – to cloak, to appear as something or someone else, like I just showed you. And we learned to fight." He intertwined her fingers with his again. "We hate being different. All of us would have fixed ourselves if we could have."

"Wow. And *both* of my sisters...?"

He massaged the vee between her eyebrows with his forefinger. "Yes. Think about it. I'm sure you'll see it, now that you know about me." He kissed her cheek. "I know this probably doesn't make sense to you yet. And honestly, I don't think you and I getting together would be such a big deal – even with Solange and Sylva already co-opted in – if the community wasn't so nervous these days. I mean, yeah, I get why government doesn't like the idea of us taking three humans from the same family. But I really believe if we didn't have so much other crap going on – a new monarch, a new government figuring things out, rebels like myself popping up left and right – I think we'd be accepted. Or we could at least elbow our way in faster."

Maya took measure of his conviction, searching for optimism she couldn't produce on her own and hoping he might supply it for her. But based on her most recent experiences? Her voice hitched when she next spoke. "I won't be on the run for the rest of my life, Aiden."

He immediately relieved her, dulling the sharp edges of her distress as only he could. She regarded him more calmly.

Aiden considered a distant point over her shoulder. "I can't promise anything, but I believe we only need to hide for a while. The longer we're bonded, the more likely we'll deter my people from interfering. And I do think Carmen will back us." He shifted away and gripped her arms. "The bigger threat to us is Thad's manhunt. For you. That's an especially good reason to lie low for a spell."

Maya gaze dropped. "Do you think we'll ever be able to do something normal? Like rent an apartment, go to a concert, or order takeout? Without the threat of someone shooting at us, I mean."

"Let's work on that," Aiden agreed, and this time Maya heard the optimism she sought. "Let's both believe we'll get through this mess. In fact, I can offer you this: we *will* get there. That's a promise." He rubbed one of her earlobes between his thumb and forefinger. "I'm so sure of us. I think if we both picture what we want, there's no chance we *won't* have it – the apartment, the concerts, the takeout. Maybe a dog." He grinned. "I want the whole catastrophe with you."

Maya envisioned the life he'd just described, and bliss spread within her center. She could see such a future in detail... and for once believed she and Aiden would find their way toward it. Her tone reflected her intent. "I want it all. More than anything."

"Then that's what we'll have," Aiden replied confidently. He sat up, swung his feet over the edge of the bed to rest on the floor, then dragged her into his lap. "What say we go hunt down some breakfast? I'm starving."

Maya felt the heaviness of their darker considerations lift away from them. She stretched, then levered herself up and onto her feet. She stood, clasped Aiden's hand and pulled. "Me, too. I could eat a tree."

"Nah. There's a café a quarter mile from here, and I'm told they serve the best hash east of the Mississippi. Possibly the best waffles."

Maya squinted. "My mama holds that title, mister. Although I'm willing to conduct a review."

Aiden snagged his shirt off the floor and began to dress. "All right, then. Waffle research it is. Let's get out of here."

Chapter Twelve

Xanthe approached Griffins Bay – and the real object of her visit, Peter – from the ocean, having decided to search out her former colleague for a chat about her aggravating work problems. No, that wasn't true. She hadn't decided anything, was following this urge on instinct, not reason; although she thought a conversation with her former prince might resolve her deepening anxiety over her erratic loyalties these days. And Peter knew her and the burden of her professional obligations as well as anyone.

Earlier that day she'd sensed he was near the Blake home, and this thread of perception, slight though it was, had given her adequate impetus to leave her offices at Shaddox and undertake her current swim. She'd had to be sneaky in her exit from the palace since others there continued to ask her about him – they hadn't stopped since they'd learned of his resurrection almost eight years ago. Peter apparently didn't want to communicate with anyone, which stopped no one from trying to wheedle a meeting with him out of her.

They were kind of cute, often inventing some weak but plausible need for reconnection with their one-time regent – would he like any personal items from his life before exile? So-and-so had been an intimate and was frantic with worry for him, and could he or she get in touch? Surely she, Xanthe, could facilitate an encounter.

She couldn't, but she didn't blame any of them for trying. She understood their artless pandering, which was a combination of genuine concern and an over-zealousness none of them could help, both of which would be alleviated if Peter would deign to visit the seat of siren government and show his face. He wouldn't and didn't.

At first, she'd tried to persuade him with the contention he'd be left alone sooner if he'd cater to his former subjects in this matter; if he'd let himself be seen and answer a few questions to allay everyone's curiosity. "You've been the center of our common life for over a century, and the drama surrounding your return is too seductive," she'd argued. And it was true: even the most stable among them yearned to ferret out for themselves the truth in this part of their community's history, to establish a more definitive resolution than the one they'd been given. Or at least come up with a palatable way to consider all that had happened since Peter's faux suicide.

Peter hadn't disagreed, but neither did he comply with their incessant requests for an audience. "I'll think about it," he'd answer blandly, or he'd say nothing at all, showing Xanthe he couldn't care less about others' need for relief, her own included. After her bids to lure him into a public appearance failed, she hadn't known what to say to sirens who solicited her for a get-together. At this point, she just wished they'd stop pestering her.

"I have no influence on him," she stated again and again. "I don't know when – or even if – he'll visit Shaddox. Ever." Their eager nods were not an acknowledgment, because they acted as if she hadn't spoken. She continued to be approached by folks who thought she had a unique in with Peter Loughlin.

She suspected she had more of an in than Peter let on, though. Because while she never had any indication where he was when others asked, she did sense him when she wished to locate him herself. *Perhaps because he allows me this access?* She wondered.

Several years ago, she'd asked him about the special radar between them. "Why can I always find you?"

"I will talk with *you* anytime," Peter had replied… and that was all he'd say on the subject. She'd studied him to determine what he might be thinking but couldn't guess. Although, he had professed loneliness for his own kind when she'd come upon him murdering their viceroy all those years ago. Peter drew her attention back to him. "You have nothing to worry about from me, Xanthe," he asserted. "We've known each other a long time, and talking with you is a pleasure of mine. My reasons are that simple."

"If you say so…?" Since she also noticed the easiness between them, she was inclined to believe him. After all, how many longtime, upper-level siren bureaucrats like the two of them were there, floating around these days? Not many.

She couldn't help but feel wary around Peter given his past, epic deviances, though.

"Truly. You are safe in my company," he insisted.

"Mmm," she'd responded, wishing she were more convinced.

But back to her current personal crisis and the reason behind her impending visit to her old boss. She'd elected to search for him in Griffins Bay on the same whim that brought her to him every time no matter where he was, although she was aware he often dropped by the Blakes' to check on Gabe, Kate, and little Henry. And sometimes Carmen and Michael when they were beachside, which they usually weren't since their move to Shaddox.

Just outside the reef protecting the bay, Xanthe grabbed a waterpack with land supplies from one of the designated caches in the rock face.

She saw Peter from underwater just before she surfaced… and she felt his grin, his anticipation. He sat on the end of a dock at the base of the Blake beach house, one that served as a landing platform for siren visitors. It was low to the water – and often submerged during high tide, which was not the case at the moment. Peter had his linen shirt unbuttoned, the cuffs of his slacks rolled up to his knees. His bare feet dangled in the sea.

"Ah, Moonflower, how lovely to see you," he crooned when her face broke through the waves. She hooked an arm around one of the dock posts to anchor herself.

The overhead sun left Peter's face in shadow, making his expression unreadable. But this time she didn't need to rely on her observational skills to determine his frame of mind because she absorbed his emanations cleanly. Peter's emotional output, usually missing altogether, was almost like that of a normal siren today.

And he really was pleased to see her. As she examined him from her inferior vantage point, the loveliest tenderness from him washed over her, a blanket of affection that softened the prickly worry she wore these days like a sea urchin wore its spines. When she reacted with her own outreach – an automatic response usually not accepted by Peter Loughlin – she perceived a freeness within him she'd never felt before. He was relaxed, almost *open.*

This was not anything she associated with their rogue, duplicitous prince, so she stilled, combing him with her intuition for evidence of deceit. She inquired within herself as well, checking for a backlash of emptiness, the sour echo of loneliness she considered a trademark of any interaction with Peter. His usual impediments weren't there this time; or maybe they were, but penetrable for once.

"You're happy," she remarked with surprise. "And apparently, you were expecting me." As vaguely troubling as such an idea was, she couldn't help but return the smile he gave her, nor could she suppress her own upswell of affection for him, a current of warmth that left something like joy in its wake.

His verbal evasion was more typical of him. "You haven't come around in a while, and it was time for one of our visits. Here. I'll hand you up." He crouched and reached for her.

Xanthe scanned the area for boaters and swimmers, although the Blake house had been built out with mermaid visitors in mind, so even with human activity in the area, the enclosed cove and walled walkway along part of the hill provided cover. She clasped Peter's hand, then thrust powerfully upwards with her tail. Peter guided her momentum so she landed neatly beside him, on her feet this time. He released her.

She busied herself with her waterpack as she spoke. "Am I the only friend you've given a nickname? I've not heard you use one with others." His welcome still gladdened her in a way she preferred not to consider, mostly because Peter didn't flirt. And she knew – as did he – he was incapable of following up on such an effort even if he *had* intended to engage her that way. Which he likely hadn't.

He was probably just restless and bored and indulging himself with her because of their long association. Who else could he be so casual with? She was one of only three or four who knew him well, with whom he could be at ease. She recalled how she'd seen him fish in the same way with others in the past, an activity she'd attributed to latent siren reflex, no more. One could certainly not forget – her least of all – the disastrous outcomes of his past romantic ventures, first with Seneca, then Kate. Their entire population was still paying for those debacles. Which he well knew.

As usual, Peter responded as if she'd volunteered her musings even though she hadn't. "No. I don't wish to flirt with you, Xanthe. And you are my only Moonflower."

A conflicting representation, but no matter; she wasn't here for him. She needed something for herself, something she suspected only he could give her... and whether she should or not, she trusted him to provide it. She remained vaguely shy though, still avoiding his gaze as she ferreted a sundress out of her supply bag. She slipped the garment over her head and down her torso, then decided she'd best ignore what might or might not have just passed between them, since it didn't matter. "Are we walking inland? I brought clothes just in case."

For an instant, Peter released too many thoughts and feelings. Tenderness still, but now accompanied by ire and distrust and a profusion of other emotions too dense for her to disentangle. After this glimpse, he barred her from further personal entrée, which ironically calmed her since such protocol was normal for him and familiar to her. And because she didn't have to struggle to make sense of him, an assignment she'd failed at anyway on the few occasions she'd tried. Many years ago, when she'd attempted to read him – and he'd allowed her to make the effort – Xanthe had concluded Peter's psyche was too twisted, too complex. Especially for beings like her, who had not been shaped by the same formative experiences that had made him so... so unfathomably strange.

He turned toward the stairs and motioned for her to follow.

"I made iced tea and brought it to the back deck," he called over his shoulder. "Gabe and Kate and their boy are gone for the afternoon. I thought we'd enjoy some refreshments and the view." He glanced back at her. "And of course, we'll address your concerns over your future."

Xanthe surveyed the walk-up to the porch, which was high enough above them, only the balustrade showed. She and her friend, Carmen – Peter's surprise daughter who had been installed as the siren monarch after he disappeared – had solved many a personal and societal problem there, also over baked goods and beverages. When had they last made the time for such frivolity? Not since Carmen had taken the throne.

The thought depressed her. Carmen had been insanely busy, of course, but surely they could have made *some* room in their lives for those interludes they'd both so enjoyed.

Xanthe wondered if she'd unintentionally isolated herself. Maybe she'd focused too diligently – and too protectively – on her diplomatic responsibilities to the exclusion of simple camaraderie, something they all needed to thrive. The lack of it pained her, had in fact driven her to seek out the most reserved, unfriendly siren on earth. But she could think of no others in their world like him – and like her – sirens whose duties had become synonymous with personal sacrifice. To some extent, the band of miscreants she'd shipped off to be rehabilitated in Peter's security training program – Simon and Aiden among them – qualified; but she didn't think she had much in common with them. Did she? Was she just like all those rebels she'd judged so harshly? She looked up to find Peter stopped ahead, studying her progress enigmatically.

"It's unfair for you to read me when I cannot read you," she accused him. He turned without responding and resumed his climb.

Once seated on the porch, she launched directly into the discussion she'd traveled here to have. "I still struggle to settle into my work as I used to. And I'm tired of trying. The tactics I once relied on to resolve our people's conflicts no longer work, or at least no longer work well."

"Try the French macaroons," he suggested, handing her a glass of iced tea.

She smiled wryly. "That's your answer? Eat a cookie?"

"No," he said. "Although they're very good. My answer is to focus less on the problem you think you have and more on the one you actually have."

She sipped from her glass as she pondered his response. "Which would be what, in your opinion?" She wasn't defensive, truly yearned to hear his analysis concerning her diminishing efficacy, or on how she might restore her former sense of fulfillment over what she did. She even wished he would speed up his critique if he had one; if she and Peter could communicate with the same flow as other sirens, she'd already have his counsel. And possibly a solution.

She grew surly, even though she'd known Peter would deny her the broader perceptual access she relied on with others of their kind, that this conversation would be no different from any other they'd had. Still, a girl could hope. "I wish we could interact normally, so I wouldn't have to reason or guess with you," she groused. "We take too long this way."

Peter regarded her with a small smile, not unkind. "I no longer have that facility, Xanthe. I know our conversations feel one-dimensional to you. But it's a self-protection mechanism I'm unable to shut off. No one else gets around it, either. It's not just you." He looked away and his tone hardened. "And I don't find our interactions lacking.

"But let's talk more about what brought you to me." This next smile was winsome, devious. "I'm tempted not to help you, you know. I rather enjoy these interludes, and I very much like this taste you've developed for my advice." He returned his attention to the water and his expression closed again. "I find the solution obvious, although I understand why you don't." He paused before continuing carefully. "You've been trying to stabilize for seven years, am I correct?"

Xanthe scanned the horizon. "Yes. I thought my confidence would return after you stopped interrupting my abilities during that conflict with Duncan. But it didn't. I don't know what I'm doing wrong, Peter."

"Hmm. And have you considered the problem may lie elsewhere? That you aren't to blame for what you see as your shortcomings?"

"No. I've done this job for decades. I've proven myself capable too many times and in too many situations. I'm not boasting, but the intricacies of diplomacy were always easy for me, a gift I could count on and oversight no one else could provide. There's nothing so different about how we are now, how we govern, to have caused me to weaken as I have."

Peter's response was swift. "You are not weak. Everyone looks to you as they always have. You are still revered."

"Perhaps...? In that I'm still doing my job, I suppose I still *can* do it. But I don't have the sureness I once did. Or maybe control. Regardless, I never leave a situation resolved to my satisfaction as I once did." When she considered him again, she was struck by the sharpness in his regard, how thoroughly he saw into her. She dropped her gaze. "I expect if you were still governing, you would have dismissed me by now."

"Not at all. But we would have talked sooner about what you want to do instead."

She fidgeted with her hands. "What would that be, do you think? Because there's nothing else I can do." She emitted a small, sad laugh. "This is all I've ever done. Ever *been*."

Having spoken these words aloud, Xanthe's mood lightened. Maybe because she'd confessed herself to a friend, even one she shouldn't trust. Maybe because she'd finally given voice to an idea she'd fought ever since the Duncan Fleming fiasco, an idea she'd found impossible to confront. She experienced the unknotting of an ugly constriction within her.

Under Peter's steady gaze, she also felt her concentration loosen, as if she teetered on the edge of hypnosis.

Her focus wandered off, so while she still understood where she was and with whom, she began to picture herself outside of her current reality, and as separate from her usual understanding of herself. She became dissociated from old wants, old ideas, even old accomplishments. And how liberating to see herself as something other than a roster of accolades, as existing outside the confines of leadership and self-discipline, regardless of how fulfilling or motivating her pursuits used to be.

"It isn't all you are, Xanthe. It just isn't. Which is really why you're having a hard time." Peter's voice had become surreal to her, as if he were an echo on the water instead of solid and seated beside her. Although, when she forced herself to pay attention, she realized he'd moved from his chair; he was, in fact, kneeling at her feet. He'd taken her hands in his, his palms beneath hers, his thumbs caressing her knuckles. She raised her eyes to his, which were intent and… mesmerizing. And mere inches from her own.

"What are you doing?" She wasn't concerned, just curious in the same way she'd be over a weather report, or mundane gossip passed by the palace staff at Shaddox. Not as if she were pondering the deconstruction of her identity.

"You came to me for help. I'm helping you."

What a lovely man, and how kind of him to apply himself to matters he had no real stake in. For the thousandth time, she reflected on the colossal hole his absence had left in their community, on how sorely she missed his prodigious intelligence at the helm of their siren ship. Maybe the shallowing of her abilities was related to his departure? She considered how all their governmental efforts felt more tenuous without Peter backing them up.

This made her jealous, even a little resentful, since her own inadequacies fell into sharper relief against the memory – and current demonstration – of Peter's competence. For the first time ever, she wished she were less like herself, more like Peter Loughlin.

Peter snorted and muttered something she didn't catch, although she knew it was unflattering. But he stayed in front of her, tightened his grip on her hands, and faced her again. He re-secured her gaze, his own strange and probing, a force emanating from him that made her feel... like she mattered in this world. Apart from what she did. She also suspected Peter was in the process of manipulating her, and... hmm. She should probably be concerned about that?

She wasn't. Curiosity superseded her desire for the more comfortable engagement tactics she knew, where she would parse and analyze another's suggestions before accepting them as her own. She also couldn't bear the thought of him pulling away at the moment, and not just because he'd reached in and unwound the tense ball of nerves inside her. Peter Loughlin was about to demonstrate something critical to her, something to explicate her troubles *and* show her the path away from them. With his guidance, she knew she wouldn't lose her way; or if she did stray, she could count on him not to leave her destroyed.

Because he cared for her.

At which point worry snaked through her burgeoning sense of hope. She perceived a deeper, possibly terrifying revelation forcing its way to her from behind his effort, one that loomed like a prehistoric, siren-eating carnivore with her on its lunch menu. The threat was related to Peter, specifically to his upbringing, which she'd heard had been unconscionable. A close – as in she would actually feel what he'd felt – review of his childhood persecutions? She recoiled. She was here for her own melodrama, not his.

You need to see this, Xanthe. Others' idiosyncrasies, yours included, have proliferated from mine, from what happened to me. He smiled kindly. *I can see you're uneasy, though, so I promise: I'll be careful with you.*

Xanthe's relief shamed her. She shouldn't wish to evade him... and she should, given the scope of societal problems she'd tackled in the past, be beyond such petty worrying. Peter again soothed her. *You're wise to approach our effort cautiously. What we're doing is harder for you because it's personal, not one of your normal endeavors. But you mustn't fret, Moonflower. I'll take care of you.*

She felt his hold on her consciousness close in like a fisherman's net around its catch. He was about to haul her up and out of her rigid self-control... but again he kept her from retreating. Thankfully, he also kept her from panic. *I've got you, Xanthe. Trust me. Now. Onward.*

Their surroundings darkened, then faded, pushing away what she sensed and thought, including the rote personal contemplations that had spurred her journey here in the first place. *Onward*, she conceded.

Releasing herself to Peter's guidance might gain her insight later, but it also revealed an immediate truth, one that kept her further invested in their hunt. With the insulation Peter provided, she could see how personally ravaging her anxiety had become to her, how much it had whittled away at her spirit like a parasitic entity, maybe a tumor. She recalled the many occasions she'd reflected on just this analogy, when she'd truly believed she'd wither and die from her inabilities... and worse, no one else cared enough about her for such an outcome to matter, not really.

For the time being, however, Peter had divested her of her tumor. She also sensed a real opportunity for a permanent excision, felt honest hope for the first time in ages. The last vestiges of her need to direct her own actions faded into nothingness...

...and pure relief overtook her. *Ahhhhh*, she sighed.

Her body pitched gently forward, and she allowed her forehead to rest on Peter's shoulder. A rational voice inside her – and this was the coping mechanism *she* was unable to turn off – still counseled her against such surrender.

But true recovery tantalized. She *could* follow Peter's lead without knowing the outcome, because he was uniquely knowledgeable about her function specifically as well as insightful in general. She could accept his encouragements without question because he had nothing to gain by lying to her; and she would ask for no assurances as to how she'd feel afterward even if this experience taxed her. She'd picked herself up after impossible negotiations many, many times during her career.

He'd also promised to take care of her, and she believed he would.

She felt Peter's smile against her hair and leaned further into him. Who was she kidding? They both knew the path she would take. Peter cupped the back of her head with his palm, his touch soft, light. And protective, which further quieted her pesky and circuitous internal dialogue.

A delicious peace ensued. She'd forgotten how it felt to be well within her own skin. *Thank you*, she told him, feeling like she might cry.

She was cut from her emotional straight jacket for the first time in forever, meaning her confidence – as well as hope for a lasting reprieve from her troubles – quickly ballooned, pushing gratitude away to make way for her more voracious hopes for the day. Within seconds, her mind whirred with fresh options for improvement on the job. Perhaps Peter could bolster her outreach or align his powers of suggestion with hers to make her governing advice better accepted. Or maybe he could adjust her perceptions so she performed with improved clarity. She didn't doubt Peter could facilitate the end of all her vexing work issues, that he was the key to her reclaiming her former prowess.

Yes! she thought excitedly. *You can fix me! Make me as I used to be!*

Peter peered at her with mistrust. "Now… what is it you think you want?" Then hastily, "No – don't answer. I think I know. And you're way off, Moonflower. Your 'work issues,' as you term them, aren't the problem."

Xanthe frowned, because she didn't know what he meant and couldn't think of an alternative to her own conclusions. Meaning, as she tended to with everyone, she sent out a tendril of inquiry, even though she knew better than to expect feedback from the man before her.

To her astonishment Peter responded this time, except his release was bigger, a kaleidoscope of output beyond her capacity to process, at least not all at once. It was the richest array of thoughts and feelings she'd ever intuited from anyone, humans included; and it was by far the strongest, most unedited emanation she'd *ever* received from their former prince.

She perceived him as she would light refracted through a prism, a thousand disparate rays too abundant for her mind to organize. Darting flashes of loyalty, devotion, yearning, irritation, amusement – they bombarded her. She caught random opinions he'd never shared with her, on the blindness pervading siren government and the crippling addiction they all had to safety; to beliefs concerning societal transparency and siren superiority over humans. Briefly, she glimpsed a core of concentration reserved for her: her beauty fascinated him, always had. He'd harbored personal curiosity over her past the entire time she'd known him, and he wondered why she'd never bonded. He'd spent *a lot* of time thinking about her.

In fact, he held particular affection for her, which hit her like a rush of cool water in a too-warm stream, the resulting sensation a sweet, dark ripple through her center.

But the whole of it soon became too much, meaning she at last comprehended how difficult a typical siren exchange must be for him; not because he was incapable, but because of all he contained.

His signature was too dense – for her and presumably the rest of them – to read. And here she'd considered his approach to sharing one-dimensional. He must laugh at what to her felt like compound communications with others.

You could relate to me, Xanthe, Peter countered silently, and she was touched by his belief in her. He believed she had the ability to make sense of him? Well, if he thought so, it might be true. Moreover, he wished she would try.

So she did.

Whatever new dynamic they'd established during her visit today continued as she – miraculously, in her estimation – eased into a communion with Peter she'd never before achieved. Or could have conceived of with him since he hadn't previously opened himself up to her. Maybe because he'd slowed everything down, was showing her the components of his make-up in a way she could accept.

And, goodness. His inner workings were a marvel – of complexity as well as talent, although he'd insulated himself so thoroughly she struggled to recognize all his capacities, even with his help. She felt as if she'd entered the meticulously maintained, mystically protected castle of a genius recluse; someone extraordinary, lonely, but refreshingly unburdened by mediocrity. His emotional make-up was fantastical, his comprehension of himself and others expansive, truly bordering on omniscient. This separate part of him was its own realm, an ancient, ivied courtyard within an immense wall, one where no others were permitted to trespass.

What a fascinating, beautiful, terrible life.

The experience humbled her as much as it awed, although the further she went, the more she fought a rise of hysteria, an itch to turn away and swim back to Shaddox as fast as she could... because she'd just realized his inclusion of her carried with it a demand. He was willing to help her only if she promised something in return.

The dirty sneak.

Chapter Thirteen

Thad no longer wished to address his problems alone. But with Nate already intolerably cozy – and Thad feared they were both being watched, in which case it wouldn't do to appear any closer – he only had one other option. He certainly couldn't confide in anyone outside the family, since no one else would understand why he'd made the choices he had. Even longtime friends who knew of his personal travails wouldn't get it, and never mind the reaction he'd receive from the rest of America.

"I had to take control of my life after my wife's illness, and I wanted a more expansive persona than the one assigned to me," he imagined saying. He could picture the blank stares he'd receive in response. And the pitchfork-toting mob that might hunt him afterwards. So, no.

Stu had yearned for his collegiality since adolescence, which was another reason Thad called him in, although chances for solidarity would likely evaporate if Thad led with his plan to have Maya murdered. That still hadn't been accomplished, even though she'd been located soon after Thad had called in the hit, and the last he'd heard, an assassin was on his way to her. This time, however, she'd made a more cunning disappearance than the one after their tête-à-tête in his office, because *no one* could find her, not how she escaped, not where she'd holed up. Perhaps the feds had entered her into witness protection, but in that case, why was he still here? If she had ratted him out, where was the swarm of officers appropriating his computers and cell phone? Where was his arrest? And the most convincing absence of all: where were the media vultures?

He bolstered his spirits with the knowledge his fund was easing its way into legitimacy at this very moment, and he and Nate had carefully avoided leaving a paper trail... so perhaps they'd dodged government attention. An audit would still land him in trouble, since electronic trades were publicly recorded, and a capable investigator would know to cross check their dates against the coincidental withdraws and transfers Thad had made from his personal accounts.

If she'd known what she saw that night in his office, Maya could still undermine his efforts.

He set these musings aside when his son entered his office. On the phone, Stu had exhibited less enthusiasm for a meeting than Thad had anticipated, a condition which seemed to extend to his arrival now. His son's manner was too careful, his perusal too sharp as he paused inside the threshold.

Thad made an immediate effort to seem congenial. He smiled warmly, although the action felt like it might crack his face. Stu's frown deepened. "Dad, are you okay?"

Thad inspected his shoes. No. No, he wasn't, not that he'd wanted the answer to be so obvious. Apparently he wasn't projecting the image he'd intended. He stood abruptly, gunning for a distraction – both from his unease and Stu's scrutiny. Maybe if he moved around, focused on something other than his nerves, he'd regain them.

He walked toward Stu, his movements disjointed, as if he no longer possessed the basic coordination to ambulate. He patted his son on the back, ushered him forward, then shut the door behind him and turned the deadbolt.

Stu shrugged Thad off and asked sharply, "Aren't we the only ones in the penthouse? Why the lockdown?"

Thad rubbed a hand across his face. Stu had not come to him eager and open and hungry for the fellowship Thad had tempted him with. In fact his son seemed impatient with him, which meant a direct start to this conversation might be his only option for having it at all.

Thad was glad he could still claim vicarious innocence over Maya's elimination, even though he'd trade it in a second for the certainty the threat hanging over him was removed. He returned to stand behind his desk.

"I have a problem," he began. "One we need to keep between us. I'll feel more comfortable with the door locked, not that it's necessary. Please have a seat." Stu remained on his feet, vaguely seemed poised to walk away. Thad felt his confidence in the outcome of this interaction further erode. He sank into his office chair... and began to truly fall apart. He fidgeted, looking everywhere but at his son.

He didn't know how to direct this talk toward the only conclusion he could afford for it to have, with Stu swearing loyalty and committing himself – sincerely this time – to locating Maya. As Thad waited for a perfect script to float down from heaven and accomplish this for him, an edgy silence grew between them, one Stu did not attempt to alleviate. Judging by his son's uncompromising stare, Stu rather wanted his dad's discomfort.

Thad burst forth with words that had made sense when rehearsed a while ago, but sounded ridiculous upon their utterance. "See, the thing is, I can't let this go on much longer. Our livelihood is genuinely at stake." Thad interlaced his fingers and placed his hands on the desk in front of him. He eyed Stu blearily, his face feeling creviced and ancient. Further reducing, he was sure, the appearance of sanity he badly needed in this moment. His gaze continued to dart around the room in the hopes something in it would right him, settle him down.

Nothing did. His attention alit instead on his own shirtfront, which was wrinkled and bore a spot, possibly from breakfast.

Meaning he could add sub-par grooming to his growing list of image failures.

"Dad." Thad fixed his gaze on his son. "You're a wreck. You look like you did when Mom was dying. What's going on?"

Thad removed his glasses and began to clean the lenses. "I need to find Maya. She's disappeared again." He chuckled nervously, then resettled his specs over his nose. "My men haven't been able to get to her."

Stu became dangerously still. "What do mean, 'get to her'?"

Thad leveled an even stare at him. "She's the only one who's seen evidence that could be used against me. Against us."

Stu shook his head slowly. "No, Dad. We know where she is, and we know by now she's not dangerous."

Thad leaned back in his chair, hoping to appear more confident. "She met with someone, Stu. My men saw it. Then she visited me at my club. Brought a gun with her. There was no way she should have been able to get past security with a weapon. She threatened me in the dining room. *In front of the entire restaurant*."

Stu's response was too measured, too slow in coming. Where was the outrage? The worry on his behalf? "Well, if she didn't shoot you, she must not have meant to kill you. Because if she didn't pull the trigger…?"

Thad pinched the bridge of his nose. "That night I found her in here… I realize I should have fully explained what the implications were."

And then he confessed everything, more than he ever had to anyone about his and Nate's investment company, its aspirational approach to marketing, and on how he'd been scrambling to cover dividends to keep everyone happy. He explained exactly what Maya had seen on his desk the evening she disappeared, and how, for all he knew, she'd already shared a photo of Nate's note with the authorities.

Stu gaped. And, in Thad's opinion, focused on the wrong component of the story. "You're running a Ponzi scheme."

Thad recoiled at the term and made to object, but Stu spoke over him. "You. A man with a trust fund that could bankroll a small country." His features hardened. "Your business decisions are your problem, Dad. Not Maya's."

"I know that's how it looks, but we're at a delicate transition. I can get the portfolio solvent, make everything above-board and stabilize our outcomes. I just need more time. And Maya... she could ruin everything, Stu. *Everything.*"

Stu's rejoinder was swift. "This is not 'our' effort, Dad. It's yours. You don't want to see it that way, but it's the truth." He braced both palms on the desk and leaned forward... and Thad badly wished he didn't perceive his son's posture as threatening. But Stu's expression was unequivocally judgmental. Against him! His own father! It was humorous in a sad kind of way, how after the mountain of personal slights Stu had heaped on Maya over the years – after his singular and unrelenting displays of self-absorption during their entire marriage – he would decide to be chivalrous *now*.

"Dad. Listen to me: leave Maya out of this. Even if she found something that night – and I don't believe for a second she knew what that note actually meant – you would have heard from the authorities by now."

Thad nodded. "Yes. I've thought of that. But then, where is she, Stu? Why else would she run?" He pictured her at this very moment discussing him with SEC agents in some drab, 80s-era office setting. Stu interrupted his vision.

"Maya is *not* the problem here, Dad. You want her to be, and I understand why. You want to believe if she's out of the way, you're in the clear. But she's not the reason you feel like you're in trouble. You think if you contain her, your business with Nate will be all right? You're lying to yourself."

Thad again studied his hands. "Stu. You have to believe me. I do know what I'm doing. If it was just me..." He cleared his throat. "If it was just me, I'd come clean, take the fall. But it's not." Stu prepared to protest again, but Thad stopped him. "I've been entrusted with others' fortunes too, Stu. And Maya's the only outsider who's seen proof of a problem. And I repeat – we've seen her talking with someone."

"*This has nothing to do with Maya*!" Stu shouted, a flush of red running up his neck.

Thad retreated into the back of his chair, regretting his assumption Stu would want to help him. Or, rather, regretting what felt like his son's betrayal, that he would side with a woman who'd already left him.

Thad should have suspected this possibility before he called. Stu had, after all, his own transgressions to defend where Maya was concerned, meaning Thad now found his son's sanctimony especially misplaced. How easily Stu sidestepped his own misbehavior here, focusing instead on Thad's and making Maya the victim. "You didn't take up for her once during your marriage," Thad pointed out acidly.

Stu blinked... and Thad was gratified to see some of the starch wilt from Stu's posture. "Well. That's not something I'm proud of," Stu confessed. "I should have stood up for her sooner. But then I had my own personal problems."

"You mean your infidelities?"

"Yes, although I never meant to drive Maya away, didn't want the divorce. My issue was... I don't know. I'd prefer to call it promiscuity."

Thad guffawed. "Promiscuity is for the lower classes. Now, depravity? *That* you have to be able to afford." Stu's face stiffened again in disapproval, and Thad wished he hadn't joked, hadn't made one more grab for camaraderie.

It was just that he was so tired, too tired to make the quick, accurate decisions that had guided him before in difficult times. Perhaps he hadn't realized all he'd hoped for from this meeting, how badly he wanted his son's support or even sympathy. Not for Stu to actually do anything for him.

Well. Stu *could* help more, since he might have sway with his errant ex-wife that Thad didn't. But Stu's anemic attempts while

Maya was still in the city, combined with his angry response now, illustrated how unforthcoming such help was likely to be.

Thad counseled himself to back off, to be the father here. Which led him to a new consideration: his order to have Maya taken out could end up helping his son, since his marriage had been such an unhappy one… and wouldn't Stu be relieved to never have the reminders of failure Maya's presence might prompt? Stu might not believe so now, but he would likely appreciate such finality after the fact.

Apparently this prospect hadn't occurred to his son, however, or wouldn't be enough to compel him to accept Thad's method of resolution. Which he hadn't shared for obvious reasons. Stu looked pretty mad at him, too, maybe enough to find Maya and warn her. Hmm. Thad had to act against *that* possibility right now. He adopted what he hoped was an empathetic expression.

"You're right, of course. Don't pay me any mind – I'm just tired. And I'm sorry for troubling you with my personal business, which I'll straighten out. Some other way, I promise."

Stu eyed him suspiciously. "Do you swear, Dad? Because I don't want you to go off half cocked after I leave. I worry I'll be visiting you in prison as it is."

Thad stared out the window. "Would you believe you're the second person recently to suggest such a thing." He faced Stu with a firm smile. "Tsk-tsk. Such a lack of faith in me."

"It's not a lack of faith. It's basic knowledge of the law and how it treats people who perpetrate fraud." Stu's stance softened. "It's not who you are, Dad. I just don't want you to make this situation any worse than it is."

Thad templed his fingers in front of him. "Well. I regret involving you. Rest assured, I'll take care of everything on my own. I truly hope to put this whole interlude behind us soon."

Stuart pushed himself away from the desk, although Thad thought he didn't seem altogether mollified since he still studied him like he was a science experiment gone bad. "I need to get back to the office," he commented glumly.

Thad shooed him away. "Run along." Stu considered him for another few seconds, then walked to the door. He turned when he had his hand on the doorknob. "I mean it, Dad. Leave Maya out of this."

"I will. But do call me if you hear from her." Thad hoped his reply came off as caring, as if he worried for his former daughter-in-law. Stu opened his mouth to speak... then shut it and regarded him unhappily. He left without another comment, closing the door behind him.

Thad checked his phone for messages and finding none, dove into preparations for an upcoming meeting with his executive committee at HWP. The frequency of these meetings had stepped up sharply for him, ever since last month when more and more inflammatory public statements – twists on the standard corporate line – were attributed to him, albeit falsely.

Thad mused over how people overlooked the truth when they were upset, even understood the renewed calls for his removal, unfounded though they were. The most expedient way for his company to solve what their corporate communications team called its 'problems of perception' would be to fire him... and it sure seemed as though he was reporting so someone else could step in and take over. He'd also received a forwarded email the previous day from a colleague on the board, a missive he was not supposed to see regarding a performance review the board intended to conduct shortly. Nothing in it was explicit, but Thad thought it raised the question of an imminent end to his tenure. The head of Human Resources had been copied on the original email, which was a sure signal.

He'd known dismissal might be in his future, of course. But he still hoped the company's strong stock performance under his watch counterbalanced all the bad press.

He decided he couldn't worry about it, not in light of where his real attention needed to be. With just a few more discreet transfers in the coming weeks, he would hide any troubling inconsistencies in his side business, eliminate the one person who could incriminate him, and then leave the Hell Well on his own terms.

Chapter Fourteen

Still in her dream progression of problem-solving with her former prince and boss, Xanthe no longer perceived them as sitting on the Blake porch overlooking the ocean. Instead, she walked in an illusion she couldn't dispel: Peter's high-walled inner courtyard. If she hadn't felt trapped within it, she could have better admired its gothic charm, its haunting beauty.

Peter himself appeared beside her as a strolling companion. He walked to her left, his hands clasped behind him, posture erect, eyes forward as he contemplated the far limit of his sanctuary. Xanthe stole furtive glances at him, as well as at the gigantic stone periphery, where she searched for an exit.

She found none... and she wondered if Peter's silence, his air of patience, had to do with him waiting for her to come to this realization, how there would be no out until he decided to show her one. It had to be the case. And with the pretense of freedom eliminated, she stopped walking, planted her feet and crossed her arms. She stood as tall as she could, even knowing she'd hardly intimidate someone of Peter's stature. She'd seen this tactic work before, although she was still struggling to apprehend human social rules revolving around interpersonal competitiveness. Still, she hardened her expression, which, judging from Peter's lack of response, accomplished precisely nothing.

She decided to go back to what she knew, which was communication without these odd adornments. She relaxed her stance and commanded, "Tell me what you want from me, Peter."

"Yes. I *would* like your assistance with something," he conceded smoothly. Too smoothly. "I'm sorry to ask," and Xanthe thought he didn't seem at all sorry, "but at least my favor won't require your attention for a while, yet. Meaning you'll still have time to run off and find yourself." His regard became affectionate, indulgent; and again she wondered at her own response to it.

Because she wanted nothing so badly in this moment as to please him, a revelation that appalled her. *He's trying to enthrall me!* she realized with disgust.

And she wasn't sure what his comment about 'finding herself' meant, but she honestly didn't want to know. She forced her gaze away in an attempt to close off at least one of her senses, maybe escape some of his enticement. She instantly regretted her full complicity earlier, how it seemed to preclude objectivity after the fact. She now felt like a small fish caught in a violent current she had no hope of swimming against.

She spoke aloud, counting on the sound of her own voice to re-establish her sense of herself. "I want you to explain *exactly* what you intend, Peter," she said as sternly as she could. Because in the absence of actual poise, posturing seemed like her best option.

Peter faced her and took one of her hands in his, entwining their fingers. She became riveted to the sight, adored such a presumption and the closeness it implied... and she really shouldn't have.

Peter interrupted her thoughts. "Your attention, please, Xanthe." He was way too sure of himself, and this caused a flare of genuine irritation. She still obeyed automatically, but only because she couldn't help it. Her displeasure added an acidic burn to their dream encounter, which gratified her since anything at all she could do for herself in this situation was an accomplishment. Her eyes pivoted from their joined hands to his face. He nodded once, as if pleased with her. Then he continued spouting his half-explanations.

"Just as I'm your personal improvement counselor today, you can be mine on another front. I'd like your advice on a foreign threat to our community."

She was seized by intense interest, stronger than she'd generally have, so she knew her enthusiasm was enhanced… and she couldn't find a satisfying answer to what was becoming the predominant question of the day: why would Peter influence her in such a way? This time, he referenced, possibly, a matter of state. An area where she had all kinds of authority and he had exactly none. She attempted to withhold herself – again, to no effect – her heart rate elevated, her eagerness for more of his capers super-charged. He'd spoken to her breezily, as if she didn't struggle against herself. Or him. "Peter…" she warned.

He talked on pleasantly, without acknowledging her discomfort. "I'll be asking you to look into a certain party to the south, perhaps pay him a visit with me." Xanthe wrested her hand from his.

Seriously, *why* was he so keen to engage her? Peter pretended the dynamic she questioned – and failed to manage – didn't exist. "Then I'd like to consult with you," he went on, "and we can decide together how to contain him. I don't want to involve others because I don't want to draw our community's attention to him, which will exacerbate the problem he poses. So few of us are able to act with discretion in these cases, and you're one who can. You've also dealt deftly before with the criminally ambitious, individuals willing to hurt us for personal gain. Meaning your experience will be helpful."

"Why not turn the issue over to me entirely? This sounds as if it belongs under my purview, not yours."

"Because you'll need help this time, some support. Or perhaps back-up I'm keen to provide." His gaze upon her was charming, solicitous. "We don't know yet, you and I." She opened her mouth to protest but he pre-empted her. "I won't have you going in by yourself, Xanthe. Not with your vulnerabilities."

Well. She wasn't about to delve into what Peter saw as her vulnerabilities, which she feared encompassed the entirety of her current job description. Gifted as he was, however, he'd never executed complex problem-solving at the state level as she had – in fact, he'd been one of the criminally ambitious culprits he'd just maligned, trampling over others in pursuit of his own fulfillment. She didn't believe he was even capable of compromise.

She was desperate to obtain the personal resolution he'd tempted her with, however, even knowing he used this desire against her. What an underhanded ploy, promising redemption then withholding it to coerce her. Peter smiled down at her serenely, without an atom of remorse. She glared back.

"This is extortion," she observed coldly.

"You can decline, of course," he said with a small, knowing smile.

Ha. A chance to relieve her professional angst was irresistible, enough for her to ignore the troubling prospect of making a fool of herself, which he well knew. Still, she attempted to influence their terms. "You'll alleviate my troubles now in exchange for open-ended support – for a situation you will not fully explain to me – later?" She drummed her fingertips on her biceps. "Does it occur to you the problem may require more than us charging in and figuring things out in the moment? That diplomacy – for which you are ill-suited – should be explored first?"

"Moonflower," he remonstrated. "I'm not sure how much – or little – statesmanship will be required. Barging in might be the very best way to deal with our South American trouble-maker. But I hope to engage you in this effort so we'll have either option. I know I have no gift for negotiation – I don't care about a fair transaction, only that my – or our – interests prevail." This time his grin was sly. "I'm actually doing you a favor. I thought you'd appreciate the opportunity to follow protocol before I take matters into my own hands."

He was definitely maneuvering her... and his fake solicitude – meant, she was sure, as encouragement – should have sent her dashing for the water.

But she couldn't leave, not until she attempted the revelation behind his offer, the one he dangled before her like a delicious but possibly imaginary filet of swordfish. She gave in grudgingly, her concession bitter in her mouth as she gave it. "You *will* deal honorably with me, Peter."

His facile reply did not reassure her. "Done," he said quickly. "And I won't misuse you." A teasing light entered his eyes. "Although I'm surprised at your indignation. I always have ulterior motives, Xanthe." He inclined himself toward her. "It's time you took a gamble on me, don't you think?"

She knew then she'd forfeited everything he'd wanted from her. That devious smile... he gloated like he'd just won a bet.

"It's beneath you to be petty," she chided, but she wasn't truly angry with him, and her own smile leaked through. "If I find you're manipulating me for ill, I'm out." She wasn't sure this was true, but she felt better saying it.

"I would never," he said, drawing himself up... and she believed his outrage was authentic, that he carried within him enough latent integrity to warrant her confidence in him in this matter.

"You're here for selfish reasons, too," he reminded her. "Haven't your own preoccupations supplanted the needs of the community for the past several years?"

Oh, now, that was low, although she conceded his point with a stiff nod. "Yes," Peter acknowledged crisply. Then with more warmth, "Let's finish this, shall we? Get you the answers you came for."

Despite the dubious bargain she'd just made – or rather, her worry over it – she released herself to him easily, focusing on the potential saving of her professional abilities and the freedom from worry she would soon feel. She still had misgivings... ones she was right to have, she reminded herself, since she was about to traipse into the psyche of a powerful, erstwhile psychotic.

He answered that thought with a scathing stare. "Hardly," he clipped. Then his features softened... and she fell into another of his directed trances. *This is going to work,* he promised. *You'll be so happy you came to me, Xanthe.*

Her reservations disappeared as before, her respect for Peter's abilities again dominating her awareness. Because he was dazzlingly gifted. The sheer scope of his talent was unprecedented, so fantastic it negated, in her opinion, every single one of Peter's past crimes. She regretted once more his absence at the palace, the loss of his leadership. The breadth of what he could accomplish would be worth the risk of having him in power.

She didn't even try to withhold her admiration. *What you can do... it's breathtaking. So beautiful.*

And it really was. She also discovered exactly why and how his approach to communication differed from that of other sirens, and his motivation was simple: he'd had to learn to connect in another way. He'd been denied the kind of emotional access to his parents – in this instance his mother – other siren children were given as a matter of course, access vital to the growth and happiness of every young waterling. He'd found, rather cleverly she thought, workable alternatives.

But at such a cost.

The despair he must have felt! How had she dismissed it when they were growing up? How could she have noticed anything else at all about him? She'd been superficially aware he struggled at home but she'd really had no idea, had assumed the perks of royalty were compensatory for Kenna's hands-off parenting approach, especially since she remained close by. As a girl, Xanthe had understood Peter's adaptations as she had other information peripheral to herself, like abstract scientific theories memorized for a test and then forgotten. Experiencing Peter's privations from within his own memory had her reliving his trials as if they'd been her own.

Peter released her consciousness, allowing her to retreat until she could once again distinguish her thoughts from his.

She couldn't regain her former perspective, however, couldn't resurrect the same ignorance she'd sheltered under before. Peter's misery when he was a mere baby, freshly experienced as if it had just happened, destroyed her, crushing the rationale she'd assigned to him all these years. Which threw her into a sea of regret that felt bottomless.

She utterly forgave his twisted choices as a grown man. He'd been fighting for his very survival.

Sadly, his superior abilities – his salvation when it came to navigating his emotionally bereft environment – also had an obstructive effect with everyone else, separating him forever from the closeness with others he'd craved. Because they'd all, Xanthe included, objectified him, classified him as someone better than themselves, something other. In doing so, they'd denied him access to the community he'd needed.

Of course they'd set him apart. His brilliance had shone so brightly it blinded, meaning he'd become more icon than individual, a flag they waved at each other to negate their own insecurities. Like evidence in a trial, Peter Loughlin as Exhibit A had shut down all arguments against the path siren society was collectively on, had likely obscured the troubling developments they – she, especially – should have caught much sooner.

What upset her the most, though, was the personal cost of such treatment to Peter, himself. They'd enclosed him in a kind of societal cage where his every action was dissected and judged, and the only emotional feedback he received was expectation. How exhausting. How appallingly cruel.

Just before she lost herself in sorrow, Peter delivered them back to his courtyard garden, which she now perceived differently. No longer an eerie place of confinement she couldn't escape, she appreciated its solace, its peace. Here was Peter's refuge, the stillness within him she'd always sensed but never understood. He wore it as he would armor, and she saw how good it was that he had it, as well as the reasons behind the stunning detail he'd given it.

She wondered how often in the past he'd interacted with her from here, where he would have appeared outwardly present but wasn't, not fully.

Still, she understood he'd had to conduct himself thusly, to deflect or at least not absorb the constant solicitation he received from their people; from sirens seeking his support but oblivious to his need for reciprocity. As a child, how had he coped? Was this what had first driven him to cloak?

In answer, she felt his further withdrawal... and sensed her own disappearance right alongside. Which she had not believed was possible. *Ah, but it is, Xanthe,* he countered, drawing her further into a dark, shaded place within herself. A part of herself she'd never realized was there. She stilled completely to observe every nuance of this amazing experience.

She couldn't help but be distracted by his skill in drawing her in with him, though. Peter cloaked automatically, slipped away as easily as she blinked or breathed. She *felt* herself fade... and with all he'd shared with her today, she finally comprehended the why of it all, the ultimate price he'd paid in response to the unreasonable context he'd grown up in.

He'd hidden himself in order to not die from anguish and never mind any hopes he'd nursed for the normal interactions she and everyone else took for granted. Xanthe wept anew for the loneliness he'd endured, feeling not only sorrow this time, but also anger at Kenna, her former queen. If not her, then *some* adult should have stood up for him, protected him. This called forth an even uglier truth: she herself should have championed him, certainly when she became a stateswoman and could have eradicated the societal constructs that put aristocrats and their children in such opposition to one another. She should have paid better attention to her community's practices when it came to the monarchy, which she'd noticed but hadn't thought consequential enough to displace other duties. Michael Blake hadn't flinched from reporting the problem in all its atrocity. Indeed, he'd recommended immediate redress by her and everyone with the power to help.

She should have listened to him. Instead, she'd concerned herself with public perceptions, with the bureaucratic fallout from Kenna's suicide and Peter's fight with Gabe in the central pool. How heartless, how shallow she'd been.

Peter reacted unkindly to her display of remorse. It seemed he could not accept her compassion, was in fact angry with her for feeling any responsibility for his circumstances. "Do *not* feel sorry for me," he commanded. "It was long ago, and your regret changes nothing."

Xanthe wiped her tears as she struggled to acquiesce. She couldn't argue with him, understanding well the deleterious effects pity could have. Defining Peter as a victim here and now imprisoned him in such a definition, compounding the abuse he'd withstood so it encompassed his future, not just his past. She reflected on her own unwillingness to court sympathy, how she'd tried to hide her own struggles back at the palace for similar reasons.

Regardless, the characterizations she'd formerly attributed to the man before her were no longer broad enough. They didn't encompass all that Peter had become – his beauty and strength, his intelligence, his stupefying competencies. His resistance to the incessant, ignorant, and occasionally damaging solicitations from people who wanted him to commit himself to solving their problems. Like herself.

Shamed, she tried to jerk away, but he held onto her hands. *No, Moonflower. You ask nothing of me I don't want to give you. Believe me, I know how to say 'no.'*

She relented, then forced her attention toward the more practical revelations of his demonstration, away from the awfulness he'd been subjected to as a boy, picking out the objective components he'd just revealed. Peter's anger dissipated, and Xanthe's sense of wonder returned.

The mechanics of cloaking, which had seemed like magic mere hours ago, were actually rooted in an empirical process. She identified the sequence first, how Peter – and presumably all other cloakers – quantified and manipulated perception initially, then advanced his particular illusion. He slowed a cloak for her so she could observe each step in making her accept a suggestion of his choice. It was astonishing. She knew from experience Peter's efforts could involve multiple individuals – a skill for which he was no longer completely unique, but still. And unlike other cloakers who could only manipulate one or two people at a time, Peter was able to project broadly.

A feat that had allowed him to kidnap and even kill, all while avoiding detection.

Regardless of those darker manifestations, his mastery captivated her. Xanthe's own illusions – where she appeared to a human as a seal or dolphin – were *nothing* by comparison.

"I've heard no one does this as well as you, that no other cloaker has your depth of talent."

Peter tilted his head, almost in apology. "My siren trainees know. But no, I have no true equal." His statement was not a boast. In it she recognized again the cavernous loneliness he harbored, the one that had ultimately driven him to corruption.

Xanthe's disgust returned, because what an impossible set of circumstances for a child. "Ah-ah." Peter wagged a finger in front of her. "These thoughts help neither of us, Xanthe, and I'm no longer defenseless. Come. Let's continue."

He returned them to his inner garden, where she now sought refuge just as he did. Again, she had the impression no one else had seen Peter this way, that she was the first he'd ever allowed so close. She reached for him reflexively, the need to comfort and connect pushing her past his warnings against sympathy… and this time he accepted her effort. Or at least he didn't withdraw, and physically, he pulled her closer, flattening the hand she'd placed on his chest with his own. "All right, Moonflower. If you must to feel better."

He was comforting *her*?

He freed her completely from his control, and as she came into herself again she wondered why he would reveal himself to her in this way, and why now. What did his tragedy have to do with her career? She was aware of their actual surroundings now, the broad ceiling of the Blake porch that shaded them, the sound and scent of the ocean as they faced each other by the balustrade.

"My circumstances and how I acted threw everyone in the community into turmoil, you included," he replied. "I changed the way sirens saw themselves, created the biggest rift between 'self' and 'the collective' in our history. You'll understand why you can't go back to the way you were – and I believe you're fighting yourself on this – by studying what happened to me. And by thinking more on the self-actualization trend that became popular after I took Kate."

His explanation both satisfied and saddened her. Satisfied because, now that she thought about it, their people's rebellious behaviors *had* coincided with his public breakdown. Yes, increased interaction with humans had played a role, but Peter's foray into deviance was the broadest point of departure, the launch of the biggest society-wide proliferation of selfishness in their history.

She was saddened because she *did* see similarities between her motivations and his… and she would have preferred not to.

Fundamentally she remained confused, however; Peter's sanity, no matter how convincingly portrayed, had always been suspect in her opinion. He'd demonstrated this by displaying truly bizarre logic on several occasions, most notably the time he'd stolen another's mate and thought he could thereby transform his life. Since his disappearance after that stunt, she'd had many, many colleagues and friends treat her in the same circumspect way she'd treated Peter. As in, carefully, so as not to trigger a destructive outburst.

Yes, he mused drily. *Insisting on the wrong thing for yourself does tend to have negative results.*

Whatever that meant.

How alike were they? Was she kidding herself about her continued suitability in siren government? And while she hated to ask the obvious question, she apparently needed to: if she wasn't going to lead the bureaucracy any longer, what would she do instead?

She knew Peter might take offense at her distaste – for both her judgment of him and for her need to rationalize against sharing any of his proclivities – but she couldn't care. Because if she was as unstable as Peter, there would be no professional resurrection. In that case, she *should* step down.

She argued with herself, checking Peter's responses as she did. As expected, he understood what she clung to... but she still clung.

Their personalities were different. Also, even though they'd shared corollary professional responsibilities, Peter had labored under personal hardship *and* the monumental public burden that came with his title. She'd only wrestled with the monumental public burden part. Her posture sagged.

They were all lucky he hadn't destroyed them entirely.

"I wouldn't be so quick to differentiate us, Xanthe," Peter observed. "In terms of deprivation, where is your family? What happened to your formative relationships, the ones other sirens rely on to go forth in society every day? Where is your husband, the children you never had? Why did you never bond?"

Because... because she was different, that's why! Because her contributions, once she'd started working, had taken precedence. Because she'd received a higher call to office and she'd answered it. And she'd wanted to! She'd made intelligent, loving choices, ones that put others first and her own needs last, which was admirable and good, right?

"Not in my experience," he murmured. "You answered a 'higher call,' as you term it, so you're better off? You think I didn't force myself to rise to the needs of my office, and for the same reasons?"

"You had no choice," Xanthe retorted. "You were born into your role. I wasn't."

He opened his mouth to respond but she stopped him. "Don't," she said. She already knew the arguments he would make, not because of the intuitive access he'd allowed her but because she'd had to repeat them to herself over the years.

And she knew her resistance was internal to her, not a point of debate he or anyone else could talk her away from.

He reached for her, but she stepped back. "I don't want to learn more," she confessed, and she cringed at the desolation in her voice, the sadness marking the realization she couldn't un-have at this point. She hugged herself and looked away as he cupped her shoulders anyway, her eyes darting toward the sea, the horizon, something to remind her of the world that had so recently made sense to her.

Her field trip here had yielded more than she could have guessed, and not at all what she'd hoped. Going forward, she would have to think about how – not if – she would abandon the only life she'd ever known.

Peter pulled her to him… and she let him, although she curled her hands between them. Still, she felt his strength, the core of tenacity within him that had both protected and driven him.

He was right: part of his truth was also her own. And she had that same strength, the same determination.

She had not served as Peter had, but she *had* taken on more of her people's troubles than she could withstand. And everyone had let her, just as they'd let Peter carry responsibilities no one person should or could. He'd eventually realized this injustice and refused his role, had walked away from them all. In this moment, she understood why.

She and Peter had both protected themselves behind bureaucratic protocols, but he'd known when to retreat. She'd considered herself an open resource for absolutely anyone who needed her, had said 'yes' to every inconsequential task anyone proposed. *How very foolish of me.*

Peter didn't disagree. "Do you see the impossible situation you put yourself in? And forgive the suggestion, but the hubris of assuming you can fix everything?"

She had no argument to offer, which meant she no longer believed in her profession as she had, and she wouldn't have the same efficacy. She reflected again on her frustrations, on how long it had been since she'd found joy in her position. She'd wanted to believe she could re-find the passion she'd once had by focusing herself... and now she knew she wouldn't.

She would never feel the same in her role because the work wasn't the same, and she wasn't the same. Fighting against those two truths would not change them. She disengaged from Peter.

"I have to leave. I'm going to take a break from Shaddox, stay ashore for a while. Maybe look for something else to do." Her mouth trembled against the effort it took to smile at him. "I can see I need to make a bigger change. Thank you for showing me the errors in my thinking."

Peter appeared eerily, preternaturally still, as if he was hunting. "Would you like me to go with you? You will not likely do well on your own right now, Xanthe..." She shook her head once, and he retreated, which she regretted. She had an epiphany to process, though, one she refused to be distracted from. Peter's interests would have to wait.

"I'd prefer to come to terms with my dilemma myself," she replied. "I need to... to choose what I'm going to do with myself. With my life."

Peter continued to study her. "This is new behavior for you, you know. What did you always tell me? Sirens reach out, and in distress they reach out harder." He caught her gaze in his. "Will you do me the kindness of staying in touch? Tell me where you go, and check in with me before you move on?"

"The only place I can go where I won't be beset with my former responsibilities is inland. I'm not going to resign yet. I'll use Aiden as an excuse to disappear, say I'm following up personally to determine the impact of his obsession with Maya

Wilkes." Peter revealed nothing, but she thought he looked sheepish, which made her suspicious. "Do you know where he is?"

Peter hesitated before answering her. "He hasn't confided in me, but yes. I know."

"He's with Maya, right?" Peter nodded once.

Xanthe pressed her fingertips to her eyes. "I suspected he wouldn't be able to stay away. If I asked you, would you apprehend him for me? Give us one more chance to dissuade him?"

"I don't believe such interference will accomplish anything. But yes, I could." He appeared full of opinions, which, thankfully, he chose not to share. After a few seconds he promised, "I'll bring him in, Xanthe. Because you've asked it of me."

Xanthe instantly doubted the wisdom of her request. She suspected she'd been overly strident in her opposition to a union neither party seemed able to avoid, and that her request was not only futile, but unkind. Aiden wasn't a criminal, just a siren man in love.

At least Maya was the last Wilkes daughter available for seduction. If two of the three women in that family were already married in, what was one more? Why not let them all live out their bonds and be happy? That's what they would do, anyway, even with the threat of division and ostracism hovering over them.

She drew herself up, feeling much heavier that she had on her swim here. The components of her sadness were different, but the result – her sense of encumbrance, the lack of resolution – was not. She considered taking Peter up on his offer of companionship… but decided she wouldn't. If she needed him, she'd call.

"Thank you, so much, for…" She stopped here, because while she was grateful for the clarity she'd gained in his company, the outcome was not anything she wanted. At least he'd given her something good, too, shown her something difficult and profoundly private within himself; and she'd faced her fears and weaknesses because of his demonstration. He'd cast her challenge in a different light and offered an alternative understanding to the one she'd had.

She regarded him mutely. A simple 'thank you' was so inadequate for all that had passed between them today... and there was something new in their communion she recognized but wouldn't examine. Not yet.

He smoothed her hair. "Be good, Moonflower," he instructed, and his eyes held a sincerity she found endearing, if a little confusing.

She retrieved the empty waterpack from the floor by her chair and tucked it under her arm. "I'll call. I promise." She walked stiffly down the stairs toward the pier, shedding her sundress and, as much as she could, her pall of disappointment as she approached the water. She dove cleanly into the waves, still feeling Peter's gaze from above. She returned her supplies to the cache outside the bay, then sped toward deeper water. She turned northward when she could no longer sense him.

Chapter Fifteen

"I think your sperm ate my brain."

Maya made this pronouncement to the ceiling while lying on her back, palms resting on her midriff. "Seriously. I'm completely blissed out and stupid." Aiden remained silent beside her, although she thought she noticed a slight tremor in the mattress. Was he laughing?

She swiveled her head to see. His eyes were closed, his face relaxed in an imitation of sleep. She picked up one of his hands and let it drop to the bed, which it did nervelessly. Her eyes narrowed. "Are you playing me?" She curled onto her side and braced her head on one of her hands. She checked his pulse, then snorted. "You are not asleep."

Aiden opened his eyes and grinned. "How would you know?"

"Your pulse. Your resting heart rate is too high."

He raised one eyebrow. "Because you studied siren heart rates in med school?"

"Well. You've got me there."

They regarded each other quietly, calmly, and, for the first time since they'd begun their escape from reality, without fogginess, at least on her side of things. Aiden reached out to run a forefinger along her hairline, then over her ear. He wore an engrossed expression that overfilled her heart and brought a sting of tears behind her nose.

"We got away," Aiden remarked, and his expression darkened. "We'll have to work to stay that way, though."

Maya's good mood also sank. More sneaking around and avoiding everyone? She couldn't even think about it. "Do we have to run?" she lamented. "Can't we go somewhere and just... just *be?*"

Aiden's smile twisted. "I'm not supposed to be with you, Maya," he reminded her. "After Sylvia married in, I was told not to even think of you." He drew away from her, although his gaze on her face remained steady. Maya kept quiet, reflecting again on the fact that both her sisters had married sirens and she'd never noticed. Knowing what she did now, how had she missed something so obvious?

For the moment, though, she wanted to figure things out with the siren in front of her, not the pair she was apparently related to through marriage. "So... what do we need to do to come into the light?"

"I made a good show of toeing the line," Aiden reported. "With the training I've had – and I'm a solid operative – I've become valuable to the community. Which I believe buys me some goodwill." He smiled at her. "After your wedding, I left town, even let Carmen set me up with a couple of other women." Maya stiffened, and he grimaced. "*Epic* waste of time," he assured her, "although I think that showed loyalty, too. Fake loyalty, but still. And I just got back from snowing them all some more."

"You left at a kind of critical time, though," Maya remarked. "Not that I wasn't grateful for your help before, and for the hideout."

Aiden shook his head. "No choice. I had to inform everyone on my findings, a trip I'd already put off. If I'd declined again, they would have come to fetch me. So, I had to protect my front if I meant to return."

Maya looked away. All that time she'd spent waiting, feeling like a loser. All the lies between them, starting with the big one she'd told herself on her wedding day, that her marriage to Stu was the answer. But if an entire race of people were against her and Aiden being together, she couldn't count on a happy ending to this little interlude, either, no matter how strongly they felt about each other. "I still wish I'd known everything up front."

Aiden stilled, and his eyes widened. "You think I duped you."

She waved her hand. "It's nothing. I've been lying to myself – and vicariously to you and everyone else – for ten years. It's a relief to finally own up."

His next words were bitter. "I still can't believe you married that loser, Maya. Actually marched down the aisle and promised yourself to him. You apparently had to work some things out on your own there, because if I'd let you know it was me playing bodyguard... well, you would have turned me away so you could go to counseling. Or 'try harder' or some other nonsense. And then my zoo keepers would have come for me and made sure we never, never had our shot."

She sniffled softly, wishing she didn't feel his regret on top of hers. "I know, love," he conceded. "I'm sorry – Stu and that whole thing... you're right, it was his fault you were unhappy. And if I'd come clean when you were in college, you wouldn't have gone to him in the first place. But I couldn't."

"How could you even stand me? I was so awful." She averted her face, her chin tucked, her cheek against his breast.

"Don't be embarrassed, Maya, please," and she took in his torment when she peeked at him. "You have no idea what it was like for me to stand by and watch Stu lay his crap on you."

"It wasn't all him," she protested darkly.

Aiden's mouth flattened into a straight line. "Yes. It was. He was dickwad and a coward, how he used you." His eyes took on a frightening intensity and his body tightened. "I could gut him. Like a mackerel."

Maya retreated and shook her head. "I'm not lily white, Aiden. My reasons for marrying him, and then thinking I could fix it..."

Aiden put a finger over her lips. "I know all your reasons, Maya. I was there every time you talked yourself into staying. But he pushed you into that situation. Someone less loyal would have walked a lot sooner."

She snorted. "Someone less pig-headed, you mean." Maya thought on how frantically she'd fought for her marriage – and the less-than upstanding reasons behind her motivations – and she blushed from shame.

Aiden smiled kindly. "You think I should judge you," he stated, and she gave a small, almost imperceptible nod. "I don't. And I won't." Then more lightly, "Now, if we're talking about how long it took you to *finally* leave, that I judge. Because you were nine kinds of stubborn, Maya Wilkes."

She didn't disagree, but she felt better knowing everything, having a complete understanding of what she and Aiden had done to each other and why. She straightened her spine and decided she could afford to be playful now. "Persistence is a virtue," she informed him archly. Then, before he could weigh in she asked, "I'm assuming you're here with some sort of permission, but what exactly happened in New York? I mean, you told me Thad had a contract out on me, but why all the drama on the bridge?"

"Basically, your killer was coming, and I didn't have time to get to you. So I called to you, and thanks for coming, by the way." He squeezed her, and she laughed. "We put on a show for about three hundred New Yorkers, not counting whatever aired on television that night. And any social media posts." He frowned. "I'm in big trouble for that, for sure." His brow smoothed once again. "But we're not going back."

"No. We're not," she agreed. "How much time do you think we have before the mermaids come for us?"

"Sirens," he corrected quickly. "*Mermaid* is soooo last century. Too girly, too." He smiled briefly. "I can't say how much, but not a lot. I'm a pretty good cloaker, and I can sense the presence of another... so no one's come around yet. But some of my brothers-in-arms are as well trained as I am. One or more of them might get the jump on me. Our best bet is to run. Find a hideout."

Maya felt the haze of happiness she'd awoken with dissipate, although she reminded herself this situation wasn't as awful as the one she'd wrestled with in New York. Running away with Aiden was so very preferable to hiding without him.

More delay jeopardized her residency, though, assuming she'd be allowed to resume it; and the prospect of continuing to keep away from her sisters, her parents, her friend Kate… she couldn't defend against the depression these thoughts caused.

"Is it ever going to end, the running?" she asked. "I can't live like this, Aiden."

"I know, love. I really do. A few things need to happen, and they *will* happen. First, someone's gonna have to figure out how to stop the assassin Thad hired to hunt you. Last I heard, communication was cut until the job's done… and we have no idea who he is. Or where. Second, my community needs to accept our bond and let us be us. Thad will get caught, and he'll be the key to stopping whoever is after you. So I'm less worried now that you're out of his reach, although I still want to be careful. The siren acceptance issue is trickier, but I think I can get a couple higher-ups to back me. My aunt – the queen – for one. My brother's another one. Gabe's my next pitch."

Maya started. "*Gabe?*" Aiden watched her intently.

"Think about it."

"You've got to be kidding me," she intoned. "Gabe is…? Well, of course he is. I mean, he looks just like you guys. Meaning Kate… and oh my God that kidnapping…" Kate's favorite epithet bubbled out of her unbidden. "Holy cats." She allowed herself a few seconds to recover then continued, "So pretty much everyone I know is either a siren or married to one." She scowled. "And my sisters and best friend have been lying to me half my life. Which I'll be addressing with them shortly."

Aiden took her face in his hands. "They couldn't say anything, Maya. Sirens who talk are banished. It's literally a death sentence."

Maya huffed. "Vicious much? And… *why*? Why stay hidden in the first place?"

Aiden's expression became grim, and he didn't answer her. Instead, he trapped one of her hands to his chest in a way she was becoming used to and stared into her eyes, also a familiar gesture... although this encounter felt perilous.

The strangest reverie overtook her.

Some ancient setting, comprised of a couple dozen people in rough homespun gathered on a beach. Were they Roman? Gaelic? She had no way of knowing. Nor could she have guessed the year, but it was in a previous century.

Ireland. Five hundred years ago, Aiden supplied, a soft aside that didn't interrupt the vision before her.

The group was fronted by a guy with the studied charm of a modern-day televangelist. He sported a head of glorious white locks which lifted dramatically in the wind coming off the sea. He concentrated with a devout, regal, and to Maya's mind, contrived demeanor, his strong features angled as if for a camera. He was creating an effect and he knew it.

The man reached one hand toward the ocean, palm up, shoulder extended.

A ritual? she guessed.

Yes. It was called a Summoning.

The heavy clouds threatened rain while the ocean below churned restlessly, the entire backdrop a sullen grey that lent a dark anticipation to the proceedings. The man's white hair appeared stark against the charcoal water, his face ominous under the iron sky. The crowd cowered and watched from behind him, scanning the water hungrily. As if they were starving and their leader was about to raise a banquet for them from the waves.

You're not far off, Aiden remarked. *Watch.*

A handful of sirens surfaced. Maya expected this, although she couldn't say why. In the scenario Aiden played for her, the peasants huddled and gasped at the sight. They seemed apprehensive, yet they shuffled closer to the water.

The rest of the demonstration horrified her.

At the urging of their human concertmaster, the crowd waded knee-deep into the shallows, at which point the sirens transformed and rushed them. Both groups crooned and keened as they engaged with small touches – stroking someone's hair or cheek, grasping forearms, clasping hands. But the ratio of people to sirens was high, four or more to one, and Maya saw the exact moment the interaction overwhelmed the mermaid contingent. With frantic, caged looks, they looked back toward the sea. Several began to cry, and although Maya didn't know what language they spoke, she understood perfectly what the sirens said.

Too much! You must let me go! And when the humans didn't, more desperate cries of, *Release me to the water, I beg you!*

"Hold them!" the leader commanded.

Maya watched an appalling mania overtake the humans, where three or four of them clung to a siren who quickly became distraught and struggled against them. And while the sirens still seemed physically gentle – Maya had to wonder why they didn't just throw the people restraining them off and speed away – the humans behaved like tyrants, screaming over each other for individual attention and brutally twisting their captives as they fought over them. The mermaids covered their ears, pleaded for kindness, and all of them wept. Even sensed as a distant memory, Maya felt their anguish and longed to free them.

Aiden explained. *We can't shake them off because we are compelled by human need. The people fighting over the sirens know this, and they spur each other on to up the emotional ante. This – and the fact that there are four to one – weakens us.* Maya turned away, ashamed even though she wasn't part of the torture and didn't support it. She still felt responsible.

Watch, Aiden insisted again. Maya forced her attention back to the unfolding drama. She could hardly make herself do it... and she soon wished she hadn't. Because the worst was yet to come.

It happened so fast. One lone siren managed to disentangle herself, but before she could twist away, the white-haired leader stepped in. In a single move, he snatched the dagger from the

OUTRUSH

tether at her waist, and without hesitation, plunged it high into her torso.

All the air left Maya's body, as if she'd been the one stabbed instead of this apparition from the past. Her mouth opened soundlessly, a perfect reflection of the mermaid's silent, airless scream. The victim shuddered violently, stilled, shuddered again, and then dissolved in what appeared to be a burst of fine, iridescent dust.

The onlookers, human and otherwise, froze in whatever postures they'd been in before the execution, everyone's gaze riveted to the spot where the siren woman had been.

Afterwards, a gruesome sort of peace descended on the humans, who looked creepily euphoric in Maya's opinion. But at least they released their remaining sirens and stepped away. By contrast, the surviving mermaids shrieked and cried and tore at their hair, until first one, then another, exploded into the same glittery sand as their murdered sister. The last three sirens fell into the water and disappeared. The scene faded.

Maya came to slowly, perceiving first the bright sunlight in their room, then Aiden's arms around her, his physical warmth loving and alive, a vivid contradiction to the horror she'd just witnessed. Even so, the coldness in her heart remained as the image of the dying siren replayed again and again in her mind. Aiden brushed her cheeks with his thumbs.

"I'm sorry. I just wanted to explain why we keep our society a secret," Aiden explained. "I'm told every human mate asks this question. Kate and your sisters wondered, too. So I shared a memory, one given to every living siren when they're old enough, to explain why we hide. Why we stay away.

"What you saw was one of dozens of such rituals that used to be conducted, possibly still are," Aiden continued. "Doesn't matter the time period or the place: there's always some greedy or sick or power-hungry human..." Aiden appeared to struggle with his anger. When he gazed at her again, he said, "It's never, never worked out for us. And so to protect ourselves, we've learned to

183

lie, to look like something other than what we are when you see us in the water."

Maya was angry, too, although she continued to mourn for the sirens whose demise she'd just seen. She wiped her tears with the bed sheet. "I wish I could have stopped them. Who was he, the man who stabbed one of you? What did he hope to gain?"

"Some of you exert a stronger pull than others, and he was one of them, a facility he discovered as a boy wading in the sea. He decided to capitalize on it, make himself into a kind of mystic and assume power in his community. He could show up at the water's edge and send out a call, and we would come. The Summoning you saw was an annual event with only a select few permitted to attend even though hundreds paid him for the chance. He told his followers the sacrifice brought good luck to the village and to those on the beach, specifically. Since interaction between sirens and humans does leave a unique sort of fulfillment behind, one that feels like magic to both parties, people believed him."

Maya pressed the heels of her hands to her eyes in an effort to un-see the carnage Aiden had showed her. "It was horrifying. I didn't have anything to do with it, yet I feel like I did. Like I knifed that poor girl myself."

Aiden covered her hands, flattened them between his as if in prayer, and pulled their fingers beneath his chin. "It's not your fault. I didn't show it to you to make you feel guilty. There are less disturbing stories I could share… but I think you understand the need to be careful now, right?"

Maya nodded once. "I'm afraid I understand perfectly." Silence stretched between them.

Aiden spoke first. "We can't protect everyone in the water – we're too dispersed. So we enacted a law requiring us to hide." He dropped one of her hands to thread his fingers through her hair until she experienced a release of the tension she held. She turned her mouth to his palm and kissed it. "I'm so sorry, Aiden. For what we did. For how we are."

"Ah, love. It's not you, not anyone you know. Humans in groups make all the trouble, not individuals, really. Religious groups, cause-related groups, governments." He gestured between them. "Like this, we're great. Better than great. When the connection is personal – between couples or families – we've never had a problem."

Maya remained unconvinced. "But that was just so awful, Aiden. I can't help but wonder why you would *ever* be with us. I mean, why show yourselves at all?"

"Because we need you. You don't feel it? What's between us?"

Maya made a wry face. "You know I do."

Out of context, the idea she could become so desperate for someone – or he for her – was preposterous. Were she reading a medical passage that described their attachment, she'd diagnose them with a disorder and send them for counseling. Possibly prescribe medication. Aiden, as usual, knew her thoughts. He considered her intently.

"Yes. The experience is different in person, and not easy to explain. If you want to talk science though, genetics are a factor. Our population is small and we don't reproduce as often as you. We also need the diversity people offer, which is another reason we co-opt you, get you to marry in. But. We're forbidden from outing ourselves, except to mates."

"Fair enough. I see why, and I won't ask again."

She was grateful for the next few minutes Aiden spent helping her recover, first from the too-graphic horror of the Summoning, and then from the emotional turmoil it created between them, an interruption in their intimacy that left her anxious and unstable. It was the first such disruption since their swim away from society and the first time they'd truly contemplated anything other than each other. During Aiden's remembrance, they'd both retreated and lost the transparent, easy sharing she already relied on to feel whole. In its absence, Maya found herself once again on the edge of desperation, fearful for her future.

"Yes," Aiden muttered, agreeing... and his understanding, his desire to erase the divide between them, helped. He also caressed her constantly – her hair, her cheek, her brow, her ear, until eventually she could banish the story he'd shared back to the past where it belonged. Their connection resettled itself between them. She relaxed, smiled, and stretched.

"Let's move around," she suggested. "Get outside and make a plan." Aiden returned her smile and released her. They rose to ready themselves for the day.

Chapter Sixteen

Stu believed he might have at last evolved past his baser compulsions, grown beyond the insecurity-driven lust that had characterized the entirety of his adult life. And sublimated his ability to show up emotionally, in his marriage to Maya among other places.

He'd left his dad's penthouse enervated but without the urge to expend his dissatisfaction in the usual way. Instead, he floated on a pleasant but unfamiliar calm, grounded by the conviction he would soon prove himself to be a stand-up, admirable man.

As of today, the internal friction that typically launched his more prurient and increasingly depressing pursuits took a back seat to moral certitude. How refreshing.

He scanned the newsfeed on his phone as he stood in line for espresso at the corner café, paying special attention to a blurry image of a couple mid-descent into the East River, one of them with a tail-like appendage curved around the other. **"Fish Man Takes Hostage, Jumps from Bridge,"** the headline read. He checked the byline associated with the notification, frowning because his wireless usually filtered out such drivel. It was probably some publicity hound in costume seeking attention. The story must have gained traction among a sizeable enough audience to rate mainstream exposure, though. He touched the screen to read the full text.

The couple pictured felt familiar to him, but their features, their whole bodies, were indistinct... which made sense when he read the photo credit. A bystander had apparently snapped the shot from his phone and while in motion. Although the vantage point was perfect – the frame showed the whole thing, including the crowded bridge, the plummeting couple, and the grey expanse of river below them – the details were grainy and obscured.

According to the report, the jumpers were either dead or had fled via tributaries, which reached into Appalachia. Recovery teams were combing the area for bodies, but none had been found. Stu scrolled to the end of the story... which concluded with a photo of Maya.

It was older but a good close-up, her volleyball portrait from her senior year at Penn State. As if the image wasn't clear enough – and it absolutely was – the cutline listed specifics: name, age, height and coloring. The article closed with a quote from his father, *"We are worried and anxious for her to be found," said Thad Evans, CEO of Health & Wellness Prescriptives and father-in-law to Ms. Evans. "We will, of course, offer a reward to anyone who can help bring her safely home."*

Stu was unsurprised to see further evidence of his father's manipulative exhortations; was only a little offended to discover he'd once again sidestepped a full explanation of his plans where Maya was concerned. In truth, Stu had known not to trust him, and upon exiting his dad's office had resolved to remove whatever threat his dad intended toward his ex-wife.

Thad wasn't going to like it, but Stu was about to publicly oppose him.

The outcome Thad wanted to avoid... well, Stu was pretty sure it was imminent, anyway. Stu was just going to see the issue resolved sooner rather than later. And he was going to do the right thing. For once.

At Aiden's urging, they collected their meager belongings – which fit in Aiden's small and unobtrusive "waterpack" – closed the door to their borrowed cabin and began to hike eastward toward an undisclosed destination. The most she got out of Aiden was, "I feel something, possibly an inquiry from one or more of us, so we should get moving. I'll get a better read outside, and I don't want to wait here for an ambush."

"Ambush?" Maya squeaked.

"It won't be if we're not here. I'll be able to put out feelers and know if another siren is tracking us. I hope."

Maya felt alarmed enough to stop walking. "Should I be worried?"

"No, hon," Aiden replied gently, taking her hand and drawing her onward. "I sense someone familiar, someone – or someones – I know. Not the government, not the guard." His next statement felt more fateful, however. "I don't want to leave you, Maya, but if I can co-opt Carmen's blessing with you tucked away somewhere safe..." He appeared to deliberate whether or not to explain himself.

"Tell me," Maya insisted. "You're saying you'd voluntarily go back alone? Which would accomplish what?"

"I don't know yet. But we're established – the bond between us, I mean, so my people will dislike separating us. Something else has changed from back home, too. It feels looser, which might help us." He focused on her until his confidence bolstered her own. Her strides lengthened as she relaxed, their faster pace resumed. They followed a country road into a forest.

After an hour in the woods, they exited to open farmland sparsely peppered with clapboard homesteads and periodic groves of trees. Aiden indicated a cluster of rustic buildings in the distance that looked to be either the humble beginnings or lackluster remains of a rudimentary town. Above a lone, modest storefront stood an elevated sign with faded print that read, "Gas – Café – Sundries."

"We'll stop there for water and supplies," Aiden announced. "And a map, since I don't know this area."

Once inside the shop, Maya retrieved bottled water from a bank of refrigerators along the back wall, as well as some cheese, beef sticks and fruit from the small grocery area. She then searched the personal care aisle for insect repellent. As she studied one of the labels, she noticed Aiden straighten suddenly at the end cap closest to her. He focused on a point over her shoulder, moved to her side, then tucked her slightly behind him. Where their bodies touched, she felt his apprehension like she would a vibration from her phone.

Maya checked to see what had captured his attention... and watched the approach of the most bizarre human being she had ever seen.

"Xanthe," Aiden grated. Whoever this newcomer was, he was not happy to see her.

Even so, Maya gaped in fascination. She knew her stare was rude, but she couldn't help herself. How had she not immediately noticed this woman's entrance into the store? Her wildness broadcast itself like a ten-thousand-watt marquis, a buzzing energy Maya could feel in the air around her. The four other people in the store also stood rapt and immobilized, so she wasn't imagining things.

The woman looked a pearl-dusted alien – glowing and gorgeous, but straight-up unreal. Maya catalogued her features to pinpoint which part of her enthralled the most. Her hair? She sported outrageous tresses, thick white-blond locks that fell in marcel curls to her waist. *No one* had hair like that. If you could look past it – and you couldn't – her eyes were her next most shocking characteristic. Or rather, their off-putting intensity. They reminded Maya of a big game cat, maybe a leopard on the hunt. Maya checked Aiden's reaction to her... and immediately noticed their similarities.

Xanthe was definitely a siren, albeit a less tame, less human version of those Maya had met.

"I'm not here to apprehend you," Xanthe announced to Aiden, then offered him a benevolent smile, as if she expected gratitude.

Aiden relaxed incrementally. "Then why *are* you here?"

Xanthe shrugged. "I was curious."

"You left your government post on a whim?" Aiden's eyes narrowed. "I'm afraid I don't believe you."

Xanthe looked bored. "I'm apparently going through what humans call a 'midlife crisis.' I'm considering other career options, other ways of living, so I'm on a bit of tour. You provided an excuse to come ashore. I also wanted to see your situation for myself, since I so failed to manage you remotely."

This time, Maya studied Xanthe for mental imbalance. A midlife crisis? The woman was maybe thirty.

"I'm a hundred and ten," Xanthe offered without any verbal prompt from Maya, and in the same offhanded way she might have mentioned she preferred tea to coffee. Maya's gaze pivoted to Aiden, who kept his attention on Xanthe when he responded, "We live to be three hundred, sometimes three hundred and fifty, Maya."

Sure. As if that made any sense. "Of course you do."

Xanthe either didn't notice or didn't care about her own personal shock factor. Perhaps she wasn't aware of the effect she had? She perused the store, asking, "Do you both work here?" Maya's laughter escaped her like a hiccup before she could suppress it. She and Aiden had in fact just talked about laying low, working some anonymous, menial job to avoid being found by other sirens. That plan was obviously a fail.

To Maya's surprise, Aiden laughed openly. "You wouldn't want to work in a human convenience story, Xanthe. Trust me on this."

Xanthe bristled. "Well, I wouldn't know. I'm interested in something with less responsibility. Something where my performance won't have dire consequences for our entire population. I'm tired of my own importance."

Aiden controlled his amusement and apologized for any offense. "But this isn't the answer for you, I promise," he concluded. "I'm truly sorry to hear you're struggling, Xanthe."

Xanthe waved her hand dissmissively. "It's fine. But you should know, last week, I asked Peter to find you and put a stop to your romantic…" and here she paused to search for the right descriptor, eventually settling on, "campaign."

Maya felt incriminated by Xanthe's statement, her disapproval oiling their shared space like a layer of rancid fry grease. A thrill of genuine fear shot through her… because Xanthe looked capable of serious damage. Was waterboarding a possibility here? Maybe. Xanthe's next words were for Aiden although she studied Maya while she spoke.

"The lies you told us are as I suspected." When Xanthe's discomfiting focus finally moved away, Maya filled her lungs desperately.

Xanthe perused the bank of freezers along the back wall. Her expression became equivocal, her smile bitter as she mused, "But then why wouldn't you lie to be with your one, true love?"

Aiden started leaking worry. Maya wondered if Xanthe had some sort of superpower that enabled her to scare the wits out of all creatures, even strong, gifted sirens like Aiden. But then he spoke, and Maya pieced together the real source of his agitation: his boss back home, who, if the tension in the room was anything to go by, intimidated him more than the woman before them.

"Peter Loughlin is coming for me," he stated carefully.

"Yes," Xanthe confirmed. She walked to a shelf one aisle over while Aiden eyed the exit. "I suspect he's romantically motivated, just as you've been," she offered. Aiden grabbed Maya's hand and shifted his weight as if to run.

Xanthe remained unperturbed, though, retrieving a jar of facial cream in front of her, then ripping through the packaging. The clerk by the register voiced a feeble protest until Xanthe glowered his way, at which point he squeaked once, then shut up. Xanthe returned to her cream, sniffing delicately before pulling a face. She set the open jar back on its shelf and picked up a competing brand, dispatching with the second box in the same way she had the first. The scent of this one appeared to be more to her liking, and she scooped out a fingerful. She began applying it to her cheeks and forehead.

"I'm not altogether certain – after all this *is* Peter we're talking about – but my impression is he's considering a bid for my affections, which is worrisome. Aside from the fact that I might very well be wrong – he did not behave decisively – my own feelings on the matter are unclear to me. So. With that on top of my career considerations, I've decided to disappear for a while." She replaced her moisturizer on the shelf and faced Maya and Aiden again. A whitish streak of unblended lotion ran from her temple to her chin... and Maya decided there was no good way to interrupt a woman on an existential rant with a comment about her appearance. She kept her observation to herself.

Xanthe studied her briefly, then, in a gesture of impatience, swiped away most of the smear. After a scowl that included Xanthe baring her teeth – and left Maya terrified – she continued her monologue. "Well, not disappear, since I'm not hiding per se. Peter or others could locate me with a little effort.

"But I've decided to roam free, be unaccountable while I contemplate this next phase of my life." She addressed Aiden. "If *I* can find you, though, I expect Peter will be here shortly, assuming he intends to come. Although I believe he planned to start his search tomorrow? I'm not sure. But you may still have a little time." She tilted her head uncertainly and peered toward the front of the store. "Maybe."

Aiden remained tense. "Does he mean to take me in?"

Xanthe shrugged. "I don't really know, Aiden. He may not find your antics worth addressing. And I no longer care." Her smile was noncommittal, a placeholder in their conversation rather than an expression of anything meaningful. Maya thought she seemed too detached... and she doubted they could count on her protection. Xanthe's smile became, if not warm, then at least less frightening.

"I will tell you I don't feel as strongly as I once did about your interests. About your courting one of the Wilkes' daughters, I mean."

Aiden was not mollified. "We're bonded, Xanthe. Whatever leadership thinks, the issue's decided."

"You knew she was forbidden, Aiden," Xanthe rejoined harshly. "And you were aware of the implications of acting against our directive. I've asked Peter to take care of it and I have no idea what he intends, for you or her. Nor will I intervene if you don't care for his decision."

Aiden's anger thickened the air, which Maya would have found un-breathable without Xanthe's next words, which seemed to contain a small gift.

"I did contact my nephew, Baxter, in preparation for..." Here Xanthe's gaze flickered toward Maya then slid away, and some exchange occurred between her and Aiden. "He lives in these parts and might be helpful." At least Maya detected, if not true empathy, a softening of her earlier rebuke. Aiden relaxed a little. "Anyway, Baxter could look out for her for a spell."

Foreboding began to beat like a trapped bird high in Maya's chest. She swiftly challenged the undefined proposition hanging between them all. "I will not go from hiding from my father-in-law to running away from siren government, guys. My life is not collateral for anyone who feels like spending it, and I'm sick of everyone assuming it is."

Xanthe offered her a short nod that felt like a show of respect, but she still communicated with Aiden. "Perhaps you should talk with Peter, see if you can help him in exchange for lenience. He's taken an interest in some diplomatic issue down south, one he wants to resolve mostly on his own. I'm sure he'd appreciate help from another cloaker, especially one comfortable with criminality."

Maya couldn't read what next passed between the two of them but the harsh lines of Aiden's face disappeared. "I appreciate the warning, and the advice," he conceded. To Maya he said, "We have to go. Right now."

"Good luck," Xanthe murmured as they passed. From her expression, Maya doubted they'd have any.

But departing from the store – just the act of physically separating themselves from whatever Xanthe had brought in with her – left Maya in a state of mild euphoria. They'd escaped! They were, at this very moment, claiming their freedom! Unlike the other evasions she'd executed in recent months, this one felt providential, as if they'd already outpaced their next challenge and would emerge victorious. They would stay together and avoid capture by a formidable siren named Peter, who Maya very much hoped never to meet.

Also, without the world intervening – his world, her world – they were back to just the two of them, which Maya preferred. Aiden strode purposefully, as if he knew exactly where they needed to go. Good. She'd let him lead them and trust in Providence.

They entered a forest whose limits she was unable to determine. The canopy of tree limbs above them lent to her sense of protection, their shade seeming to offer yet more evidence the world might hide them from all the bad guys. She and Aiden slowed their pace.

Maya didn't want them to search out Xanthe's nephew. She didn't relish the prospect of any more jabs at their intimate bubble… yet she couldn't bring herself to ask where they were headed.

She asked an easier question, instead. "Who's Baxter?"

Aiden glanced her way, cocked an eyebrow before returning his attention to the path ahead. "A relative of Xanthe, which I know is no endorsement. He's been a friendly in the past, though. If Peter lures me away, at least I'll know where to start looking for you." He paused and turned his face eastward. "God. I think I even sense him."

Instantly, Maya's well-being caved. She scanned their surroundings, seeing and sensing no one. "Who? Baxter?"

Aiden shook his head. "Peter."

He was unalarmed, which Maya decided to accept as encouragement. Because she was desperate not to feel oppressed again. Maybe this would be one small, final – the very last – impediment between hiding and a normal, free existence. She checked the position of the sun, which she could just make out through the trees. They were still headed east.

Toward the water.

She worried her lower lip. "Won't they know we'd try for the coast?"

"Yes." He regarded her... as if he was apologizing. "We're going to have to try Xanthe's approach, love."

Maya stopped walking. Here again her stupid, stupid hopefulness would result in yet another deviation from fulfillment, and she wouldn't enforce putting yet more distance between where she was and where she wanted to be. Her desire for that 'normal' life she'd so recently described to Aiden? It constantly ended in disappointment, no matter how many times she attempted to steer her situation. Instead of the freedom she'd envisioned not two minutes ago, she now guessed this jaunt would end exactly as her others had. Meaning she couldn't see the point of continuing.

Aiden moved to comfort her, but the peripheral presence in the woods – or rather, presences, since he intuited more than one – pulled on his attention before he reached her. One of their followers could only be Simon, his emotional signature too familiar to him for deception to work, cloaking included. The other might be Peter? Although if it was, Aiden wouldn't know. The guy could cloak better than anyone. Those he'd trained understood just how awesome his capabilities were – none of them could find the guy if he didn't want to be found. For that matter, Aiden wouldn't know if Peter was here at all... meaning Simon's companion was likely another of Aiden's siren security comrades. Peter would reveal himself if – and only if – he felt like it.

Aiden had become certain of an impending disruption soon after they left the store, had felt definitively the pursuit they were under. But as he'd thought through the possibility Xanthe had hinted at, where he might negotiate an end to their exile, he decided he was up for talking. Of course he regretted the disheartening prospect of another separation from Maya, but he resolved to view whatever came at him in proactive terms, as an effort he could direct. He wondered if Baxter was part of the nearby siren posse, and if he could be trusted to keep Maya safe. Aiden rested his hands on Maya's shoulders.

"This is going to work," he vowed. She closed her eyes, her mouth tightened in a bitter slash.

She argued with him. "We're already together. I know your secrets. Other people – your people – can tell we're bonded, right? Isn't that what you said? We'll convince them I'm not a threat and I can go with you."

"I don't think..." He swiveled his gaze ahead and listened for footfalls in the leaves. "They're close," he informed her. He studied the area around them, letting his senses range. He confirmed Simon's proximity as well as the approach of two others. He also felt their instructions to stay put.

Simon's voice reached him first. *Don't make us chase you. Just stop. It's not going to be so bad, and Peter's with us. You're as good as caught.*

Maybe not – Aiden wasn't convinced he couldn't outrun them. But he wouldn't get away with Maya at his side… and that sealed his fate. He would hear them out, which meant he had only a minute to take care of his girl. As he registered the ambient sounds of the woods around them, he thought of a way to make their parting easier.

He cupped her face in his hands. "You're going to be fine, Maya. We're going to get everything we want if I do this." She looked down and shrugged.

For both of them, he envisioned a different scenario, led her on a daydream that put them near the ocean instead of here, miles away from it. His vast, deep blue ocean. He inclined his head back and inhaled.

Trying to scent the water.

Ah. There it was, a hint of salt, a weighted coolness in the air.

"Look up, Maya," he instructed, and she raised her gaze, then closed her eyes. The high boughs swayed in the wind, the leaves rustling and whispery as they moved. Flickers of sunlight played behind their eyelids in flashes of red and orange, a dappled, fleeting warmth across their faces.

He imagined a vivid seaside environment instead of the forest. He connected the sound of the leaves in the wind to the rush and pull of the tide, a rhythmic surge and retreat that enticed them further into his illusion. The filtered flights of sunlight became glimmers on the sea's surface, the movement of air a breeze off the water. He made the vision so immersive, they floated within it.

Aiden released her, and she opened her eyes to find him smiling down at her. "Better?" he asked.

"We're going to be okay," she responded with only a little uncertainty lurking behind her assertion. "All I hear and feel is the sea."

"Good." Aiden shifted his concentration to Simon's approach. His brother was seconds away. He once again brought his palm to Maya's cheek. "We're out of time, love." He kissed her. "I *will* come back for you."

"Okay." She said it easily, because she didn't believe he would truly leave her.

Even as she kept the impression of him by her, though, his image faded, which didn't add up… and then she couldn't think past the thundering resonance within her, like the surge and retreat of waves against the shore. The light that had sparkled so benevolently a few moments ago intensified until it bleached, then whited out her vision. She squeezed her eyelids closed against the glare.

She realized Aiden had disappeared… but couldn't see to look for him. Another presence – or was it more than one? – formed near her. She pivoted on her heel and ran blindly. She bumped into a tree and slid in the mud, but she scrambled forward. "Leave us alone!" she yelled. "Let us go!"

This is his choice, Maya. But everything's going to be okay, one of them soothed.

She stopped, braced her hands on her knees and sought to orient herself. She wanted to believe whoever tried to calm her, but the attempt felt like a subtle dupe if not a blatant lie. Aiden had abandoned her? He wouldn't. She stood straight and opened her eyes, her sight restoring itself by degrees. The blurry shapes in front of her took on clarity. None of them were Aiden.

Tears of betrayal seared her sinuses, although she fought their production, resisted supplying any evidence that would make her appear weak in front of this new group of manipulators. It seemed to be comprised of a leader; and two or three indistinct others. God, she was so angry. If she had a machete she'd use it on every man around her – Aiden, too, if she could find him, a thought that amused the stranger she faced. She focused on him, noting he shared something of the terrifyingly wild mien Xanthe had also exhibited. He was also vaguely regal. She knew he read her private emotions as Aiden did, so he was definitely a siren. Was this Peter?

Maya didn't care; he was here and Aiden was gone she willed them all dead. "Leave. Me. Alone," she grated.

"Aiden will be fine, you'll be fine. We're taking you somewhere safe from Stu and Thad, someplace you won't need Aiden's help for a while," the man reported.

Her internal rebellion dulled. She felt her resistance bleed out of her a little, the loss of control hurting like a physical cut. *No*, she begged. She couldn't help it. *Please don't make me hide again.*

Ah, sweet Maya, her pursuer crooned. *Don't worry. We'll make your memories go away, at least for now.*

Her vision dimmed just as it had under Aiden's guidance, the world flattening this time into a gray abyss. A new dream overtook her, one of a verdant, hilled countryside around a tiny, bucolic outpost by a river. The pace of life there was peaceful, the people comfortably anonymous.

The image quieted her and removed some of her sense of loss. What had she wanted to do instead of go there? And who had she worried would leave her? She couldn't recall.

She felt the most uplifting release from... some heavy distress she'd been under, which meant letting go was so much more preferable. Maya gave herself to the current pulling on her. In the space of a few moments, she'd moved away from the forest and this time of trouble. In a few more seconds, she'd forgotten her anxiety.

Shall we go down to the village, Maya? A man's hand settled at the small of her back to urge her forward.

Yes. I'm ready now, she told him. She walked eastward, anticipating the contentment her guide promised.

Far off I could hear the bellow of a sea elephant. But suddenly, as I thought of Tutok, the island seemed very quiet.

From "Island of the Blue Dolphins" by Scott O'Dell

PART THREE

Chapter Seventeen

For all the years Aiden had spent wishing for acceptance, the sensation of finally having it chafed, put him off balance. Because here he was, at the seat of siren government on Shaddox Island, not sneaking around, not hiding his dissidence, not lying about his romantic proclivities… and no one cared. Even weirder, he'd been adopted into the leadership circle, meaning he was treated with deference. And that was a straight-up head trip.

Maybe they were coercing him. Maybe they wanted his help with their little South American problem and everything would return to normal after he and Peter & Company made their foray. But for the first time since boyhood, Aiden was welcomed enthusiastically into traditional siren society, although no one shared the rationale behind the sudden rise in his approval rating. He'd asked for no concessions, made no arguments for himself… and no one had explained a thing to him. Nonetheless, the administration had performed a one-eighty on its treatment of him, deciding not just to let him be, but to actively help him. He distrusted all of them.

He'd mused over this switch-up privately and kept his habits of evasion obviously on display, which Peter alone decided to notice. He'd been the first to enlighten Aiden as to why he was being courted, had even offered unsolicited counsel on how Aiden could engage to his advantage. Of course, the guy referred to his own history for justification, said he understood why Aiden continued to slink around. "I am also unable to interact normally with others to this day," Peter had offered conspiratorially. Was that what Aiden had to look forward to? Because, ouch. He wondered if he might have to live apart from everyone after all – with the exception of Maya, who he intended to steal upon completion of his upcoming assignment.

Hence his surliness, even toward his Aunt Carmen, who had been nothing but gracious and had militantly pushed for acceptance of his union. Like Peter, she didn't hold his distrust against him; he remained free to roam at large within the palace, with no one assigned to spy on him or guard him. It all felt wrong.

After a few days, he challenged Peter to deny the whole thing was a trap. "Tell me again I'll be free when this is all over, that you're not all buttering me up just so I'll help."

"We're not," Peter assured him. "This isn't much about you, Aiden, other than our respect for your skills, which I've told everyone we need. That's to your benefit, by the way. You headed one of the successful containment missions after Duncan's video campaign. You've been immersed in human security protocols these past several years, *and* you're a talented cloaker. So you've become valuable, which trumps your quasi-criminal leanings. I've sold everyone on this perspective. You're free to thank me."

"Hmm. Well, thank you? And, yeah, but I didn't do a single thing to warrant all this sucking up. That Duncan mission was eight years ago and I've been a pariah this entire time. Also, I *still* haven't been briefed on why we need a strike squad in the first place."

"I'll get to the specifics of our trip, but as for the shift in how you're perceived, again, I negotiated on your behalf. Thoroughly. As in you couldn't be more covered." Peter's expression darkened. "Which you did not make easy for me, I must say, what with that reckless demonstration on that bridge in New York, your grandstanding, the traffic jam you caused – not to mention actual photos of your lovers' plunge into the river. Did you even *try* to scrub anyone's memory? Did it occur to you to cloak when you made that jump?"

"Peter, bona fide gunmen were after my girl and I had *seconds* to get her away. I wanted their focus on me, not her."

Peter's lips thinned. "You are *not* forgiven for that, Aiden, no matter how urgent your other priorities seemed. You acted selfishly – and very irresponsibly – with that display. It took a team of twenty of us to take that story out of the mainstream, and there are still photos from people's cell phones floating around."

Aiden attempted to defend himself again. "Look, Peter…"

But Peter was in no mood to listen. "No. You can't make the outcome of that farce any different by explaining it to me, Aiden. I know what drove you. It's no excuse. If you'd used your head at all, you could have avoided making a scene. You didn't."

Aiden still didn't regret his actions, but neither was he going to justify his behavior to people who viewed siren comportment through such a rigid, narrow lens. He'd wanted to keep Maya breathing, and would change nothing about what he'd done if he could go back. He pretended to make nice, though. "Fine. I promise to make better choices the next time I have to protect my mate from assassins."

Peter glowered at him but continued with less antagonism. "The narrative from your antics has been sidelined for the most part – you're now part of fringe American lore, one of those nonsense stories that appeal to conspiracy theorists. Again, you're welcome. And you're lucky you're not on trial for banishment."

"Great. Which brings us back to my initial question. Why am I here rubbing elbows with those in charge?"

Peter sighed and pinched the bridge of his nose. "I really am trying to help you, you know. Also, our cooperation on this issue – where I show I can work and play well with others – will benefit me."

"You're using this opportunity to reintegrate," Aiden guessed.

Peter grimaced delicately. "Not really. Let's just say I have an interest in securing Xanthe's good opinion of me."

Aiden waited for Peter to elaborate, which, not surprisingly, he didn't... and Aiden was irritated enough to needle the man. "I wasn't aware you were on the outs. And if she's the reason for this circus, where is she?"

"Ah-ah," Peter scolded as if Aiden was a child guilty of sneaking sweets. And he displayed that creepy, subversive smile Aiden had never been able to witness without alarm. *"That's* a state secret." He looked away. "She's not here, nor will she be," he went on briskly. "I'm facilitating our effort, and I'm not ready to share the reasons behind my decisions. But I will say I want resolution for her when she returns. So she has one less deviant to trip over."

Aiden understood he wouldn't be taken into Peter's confidence on this issue, and that Peter would not be drawn into a fight. "Fine," he conceded. "What's the gig? What are we after?"

Peter launched into an overview of the strangeness he'd uncovered in Cerro Lejano, the small town in South America that served as the final launching place for travellers on their way to the siren outpost in Antarctica. Aiden was familiar with the town, since he'd served on the original excavation team sent to ready the place for siren visitors. He remembered exactly the situation Peter described, too, how the residents had seemed drugged or inbred, or... *something.*

"Yes. Everyone reported the same issue," Peter agreed. "When I focused on the anomaly on my way by, I discovered a low-level, constant inquiry in the water, too. It was so subtle, I'm sure no one else caught it... Anyway, I followed it to its source, which was, indeed, Cerro Lejano. And I found the same oddities in the village you all did – the emotional coldness, the suppressed broadcasts of every person I encountered, even the children. It felt like siren tampering to me, and while I didn't sense a threat per se, it was troubling enough to warrant further attention."

"What's the cause?" Aiden asked. "And also, why do we care?"

Peter ignored Aiden's sarcasm, but he did answer his question. "The situation is rooted in human-siren dynamics, but sirens are not the perpetrators. I didn't stay to investigate – and I cloaked the little time I was there, so I collected indirect information. Although, of course, it was very good." Peter's smile was self-deprecatory. "I identified our culprit, a human Caller who harvests adoration from sirens when he can get it but siphons off of – and controls – the human population otherwise. Like a parasite. What he's taken from each individual sickens me, especially the children. They're deliberately lifeless.

"But it's quite the set-up. Our villain – he goes by Alvaro Bartolomé and I've yet to meet him – has cultivated an entire human village to serve him, using all the usual religious threats. The townspeople think he's a deity – an abusive, controlling one they don't want to upset. He uses fear, feeds on them, or on their adoration, similar to a siren-human dynamic except it's... off. That's another component of Mr. Bartolomé's scheme I want to study."

"A Caller who manipulates sirens and the people around him for power. That's not new, Peter. What's he after? And why didn't you take him out on your own?"

Peter regarded Aiden reprovingly. Aiden felt like he'd given the wrong answer in class. Peter sighed. "I'll get to that when I'm ready, Aiden."

He continued. "Anyway, effusiveness – celebrations or sadness, or overt expressions of any kind on the part of the townspeople – attracts him. So the villagers keep themselves on a kind of emotional lockdown, even schooling their little ones not to broadcast themselves."

"Because...?" Aiden prompted.

"Because anyone who displays passion is co-opted into Alvaro's service, and once they leave the village, they're never heard from again."

"Yikes."

"Yes. I believe Alvaro's goal is longevity, and he's gotten it so far, although I don't know how. But I'd estimate him to be over two hundred. He's highly intuitive – I caught that much – and he hides, doesn't live among his people. In fact, they rarely see him...

and I could not intuit a clear physical definition of the man, despite querying several sources, which was another inconsistency I haven't encountered before. I know sirens are involved in his scheme, but I'm not sure how. So. I think a reconnaissance effort with a capable security force will help us define the whole of the problem. The approach will also mean positive attention for our little force, and it will show goodwill on my part if I'm part of a team."

Aiden's need for understanding flared again and he wished it wouldn't have. Peter must know he courted such nosiness given how inquisitive they all were. For once, Peter had referenced the obvious issue of his fringe status in the community, and he was acting with seemingly sincere concern for rules he'd gone to great lengths to disdain. Which made Aiden even more curious.

Peter almost seemed nervous under Aiden's regard, which was out of character for him. "I mean, I – or we – can resolve this however we'd like," he muttered. "But afterwards, I want Xanthe to feel good about how we manage ourselves."

"You realize you could have found him yourself, killed him off, and placed your accomplishment at Xanthe's feet. Like a gift." Peter shuttered his output as only he could, responding with an ambiguous stare.

Ah. This truly did have more to do with Xanthe than Peter was letting on. Aiden shrugged and returned his attention to his own role in their upcoming trip. "An actual Caller. In this day and age." He shook his head. "I literally just shared our standard Summoning story with Maya last week, so she'd understand why we resist integration with people."

"Our South American miscreant runs the same type of program, I'm afraid," Peter agreed. "He's doing all the usual things, which explains why you feel like you're in a cult when you're down there."

Aiden laughed humorlessly. "Because it's a cult. Which should trump your concerns for Xanthe..."

"…and yet it won't," Peter cut in. "I will not be moved on this, Aiden, so don't bother bringing it up again. As I said earlier, I have my own reasons for this decision, ones I'm still mulling over. I'll share if and when I care to, which might be never. And again, supporting my plans is to your advantage."

"Fine. Who all is going, and what do we do when we get there?"

"I'm taking you and Simon, and four others. I want a thorough, covert investigation of the area. Then I'll report back to the bureaucracy, and we'll act based on whatever consensus emerges."

"Then let's go. I want to go get Maya like yesterday. And I *really* want to show her ex-laws what I think of their treatment of her."

The menace behind Peter's laugh perfectly reflected Aiden's own at the prospect of confronting Thad and Stu. "I'm glad someone else gets it," Aiden remarked. "But I'm sick of stalling, so let's get this deal done."

"Ah, the impatience of youth," Peter intoned, earning him a glare from Aiden. "Worry not, soldier," Peter soothed. "I've got Maya under watch with orders to wait for us should something happen. No other romantic prospects are permitted near her, and you'll have your shot at her detractors. We're clear to travel south, and your brother is meeting us at the airport later today."

"I'll get my gear," Aiden replied, then went to search for a spare waterpack.

Chapter Eighteen

Except for an occasional, gripping, and inexplicable sense of loss, Maya was happier than she'd been in a long while. She could even see herself settling here permanently.

She'd have to achieve inner peace over the huge holes in her memory, though, the ones concerning her journey and arrival here and the foundation of a niggling insecurity complex that had her hungering for an MRI, possibly psychoanalysis. Because honestly, why couldn't she remember what had happened to her?

She reasoned the freedom she enjoyed in this hidden hamlet trumped the exposure she'd risk if she reached outside of it, though, even to sneak in an x-ray. So, she breezily pretended she didn't have a brain tumor leaching away her faculties, and acted as if her sanity was intact.

She had the residents of this odd place to thank for her delusion.

She could recall certain components of her impetus to leave New York, such as her unsalvageable marriage, and her fevered escape from the goons her father-in-law had hired to stalk her. When she thought of that, her heart rate increased and she began to sweat, a kind of physical re-enactment she experienced whenever she imagined her sprint across... some bridge. She had no idea what came after, only that she'd run away.

Even so, she didn't question why she'd left, didn't dismiss the oppression that had convinced her to bail on every single component of her former life. She just wished she knew something about the specifics, which had to have been pretty important or she wouldn't be sitting here in the middle of nowhere. She couldn't call anything up, though, nor could she work out the timetable between her getaway and arrival here. Those days and happenings, whatever they were, had disappeared as if they'd been surgically removed, like an amputated limb whose absence now itched.

She had a visceral sense that she'd also forgotten a vital component of her escape, something or someone she needed like she needed air. She believed this was the basis of her intermittent grief.

Mostly, she remembered her confrontation with Thad at his club, which she should not have been able to pull off. How had she carted a gun through security, then pointed it, unconcealed, at one of the club's most prominent members? She had, though. A friend should probably have talked her out of that idea. Maybe if they had, she wouldn't have provoked Thad to such an extent, wouldn't be hiding out from the contract hit he'd put on her.

The more practical reasons for anonymity aside – the avoidance of her own murder was a biggie – she loved it here in Lehland. Most days, she decided how she'd gotten here didn't much matter.

The place wasn't even a legal town, was more a beefed-up truck stop comprised of a bar, a gas station, a general store, and a church no one seemed to go to. A sparse number of cottages, hers among them, peppered a quarter mile circle around the "commercial center" willy-nilly, without thought to symmetry or becoming a neighborhood. There certainly was no citified grid, no standard north-south or east-west orientations to make the place look like it was planned.

Locals drifted into the store daily from abodes unseen, though, so who knew how many people considered themselves Lehlanders? The municipality conceivably extended for miles.

This, at least, she had partly figured out. The whole of the community, hidden portions included, lay tucked in a triangle of land bordered by a dense, seemingly infinite forest to the southeast; the Appalachian mountain range to the northwest; and a winding tributary – locals called it the Bight – to the northeast. Population-wise, Lehland revolved around six families with old ties to the land – as in nine or ten generations old – along with their physically undifferentiated children of indeterminate number. Like maybe someone at the county hospital, wherever that was, had decided wild-eyed, russet-haired babies with snub noses were the only kind they'd let out of the maternity ward. The kids formed a sort of gravitational center to town life, though, since everyone took some responsibility for looking after them, related or not.

A fair many also took incidental care of Maya, checking in to see she had firewood and leaving baked goods or casseroles on her counter. It no longer startled her to have people wander in and out as they pleased; and anyway, whatever locks her home once possessed no longer existed. No one else worried over the situation, so she didn't, either.

At least the townsfolk provided entertainment with their iconic, insular affectations. She yearned to describe them to her friend, Kate, who she knew would find their antics as comical as she did. She'd start with Betty Sue and Norma, a pair of sisters who brokered gossip with the intensity of traders on the New York Stock Exchange floor. It was best not to try and evade them when they bustled your way with a question or to offer advice, because they would back you up against a wall. The positions of firefighter, game warden, and local constable were filled by one Dorsel Aberdeen, and yes, he took bribes to look the other way when one of the founding family members took an extra deer or made moonshine or held an unsanctioned bonfire. Lehland even had its stereotypical town drunk, replete with sad, watery blue eyes, a stained chambray shirt, and rusted out pick-up he lived in if you didn't count the local bar. He would accept help from no one, reputedly had a cabin nearby he was escorted to again and again.

Despite his assurances he would, 'stay home and sleep it off this time,' he could always be found in his truck across the street from the bar, dozing while he waited for it to open. Maya sometimes brought him coffee on her way to work in the morning.

Baxter was her favorite character whether he should have been or not. Maybe he was just the most enigmatic and therefore pulled hardest at her imagination. She shouldn't have been drawn to him, though, since he lurked, disappeared at random, and no one had much information on him. He could be a serial killer for all she knew. Still, sometimes she sought him out, his taciturn presence calming to her. Go figure. For a living, he bartered and sold fish at the general store, which saw so little traffic Maya couldn't imagine how he supported himself.

But the beating heart of Lehland was irrefutably Amelia Hadley, the only other transplant aside from Maya, although Amelia had moved in twenty-five years ago. From Maya's perspective, Amelia had made herself indispensable, was the local Atlas holding up the entire place on her back. She cared for everyone, and everyone relied on her in some way, a circumstance Maya mostly attributed to her heroic gardening habits. From what Maya could tell, Amelia's gardens had supplanted county meal services and biology classes for local high schoolers; and they served as an ad hoc daycare for the horde of little ones who came each morning, no parents in tow. Amelia fed everyone breakfast out of her big, American foursquare kitchen starting at seven a.m. Childcare thereafter was overseen in a hands-off manner by older siblings or cousins or whoever else showed up, which people did as if telepathically called, coming and leaving like ghosts. The kids didn't bother anyone, and no one kept any set schedule Maya could discern.

Amelia was a fan of hers, although Maya had been welcomed coolly at first despite her sponsorship. But Maya's status elevated instantly when she revealed her close brush with doctorhood. Lehland currently had no medical practitioners close by, which proved to be the turning point for Maya's popularity and no one cared in the least that she hadn't quite finished her residency, hadn't actually practiced outside a supervised setting. "I mean, I am an M.D., I just don't want to misrepresent myself," she'd reported, a truth she suspected mattered to her and no one else.

She didn't know how word spread so quickly, either, but the day after her announcement, she awoke to find a line of locals stretching from her front porch across her yard; people looking for help with some ailment or another, illnesses they later described to her as "tender throats" or "a scratchy lung." Or her favorite, "foot barnacles." She startled when she first saw them all, standing silent and morose as zombies, and she had no idea how long they'd been there. Why hadn't anyone knocked? Anyway, when she informed them she didn't have the tools or facility to treat anyone – she didn't even have a first-aid kit on her and what did that say about how far removed she'd become from who she'd been – they shuffled off without complaint to Amelia's house.

The next morning, Amelia herself knocked on Maya's door, handed her a cup of coffee and a homemade cinnamon roll balanced on a napkin, then walked her to a large-ish outbuilding on the south side of her property. It was brick and newly tuck-pointed, teeming with industrious cleaner-uppers… which left Maya prickling with a sense of destiny. From the large chimney, Maya guessed the edifice had served as the original kitchen to the main house in some previous century.

At present, though, mystery elves had outfitted it with basic doctoring materials: two metal cabinets stocked with medical supplies that were likely ideal in the 1950s; an antique but serviceable wooden filing chest; and basic scopes and diagnostic tools. Someone had even hung anatomy charts and a list of hygiene directives on the wall – wash your hands, cover your cough, eat your fruits and vegetables.

She was impressed, but she also truly wondered where they'd come up with a regulation exam table in the last 24 hours, even if the design was prehistoric. "I mean, my God. That mauve leatherette..." she murmured. She questioned how long Lehland had been without a physician.

"Is your last doctor laying butchered in a shallow grave?" she asked Amelia, only partially joking. "It's kind of creeping me out how fast you guys put this together."

"Pfft. You city folk need to learn to trust. One of the ladies used to volunteer in a rural clinic two towns over, and I think she called in some favors. We've never had a doctor in Lehland. And don't be such a Suspicious Sue."

"Says the girl who used to work on Wall Street," Maya retorted, but she relaxed her stance. "I guess I'm a little excited to do this, although I'm going to need some research options, since I'm going it alone here. Any chance I can get internet access?"

Amelia was already shaking her head before Maya completed her question. "You know we can't take that risk, honey. You're here to hide first, which means not be tracked, and second – so much second it might as well be a hundred and eighth – to practice medicine." She pointed toward a kick-out nook on the back wall. "There's a complete set of medical encyclopedias – the best America had to offer in 1973 – on the shelves over there. They're going to have to suffice."

"What if I want to order vaccines or talk to a pharmacist?"

"You let me know if there's something you need and we'll see about getting it for you," Amelia advised. "If we can't, we'll make do. It's not like we're not all used to going without around here."

Maya was tentatively up for the challenge of dispensing small-time, small-town medical advice, even if it was the only professional opportunity on offer. The constant life-or-death scenarios she'd faced in New York had required a level of vigilance that had excited her, but they'd also drained her of her capacity to commit herself much outside the E.R., a situation that had suited her fine when she'd been avoiding her marital problems and the sadness they'd caused.

Free of those, however, Maya had rediscovered her appetite for a more expansive reality; for activities beyond the constant heroics of running triage and saving lives. Safely away from the emotional box she'd lived in through most of her twenties, she dusted off her pre-adult motivations, those initial musings she'd given the prospect of a career as a physician when she'd been trying to figure herself out. As she'd considered medical school during her senior year at Penn State, she'd envisioned herself ten or fifteen years after the fact, and what she'd pictured was very close to her current situation – tending a small practice within a community where she could invest herself personally as well as professionally. The only missing components were a husband and children of her own, a possibility she'd lost enthusiasm for at present because the idea prodded that bruise in her heart she couldn't ascribe. She'd also hoped for some sort of tie-in with her athletic interests. She wondered if the local high school would let her coach a girls' volleyball team.

And this was where Maya started to imagine settling here, even if she would prefer a more sophisticated clinic than the one she'd been given. Maybe she could add imaging equipment and a basic surgery? And find someone to work with, as much for collegiality as to broaden her concentration of services. When it was safe to do so, she wanted to talk with her friend Kate's husband, Gabe, a physician who had set up a primary care clinic in Griffins Bay. She wondered if she could talk them into moving here... although they seemed pretty married to their ocean proximity, so, probably not. But she might try.

When she could set her misgivings aside – and she usually could – Maya recognized within herself a hopefulness she'd been without for a long, long time. Unused to contentment as she was, she didn't trust it, meaning she could probably be happier, because she still greeted nonthreatening interactions with pleasure-killing suspicion. She knew her skepticism wasn't warranted, but she couldn't help but feel it.

Even so, everything had become much improved with the addition of patients to her routine – generically sick, mildly compromised patients; not drug addicts or gang affiliates courting death all day, every day. Maya flexed her hard-earned professional muscles and still had personal time to spend as she liked. Better yet, she walked free here, never once had to worry if anyone she encountered was out to kill her, which was such a lovely change. For the first time since childhood, Maya let her interests – not her schedule, not her fears – guide her forward.

Which opened up a portion of her psyche she hadn't accessed in forever, the part of her that hungered for banal pleasures she'd foregone in order to power through school and distract herself from her demoralizing personal life. Here, even with her patient responsibilities, she had extra hours on her hands. She didn't have enough work to warrant her constant, on-site presence at the clinic, so she often ran errands between patient appointments or went out for a stroll, or read through one of the cookbooks in Amelia's enormous collection. If someone needed her and she was out, she could always be located. She took advantage of her new freedoms, creating time for them as she chose. Sometimes, she just sat on the porch swing, rocked herself and contemplated the horizon, thanking Providence for kerplopping her in this protected oasis.

One morning while pulling an especially tenacious series of weeds from Amelia's carrot patch, Maya pondered the fortuitousness of her current set-up; how apart from her recent stint as a persecuted hermit in New York, all of her life's experiences seemed to have circled back on her here. Small-town in the Mid-Atlantic? Check. Slower paced with limited traffic? Check and double-check. Amelia factored heavily in these musings, too, since she was much like her own mother with bits of her sisters and best friend, Kate, thrown in. She enjoyed her own company, for instance; was an adept creator of creature comforts both for herself and others, and was unapologetically herself. And she had an agile mind, a wit that channeled the personality of every female she'd grown up with, which was probably why Maya had felt immediately close to her.

But Maya's feelings of familiarity went beyond Lehland's locale, and beyond the reflections of others she saw in its inhabitants. It was like the place was an actual clone of Griffins Bay, except it was one-tenth the size and hours from the coast. Still, the air itself sang of the ocean, as if you could walk to it. The Bight was freshwater... but Maya could sometimes swear she tasted salt when she inhaled. Also, according to a beachy definition she'd developed during childhood, time here could advance strangely, as if it obeyed separate laws of physics. With certain townspeople, too – mostly Baxter – she felt her emotions pulled out of her whether she wanted to share them or not, an experience that seemed natural because she'd had dozens just like it as a child. As well as more recently... although here her thoughts again ran into her mental blockade.

Oddly – since she'd been so lonesome when she'd been caged up in the city – she was most grateful for the isolation here. It felt like safety. She began to feel like she belonged with the few people she knew, an impression that was magnified one day not long after her clinic opened, when she spied a threesome of disoriented strangers. The men stumbled toward the woods almost as if they were fleeing.

As a physician, she'd immediately been concerned because they'd appeared compromised – although maybe they were just drunk – and none of them carried supplies into the forbidding, darkening expanse of timber they scrambled toward. For all she knew, they would be eaten by squirrels upon entry... and no one would ever find the bodies.

The people around her that afternoon seemed to hope for such an outcome.

Baxter was the ring leader and had stopped her from interfering. She'd exited the general store with her supply of milk, tea, and a handful of butterscotch candies, was unfolding one from its golden wrapper as she stepped onto the front walkway. The sun was perhaps an hour from setting, casting an oblique, copper glow on the faces of those gathered on the gravel road in front of the store. In fact, the whole world appeared drenched in honey, although the atmosphere was anything but sweet.

Baxter and three others, people whose names she'd been given several times but could never seem to recall, gave her their backs when she joined them, forming a sort of wall in front of her. Good thing she was tall enough to peek through their shoulders. Another man came seconds after she did and remarked, "I thought there was another one." Baxter glanced sharply at the newcomer and shook his head once. Then all four resumed their vigil, their postures challenging – chests out, bodies inclined forward. She hadn't heard a skirmish while she shopped... but she became certain the hikers had been forced to leave. Her attendants inspected the retreating forms menacingly.

"Who...?" she started to ask. Baxter gripped her arm and she fell silent. He pulled her into his side, keeping his attention on his quarry.

Maya sank into catatonia, couldn't thereafter muster her former concern or curiosity. She rested her cheek on Baxter's shoulder, his arm circling her lightly, and she sighed. She vaguely remembered being led away.

The hikers had never returned, and no one brought them up. She thought of them sporadically, though, more when she began to hear muffled thuds in the night, as if someone banged against a wall in Amelia's house across the way. Sometimes, she thought she heard a man weeping. But she never saw anyone, and Amelia assured her everything was, "as normal as ever," which hardly meant anything. "Maybe you're hearing a ghost? These parts are said to be haunted, you know," Amelia informed her.

The emotional context surrounding her almost-encounter with the visitors remained with her for another reason, as well: her interaction with Baxter in the aftermath. She wouldn't have predicted she'd cozy up to the guy like she had... and then he'd drawn her to him, held her close as if the gesture made sense to him. She hadn't felt attracted to him otherwise, still didn't think either of them entertained amorous possibilities with the other.

Even so, she'd once broached the subject of the "invasion" with him in the hopes of gaining a better understanding of it.

"What was up with those three guys who wandered through Lehland the other day?" She felt her memory of the event grow fuzzy under Baxter's regard. He didn't answer her.

He never explained, either, which was at least normal for him. But the fact that he'd held her remained noteworthy. Her subsequent trance was something else to ponder.

Or not, she concluded.

Her response that afternoon hadn't been completely unique, however, since she'd behaved identically – and so had he – on one other occasion, where their closeness overtook her and upset her already murky understanding of her interpersonal dynamics in Lehland.

Baxter had arrived agitated and out of breath on the banks of the Bight where she been standing for… she didn't know how long. Perhaps hours. She'd hungered for the river constantly at some level since waking up in in her cottage, especially when that inexplicable sadness overtook her. Contemplation of the Bight righted everything, its black surface heavy with secrets, the answers to which would bring her peace. The slow, glassy roil should have warned her away, since she knew an unpredictable current ran beneath…

…but she longed to swim in it.

She imagined the invigorating rush she'd feel against her skin, the delicious release from earth-bound practicalities she'd feel. She rehearsed the story of all that would happen to her, about the journey she would take as the river carried her until it expelled her into the Atlantic. The prospect hypnotized her.

Baxter appeared out of nowhere, silent as usual… and her compulsion to fling herself forward bled out of her when he placed a hand on the back of her neck. In a few moments, he led her from the shoreline and they returned to town. She hadn't been back to the riverbank alone since.

But the response Baxter drew from her, both by the Bight and during the few other times they'd touched, harrowed her in quiet moments. Their interactions – his very presence – reminded her of her buried loss. Beneath the calm front she wore, her questions simmered like molten iron in a too-small crucible, its scalding potential a worrisome threat to her contentment. This was when she most longed for the river or yearned for rain, when her senses reached for anything reminiscent of the sea.

Chapter Nineteen

Cerro Lejano hadn't improved since Aiden's visit several years ago. It was, if possible, even more charmless than he remembered. Back then, he and his crew had been focused on the next leg of their trip – Antarctica and making it into a habitable siren outpost – not this place, so they hadn't paid close attention. Still, he and Simon had noticed how bizarrely everyone behaved. They'd reasoned the differences they saw were due to insularity, were maybe normal in a remote, ethnically uniform village with little to no wireless coverage. Then they'd spent a year chiseling out ice caves further south and had forgotten the matter.

Having come expressly to study the town this time, Aiden conceded the dynamic here deviated widely from anything else he knew even allowing for his earlier rationalizations.

As Peter suspected, a Caller was causing all the problems, had been for the better part of two hundred years. Which made them all wonder if he was human? It was one of the things they needed to check out.

Their mission included Aiden and seven others, Simon among them. Led by Peter, they'd intended to troll the locals like a pack of journalists, reasoning they could inquire more efficiently if all of them worked the crowd together. They'd had to abandon that plan after their first afternoon.

"Do you recall getting hated on like this the last time?" Simon asked him the morning of their second full day. The pair had been dispatched to find coffees and buñelos con miel, a fried breakfast bread drizzled with honey that had promptly become everyone's new favorite thing. Today's order had been for triple rations.

On their way to the café, townspeople crossed the street in an obvious effort to avoid them, then scurried into their shops or homes and quickly closed their doors. Many of them spat on the pavement in Simon and Aiden's direction before disappearing.

"No. I don't," Aiden replied. He would have characterized their reception here before as circumspect but not hostile. Nothing like this.

They'd arrived late at night two evenings ago, but even in the darkness they'd fielded local disapproval. Every single villager who saw them hissed and scuttled away when they approached, except for the hotel staff and restaurant workers obliged to attend them. Even from them they'd heard, "Vete, pescados."

"Are they calling us 'fish'?" one of their group asked incredulously.

Peter, who in Aiden's opinion was the ultimate cynic – Aiden couldn't imagine the guy being surprised by anything, ever – studied the vacated lobby around him in astonishment. "Yes. They are," he replied.

The experience repeated itself the following day until the team realized no one was willing to get anywhere near them when they marched along en masse.

"God. They're like cockroaches when the light goes on," Simon commented after they'd cleared an entire block within seconds of stepping onto the street.

"Indeed. We're going to have to split up," Peter concluded. "Our siren appeal isn't working, which I must say I've never personally seen happen." He studied each member of his squad. "See what you can manage individually. Maybe we'll be more inconspicuous that way. We'll reconvene at the hotel at six."

Stealth proved more fruitful. Aiden and Simon claimed the southwest neighborhoods, separating in the middle of their territory with an agreement to return to the hotel together. Aiden first made his way through a deserted alley, rehearsing the persona he would present. He cloaked lightly to dull his oceanic markers... and then decided to add actual acting to his schtick. He would cultivate empathy by posing as someone caught in Bartolomé's pull.

It was a good decision.

He collected several villagers within minutes, their trust readily offered when he came off as a wanderer from the hills driven to investigate the worrisome emotional energy of this place. Was he wrong to come? What was the basis of the oddness he felt here? His new friends opened up to him.

As his Spanish wasn't great, he conducted the majority of his inquiry through touch, with a hand on someone's back or by grasping forearms, which thankfully they accepted. Maybe because he solicited only for information, not the emotional output Bartolomé trolled for.

They worried for him, and they all but sang of Cerro Lejano's problems. They also didn't notice how they delivered their story, that it wasn't verbal, meaning Aiden understood everything, which was a plus.

Peter was right: Bartolomé and his pseudo religion were the foundation beneath everyone's extreme emotional reticence. Under the guise of spiritual guidance, Bartolomé proclaimed himself, of all things, a god of the sea, and everyone within the area was obliged to serve his interests if they wanted to avoid hurricanes and tsunamis and other sea-time ravages. He portrayed these disasters as God's wrath against the noncompliant, the impure of heart.

Few in the area believed him to be divine... however, he had lived an awfully long time – centenarians in the town could attest to his evergreen presence, how their parents had accommodated him, too.

He hosted public "presentation parties" in the village square every few years, insisting on revelry for all. Inevitably, the more vivacious among them earned a spot in private service to him after these events, which no family member wanted for their children because they were never seen again.

As for Bartolomé's assertion he was one with the sea... well, Aiden wasn't able to glean anything conclusive when he grilled his subjects. *Is he a... I mean, has anyone ever seen him swim and perhaps, ah, transform into something with a tail?*

"No. No es tritón."

Okay, then.

No one dared express skepticism, though, either over Bartolmé's divinity claims or the purported glory he conferred on those he selected to follow him home. He *had* made life unpleasant in the past and *could* influence inhabitants beyond their misgivings, beyond even their will to protect children if they were in his presence. So he had some kind of mystical mojo going on, one all in Cerro Lejano protected themselves against.

Then there were reports on the "fish people" Bartolomé occasionally, if infrequently, called from the sea... and Aiden realized his interviewees were speaking casually of sirens they'd seen. Everyone had seen at least one, their memories coming across clearly and unedited by siren influence. In fact, word on the street was a whole contingent had moved in two days ago and was walking around town trying to get people to talk. Aiden should watch out and avoid them for his own safety.

"Er... I'll see what I can do..."

Bartolomé's demonstrations were mostly viewed for what they were – theater – but the locals placated him as they would any tyrant because they feared him. They schooled their children into emotional blankness whenever they went out so as to avoid attracting attention. One of the men Aiden interviewed shared his belief the people Bartolomé took were killed.

Aiden feared he could be right.

Where is he? Where does he live? Aiden inquired again and again… and this was when his hold broke every time, when his respondents fled no matter what tricks he applied to coerce them. Which meant they'd become inured, probably because Bartolomé had used the same techniques too hard and too often.

Everyone reported similar findings when the team gathered again. They also all agreed on a verdict: Bartolomé needed to go.

"I think the man is human, and I believe him to be a Caller," Peter shared. "I'm guessing – and before we came, I inquired among sirens who've had family members go missing in this area – he prefers siren hostages. But he must know he'd be hunted by us if he isn't careful. We've killed everyone like him in history, at least to my knowledge. I'm aware of no other living Callers. So I'd guess he's using human replacements for his nefarious ends. Which I'm not one hundred percent clear on yet. But I will be."

Simon's expression turned sour. "Whether he's hunting sirens or not, dude is a sick bastard." The rest of the group murmured their agreement.

"I think we know enough to take him out now," Aiden stated. "We don't need all the details, don't need a full list of crimes. Let's just end him." All members of the party again voiced approval, with the exception of Peter.

"I prefer to take over from here, gentlemen," he said apologetically. Aiden became annoyed.

"Not to complain, but again, you could have figured that out before hauling us all down here. You certainly don't need our help with an assassination. He's human? You'd waste him in under two minutes. The rest of us could be back home, dealing with our own crazy." He took in Simon's derisive smirk and glared. "*Of course* I'm anxious to go after Maya. Idiot."

"I could *not* have figured out what we learned today on my own," Peter disagreed. "At least not as quickly." He addressed Aiden. "I've already explained how this mission will confer legitimacy on you and your choice of mate." Peter scanned the rest of the team. "To an extent, our efforts help all of you in some way." His attention went to Aiden again. "As for my other reasons, I've decided it's better to take matters into my own hands after all." He studied the ocean over Aiden's shoulder.

"Peter..." Simon began warningly, and all of them felt the precursor to an argument brewing.

Peter maintained his stare and spoke as if he hadn't heard. "In part, I'm simply curious," he offered. "I don't have anything truly challenging to apply myself toward at the moment, and I want to learn more about this man who can mimic us, call to us and kill us. All while controlling a population of humans he isn't physically among." He smiled at Aiden... and Aiden could see the puzzle Bartolomé posed did, in fact, invigorate their former prince. Privately, Aiden also acknowledged the idea of a confrontation between the two got his blood up. Peter was so freaking powerful and Bartolomé sounded like such a pig... well, Aiden might like to see Peter handle him. "How will you find him?" Aiden asked.

"Send him fishing, of course." Peter grinned. "I can make my presence known off the coast, and someone like me in the water... well, Bartolomé won't be able to resist trying to call me in. I intend to let him."

"Shouldn't we back you up? Since we're already here?" one of the other group members asked. Aiden noticed everyone's excitement had elevated, not just his own, over the prospect of seeing Peter eliminate his opponent.

Peter deliberated a moment before answering. "I'd prefer to have you all travel back to your respective posts." He glanced at each of them. "You're right – I don't need help... and I'd prefer not to risk any of you. I'll report back to the powers that be on how invaluable you all were in Bartolomé's removal."

Several in the group guffawed, and Aiden knew he spoke for all of them when he responded. "Risk? Seriously? All of us against one human? You're high."

Peter laughed. "Aiden, my friend, I expect this encounter will make me high, and that's part of why I want to do this. I cannot wait to study this man, then see how quickly I can kill him. It will be a kind of personal contest, using abilities I don't exercise often." He clasped Aiden's shoulder but addressed everyone. "If – and I don't think it's much of a possibility – Bartolomé has tactics we can't defend against, I'd prefer not to give him access to my top talent. The community back home needs a security contingent, and while one of us can disappear, all of us cannot." He retreated. "So. I'd like you all to head out. Go back to your families, resume the responsibilities I gave you after your training. I'll take care of this newest..." Peter waved a hand in front of him, "person of interest, let's say."

Aiden felt their collective disappointment. "You mean we don't get to stay for the fun part? And I thought you wanted to wait, show Xanthe how civilized you are."

Peter regarded him thoughtfully. "Yes. I did. But now I believe I misspoke. Bartolomé doesn't sound as if he would conduct himself diplomatically, definitely not according to Xanthe's refined sensibilities. If she were to come down here, and if he were to..." Peter stilled, and menace thickened the air in the room. Aiden – along with the rest of them – tensed, as if for a fight.

Peter relaxed and smiled kindly at them, although he retained a sharpness in his expression that kept them all alert. "Let's just say I've changed my mind."

They all shifted on their feet. "Will you report to us when you come home? Tell us exactly how you kill him?" one of them asked.

Peter chuckled. "Bloodlust from a group of sirens. I never thought I'd see the day, but I must admit, I like it." He composed himself before adding, "Yes. We'll meet when I return and I promise to impart every detail of our encounter." He turned toward Simon and Aiden. "Will one of you get in touch with Xanthe for me? I won't mind if you represent me as brave and an effective force for good in this matter..."

Aiden choked on a laugh, but he rallied to respond as he should. He couldn't help teasing his commander a little, however. "I will. I'll tell her you changed your mind about including her but made a clean kill. Because you care for her." He smirked but took two steps back. In case he needed to run.

Peter arched a brow. "Do you really want to have a conversation about misplaced attachments, Aiden? About ideal methods of courting?"

Aiden grinned and extended his palms. "No – dude, it's fine. I'm actually kind of jazzed for you."

Simon apparently decided further conciliation was needed between them because he moved to Aiden's side. "Of course we'll we do our best to make you look good in our report," he promised. Peter's glare faded. "You're all dismissed," he concluded... after which he turned and walked away.

As they exited the lobby, Simon snickered. "Peter and Xanthe? I can't picture it," he mused.

"Right?" Aiden responded. "I can't see either of them in any relationship, never mind with each other." But he became solemn as he considered the messiness of his own personal life, his drive to make Maya Wilkes his mate. He really was no one to judge. He thought instead on his imminent trip back to her. God. After so many years sneaking around and lying, he couldn't believe the interdiction against them was gone.

Simon flung an arm over his shoulders. "It'll be okay, little brother. You've all but got her."

Aiden forgot everything else – Cerro Lejano and Bartolomé, Peter and Xanthe, his brother's presence at his side – as hope surged within him. His impossible, implausible decade-long suit might be won at long last. How had he thought he could stay here a minute more?

"I can't wait. I have to get back."

Simon grinned and pushed his chest. "Go, then. Go get her."

Chapter Twenty

Whether or not she intended to stay in Lehland – and she was increasingly warm to the idea – Maya's only complaint continued to be her lack of understanding over why she was there at all. In quiet hours, she still fought for the placid ignorance required to maintain her contentment.

She likened herself to a pinball rolling around in her own life, with no edges to catch on the surface under her, her progression frictionless and fleeting and managed by some unseen player arbitrarily flipping her along. She had to worry where the final sinkhole was, how this game would end.

She didn't complain, though, and she tried to live in the moment, an endeavor at which she mostly succeeded. Unlike her time in New York – where she'd experienced the exact same variety of frustration except a lot more profoundly – she really did look forward to each day here. And anyway, her former attempts to mold the life she'd wanted at one time? Well, she told herself she needed to give all that up. The abiding peace she received in exchange for her surrender to unpredictability made this option the most sensible one. She hid her concerns when she had them and she pretended the future didn't matter.

Everyone in the area now called her "Doc" – not Mrs. Evans, not even Maya – and the identifier helped her feel even more distanced from the confusion within her. Which helped. She also continued to indulge enthusiastically in her leisure pursuits, in the pleasure of small things whose purpose was personal gratification instead of self-improvement. Her most recent preoccupation, baking, surprised her since she wouldn't have thought she could become absorbed in such a diversion. Evidenced by the fact that she never had. But the effort proved both a catharsis and a comfort, though; and it was another tie to childhood, too, since her sister was a pastry chef with her own café. Maya wished she could present Sylvia with a sample of her efforts and vowed one day she would.

Mostly, though, Maya enjoyed reacquainting herself with a version of life she'd long forgotten, in re-forming the definition of herself she'd recently adhered to as wife, medical student, rich society girl. Fugitive. In a sense, she was relieved she could accomplish this with butter, sugar and flour, meaning she didn't have to take up cliff diving or go off to become a space colonist or something.

A mournfulness, like a parasitic hole in her center, still nagged from time to time, although even this component of her existence had normalized. Anymore, it was just a faint sadness underneath her days, one more loss she'd accustomed herself to.

As she reviewed the previous week's cases on her front porch one Saturday morning, she froze at the sound of two women in conversation, unseen but approaching from behind the house. Maya held her breath… because one of them sounded an awful lot like her friend, Kate.

"Oooo, Amelia, thank you again, so much, for inviting me! I've been wanting to visit for the longest time."

Blood thudded in Maya's head, muting the women's voices and consequently her ability to verify her suspicion. She stood and faced the direction she thought her friend to be… and watched Kate and Amelia materialize around the corner of her house, Kate waving excitedly. Maya dropped her files onto the deck and ran down the steps.

"Kate Blake, you rotten, worthless friend! Where have you *been*?!" she called, her voice breaking. She reached for Kate and pulled her into a rough hug, both of them hiccupping through laughter and sobs.

Kate wiped her eyes. "Oh, I've been following your drama from afar, don't you worry," she assured her. "If I could have come a second sooner, I would have." She inclined her head toward Amelia. "But Ms. Hadley has been providing me with secret updates."

Maya searched the two of them warily. "Y'all have been talking behind my back?"

Amelia winced but defended herself. "There were no secrets! I was told to be careful, especially while you settled in. But I had Kate's cell number and a little background on you two. I was just waiting for the right time to have her over."

"Fear not, Wilkes. Your time of trial is almost at an end," Kate proclaimed, crooking an elbow around Maya's. "In the meantime, I've come to sort you out." The three of them walked to the back door of Amelia's house while Maya silently attempted to guess at Kate's intentions. Her time of trial?

"I have fresh coffee on, and I made pound cake," Amelia announced. "After we've refreshed ourselves, I propose we can tomatoes and steam a few batches of green beans for the freezer." She beamed at Kate. "Maya tells me you know your way around a stove."

"Ah it all becomes clear," Maya intoned, throwing Amelia an accusatory glance before informing Kate, "You've been drafted as a kitchen slave like the rest of us." She gestured at Amelia with her chin. "Amelia has a one-track mind and manipulates everyone she meets into helping with food preservation. Apparently she recruits from the coast now. Don't be fooled! She'll get hours of work out of us! For the low price of coffee and a slice of cake!"

Amelia sniffed. "I have other kitchen slaves. This one knows what she's doing. This one can gossip and make the work go fast. Baxter would glare at us and say nothing and ruin the mood.

Dorsel hasn't bathed in... I don't really know how long... and Norma and Betty Sue? The mere idea of getting picked apart by those two... well, it exhausts me. We'd beg to die before we peeled our first Roma." She smiled primly Maya's way. "So, you're welcome."

"I don't mind," Kate interjected. "It'll be a fun way to catch up. I'll also demand canned tomatoes in payment, which my family will love." She flicked Maya's arm with her forefinger. "And you've been quarantined long enough. I want my girlfriend back, even if it means forced labor." Her whole demeanor brightened as she bubbled forth with, "Just a few more days 'til freedom!" Amelia shot her an ominous look... after which Kate appeared to regret her outburst. "I mean, you're settling in so well here so you'll probably want to stay..."

Maya waited several long seconds for enlightenment, which neither of her companions provided. "What are you talking about, Blake?"

Kate nabbed coffee cups for each of them from a cupboard while Amelia started plating the cake. "You'll see," Kate said smugly.

Maya sighed and gazed out the window toward the green sea, the forest that stretched limitlessly eastward. She nursed a sudden compulsion to walk into it, torn between the desire to stay here and catch up with her friend, and annoyance over what Kate had just revealed: that she was among the nearly comprehensive group of people who knew more about her circumstances than she did. More than anyone, Kate should be on her side.

Maya grimaced. If she wanted to, she could trot into those dark woods and become very difficult to find. She would exit somewhere inconspicuous, choose a new identity and never but never again suffer through a life filled with deception. The prospect left her with a shallow sense of vindication.

Amelia set a plate in front of her and rested a hand on her shoulder, saying kindly, "Don't listen to her, Maya. She's not part of any conspiracy against you." Her glance at Kate came off as a sharp reprimand. "And you were told not to meddle, missy."

Some of Maya's anger dissipated. Maybe Kate wasn't among those scheming to keep her contained and stupid. Still, a demonstration of allegiance would not be amiss. And if Kate knew something? Well, of all the people on the planet who might have a soft spot she could play on...

"Who told you not to meddle?" Maya challenged, gripping Kate's wrist in case she tried to wriggle away.

Kate eyed Maya's hold on her arm. "Uh oh," she muttered. Amelia stamped one of her feet. "Listen up, you two! This is *not* what we should be talking about and I *won't* have this conversation in my kitchen!"

Maya cast her a brittle smile and offered sweetly, "We can have it outside then. Or at my house if you want." Turning to Kate, she begged, "Girlfriend, you gotta give me something. I can't spend the rest of my life worrying I got a secret lobotomy somewhere..."

"Stop it! Or I'm calling Baxter!" Amelia threatened, and Kate wrested herself from Maya and clutched Amelia's wrist. "Hold on a sec. This can be okay – just listen to me, both of you." Amelia's scowl faded, but not much.

"Maya," Kate began, "I don't know a lot, but I do know you're being protected by people who love you, and that you'll be one hundred percent in the know very soon." She peeked at Amelia – who was shaking her head slowly at her – and ventured, "Also, there's someone in particular looking out for you, and he'll be here in a few days."

Amelia sagged into one of the kitchen chairs, cocked her elbows on the table and covered her face with her hands. "You two are going to get me in so much trouble."

Kate patted her. "I don't think so, Amelia. It'll only be two more days, three at most, and then he'll be here... We're not saying much, just a little. Just to be kind."

Maya gazed from one woman to the next as too much silence filled the next several seconds. "You realize neither of you are making sense, right? You haven't told me anything other than there's 'something' going on I don't know about, and hello, that's not news." She frowned at Kate. "You *could* clue me in on this 'he' who's on his way. Who is it? How do I know him?"

Amelia brought her head up from her hands and addressed Kate. "That's it. Now I *have* to call Baxter."

"No, you don't!" Kate insisted. To Maya, she said, "An old friend. Someone you met in Griffins Bay but haven't seen lately. You'll recognize him right away... and... and you'll be very happy." She smiled at Amelia as if pleased with herself. "There. See? Now everyone feels better."

"I really don't," Amelia replied darkly.

"I don't, either," Maya added, although that wasn't true. Kate, she knew, wanted the best for her, so if she had confidence in her near future, so would Maya.

"Well I do," Kate maintained. "And Amelia's right: we need to talk about something else. We have a ton of other catching up to do, so let's get to it."

Maya capitulated. "Fine. Whatever." She reached for her coffee cup. A few more days of waiting to know more? She'd already dismissed self-direction as a fantasy, so this conversation didn't matter. "But if three more days go by and nothing's changed, you're both in for it," she warned. She rubbed her eyes and sighed. "Okay, Blake – catch me up. What's going on with our peeps?"

The rest of the afternoon passed in a haze of semi-euphoria for Maya. The canning almost took care of itself – as Amelia had guessed, their conversation did make the work go quickly – and Kate's physical presence combined with her updates on everyone they both knew killed any lingering misgivings Maya had, at least temporarily. Amelia surprised Maya with her active participation in their talk; she apparently knew the people Kate discussed, although Maya couldn't figure out how. But that meant everyone was included, which added to the overall easiness of the afternoon.

The news Kate shared was good. John and Cara were busy with Everett, John's thriving practice, and Cara's work at the library.

Jeremy and Alicia were on a trip to the Greek Isles – Kate displayed pictures from her phone – and Maya pretended she didn't care that her parents were sending her friend happy pictures of their life while their own daughter flailed around alone and unloved. Kate read Maya's sentiments accurately because she said, "They've been duped every bit as much as you have, Maya. They think everything is just fine." Then before Maya could delve, Kate continued with news of Maya's sisters.

Solange and Luke each juggled jobs and their two kids in Boston, professing to be "crazy happy" despite their overloaded days. "They even got a puppy," Kate revealed with a laugh. "Solange told me the kids have been begging, and she and Luke finally caved, saying one more dependent didn't matter at this point."

Sylvia and Simon were pregnant with baby number three and, according to Kate, acted like they were the only two people on the planet ever to have conceived. Maya sensed an edge of resentment beneath this last revelation, one she should perhaps leave alone but couldn't, not when she didn't know when she'd next see or talk with Kate again.

"Kate, honey, what do I hear in all that? Are you and Sylvia fighting?"

Kate studied her lap. "No. I'm jealous," she confessed, then peeked at Maya before looking down to pick at her cuticles. "We want another one, but between Gabe being gone for various… er, obligations… and… I don't know, it just hasn't happened."

Amelia who as far as Maya knew was childless, responded first. "That's unusual for a couple like you, isn't it?"

"It is," Kate confirmed, "but we kind of chose to wait, too, while everything with Gabe's work and family stabilized. Which means when people announce they're expecting these days, I get to feel like a schmuck and wish it was us instead."

"You two are speaking in code again," Maya reminded them, then checked her phone. "And I'm going to scoot over to the clinic to meet my one patient today about his sinuses." She turned to Kate. "Are you staying with me tonight?"

Kate shook her head. "Nope. Amelia wants me under watch here, and no, I'm not going to explain that. Maybe you could stay here instead?"

Maya made an instant decision. "Yes. I'll bring my pj's and we'll have a slumber party." Amelia ladled fresh tomato sauce into a separate pot. "I'll throw on some spaghetti sauce." Maya stood to leave, washed her hands and made for the door. "Back in a couple of hours, girls."

Later that night, after the three of them had killed a bottle and a half of wine, eaten spaghetti like marathon runners before a race, and laughed until they clutched their sides in agony, Maya snuggled under the down comforter in one of the second-floor guest bedrooms. Full and drowsy, she was nearly asleep when she heard a series of dull thuds, as if someone pounded on a distant wall; then several muted groans, originating from either the main floor or lower. Hurried footsteps sounded across the first level then down the cellar stairs... and then the pounding and groans stopped.

Maya awoke instantly, but she remained in her bed and listened. She checked the clock on her nightstand. After ten minutes, whoever was creeping around below made their way quietly up the stairs and stopped outside her bedroom. Maya turned to her side away from the door, which Amelia cracked open to whisper, "Maya?" Maya kept her breaths deep and slow and did not respond. Amelia closed the door and tiptoed away. Maya waited a half-hour longer before slipping out of bed.

Amelia's house was more than a century old, meaning it featured the innumerable and unpredictable creaks of age. Maya kept near the walls for the most stable, least used floor boards for each step. She still made noise, although it must have sounded natural enough since she succeeded in her quest to reach the kitchen without anyone checking on her. At the sink, she paused to make sure she was alone. This would be her last chance to lie, to tell Amelia or Kate, should they appear, she'd awoken for a glass of water.

The stairwell leading down to the basement yawned with sinister silence, exhibiting the exact same gloom that was the precursor to someone being butchered in every horror film Maya had ever seen. Yet here she was, making the same fateful choice as all those other idiot heroines, who left light and escape routes to venture into the dark unknown. She held her breath as she crept down the steps.

Her eyes accustomed themselves thanks to a glow of moonlight filtering through transoms along the south wall. At least she could perceive the dark shape of the boiler and a few odd pieces of furniture well enough to avoid running into them. She heard shuffling and a sigh out of a room to her left and she inched toward it to investigate. On a small table outside the entrance sat an old-school baby monitor, which Maya gingerly picked up. She had no idea how those things worked… so she set it down. The table it was on was small and light, however, and the device was attached to an outlet by a long extension cord. Maya picked up the table carefully and moved it – along with the baby monitor – as far in the opposite direction as she could.

She returned to the doorway, stopping to peer in. She could see precisely nothing. She felt along the wall for a light switch and flipped it on. Florescent overheads flooded the room, revealing a cell like a lion's cage at an old-time zoo. The man locked within it rolled over on his cot, blinked at her and bolted upright, immediately straining to vocalize through his thick gag.

"Oh my God. Stu. What are you doing here?"

Stu's jailor was either new to the job or poorly trained in the ways of captivity. The cell keys hung on a peg in plain sight to the right of the doorframe – out of reach from the cage, but still.

Anyone wandering by – and the place wasn't *that* tucked away – could have sprung him. Maya stayed by the door and left the keys where they were despite Stuart's pleading looks and muffled attempts at speech.

He was bound by a rope hobble connecting his ankles, one that would allow him to take short steps but nothing more. Likewise, his hands, which were secured at the wrists in front of his body. Maya assumed he could brush his teeth in the small sink he had, and was able to take care of other personal needs. The gag and bindings were ingenious enough to deny Stu the ability to free himself, she saw, but at least he was mobile. Not so he could reach outside the bars and grab anyone, Maya was relieved to note… although she still kept back. She found the sight of him bound gratifying, which was perhaps spiteful. But she would assume guilt before innocence in this situation, believing Stu must have somehow warranted this treatment.

She suffered a moment of regret as she withstood Stu's ongoing, mute supplications for help… but whatever she might do next, she recognized the opportunity that had just presented itself. She could ascertain a few things with her former husband in a situation where she had control of him, without worry for her own safety.

"This is quite a reversal of roles, here, persecution-wise," she remarked. "Yes, I see the keys, Stu. And I might unlock you. But I might not. We need to chat first." Maya spoke in a low voice, but her gaze skitterered to the space behind her, and she stilled while she listened for activity above. Hearing nothing, she faced Stu again. "If we're discovered, we'll both be in for it," she warned. "So you'd better be quiet."

She wasn't sure how effectively Stu would be able to communicate through his gag, but there was no way she was going to remove it. She couldn't risk getting close to him, for one, even if she made him sit with his back to the bars. Mostly, though, she really, really didn't trust him. If yelling at the top of his lungs would free him, he'd sacrifice her in an instant… and she had no idea what the people who'd shackled him would do to her. Stu was a strong guy, and Amelia hadn't apprehended him by herself.

She also made the decision to leave him imprisoned after their talk. She would sneak back upstairs to her bed and pretend she had no knowledge of what Amelia hid in her dungeon until she could better figure out what was going on. She didn't want Stu to know this or he wouldn't talk. But. The less tampered-with he appeared after she left him, the better.

"I can't take your gag out, Stu. Not until I can trust you." Stu looked ridiculously sad in response, and she felt guilty. Then she remembered all the gaslighting he'd subjected her to over the years. She focused on the information she wanted.

She began with her easiest question first. "How long have you been here?"

He held up four fingers.

"Four days?" He shook his head. "Four *weeks*?" she asked incredulously. A slow nod. Well. That explained the ghostly thuds and moans she'd been hearing. The knowledge put Amelia's nervous explanations of local hauntings in a new light, the little sneak.

"Why did you come here?" She had no idea how he'd succeed in answering this one through his gag. But he was a smart guy, so she laid her inquiry out there and hoped he'd deal.

He stared steadily in her eyes – she felt he was trying to establish the fact that he planned to be honest with her – and he pointed at her.

"You came for me?" He nodded. "Why? To bring me to your father?" A head shake. "To warn me?" she pressed. Stu winced, kept eye contact with her, and tilted one hand palm down while tilting it back and forth. "So, sort of," she guessed. She considered him a few more moments before venturing, "You wanted to talk me into coming home." He closed his eyes briefly, as if in relief. He nodded. She looked away.

"I was there the night of the party, you know." He nodded again, and even muffled she understood him. "I know, Maya. I'm sorry."

His apology felt sincere, enough that she had to swallow tears. But she swallowed them, wanted to make sure he fully grasped the consequences of his trysts, so she persisted. "I saw you and Annette go into your dad's office together. And I went in after you left. I saw the desk, the impression on the surface... I know exactly what happened. And I'm sure that wasn't the first time. That Annette wasn't the first woman you seduced."

"Ah-oh," he managed to say. *I know*. His kept his eyes intent on her face. He made no evasions, offered no hollow excuses... and she vaguely thought about how this was the most straightforward Stu had been with her since they'd married. She grudgingly respected him for it. She still wanted more information, though.

"What set your dad off that night? Do you know what he put me through? Why I ran?"

"Eh," he said. *Yes*. Then he engaged in a series of charades. He outlined a flat rectangle in front of him, hip height. "The desk," she guessed, and he nodded. He indicated a back corner, then held his palms facing each other, one at the upper limit of his restraint, one at the lower. He placed the unseen object at the back corner of the desk. Maya thought back to what she could remember of Thad's desk that evening, recalling the mussed pile of papers from the corner Stu indicated on his imaginary platform. "The files," she surmised. Stu nodded again.

He pretended to remove an item from the pile, then indicated between the fake item and his own bonds. He circled one wrist then the other with the opposite hands – suggesting manacles, she thought – then moved his wrists close together, and fanned his hands away.

Maya caught on completely then. "Handcuffs," she guessed, and Stu nodded and smiled at her proudly. "Thad was engaged in something illegal and that pile contained evidence he thought I saw. He could be put in jail if caught."

Stu closed his eyes and nodded slowly. "Eh." *Yes.*

"Stu, I didn't see anything. I didn't look through his things."

"Ah-oh, 'ahy-ah." *I know, Maya.*

"Does Thad know you came for me? Did he send you?" she asked. Stu shook his head angrily. "Ah-ayhd. Uh-ee." *I came. Just me.*

Her legs felt like they might give out, so she slid along the wall behind her until she was seated on the floor. She rested the back of her head against the wall, cocked her knees, and considered Stu as she processed what he'd just told her.

She placed a hand against her mouth to quell the hysterical laughter that threatened. Her crazy stint as a fugitive in New York was based on a mistake? Thad was paranoid, so she got to be chased after by assassins, it seemed. The fallout of her decisions that night astounded her. If she'd stayed in instead of cabbing it to the penthouse to surprise Stu. If she'd arrived even a few minutes later and missed the floor show he and Annette had put on. If she hadn't gone into Thad's office, or if Thad hadn't decided to enter just when he did... God. It was like the universe had conspired against her.

Once her hysteria passed, a familiar grief welled in its place, the one she'd fought in the city when she couldn't understand why she was in hiding; the one she wrestled with here because she'd lost something precious and she didn't know how to find it, or even what it was. She felt like she was being forced to drive onto a highway while wearing a blindfold.

Her decisions, her very being, started to feel unreal to her, as if her consciousness floated separate from her and well away from any definition of normal she understood. She felt truly careless of herself for the first time possibly ever. Because no matter what she chose to do, no matter how many times she rallied herself into self-direction, she failed to attain it. She could no longer understand her compulsion to try… and she thought, maybe, this time she wouldn't.

A tiny sense of outrage brought her back to herself, however, at least enough to convince her she wouldn't give up. Not because she didn't want to – she did – but because she couldn't. She'd been in this situation too many times over the years, had consistently fought against currents carrying her places she didn't care to go even when she was exhausted. Her response this time would be no different.

As awareness of her surroundings reasserted itself, she realized Stu had patiently stood by, had waited silently while she came to terms with all he'd told her. He stood tall and still, gripping the bars between them as if to hold them up, and as if in solidarity with her.

He was on her side.

In fact, despite his compromised state and her power to change it, he hadn't made a sound in the past few minutes, hadn't clamored once for freedom while she collected herself. He'd thought of her instead of his own more perilous and certainly more immediate needs. *I can trust him*, she realized.

She'd changed her mind about something else since entering this room, too: she wanted to help him. In fact, she would. Just not until she knew the ramifications, for herself as well as him. She started to hatch a getaway plan… but she would need to perform some reconnaissance before she could execute it.

"I can't free you tonight because I don't know why you're being held, and I don't know how many townspeople are in on keeping you here. Or why I'm here, for that matter. And I don't want to run before I know we can get away." Stu tapped on the bar to get her attention, then held up four fingers on one hand, two on the other.

"Six people took you?" she surmised, and he nodded. At least she was good at reading his cues.

"I'm going to figure a way out of this for both of us," she promised. She rose to her feet. "I'll try to visit you again, but even if I can't, I'll come back for you soon." He maintained his composure, and compassion pushed her forward to where he stood. She covered his hands gripping the bars with her own. "Thank you for talking with me, Stu. I know you did the best you could." She dropped her gaze. "I'm sorry I wasn't a better wife."

He placed his forehead against bar above her face. "Oh. Ih ah-d oo, 'aya." *No, it wasn't you, Maya.* "Eye- ahd." *My fault.* She squeezed his hands once and backed away.

She felt better, more sure; and Stu looked calmer, too. "Be careful, okay? I *will* get you out of here," she vowed, feeling closer to him than she had in a long time. Then she turned out the lights, put the table with the baby monitor in its former spot, and left.

Her trek upstairs went more easily than her descent had. She filled a glass with water from the tap at the kitchen sink and drank it while contemplating the moon-bleached vista out the window. The world's flatness, its whitish-blue planes and shadows perfectly reflected her own perspective, she thought, with nothing colored in, nothing as dimensional as it should be. She would take steps, starting tomorrow, to remedy that situation.

She no longer took extraordinary care to be quiet; if anyone heard her, she would say she'd come down for a drink. She set a cup in the sink and padded back upstairs to bed. She felt in control for the first time in months, a grim sense of purpose as she settled herself under her covers. Tomorrow, she would identify who was watching her, and make a get-away plan when they weren't looking.

Chapter Twenty-One

Thad found his firing a little ironic, seeing as how the verbal insensitivity attributed to him – and the foundation on which his dismissal was based – never happened.

He was told not to engage with those people at all, however, so his company's complaint against him wasn't without justification. But he'd thought he'd been responding politely to his questioner, who'd asked what needed fixing to improve the health care system. He'd delivered the practiced company message about HWP's deep concerns for the uninsured and how hard everyone was working to cover everyone they possibly could. He'd followed it up with a comment about how his company fought alongside all American citizens, and that's what it would take: working together with everyone contributing, everyone pulling on the same team.

His remarks had been twisted into something else, but the reporter's version quickly became reality in the court of public opinion. She'd represented Thad as having insisted people needed to pay more… and some group or another had now been protesting outside corporate headquarters ever since as a consequence. Sadly, they believed his dismissal would result in the changes they wanted. *Wasted hopefulness, my friends*, he thought as he drove past them on his way out. He knew the woman likely to replace him, and she wouldn't be changing a thing.

It had been over in minutes, his tribunal seated and waiting for him as he entered the conference room. The move was mostly a public relations necessity, they explained. His courageous leadership would be remembered, his service deeply appreciated, blah-blah-blah. Here's a copy of the announcement going out later; here are the terms of separation and severance, please sign at the bottom. Handshakes all around and aren't we all paragons of civility. Bye-bye, Hell Well.

Despite his anticipation of the event, he still felt slighted. He truly didn't mind being divested of the job's responsibility, especially the disingenuous face he'd put on to carry his position forward. But he did mind feeling expendable. The emotional fallout from this impression had proved more difficult to accommodate.

His son should have been around to talk with, but Thad had been unable to reach him despite multiple attempts. Eventually, Stu's lack of communication supplanted Thad's focus on losing his job.

After four days of no contact, Thad instructed his driver to bring him to Stu's office, where he learned his son hadn't reported in for a worrisome length of time.

No one had heard from him. He hadn't called any of his colleagues, had just disappeared. Thad's inquiry at Stu's brownstone yielded the same news; possibly several week's worth of mail was piled up in the front hall no one had been in residence "in ages" according to the housekeeper.

"I assumed he was traveling or at one of your other residences, Mr. Blake," she explained.

Thad became genuinely alarmed. A barrage of untenable possibilities streamed through his thoughts, everything from Stu teaming up with Maya as part of an SEC investigation, to Stu's abduction by people hoping to ransom him. Thad consoled himself with the fact that he hadn't heard from either the SEC or any kidnappers, so perhaps Stu's disappearance was not so sinister. But then, why hadn't his son returned any of his calls? He checked their joint accounts, which showed no activity, meaning he had no idea where to begin looking. He called his security team...

...and discovered Harlowe was no longer with him. After inquiring among his staff, Thad learned almost nothing, other than that he'd been "reassigned" by the security services company he technically worked for, and any questions Thad had for him were to go through his employer. The news settled over Thad like a heavy tarp to an already dense blanket of doom. He wanted badly to run.

He resolved to keep his focus on finding his son... although perhaps he could double up on his urges and leave town under that very pretext. He hired an independent investigator to help him find a starting point.

Two days later, he had a lead: Stu had apparently left with three friends on a trip south, one he hadn't put down in his calendar and hadn't returned from, even though his companions had come back. An interview with each of them produced more questions than answers; the men vaguely, *kind of* recalled Stu being with them, although none were sure. They'd become lost in the woods, possibly somewhere in Virginia? The Carolinas? They'd stopped at a convenience store in some backwater village no one recalled the name of... and had remembered very little from that point on. There was a river close by – they'd each waxed oddly poetic on that issue. Park rangers rescued them a few days later. None in the trio could accurately characterize the timeline of their misadventure.

"When you returned from your hike, didn't any of you conduct a head count, maybe wonder if Stu was all right?" Thad's frustration made him condescending, but honestly, how could three grown men – three! – have so easily dismissed losing a fellow traveller? How could it be that not one of them questioned how little they knew of their excursion?

Thad decided to look into matters on his own... and if Stu was colluding with the authorities, Thad wouldn't be working through law enforcement to locate him. He told the rest of the world he was going to take a little driving tour along the coast, needed some time away to take stock of his life. He collected enough data to direct him to the general area from which Stu would have departed, packed a bag and cabbed it to a lot where he paid cash for a car, one he was uninspired to drive but was nondescript enough to avoid drawing attention.

Once out of the city, he pulled onto a side road and parked. He placed the handgun and magazines he'd brought along in the glove compartment, then reviewed his notes. Based on the ramblings of Stu's amnesiac co-travellers – and the snippets of news he'd caught on Maya's conjectured whereabouts – Thad had narrowed the location of his son's disappearance to a defined swath of the Mid-Atlantic. He suspected Stu had meant to track Maya down, and if that were the case, Thad would comb the area the two of them might be. He traced a rough circle in red ink on his map. The territory was sizeable enough to make his search a challenge, but he had time these days. He folded the map, stored it over his visor and restarted the car. He'd begin at the northwestern perimeter and work his way southeast.

The morning after her basement encounter with Stu, Maya struggled to appear normal over breakfast while Amelia floated subtle inquiries about what she may or may not have heard from the moaning tenant in the basement. Or rather, the questions would have been subtle had Maya been unaware of Amelia's little underground prison. As it was, all Maya could think about was the fact that Stu was bound and gagged about thirty feet from where she currently sat. And the fact that Amelia was the one keeping him there.

It was a Saturday, meaning Amelia had *not* risen at dawn to feed the hordes as she did during the week. Maya had slept well after her discovery but for too short a time, and she'd awoken enervated. She'd given up hope of adding to her rest when the first signs of dawn lightened the sky, descended to the kitchen at a barely acceptable hour, and made directly for the coffee maker. Kate appeared shortly thereafter, shuffling drowsily toward the table. "What are you doing up so crazy early?"

"Just anxious to start my day," Maya said, trying to sound nonchalant. Except she was restless and worried, so she made a pretense of looking for things in the cupboards to keep from having to sit still... and thereby avoided her longtime friend's scrutiny, which might very well uncover more than she could afford to share right now. Thankfully, Kate stayed oblivious. She slumped into a chair, propped her chin on her hand and yawned. "Another vacation day. I don't even care if that means canning a thousand pounds of tomatoes." Maya grabbed two mugs, then a carafe with coffee, poured herself a cup and set the rest on the table. She then rummaged through the fridge for a jar of Amelia's plum preserves. "Toast?" she asked. "If you have it with Amelia's jam, you'll be happy all day."

"Sign me up."

Amelia joined them then. Maya now saw her much differently than she had the previous day, but she worked to appear as if nothing had changed, hoping her pretense of ignorance could withstand breakfast with her.

Maya retrieved another mug from the counter and poured coffee for Amelia. "How did you sleep?"

"Poorly," Amelia replied, sounding bitter. She eyed Maya as she would a rat who snuck into her flour bin. "I became anxious over my houseguests, apparently." She drank deeply from her mug. "Did you both sleep?" Her inquiry came off too sharply in Maya's estimation.

"Like the dead!" Kate exclaimed. "No responsibilities hanging over me, no one needing me first thing in the morning – I completely let go and it was glorious."

Maya took her time buttering her toast so she wouldn't have to look Amelia in the eye, and she kept her tone light. "I slept great."

She took a bite of her bread. "I was thinking about taking a little hike today. Maybe in the woods or along the Bight. I feel like I've been sitting around too much, need the exercise."

Amelia dropped her butter knife. "But, er, I need your help here today. With Kate. And we might... well, there might be a special visitor coming, so you should stick around."

"Yeah? Who is it? Anyone I know?" Maya remained turned away, smiling smugly into her coffee.

Eventually, she peered over her shoulder to find Kate fidgeting. Amelia had removed her cell phone from the pocket of her robe. As neither of them answered her, Maya shrugged and returned to her toast at the counter. "Kate can come with me if she wants. I just need to check in at the clinic for a while, and then I can come back here and collect her."

"We'll both go with you!" Amelia exclaimed while texting on her phone. "To the clinic, I mean," she clarified. Kate and Amelia glanced at each other, then away.

Maya struggled not to laugh as she continued to press them, until a painful thought occurred to her: Kate might know about Stu's incarceration. So, while Amelia appeared to be the mastermind among them, Kate was not to be trusted, either. The idea brought the sting of tears to her sinuses. She retrieved a tissue from a box on top of the fridge and blew her nose to cover them. Her next words felt strained. "Why would you accompany me to the clinic? Unless one of you has a nursing degree I don't know about."

Amelia finished her text, returned the phone to her pocket and regarded Maya more calmly, her smile generous. Excellent. Maya would pay close attention to the people who showed up to tail her this morning and learn who was in on Amelia's containment scheme. Also, if her "visitor" was on his way to her – possibly today – she'd have to improvise an escape plan but quick.

Maya refilled her cup and faced them. "Ladies, I'm going home to shower, then to work. I'll wave on my way there in case you want to come with me and read twenty-year-old magazines in my lobby or whatever." Kate studied the kitchen table and made no comment. Amelia relaxed in her chair and waved her off. "We'll just wait here for you."

"See you later," Maya said with a tight smile. She left through the back door and headed to her house.

Chapter Twenty-Two

During his last moments outside the forest, Thad found he looked forward to the end he'd fought so hard to avoid. He checked the safety on his gun, then stood from behind his makeshift blind and strode in the direction of his patrollers as if he was unaware of them, as if he were out for an afternoon stroll. He carried the gun as he would a baby, one arm cradling the hand that clasped it.

He felt so light. His gaze flickered upwards.

He deemed it a perfect day – the expansive blue sky, the bright sun. Such an appropriate expression of life and freedom. He stumbled and caught himself, returning his attention to the uneven ground beneath his feet.

He'd found Stu, was currently walking away from where he'd been kept.

Thad's paranoia had guided him rightly this morning, providing him with the correct impression he might be headed into an ambush. Which was amusing when he compared this realization to the insular, phantom worries that had preoccupied him back in the city. His belief in Maya's treachery, in particular, had taken a hit this morning. Had his obsession had been misplaced? When Stu had argued Thad's circumstances were his own fault, had he been right?

Regardless, he regretted persecuting her. He imagined apologizing to her in person, understanding he might never have the chance, now.

Following his initial strategy session in his car before setting out, he'd begun by canvassing just south of the river, the Bight. He surmised – he wasn't sure why – Maya had stayed close to it when she escaped, and if she and his son were together, Stu would have used the same point of departure. As he trolled through nearby towns, he became convinced his son had taken the same route.

Still, his first few days were a bust... but then he'd encountered something odd: a road with a will of its own.

He'd parked on a shoulder in a rural area to review his map. It was dumb luck that landed him at this particular intersection, but repeated scans of his surroundings eventually made an impression on him. Straight ahead, devoid of any visual distinctions whatsoever, lay a throughway. He'd noticed it, then looked down at his map, and noticed it anew each time he raised his head.

It was as if it didn't want to be remembered, didn't wish to be travelled upon. He felt something akin to alarm each time he focused on it, and he wanted nothing so badly as to turn around and drive away, even as his instincts suggested Maya and Stu were likely ahead. He started his car, forced his misgivings aside, and drove forward.

Out of caution, he paused a mile from town, feeling he'd be too exposed on the long, open approach. Ahead lay a small cluster of buildings that looked to comprise a very modest commercial center. But he did not wish to be seen, did not care to alert anyone in the area who might take an interest in him. Or worse, identify him. He drove into a nearby grove of maples, covered his car with brush, then retrieved his backpack from the back seat and gun from the glove compartment. He trekked along a thin strand of pines edging the open farmland, the trees curving sparsely around much of the town. He kept to their shade until he reached the outskirts of the village and could cut behind a shack that seemed deserted. He hid behind a corner and watched for human activity, seeing none at first.

After several minutes, however, he saw Maya from afar, her features indistinct but her gait familiar to him. She walked from the only residence of any significance – a big American foursquare situated amid a series of vegetable gardens and a few outbuildings – toward a cottage roughly in Thad's direction. She progressed with the loose, rumpled affect of someone who'd recently been asleep, and she carried a bundle of clothing under her arm, a cup of coffee in her other hand. She disappeared into the cottage, where he saw a light go on. Twenty minutes later, she exited and headed the way she'd come, this time skirting the big house toward one of the outbuildings. Thad put a pair of binoculars to his eyes and read the sign hanging above the door. "Clinic," it said, and it bore an etching of a stethoscope. Interesting. He made his way stealthily to the cabin Maya had just vacated.

The door was unlocked... and the items strewn about the place suggested long-term habitation. A laptop charged on the kitchen counter next to a scarf Thad recognized as one he'd seen Maya wear in the city. Jackets of different weights hung on a board with hooks mounted by the door. The fridge was stocked. He opened a drawer in the kitchen and spied Maya's old keychain, the one carrying a miniature volleyball bearing the Penn State logo on it.

Thad checked the bedroom, noting the closet and dresser were stocked with clothing in Maya's size, then went through the rest of the place, even checking the attic and cellar.

He saw no sign of Stu, none of his things around to indicate he'd stayed if he'd come here. So. Maya's little home was hers alone, and if Stu had paid her a visit, he hadn't left evidence of himself.

Frustration flared. Maybe his son hadn't travelled here after all, and maybe Thad had made this pilgrimage in vain. But where else would Stu be? After expressing such disapproval back at the penthouse, truly challenging Thad for the first time in his life – and then his threatening insistence that Thad leave Maya alone – would

Stu have decided to let the matter drop? Gone on an impromptu golf trip or taken a snorkeling tour without telling anyone?

No. No, he wouldn't have. He'd been upset enough over Thad's treatment of Maya to castigate him. Thad again became certain Stu had left to search for her, although whether he'd found her was another matter. Thad needed to poke around a little more to find out.

He couldn't help but think of the descriptions Stu's last known companions had provided, of the sleepy little town by a river, of the fields and the vast forest to the east. It fit this place exactly.

Thad heard the crunch of footfalls on the gravel road outside the house. The sound was faint, so he didn't worry someone was just outside the door and about to charge through. But the lack of other noise underscored how small this place really was, how anything not an edifice or a tree would attract notice. He would not be able to blend in or appear inconspicuous here... and he wasn't ready to announce himself, certainly not while trespassing in Maya's home. He flattened himself against one of the walls to avoid being seen through the windows. He peeked through one of the panes, quickly locating the source of the gravel crunching.

Huh.

Apparently, he wasn't the only one keeping an eye on Maya this morning, a conclusion he drew after watching a man in heavy work boots tromp along the road from the direction of the river. He was dripping wet, which was odd. He also appeared to be still getting dressed, buttoning his shirt as he made his way to the front of Maya's clinic. He seemed put out, as if he was on a nuisance errand. He shook his hair out before stationing himself to the side of the clinic door, feet wide, arms crossed. He looked toward the big house and lifted his chin once; then stared to his left and made the same gesture.

Through his binoculars, Thad studied where the man had nodded, uncovering the presence of two additional sentries, one behind a shed and one stationed at a corner of the main house. Were they officers?

Thad experienced several seconds of giddiness, leaning over and bracing his hands on his knees to stifle the impetus to laugh. The men's interest in Maya could not be related to his presence, because they didn't know he was here, and if they could track her to this godforsaken outpost, they surely could have located Thad in all his prominence in New York. Perhaps Maya had embroiled herself in her own illegalities, and hence his hysteria. God. The irony.

But when he considered the men further, he lost his good humor. He realized they were not professionals – they wore no protective gear, carried no weapons, and they were too visible. One hung out on her front stoop, for crying out loud, was the most noticeable thing in Lehland, and she would see him immediately when she exited the place. Just as he had this thought, she appeared at the window, smiled, and waved at her surly attendant.

Meaning she'd probably acquired a contingent of people looking out for her, loose bodyguard types, perhaps... which led Thad directly back to his conspiracy theories. What if they were protecting her from him? What if she'd already helped the SEC build a case, had agreed to testify, and this was her hideout until his trial? That option seemed likely, because no sane person with means would choose to live here.

Here he was, though, traveling on a whim and handcuff-free. If there were charges to be made against him and someone had a strong enough case to warrant Maya's dispatch to this social and geographic oblivion... well, he wouldn't have been able to waltz out of New York as he had. He would certainly have seen something pop up on his phone, maybe heard from Nate. He checked his texts, noting his last contact with his cousin had been two days ago – a photo Nate had sent of him and a mutual acquaintance enjoying a cigar in Manhattan, both of them relaxed, smiling. Tan.

He couldn't piece together a scenario where all the components he saw made sense.

He took up his binoculars again and inspected everything he could from his limited vantage point. The town had woken up a little, with a trickle of residents entering and leaving the general store. A couple had arrived to pull weeds in one of the many garden beds outside the foursquare, and a rusty pick-up made its way down main street, eventually parking in front of what looked to be the local saloon. Thad returned his attention to the extensive tree line fronting the forest to the east. He adjusted the focus on his binoculars to increase his field of vision and searched the edge of the woods from left to right.

Still he almost missed it, dismissing the slight movement he saw as a deer, or possibly a gust of wind.

Upon closer review, however, he identified a figure in the trees. A more thorough scan revealed several more people positioning themselves for... something. Thad couldn't guess. He counted five operatives, all in charcoal body armor, all carrying weapons. They reminded him of news images he'd seen following the apprehension of one of his Wall Street acquaintances several years ago, a man he'd chatted with at various charity and professional functions but hadn't known well. This man had also tried his hand at alternative revenue enhancement for a publicly traded fund. The SEC had caught him; and because he'd threatened the lives of two people in his inner circle – not unlike Thad had with his colleague from the club and with Maya – he'd been deemed a broader security risk. The FBI had executed his actual arrest, using paramilitary officers who'd set up a perimeter to force the man's surrender at gunpoint. Thad didn't appreciate all the similarities.

The team he observed wouldn't be here for him, though. Would they?

Speculations, then rationalizations, raced wildly through his head but only got a few seconds of playtime before he heard the grind of a utility vehicle passing by. He swiveled his binoculars back to main street, refocused, and instantly became horrified: a tow truck pulled the car he'd hidden in the copse of maples. His mind filtered through the implications. He'd left no identification behind, and the car wasn't registered to him… he fingered the car key in his pants pocket.

The truck stopped in front of the church, at which point the driver and a passenger exited the cab and met at the back end where Thad's car was attached. The passenger handed the driver a wad of bills, then pointed to a nearby alley. The driver re-entered the cab of the truck, pulled the car into the alley and began to unhook it. Meanwhile, the passenger jogged to the clinic and conversed with Maya's porch-squatting friend, who signaled to his two cohorts, after which everyone made for the backside of the foursquare. Two women – Thad recognized one of them as Maya's friend from the wedding, Kate Blake – came from inside the house and joined the conversation.

A brief, animated exchange ensued, one punctuated by lots of gesturing toward the clinic, the car, and the forest to the east. The entire contingent moved quickly toward the trees, disappearing into the area where Thad had seen the black-clad security team.

He set his binoculars down on a side table, then packed them. If anyone here would know where Stu was, it would be Maya, and she was at present unattended. Thad strode out of the cottage toward the clinic, this time without care for whether he was seen. A bell at the front door announced his entrance.

He found Maya at a desk near the back, and her pleasant greeting died on her lips when he appeared. "Oh my God. Thad. What are you…"

He showed his palms, hopefully creating the impression of harmlessness. "I didn't come for you. Stu's gone missing, and I'm worried about him. Is he here?"

Maya hesitated, appearing to deliberate her response… and hope surged in Thad's chest. She knew something. "Please, Maya," he implored. "I have to find my son. Is he all right?" He watched a series of conflicting emotions play across her face, including anger – perhaps at him – and uncertainty, then a kind of hopelessness. But he was too impatient to show compassion. He doubted they had time for the conversation they were having much less anything else. "Maya," he insisted. "You were being watched and they'll be back."

"I know," she clipped. "I counted three a little bit ago."

"They're gone," Thad assured her. "But they found my car and towed it over by the church. Everyone went east, into the trees. I don't know why or for how long."

Maya stood, and after a second of indecision made for the front of the clinic. "Come with me," she said over her shoulder. "Hurry."

She paused near the back door of the big house, listened, and asked, "Did you see anyone leave this place? Two women, maybe?"

"Yes! One was your friend, Kate Blake. They went into the forest with the others."

Maya appeared vindictively pleased. "Good." She turned the knob and entered.

He followed her to a stairwell leading to a basement. Maya paused again, not quite looking at him. "I just discovered Stu here last night, and I have no idea why they took him, or who did it." She pinned him with a hard stare. "I had nothing to do with this, Thad. I pretended stupidity this morning so I could come up with a plan to free him." She waved a hand in the air down Thad's frame, head to feet. "And then you showed up."

"Maya, it's fine. Just get me to him." She opened her mouth to speak, seemed to think better of it, and turned to continue down the steps. Thad hurried after her.

He nearly toppled from relief at the sight of his son alive and whole, but he felt the smile fade from his face as he recognized hostility in Stu's own regard. Stu stood, gripping the bars at the front of his cell... and glared at Thad while Maya retrieved a set of keys off the wall by the light switch. She opened the cell door, removed Stu's gag, then retrieved an oblong piece of fabric from her pocket, from which she unwrapped a scalpel. She began the tedious task of cutting the rope manacles binding Stu's hands while Stu addressed him. "You came looking for me, not Maya, right?"

...and Thad understood immediately what his son wanted from him: affirmation he was not here to hurt Maya.

Thad hadn't thought of the option on his way from the clinic, but he thought of it now, thought of the gun he'd tucked in the back waistband of his pants. The idea of removing Maya as a potential tool for his prosecution team still appealed, although the passion behind such impetus was gone. He recognized his approach to her as the coping mechanism it was, how and why he'd assigned her the culpability he had. But his habit of blame – and the necessary diversion it had provided – still felt hard-wired. Reflex or not, he fantasized about being right and ultimately avoiding his looming disaster. He could still emerge from this unscathed.

He did want her gone, just in case.

That impulse was secondary at the moment, however... and it wasn't one he was willing to act on, anyway. Would he walk away if the hit man he'd hired showed up right now? Turn a blind eye and let her be killed? He didn't know. Thad found a hunting knife among his things and began cutting Stu's ankle restraints, with Stu watching him critically all the while. As if Thad had deliberated his murderous musings aloud.

His son's superior vantage point underscored Thad's awareness of a permanent power shift between them, one that called into question a reality Thad had considered immutable – a father-son dynamic he'd taken for granted, and the underpinnings of his own self-regard. He admired his son for breaking free of it even as he understood Stu no longer respected him. The realization delivered a crippling blow to his desire to protect himself. With Gloria gone and Stu set against him, none of the rest of it mattered.

He wanted to be cleaned of it all, to be truly honest with himself and the outside world, become a better father, a better man, someone his son would someday want to spend time with again.

He cut away the last of Stu's hobble and stood. He felt a new peace, a certainty he hadn't connected with in years. He hugged

Stu and stifled a sob. Stu returned his embrace, stiffly at first before warming. "It's going to be okay, Dad. I'm okay."

Maya gripped Thad's arm. "We have to get out of here, guys."

Thad retrieved his car key from his pocket and handed it to his son. "Take this. Maya knows where my car is. Get her out of here."

"You're coming with us," Stu commanded, already moving toward the exit.

"No," Thad countered. "The people I need to see are here."

Stu halted. "Dad…" he began, but Maya interrupted him.

"Stu, we don't have time for this. You have to get away *now*, before they come back. I don't know how many of them there are, or what they'll do to you if they find you."

Stu stared at his father. "You won't come?"

Thad shook his head once, firmly. "Go." Stu hesitated another moment, then left.

When Thad heard the upstairs door close behind them, he ascended the stairs and walked to the edge of the property facing the church. He heard the start of a motor, then watched his car speed out of the alley and head west. He turned his attention to the hulking mass of timber to the east.

He saw no activity along its front, not that he would without his binoculars. He didn't care to retrieve them, though; whoever was there and whatever their reasons for coming to this place no longer affected him, not really. He ambled toward the tree line, finally settling himself in a protected patch of high grass twenty yards from the woods.

He marveled at how calm he felt, even though he hadn't yet decided – assuming he'd correctly interpreted the tableau before him – which of the available endings for himself he most wanted. He decided he wanted his binoculars after all, though, so he unpacked them.

He watched the antics of the odd mix of individuals co-mingling behind the trees – Kate Blake, along with another woman who seemed to be her friend; the dripping bodyguard from the clinic and his partners; and the armed soldiers in black he was reasonably sure were with the FBI. Kate and her middle-aged companion were the most mobile, trotting between different agents at first. After one operative pointed at the cloud of dust behind Stu and Maya's departing vehicle, the women made a hasty return to the big house.

Thad stowed his binoculars in his satchel, then reclined in the grass and thought on small, permanent things. Of the sureness of his breath, the simple act of inhaling and exhaling. He noticed the slight wetness of the ground beneath him, its chill a pleasant counterweight to the hot overhead sun. When he closed his eyes, he imagined the rush of water over boulders in the nearby river, and the timeless implacability of the elements in general. The river, the sky, the ground he rested on – they existed outside the ridiculous machinations of the lives people constructed for themselves, Thad included. And the elements would go on existing regardless of people's triumphs or failures, their satisfactions or disappointments.

It was a powerful reminder to him how little his own cares factored, and he welcomed the relief this perspective brought him. Even if he'd misread his situation and yonder SWAT team hadn't come to arrest him, he was done struggling, done going on as he had.

He left his belongings on the ground when he rose, and made sure the safety of his gun was off. He kept the weapon visible. He didn't want to shoot anyone… and yet he experienced a thrill at the possibility of death, of raising the question plainly with his would-be captors and letting fate decide how this would end. Were these his last moments alive? Would he be spared? Imprisoned? He didn't know! It wasn't up to him! How free he was! He walked forward with a smile on his face, having abdicated the very last of his claim to power. He didn't react when they trained their guns on him and yelled for him to stop, didn't quicken or slow his pace. He didn't lay down his weapon and go to his knees as they asked, not when he walked at last as a carefree, honest man. He regarded the soldiers warmly, loving them for making this sensation possible, for taking away the last of his misguided perceptions about his own humanity. A glorious joy burst in his chest, so sweet it burned. He'd never, never felt so alive. He fell to the ground smiling, grateful for the deafening report of a gun and the pain that came after.

Chapter Twenty-Three

"Stu. Stop for a minute." For all the frenzy surrounding their escape – which was not yet accomplished – Maya spoke calmly. Stu ignored her and sped forward.

"Seriously, stop the car. I'm getting out." That got his attention. He halted abruptly in the middle of the road, jolting them both against their seat belts and kicking up gravel under the tires. He kept a tight grip on the steering wheel but faced her.

"To do what?"

Maya checked behind her, judging the return distance to Lehland at around two miles. She could easily walk it. She unbuckled herself and pulled the latch to open the door so she wouldn't lose her chance to leave, although she remained in her seat. "I have to go back. I... I don't belong here with you. And you don't need to worry about me."

Stu rubbed the back of his neck and contemplated the dash. "I'm not sure that's true, Maya. Neither of us know why I was taken hostage. Or why you're here at all." He hesitated, then reached across the seat, but he stopped himself. He gripped the steering wheel again. "And I'd like us to talk about a few things. About our marriage, about my infidelities. I want us to recover from them." He stared evenly at her. "I want to fix things, if I can. I've done a lot of thinking, Maya."

His expression was a paradox to her, reminding her as it did of his sincerity on their wedding day. It was a good look, and she understood fully the effort he'd just made – the self-honesty he'd apparently practiced since her departure. He'd at some point acknowledged and regretted his actions, and he wished to make amends, perhaps rebuild something between them. My God, what she would have given for such an offer at any other time over the past eight years.

But when she braced herself against the internal response she expected, against the emotional backlash his words would have prompted even six months ago, she experienced nothing – no burst of joy, no surge of hope, not even anger or disappointment. Instead, she felt a sort of distant curiosity, as she would for the death of a relative she'd met but never spent time with.

"I'm not sure that's a good idea, Stu," she replied gently. Before he could argue with her, she continued, "You don't owe me any explanations, truly. I'm at least partially to blame for why we didn't make it."

"You're not," Stu disagreed swiftly.

"I am," she maintained. "I started off wrong, perhaps wanted the wrong things from you, for us. And I never relented, not even when I really, really should have." Her gaze swept the surroundings outside the car before returning her attention to him. "But I forgive you, if you need to hear that from me. For being unfaithful. I know you did the best you could." She reached over the center console to clasp his hand.

Stu closed his eyes, brought their joined hands to his face and pressed his lips to her knuckles. "I don't deserve that, but thank you," he murmured.

"I won't go back with you, Stu," she insisted kindly, and his eyes opened. "I really do wish we'd been able to work things out, and I'm very sorry they didn't, but... I don't feel anything for us anymore." He started to protest, but Maya remained firm. "I don't have any interest in revisiting how we failed, Stu, none at all, because it doesn't matter to me any longer. It's just too late. But

I'm… I'm proud of you. For coming after me, and for what you just said." She pulled her hand from his and placed it back in her lap. "I think I don't want what I once did, and I can't lie to either of us and say I do."

Stu regarded her levelly. "We should try, Maya, really try. I'd be better this time." He lifted his chin. "I haven't been with another woman in months. My head is clear. And I don't want the same things anymore, either."

Maya suppressed a small smile, because part of those "months" of abstinence Stu boasted of had occurred while he was incarcerated and without opportunity. And the few weeks he'd spent examining himself beforehand? She knew from her experience with other addicts he was unlikely to be on the other side of his addiction for a long, long while.

She was no longer the person to help him get there, though.

"I won't be in our marriage again, Stu, regardless of how it could have been better, or how it might improve. I've already started a new life for myself, one I want too much."

A look of suspicion clouded his features. "Are you… I mean, have you started seeing…"

"No," she hurried to say. "There's no one else." She pivoted her face away from Stu's regard, which she worried would reveal to both of them her evasion, even though she couldn't recall anything about the man she wanted, one she missed terribly despite having no memory of him at all.

Regardless, she reminded herself this conversation was about Stu's desire for reconciliation, not her own circumstances. Moreover, she was not his therapist, not his physician, and even if he would accept advice from her in this moment, it was not her place to give it.

"You'll be stronger without me," she predicted. "And I don't want to be your crutch, or you to be mine."

His expression became speculative. "At least let me take you back to the city, help you get set up so you can finish your residency. Get you away from the crazy swamp people in

Lehland." She giggled. But she saw his attempt at manipulation for what it was.

"I wasn't put in a cage," she reminded him. "Those people rely on me, and whatever their motivations, they care about me. You don't have to worry about me coming to harm here." Before he could mount a rebuttal, she slid out of the car, pausing with the door open.

"For what it's worth, I'm glad you came looking for me, that you wanted to help me," she remarked. "It makes this easier, our goodbye."

Stu ignored her, glaring at the windshield instead. "I don't like leaving you here." But he relented, perhaps because he could tell she wouldn't be convinced away. He leaned across the center console. "Promise me you'll call, even if it's just to leave a message at my office. Let me know you're okay."

"I will," she promised. "And you'd better skedaddle, Stu." She gazed at the road leading back toward town. "Be good, okay?"

He flashed her a winning grin in which she saw the ghost of the man she'd once given herself to. He would be okay... and he'd find someone new in ten minutes. "You, too, Maya. Don't forget to call, okay?"

She smiled, shut the door, and began walking back to Lehland. She heard Stu drive off.

She had time to think during her stroll, about what she would say to Kate and Amelia when she saw them, about the questions she wanted to ask them. A commotion in the trees to the east, along with snippets of shouting reached her... and then the clap of a gunshot. Maya ran.

She found Kate and Amelia in the side yard by the house, both of them facing the woods, silent. "Welcome back," Kate quipped, her eyes remaining on the scene before them.

"What happened?" Maya demanded, panting, sweating.

"They were here to arrest Thad," Amelia informed her. "It looks like they shot him."

Maya scanned the area for medics, pivoted toward her clinic, entered, and quickly packed supplies, and thank God for all that experience treating gang members in the city. She wasn't worried in the least about what she'd see. She made for one of the utility sheds, took the keys for an ATV off the wall and drove out.

Thad was in pain but alive when she reached him. "I'm a physician with gunshot wound experience," she informed the military types attending him. She knelt on the ground and opened her bag, praising the officer holding a towel to Thad's shoulder. In a glance she assessed the order of care required, part of which involved addressing her patient to gauge his state of mind. She took his hand and pressed against his wrist for a pulse. "Hi, Thad," she greeted him kindly.

"Maya!" he exclaimed, albeit weakly. "I didn't think I'd ever see you again!"

"Well it's your lucky day," she replied, giving him her sunniest smile. Then more softly, "I'm going to take care of you, okay?"

Thad started to cry, but at least he was babbling, too, which Maya took as a sign of vitality. "I made it all be about you, hon, because I didn't want it to be about me," he explained. "And then the idea of death... you know, Gloria's was so awful, and I sure didn't understand it at the time, not that I do now, but I see everything so differently, can at least feel what really happened. I couldn't back then... God, that hurts..."

Maya readied a syringe with morphine and administered it to his arm, after which Thad became quiet. "You're so good to try and save me, Maya."

Maya held his hand and stroked the hair off his forehead. "You can thank me by hanging in there, okay?"

"They'll be taking me to prison, you know," he reported, his voice becoming faint.

"Prison and alive is better than the alternative," she contended.

"Okay, Maya. Prison and alive. That's what I'll try for." Thad drifted off as a medevac hovered nearby, then landed. She helped load him onto the gurney, giving instructions to the EMTs who'd be taking him in. She stood in the field as the crew took off, shielding her eyes from the sun with one of her hands until the helicopter disappeared from sight.

Chapter Twenty-Four

Alone in her mini-office at in the back of her clinic, Maya drummed her fingertips on her desk while she fought to make sense of the capers currently underway in reception out front. From their harsh whispers – and the muted protests of the doomed supplicants trying to breach the entryway – she guessed Kate and Amelia were "secretly" turning away all her patients. For no reason she could identify. The women didn't think she could hear them? They were as subtle as rhinos in church.

Still, she knew if she questioned them about anything other than vegetables or the weather, they'd stonewall her.

In the three and a half days since Kate had arrived in Lehland – the second of which had been taken up with the appearance of Thad, the freeing of Stu, and the sudden arrival and departure of government commandos in the forest – Maya felt like she'd become perma-stuck in yet *another* alternate reality. Where the normalcy she'd so recently established hid some big, fat abnormality everyone else was in on but she was not. Kate's complicity in this state of affairs especially rankled, because where was the loyalty? So much for a quarter century of friendship.

Maya tiptoed to the door to catch the most recent of what sounded like arguments between people with laryngitis – because Amelia and Kate's whisperings were *not* quiet – and escapees from a psych ward, although at least her visitors' objections made sense.

"Y'all are batty!" the current newcomer challenged angrily. "I have an appointment with the doc!" Raspy murmurs, followed by bumps and scuffling, then, "Get your hands off me!" The sound of the front door slamming, with silence at last prevailing behind it. Maya had had enough.

Why-oh-why was she constantly burdened with crazy, incompetent overseers? She jerked open her office door and marched out.

"What are you two idiots doing?" she demanded. "You realize this is a clinic, to which patients come to be seen, right? That was my fourth appointment you just scared off, and... and just... cut it out!"

Kate and Amelia had the grace to look guilty before Amelia drew herself up. "We're only here to help with the filing. And straighten things." She tightened her lips primly then began looking, as far as Maya could tell, for some useless task to seize upon. Kate wore an overly sweet smile as she grabbed three sheets of correspondence from one of the counters and made a show of lining up the edges. Maya frowned.

"I don't have that much to catch up on, and the place was cleaned two days ago. Get out of here. Now."

"Your lights need replacing," Kate offered after her eyes darted desperately around the room. She pointed at the flush-mount centered on the room's ceiling, where it seemed one of the bulbs was, in fact, dead.

Maya narrowed her eyes at her friend and grabbed the papers from her hand. She inspected them briefly and guffawed. "These are flyers for the church supper next week. They are *not* office correspondence."

Kate sniffed. "We're leaving them all around town so people know about it." She looked affronted, too, the little faker.

Maya crossed her arms over her chest. "Listen here, you two. I don't know what you're up to and truth be told, I don't care. But I won't have you running off all my patients. You guys need to get lost." Amelia opened her mouth to argue but Maya preempted her.

"Uh-uh. No more of this crap." She glanced around her. "This place is spotless. And I'm going to change the light bulb right now so you have *nothing* more to complain about. Then you're both going to take yourselves back to Amelia's house. No arguing."

Both Amelia and Kate looked abruptly out one of the windows...

...and Maya just as abruptly understood why.

Someone approached, someone who made her feel wildly happy and caused her heart to beat faster. And also as if she might break down in tears. But since this response made no sense to her, she continued on as if she hadn't noticed anything, her companions' unresponsiveness included.

She retrieved a fresh light bulb from a supply cabinet and dragged a chair under the room's central fixture, chattering the whole while. "I cannot imagine what you hoped to accomplish by turning all those people away today but I can tell you your motivations don't matter, you must stop regardless, and Kate, could you turn the switch off by the door... No? Fine, I'll do it, and wouldn't it serve you both right if I fell and broke a foot or something right now..."

Maya climbed down from her perch to turn the light switch off. She had just re-established her feet under her on the chair when she heard someone stomping outside the entryway as if to shake mud off his shoes.

"Okay then!" Kate announced brightly, like a statue suddenly come to life. "We'll be on our way and don't you worry about your patient schedule here or anything because Amelia and I have everything covered. We'll just be up at the house and certainly won't expect you to check in..."

Kate continued talking about... something. Maya couldn't hear her over the pounding of her own blood in her ears, was hardly aware when her friends scooted out the front door. As if they'd been electrocuted. The person they'd apparently been waiting for – and the one she'd been waiting for, too – entered as they left.

She didn't know him and yet she did. As those first seconds ticked by, she found him increasingly, profoundly familiar, as if they'd been friends since she'd been a girl. From his expression, he looked like he knew her, too. And she felt... so very much coming from him. That he'd regretted their separation terribly, for instance.

She'd once loved this man, she realized, could feel her devotion to him freshly, poignantly, until it transitioned from past to present. And wouldn't it be awesome if she could remember anything at all about them as a couple. Or think of his name.

His breath was heavy from exertion. And his hair – his whole person – dripped water. She vaguely noticed his clothes clung to him like he'd worn them in the shower.

"Maya," he said, managing to look both vulnerable and sure, a man contemplating a tenuous negotiation, but one he could win. "Come to me."

The words were a sharp prod at that bruised, dark spot in her feelings, and she played with them silently in her mouth. *Come to me.* She became certain he'd said this to her before. Yes. The phrase was tied to Thad's attempt on her life and her battle with anxiety in New York. To her failed marriage, too.

And hope. She'd hoped for so much when she'd run to him before.

She was too unsure of herself in this situation, however, too shy of what she didn't understand... and so she remained frozen on her chair, unable to come down, take that next step forward.

"Okay, love. I'll come to you."

He approached her with care, which she appreciated since she felt fragile. She might prefer to bolt, to protect her recently built life where she belonged somewhere and participated in things that meant something to her. He radiated promise, though, like a beacon whose light penetrated an interior gloom she disliked but had come to accept. He ran his hands up the outsides of her thighs, then wrapped one arm around her hips, his other around her waist. He pressed his face to her stomach. "God, I missed you."

She rested her palms on his shoulders and tested the name that surfaced in her memory. "Aiden?"

He ran his nose back and forth across her midriff, his eyes closed. "Yes." Then he tightened his grip on her body and lifted her from the chair. He kept her elevated, a suspension that called to her... and quieted her earlier impulse to flee.

"You should know, I'm not paying for your back surgery," she blurted, and Aiden laughed, vibrations that suffused her with heat when she'd been cold, so cold. He let her slide down his length until she stood on her feet. She tilted her face to his, fascinated with their response to each other.

"Light as a feather," he scoffed. Then he dipped his mouth to hers and kissed her.

Memories seeped languidly from some buried cistern of her past like it was cracked. Rivulets of recognition wound their way through her mind. That time he'd come into SeaCakes with Simon and made her feel so out of control. The hard expression he'd worn at her wedding to Stu, then his hand at her back as he guided her into a limousine and scanned the crowd around them for threats.

His quiet presence when she'd cried.

Her meeting with him over the East River and that glorious fall into another world. As Aiden's passions strengthened, hers did in response. The trickle of memories became an outrush.

He'd come back for her, just as he'd promised. Tears leaked from the corners of her eyes and into her hair, because she remembered everything now. She hiccupped as he nibbled and whispered against her skin, until he rested his forehead at the base of her neck. He rocked them from side to side.

Eventually, he raised his face above hers, brushed away the wetness at her temples. "Stu and Thad got away?" he asked.

"Yes. No. Well, sort of. I sprung Stu – I don't understand why he was captured and held here – but he'd come to warn me away from Thad. Thad found us... and basically turned himself in to the authorities. Stu used Thad's car to drive back to the city. I was going to go with him, but then I didn't. I came back."

"Appreciate the loyalty, although I would have come after you." He devoured her visually, scanning her features again and again; and he sifted his fingers through her hair. "Wanna get out of here and live out that fantasy we discussed?"

Distracted by the sensations rioting within her, Maya wondered what he meant. "Which one?" She sounded breathy and needy... and she didn't care. His low laugh washed through her cleanly, clarifying the muddiness of her feelings this morning. Then she remembered his people's disapproval, of their need to hide.

"That's all been resolved," Aiden reported. "We're free, Maya."

"So... we can visit Mermaid Island, and no one will arrest us?"

"Mm-hmm. And we can rent that apartment, take those walks. Get that dog."

"Ah," Maya sighed. "*That* fantasy. Which is not my favorite one at the moment." Another low laugh from Aiden.

"Tell me, love – which one do you want?"

"You. You're the myth I want, the one I've always wanted.

He squeezed her. "Anyone here you need to see before we leave?"

Maya shook her head. "I never thought I'd say this, but get me to the ocean."

He grinned. "We'll take the river."

Chapter Twenty-Five

When little girls imagined a fairytale wedding – and she'd been no different as a child – Maya was pretty sure they envisioned the kind of staging that surrounded her first walk down the aisle with Stuart Evans. Maybe they believed as she had that such a spectacle meant permanence, or in her case that it might cement the whole tenuous venture into something she could rely on, because look at all the people come to bear witness, and listen to all those legacy pronouncements. Those ten thousand professional photos weren't going anywhere, either.

In retrospect, Maya knew she'd been bullied into the occasion by her in-laws, but she'd gone along with it all because she really couldn't think of an alternative. And who knew? Maybe that legion of little girls would be right and the grand gestures of one particular afternoon would carry her relationship into the future. Maybe she'd wake up in twenty or thirty years to find her marriage in a state of placid maturity because of all they'd done and said on their wedding day.

As she contemplated her second stint as a bride, this time at the palace on Shaddox, Maya concluded none of them on the mainland had possessed big enough imaginations. Perhaps their definition of couple-hood had been too small for themselves, and hence all the effort to make her union with Stu seem bigger. Whatever the premise, the performance looked lamentably quaint in hindsight, especially considering the current extravaganza the sirens had laid out on her and Aiden's behalf. The prospect of walking into it made her dizzy.

Simon, her soon-to-be brother-in-law and stand-in male relative for part one of the proceedings, steadied her but smirked. "Buck up, little camper," he teased. "You're almost home free." Perhaps as he'd intended, she collected herself enough for a retort.

"Just for that, I'm going to throw up on you." Simon laughed.

Sylvia turned their way to hiss, "Stop it, you two." To Maya, she instructed, "But he's right. You need to get over your stage fright. It's not like you haven't faced bigger crowds in New York. Or courtside, when you played volleyball." Maya gasped in protest – this was not about stage fright – but Sylvia cut her off, addressing Simon this time. "And you, behave. You're representing Jeremy, remember?" The prompt caused Maya to relent, since Simon had, after all, volunteered to fill her father's role. No one had been able to devise a plan to include her parents in a primarily and obviously siren affair, so they'd had to improvise. She remained touched by Simon's offer to stand by her.

Simon grabbed his wife's wrist and kissed the inside of it, then spanned her pregnant tummy with his hands. "It's all good, angel. I've got her. Now run along to your place in the lineup so we can get to the fun part." Sylvia narrowed her eyes at him, but Maya could see she wasn't really angry. Sylvia hustled to where their two children waited for her.

Maya would have greatly preferred not to have any sort of public rite and had initially begged for a quiet, expedient visit to a human licensing bureau, just the two of them. Followed by a casual dinner party with ten other people at most. Her groom hadn't supported her, however, although he'd held her hand as she'd pleaded with his overexcited aunts.

"Can we just... I mean, I've already gone through this nonsense once and it made me nuts. Really – I didn't sleep or eat for almost a month from nerves. And I stitch viscera in place for a living."

Queen Carmen herself quashed the last of Maya's hopes for privacy. Or for any say at all in what came next. "This is about the community, not you, Maya," she admonished, and, really? A spectacle where she would be gussied up and on display for several thousand people was not about her? She didn't even know how to respond.

"We'll get through it, love," Aiden encouraged... and something in his approach, his tranquil warmth, convinced her to give in. He squeezed her hand. "This will be strange for me, too," he confessed. "I've always been peripheral to big community shindigs. But I know a bit about what a Shaddox wedding will mean for us. I think we'll appreciate it afterwards."

"We're decided, then," Carmen declared. She set a date two weeks out, and Aiden's relatives bustled off to make arrangements. Carmen departed, too, citing her need to attend to "issues of actual consequence."

Aiden, who was seated on a stool, pulled Maya to him so she stood between his legs, facing him. He rested his palms on her hips and concentrated on her with such weighty devotion, she lost most of her anxiety over what had just happened. She looped her arms around his shoulders and fingered the hair at the back of his neck. "What was so wrong with our plan to keep to ourselves for a while?" she complained lightly. She relived a snapshot of their swim here, the lush closeness they'd enjoyed and the sense of permanence they'd gained. Following their exit from the sea – which had included whole minutes of terror for Maya as Aiden led her through the "compound illusion" protecting Shaddox – she'd become convinced her life had finally righted itself. Her new and unencumbered happiness relegated the unhappiness of the last decade to a far-away realm disconnected from her, as if her trials had happened to someone else. She couldn't help but try to protect what they had, to avoid outside factors that could burst the bubble of contentment they'd so recently formed.

She supposed the prospect of a palace wedding was less onerous than the intrusions she'd suffered from her stalkers in New

York, or from her siren-led memory hijackers in Lehland. She sighed. "Is there somewhere more remote we can go afterwards?" Aiden chuckled. "There is... but it's cold. Trust me – you wouldn't like it."

"I might," Maya protested, but she surrendered herself to her ceremonial fate.

The same battalion of goddesses who'd shanghaied her in New York before she married Stu also showed up to prep her for today's production... and why she'd thought they were anything other than mermaids back then now baffled her. Seriously. Only someone with no observational skills whatsoever – and she was a physician trained to notice stuff – could have convinced herself these women were *not* sea creatures of some sort.

"We're not hazing you this time," one of them explained as she wove seed pearls and ribbons into Maya's hair. The one dusting Maya's face with... something... paused, and stared at her with that hungry, ardent expression Maya had come to recognize as natural siren solicitation. It made her want to take all five of them swimming.

When she was deemed ready, they stood her up in front of a mirror, and she stared at herself in amazement. "I look like you," she murmured.

"And you're waterproof, too," her hairdresser added, tweaking Maya's chin.

Maya studied the details of her appearance, enthralled. Her dress was a pale, shimmering blue with a diaphanous overlay, the garment so light she hardly registered its weight on her frame. Her skin shimmered, her eyes beckoned. She looked, in fact, exactly as lovely as the mermaid cohort surrounding her.

"You're one of us, now. A sister," an attendant told her, and Maya's eyes brimmed. To be included in such a community, to be wanted by Aiden and his people... a swell of gratitude rose and burst painfully in her chest, causing the women around her to croon and pet her until she was soothed. They drew her with them to the reception hall at the front of the palace.

Wherein she promptly lost her sense of well-being and thought again on her desire for a private event that would be dry in every sense of the word. Her sisters and Kate turned to her as she entered the hall, their admiration a balm that temporarily suspended her displeasure.

But then it all became too much, the songbirds flying in the atrium, the outrageous profusion of flowers everywhere.

The monumental crowd awaiting her just outside the palace doors. "Oh. God."

Without Sylvia's intervention, she might have turned on her heel and locked herself back in her suite.

But Simon and her ladies-in-waiting surrounded her and urged her forward, eventually stepping outside with her onto the marble terrace fronting the hall. At her appearance, the crowd cheered... and the sound resonated within her like a deep rumble of thunder. It demolished her misgivings. Instead, she became filled with anticipation for whatever would happen, and she loved, truly adored, every single person who'd come to witness the day with her. She let Simon draw her down the stairs into the gardens, into her sea of well-wishers. She beamed at everyone she passed, clasping their outstretched hands as best she could. She glided along the corridor they created for her, their whispered blessings a force of optimism that permeated them all. Flower petals floated from the sky like snow.

Their tour led them back to a wide staircase at the other side of the palace. At the encouragement of her companions, she left them to ascend on her own to a platform, then through a set of double doors. The crowd streamed in after her at a distance.

She felt the presence of her love.

She followed his pull toward the castle's center, winding her way through unfamiliar hallways, past a dizzying assortment of great rooms and offices, until she came to a massive interior courtyard comprised almost entirely of a lake.

"Welcome to the central pool." The definition registered as one she'd heard mentioned before... but she hardly thought of it, because there, waist deep in the water and grinning at her, was Aiden, bare-chested except for the tether he wore at his waist. He extended his hand to her, palm up. "Come here, love." She slipped out of her ballet flats and waded in to meet him.

"I like your dress," he offered before securing her waist with one arm. He cupped her chin with his other hand and kissed her briefly. Then he wrapped her against him and dove.

His transformation, now familiar to her – and a process she felt rather than saw – mirrored her own, equally familiar internal shift. Which she loved. She loved how they slipped away from separateness into togetherness, a unique entity that was a blend of the two of them. She loved the effect of their unity, especially when they swam, when the borders between them blurred and their capacities and strengths compounded, then magnified. She was her happiest, most competent self in these moments, as if nothing could overextend them and they could effortlessly achieve everything they hoped for.

Is the ceremony over? she inquired.

Not quite.

Others joined them in the water, their presence not altogether welcome since Maya didn't trust their over-attention during such a personal exchange. At least they stayed back.

They're here to help, Aiden promised.

When she and Aiden reached the middle of the lake, Aiden disengaged enough so they faced each other, their hands clasped between them, their bodies slightly elevated off the sea floor. An indeterminate amount of time passed... and Maya didn't fight the calmness Aiden forced on her, the insistence her attention remain on him alone while his people gathered around them.

The pool teemed with onlookers now, so many Maya couldn't contemplate their number without panicking. Aiden described what was to happen next.

We're in a circle, and they're here to support us, to recognize our bond. There's nothing you need to say or do. We'll spend a few minutes where we are, and then we'll leave the water and celebrate. It's hard to describe, but you'll understand what's happening as soon as it starts. There's nothing, not one thing, for you to worry about. His smile was sure, his confidence the only part of this situation she could make sense of. But because of it – because of him – she did trust in what would come next. She remained easy…

…until she glanced away from him and took in the size of their audience. *Ah-ah*, Aiden chided. *Eyes on me, love.* Her attention swiveled back to him.

A low hum rose from the sirens, a pleasant, hypnotic sound that further focused her on her groom and concentrated the quiet between them. Their surroundings receded.

She knew this feeling, the one where reality thinned then disappeared, leaving her and her lover cocooned in an alternate space. And Aiden was right: she understood the progression she was in now that she was in it. His faraway community, the one that had just allowed them to slip into privacy among them, chanted for their happiness and applauded their bond.

Aiden kissed her tenderly and the sound around them swelled. The energy of everyone gathered filled the water, filled them, then lifted them toward the surface. Aiden once again wrapped her tightly against him. They breached as the others surfaced alongside them, her fall back into the water with Aiden breaking their separation from their attendees. Maya's awareness expanded beyond the two of them.

They exited the water euphoric and replete, no longer defensive, no longer hesitant to claim what they were to each other. Aiden grabbed her and kissed her again, inviting ripples of laughter from those leaving the pool.

"The whole siren world approves," Aiden whispered in her ear.

"It's beautiful," Maya replied. "I think this means no more hiding, right?"

"No more hiding," Aiden confirmed, and he kissed her again.

Within minutes – and in Maya's opinion, magically – multiple doors between the palace and the inner courtyard opened, revealing a banquet of epic proportions. "It's for a *lot* of people," Aiden explained. Which went to reason. A platoon of helpers in bizarre but elaborate attire also began wheeling what looked like oversized bell hop trolleys around, each filled with an array of off-looking formal wear made from over-bright, unconventional fabrics. The wardrobes were mobbed, and within a few minutes, the gathering took on the look of a colorful, edgy, vaguely disheveled ball from another century. Where shoes were optional. Simon came forward bearing a folded linen shirt and pants, which he tossed at his brother.

"Here. My wife says to put these on," Simon instructed, then snagged a velvet smoking jacket off one of the caddies to complete his own ensemble. Aiden donned the shirt and pants, rolling up the pant cuffs to his shins. He left his shirt un-tucked and declined the offer of a suit coat. Someone handed Maya her ballet flats.

Aiden held out his hand to her. "Let's eat. I'm starved."

After sampling too many delicacies and feeding each other multiple different kinds of cake, Aiden drew Maya outside to the courtyard again. He closed one set of doors against the revelry and walked with her in silence, along the edge of the central pool and away from the party.

The moon drenched every surface in blue and silver, a cooler and obscure counterpoint to the sunny radiance inside. Following the dense sensations of the afternoon and all the people she'd interacted with, Maya preferred this, the dimness, the solitude. She regretted no part of the last several hours and would choose the same wedding day for them again, but she was ready for it all to end, ready to start her unknown, hopefully emergency-free life with her siren husband.

She felt guilty for asking, but she asked anyway. "Can we sneak away yet?"

Aiden immediately steered them toward a quiet, unattended door well away from the reception. They still hurried through the darkened passageways, eager to escape before they could be stopped. They giggled when they took their first free breath outside the front of the palace, then ran through the gardens until they reached the front of the estate.

Once clear of the gates, they slowed their pace. Maya caught Aiden's hand, swinging it between them. "Where are we going?" she asked.

"Does it matter?"

She laughed. "Not really. Just curious."

"We're going to break into the Blake cabin, since I happen to know Gabe and his family are staying in one of the royal suites."

"And after that, maybe in a week or so, then what?"

He eyed her affectionately. "Where do you want to go?"

"Anywhere with you, Aiden. Anywhere there's a clinic. But close to the ocean."

"Well. We're a package deal, you know, the ocean and I. Which means we're a trio now, since you belong, too."

"Just you, me, and the sea?" she returned wryly.

"Yes. Just us and the sea. And maybe a dog." His expression deepened. "And someday, a child or two."

Joy surged within her. "I can't wait, Aiden," she professed. "Which way to our stolen cabin?" Aiden pointed southeast, and she ran ahead, tugging him behind her. "Hurry. I want it all to start now."

But he pulled her to his side again, looping an arm around her neck. "Ah, love. We've already started," he said into her hair. "And for once, we have all kinds of time."

She realized he was right, and the urgency she felt softened. Instead she viewed her situation with awe. Autonomy after living under the constant direction of so many others, and with everything in place so they could choose what they wanted for themselves. "We really do. We actually get to call our own plays." She considered his profile, their joined hands, and the open future before them. "You know, I always preferred playing offense to defense. I'm better at it, too."

"*We're* going to be amazing at it," Aiden vowed.

The End

Author Note

Thank you for reading my story, *Outrush*, and probably for reading the two before it, *Updrift* and *Breakwater,* as well. Since you've made it this far, I hope you will also enjoy the upcoming fourth installment. This story will follow Peter and Xanthe to South America and back as they fight internal and external demons from past and present; and as they carve their own unique path to love. Here's an excerpt:

From
Crosstide
Book Four of the Mer Chronicles
by
Errin Stevens

"Xanthe. Come back to me."

She knew that voice, had been in these arms before... but maybe not. Maybe she was dreaming she was in a better situation than she actually was. She looked apprehensively over her shoulder toward the room she'd just left, the glow from the chandelier too bright, its illumination still touching her.

Like a prison searchlight when all good inmates were in bed, and she was an escapee in the yard.

She bolted deeper into the night shadows, pulling so hard on her companion, they both stumbled, and how odd for the laws of gravity to work in a scenario that didn't really exist. Her phantom Peter steadied them.

"Moonflower." His voice was gruff with emotion. He contained her struggling when all she wanted to do was run, flee to the ocean as fast as she could and find the deepest, darkest sea cave to hide in. "What did they do to you?"

Not that negotiating with a ghost would get her anywhere, but she decided there was no harm in responding. "You must be new here. If you show sadness, if you withdraw and dim yourself, they will kill you." She checked over his shoulder again and frowned. "I don't know why they aren't coming for me..."

Peter shook her, pulling her attention back to him. "Xanthe. You're safe. And they're all dead. No one will chase you."

God, but his anger was glorious, as was the unlikely assertion he'd done away with her captors. Still, she reveled in the reprieve, in the idea she had a true friend at her side. She studied his face, his ethereal beauty, then took in his confidence and self-possession, two attributes that would never survive in this place. He was so vital, so real. "What new trick is this?" she murmured, touching his cheek. He felt warm and solid, and yet couldn't be. He flattened her palm against the side of his face.

He was too physically vibrant, too enticing. He was in fact a desperate hope she couldn't afford to indulge, because to believe in him was to invite her own execution. She fought to get away, but he held her firmly... and even his strength, his illusory hold on her, was a solace. She stopped, leaned into him. Perhaps she'd snapped and her mind was forcing her into the conclusion she needed so badly, that she was loved and protected. Even so, she turned her head away, gazed toward the sea glittering under the high moon. If she could imagine Peter, she could imagine getting away from here.

Peter began to hum. The tune tugged at a memory, one she'd buried because it had made her too homesick.

A ball in a grand palace among her own people. A prince in fine dress bowing before her, his admiration evident as he paused over her hand to request a dance. Her worry at the time seemed absurd now, how she'd stewed over his interest in her and what she risked by allowing him to lead her onto the floor.

He swept her into a waltz.

The sights and sounds of that faraway time blended with the present, her old memories darkening as she and Peter glided and turned along the stone corridor. She relaxed against Peter's hand at her back for every spin, trusting him to contain their momentum. And at each step, the music from their earlier encounter also bled away... until soon, all she heard was the deep, resonant voice of her partner, his breath intimate and warm in her ear.

The vivid hues from that long-ago celebration – the gowns, the floral arrangements, the garish towers of hors d'oeuvres – went last, their brilliance fading into a colorless but deeper, more private display. She and Peter performed alone here in moonlight and shadow, like a silent movie they enacted between the arches of the arcade. She began to watch Peter's face, looking for further evidence of his actuality. His features appeared and disappeared, never displayed long enough for her to know.

At the end of the gallery, he stopped humming but kept her in his frame, as if they might dance again. He stood so close she could see nothing else, his chest heaving slightly from exertion. She watched the movement in fascination, reminiscent as it was of the waves she so longed for, the swelling, the contraction. She set her ear against his heart and let its rhythm absorb her. He cupped the back of her head.

Interview by Dove Winters: Quirky Questions with Errin Stevens

https://dovewinters.wordpress.com/2018/10/19/quirky-questions-with-errin-stevens/

I asked some quirky questions of Errin Stevens! But first the book:

Audible: http://tinyurl.com/lhayfcj
iBooks: http://tinyurl.com/mm9gk3g
Barnes & Noble: http://tinyurl.com/mfam47f
Amazon: http://tinyurl.com/kro64ew
Book Depository: http://tinyurl.com/lye3uo2
Kobo: http://tinyurl.com/nyvqwth

And social links:

Facebook: https://www.facebook.com/author.errin…
Twitter: https://twitter.com/errinstevens
Goodreads: https://www.goodreads.com/author/show…
Pinterest: https://www.pinterest.com/errinsteven…
Instagram: https://www.instagram.com/errinstevens/

Errin Stevens, you're in the spotlight! Hello, Errin!

What is the weirdest scar you have and how did you get it?
I awoke one morning when I was 25 and draped my right arm over the edge of the bed at the precise moment a wire coil poked through the mattress. The thing sliced a 2-inch, diagonal gash on the underside of my bicep… and to this day, I have a thin, satiny-white scar there. I know I should say I have the impression of a shark bite or something more interesting, but other than my appendectomy scar, that's it!

Ouch! What a way to wake up! What's the closest thing to

real magic?

I believe we humans are more intuitive than we acknowledge, to the point we really can tell exactly what another person is thinking or feeling in many cases. I played with this idea a bit in my stories by having my sirens draw their human counterparts in. But I think this is a real thing.

How interesting! Have you ever had an imaginary friend? Tell us about them.

When I was a child, I saw guardian angels – well, one angel at a time, although it wasn't necessarily the same one – standing watch inside my bedroom door while I slept. They were 7 or 8 feet tall, lean, grim and fearsome creatures, and I loved them.

Wow! I'd like to hear more about that! But moving on, what is one of your favorite quotes?

I think the Isak Dinesen quote I front "Updrift" with played a huge role in getting me to write that story in the first place: *The cure for anything is salt water – sweat, tears, or the sea.*

There is nothing quite as cleansing as a good cry! When was the last time you got the giggles at an inappropriate time?

Oh, how I miss losing myself in uncontrollable laughter! My mother and I still get caught up occasionally, but the sessions are rare. My most frequent giggle-fests used to be in church with my grandmother, who I wrote about in this little essay, Long Lost Love: https://errinstevens.com/2012/05/02/long-lost-love/

Great essay! What is your favorite smell?

I'm a scent hound, I swear, and smells tie very closely to

moods and emotions and memory for me. If I crush a little dill between my fingertips and then stick my nose in it, I'm immediately in my grandmother's backyard again, talking with her about gardening. Nothing else – not pictures, not mementos, not stories retold by relatives – brings my grandmother so vividly to mind.

I also LOOOOOVE the scent of the cologne, "Terre d'Hermes" for my husband. Seriously, I've hunted through hundreds of aftershaves and that one is the absolute best. Other smells that put me in a trance? Bring me to the lilacs, peonies, and jasmine, please.

Your nose knows what it likes! What is the last thing you do before you go to sleep?

I reflect on everything I ate during the day, from the first sip of rich, dark coffee with toast and jam, to a cookie I devoured warm from the oven, to the last bite of chicken with lemon and garlic I had at dinner. The process dissociates me from the more complicated or worrying contemplations I'm prone to, enough for my brain to quiet and let go. I stole this process for my heroine in my second book, Sylvia, to use… and I hope I described it right.

A good practice, though reading that answer made me hungry!

Thank you for participating in Quirky Questions and letting us get to know you! While I go get a cookie, follow and support Errin, and join us next Friday for more questions and cookies!
Happy reading!

CPSIA information can be obtained
at www.ICGtesting.com
Printed in the USA
BVHW031913080219
539827BV00001B/22/P